JUDAS ISLAND

A BAY TANNER MYSTERY

KATHRYN R. WALL

St. Martin's Paperbacks

JUDAS ISLAND

Copyright © 2004 by Kathryn R. Wall.
Excerpt from *Resurrection Road* © 2005 by Kathryn R. Wall.

Cover photo of house © David Muench / Corbis.
Cover photo of lake © Dana Tezarr / Photonica.

ISBN: 0-312-93481-5
EAN: 80312-93481-1

Printed in the United States of America

St. Martin's Press hardcover edition / May 2004
St. Martin's Paperbacks edition / May 2005

St. Martin's Paperbacks are published by St. Martin's Press, 175 Fifth Avenue, New York, NY 10010.

10 9 8 7 6 5 4 3 2 1

For Norman—
Here's to seventy-five more!

ACKNOWLEDGMENTS

A perceptive, caring, and dedicated editor is every writer's dream, and I have one in the person of Linda McFall. It helps that we share a somewhat quirky sense of humor because I've found you need one in this business. Publicity and marketing are twin monsters that scare most authors to death, and again Linda McFall, along with Rachel Ekstrom, has helped me navigate those treacherous waters. Thanks as well to PJ Nunn and her staff at Breakthrough Promotions for their work on my behalf.

In the course of researching *Judas Island,* I had the good fortune of being permitted to pick the brains of two very knowledgeable men: Jack Keller enlightened me on the subject of the local waterways and Coast Guard procedure, while John Dukes shared insight and information about the Port of Charleston. Any factual errors are the result of either my own misunderstanding or intentional fictional license. Thanks also to Captain Mark Poindexter and Ken Bell for a chilly but fascinating ride up the creeks and rivers that surround my island.

There are so many bookstore owners and their personnel to thank, I can't begin to name them all here, but you know who you are. There are no words to thank you for your enthusiasm and support. The same is true of my fellow writers, both published and aspiring. It really is a community in the truest sense of that word.

And finally I want to acknowledge the next two generations of my family: Kristin, Gretchen, Erik, Jennifer, and Doug; Liam, Elinor, Benjamin, and Brendan; and Josh, Taylor, and Carli. Thanks, kids. You've kept us young.

PROLOGUE

The flat bottom of the johnboat scraped across the narrow shingle as the young man leaped out into the shallows and waded ashore. The tide was on the turn, rising for the next few hours, so he tugged the wooden boat up into the scrub palmetto and hawthorn growing nearly down to the water's edge. Though without shoes, he did not feel the sharp edges of the oyster and clam shells strewn along the barely perceptible path he followed toward the interior. As a boy he had fished and shrimped and crabbed the marsh creeks and mud flats of these islands, toughening his feet as well as his spirit. Even without the light of a three-quarter moon he could have found his way unerringly to the site of the gathering.

Fifteen minutes later he paused on the edge of the clearing, surprised to find the fire circle dead and cold, the stumps and logs scattered around it empty. He had feared he would be late, Mr. Clymer having kept him beyond closing time at the Red 'n White to sweep out the storeroom and stack the last of the day's shipments. Today it had been cabbages from one of the big truck farms out near Ridgeland. He hated the smell and the way their slimy leaves stuck to the concrete of the loading dock.

So he had expected the others to have arrived before him, the fire to be already beating off the October chill, the bottle to have been passed back and forth between them at least a couple of times. And tonight he couldn't dawdle. She'd have his hide if he kept her waiting again.

The young man settled back onto his haunches in the thick underbrush, unsure of what had stirred this faint whisper of unease that prickled at the back of his neck. He sat unmoving for a long while, his still form melting into the gray and black shadows, his breath indistinguishable from the rhythmic soughing of the wind high up in the swaying pines.

A soft footfall on the carpet of needles off to his right. He tensed in alarm a second before the suffocating hood dropped over his head. He had a moment to register the unmistakable *click* of a hammer being pulled back before the heft of the rope settled around his neck.

"This is the last of them, gentlemen."

He recognized the voice immediately, low and ugly just a few inches from his ear, and he knew that he was dead.

CHAPTER ONE

I flung my arm across the wide expanse of bed, but my fingers encountered only rumpled, silky emptiness. I cracked open one eye against the shaft of sunlight seeping into the room through a chink in the wooden shutters. When I had verified that he was in fact gone, I hitched the duvet up around my bare shoulders and snuggled back down into the warmth he'd left behind.

Probably picking up the papers. I stretched and rolled over onto my side, picturing Darnay passing the time with Madame Srabian and her son over a demitasse of the thick Algerian coffee he loved. As I drifted back into a light doze, I hoped he'd remember to bring me the English-language version of the *New York Times* along with one or two of Madame's croissants. Though my French was fast improving, I still couldn't manage *Le Monde,* especially on an empty stomach . . .

It could have been an hour or only minutes later when the sharp rapping on the outside door finally penetrated my sluggish brain. I rolled out, snatching up the shirt Darnay had left draped on the bedpost the night before. Not much in the way of a robe, but at least it covered the important parts. Besides, I expected my caller would prove to be Darnay himself.

As I padded down the hallway and across the worn Aubusson carpet covering the front room of the vast apartment, I could envision him just on the other side of the massive old door: the newspapers, a huge box of pastries, and a net bag full of fruit from the little stand on the corner clutched to his chest as he fumbled for his keys.

We never had visitors except, occasionally, his chic, sour-faced sister Madeleine, and she, thank God, was spending the month at the house in Provençe.

But the smile of welcome died on my lips when I flung open the door to a young man in yellow-and-black spandex, his long orange hair flowing from beneath a bullet-shaped bicycle helmet. Unconsciously I took a step back, my fingers working of their own accord to fasten the top button of the wrinkled white shirt.

"M. Darnay, *s'il vous plaît.*"

I watched him check out the long expanse of bare leg that constituted a good part of my five-foot, ten-inch frame, his gaze lingering in a couple of places along the way, before his knowing eyes finally fastened on my face. The grin was pure French; and, because I had grown used to their frankness in my four months of living in Paris, I tried not to take offense. *"Il n'est pas chez nous. Puis-je vous aider?"*

I was pretty sure I'd gotten it right, and Darnay swore my pronunciation improved daily.

"Êtes-vous sa femme?"

"Non, seulement une amie. Pourquoi?"

Now that we'd established that Darnay was not there, and that I was not his wife but merely a friend, the courier seemed at a loss. He consulted his watch then flipped through some papers attached to a metal clipboard. Finally, with a shrug that exemplified the live-and-let-live attitude of almost everyone in this marvelous city, he thrust a pen into my hand. *"Nombre sept, mademoiselle."*

I scratched *Bay Tanner* on line seven and accepted the bulky envelope. It bore no return address, but the label looked as if it had been computer-generated. *Perhaps something he's ordered,* I thought, although a catalogue shipment would have come through the mail or by one of the overnight delivery services, not a special courier. I turned the package over in my hand then looked up, surprised to see my admirer still studying me intently. I was trying to formulate a stinging rebuke he might possibly understand when it dawned on me he was waiting for a tip.

Since I so obviously had no pockets, I left him standing in the doorway as I dropped the envelope onto the Louis XIV console table and sprinted back into the bedroom. I snatched a few francs from my wallet and paused long enough to pull on a pair of black leggings before returning to thrust the bills into the messenger's hand. He looked disappointed, whether from the size of the tip or from my more modest state of attire, I couldn't tell.

Again I studied the package, squeezing it gently in an effort to determine exactly what it might contain. It felt like a thick wad of paper, although that could have been padding for something fragile or easily crushed. Which might explain the courier. The French postal service was no better than its American counterpart when it came to complying with such optimistic requests as "Handle with Care." With a shrug I propped the envelope up against one of the heavy brass candlesticks on the console.

I was heading down the hall to our one bathroom, visions of a long soak in the mammoth, claw-footed tub sending little murmurs of anticipation vibrating in my throat, when I heard the click of the lock. Alain Darnay, burdened much as I had imagined him just a few minutes before, sidled into the entryway and pushed the door closed with a sharp thrust of his right hip. I hurried to meet him, laughing as I disentangled his long fingers from the string bag of oranges and peaches dangling from his hand.

"Thank God!" he exclaimed and dropped a brief kiss on the end of my nose. "I thought I might not make that last flight of stairs." He hurried into the narrow kitchen to deposit his other treasures on the old oak table. We took most of our meals there, despite the magnificence of the formal dining room just a few steps away.

"Here, let me help." I stacked the heavy newspapers off to one side, drew a sharp paring knife from the old wooden block on the counter, and cut the twine on the pastry box while Darnay shrugged out of his jacket.

Even in the bulky fisherman's sweater and baggy corduroy pants, he looked too thin. I had made it my mission over the past few months to feed him back into the vigorous health he had enjoyed before an encounter with a bullet nearly ended our burgeoning love affair, along with his life. That my amateur investigation into a series of gruesome murders had been the cause of this misery still lay like a hard kernel of guilt in my chest.

"Jean sends his regards," he said, rubbing his hands together to warm them as I set the kettle on for tea. Despite the time-worn words of the old song, April in Paris was turning out to be gray and decidedly cold. "He wants to know when you'll be available for his next lesson."

Madame's twelve-year-old son and I had worked out a mutual assistance pact, he for his English and I for my French. We met as often as his schoolwork allowed, usually while exploring the markets, shops, and parks which abounded in our little neighborhood of tree-lined boulevards.

"I nearly forgot," Darnay said, pausing in the midst of peeling and slicing the fruit to reach for the jacket he had slung over the back of a chair. "I picked up the *poste* on my way up. There seems to be something for you." He grinned as he waved the white envelope. "From the colonies, I believe." I snatched it from his hand just as the kettle set up its insistent whistle. "Go ahead and read it, *ma petite*. I'll make the tea."

The letter was from my father. Retired Judge Talbot Simpson, wheelchair-bound after a series of strokes, steadfastly refused to succumb to such modern conveniences as e-mail or the trans-Atlantic telephone system. While I kept in close touch with most of my friends and acquaintances via the Internet, I was still forced to wait upon the whims and vagaries of the international postal service for word from the Judge.

I spread the pages out on the table while Darnay poured tea. I marveled at the steadiness of my father's handwriting, despite his infirmity and the fact that his eightieth birthday was fast approaching. Absently I slathered butter on a still-warm croissant, smiling to myself at the gossip which had become the lifeblood of the Judge's existence in the small town of Beaufort, South Carolina, just up the road from my own home on Hilton Head Island.

Home, I thought, my eyes darting to Alain Darnay.

He had spread out the newspaper *Le Monde* across the old wooden table and sat hunched over it, absorbed by some article, while he sucked the sweet juice from a dripping section of orange.

I sighed and blew across the rim of my cup, then sipped the hot, strong tea.

As soon as he had been pronounced healed by his bosses at Interpol, who had spirited their best undercover agent away immediately after his wounding, I had sped to Paris. To this apartment, this life. Widowed nearly two years before by my husband Rob's murder, it had seemed imperative to find out if I could find it in myself to commit to another man. To Darnay. Four months later, I still didn't have an answer.

I flipped to the second page of the letter, smiling despite myself at my father's seemingly endless store of anecdotes about his old cronies in local politics and law enforcement. Including my brother-in-law, Beaufort County Sheriff's Sergeant Red Tanner, a younger, shorter version of my dead husband. Red occupied a special place in my life, the spot I would have reserved for an annoying but well-loved brother if my parents had seen fit to provide me with one. I missed him, too.

The paper rattled as Darnay turned to a new section. I looked up to find his steel-blue eyes fixed on mine. "Everything all right?"

"Fine," I answered and popped the remaining bite of croissant into my mouth.

"Bien." He bent again to his newspaper.

I read through the remaining few paragraphs, pleased to find that Lavinia Smalls, our family's housekeeper through most of my childhood and now my father's caregiver and companion, had added a few lines at the bottom. She conveyed news of my longtime friend Bitsy and her children, reported on the health and well-being of her own son and his family, and asked when I thought I might be coming home. Twice.

"Bay?" Once again I found Darnay staring at me from across the table. "Are you sure everything is fine? You look troubled, *ma petite*."

I smiled and shook my head, confused and embarrassed at the wave of longing that swept over me at Lavinia's question. *Home?* Of course it was. But Darnay's life was here. Despite having retired from Interpol, he was bound to France, not only by his father's heritage, but by the land. The small vineyard would be his as soon as his health permitted him to claim it. His sister Madeleine could barely wait to take possession of the sprawling Paris apartment.

At first we did not discuss our life together any farther than the next day, the next outing—to the palace at Versailles, to the marvelous castle at Chenonçeaux, to Monet's gardens at Giverny, no doubt bursting soon, in spite of the cold, into glorious spring color. We had both been content to let the days of rediscovering each other drift from one week into the next, both of us fearful of planning too far ahead. Life had taught us the futility of that, but sooner or later we would have to decide.

I would have to decide.

Absorbed in my own thoughts, I hadn't registered his moving until I felt his warm breath against the side of my neck. I leaned back into his arms.

"You are homesick, *n'est-ce pas?* Would you like to go for a visit?"

"Could we?" I tried to keep the excitement out of my voice, but all of a sudden the idea of it seemed to consume me. "Are you sure you're up to it? I mean, you are nearly finished with the doctors, but what about therapy? Are you strong . . . ?"

"*Sshhh! Tais-toi!*" He pressed one finger against my lips.

"Why don't you check the Internet for flights, see what can be arranged? Go on, let me finish my newspaper in peace."

I kissed the hand that trailed across my cheek then flew toward the bedroom where Alain's laptop computer rested incongruously on an ornately gilded little bureau. I could be booking flights in a matter of minutes. *By this time tomorrow,* I thought, *we could be stepping off the plane in Savannah into warmth and sunshine and the sweet scents of home.*

I checked my headlong dash down the hallway as I passed the console beneath the heavy gilt mirror. I scooped up the package and reversed my steps back into the kitchen.

"Alain, I completely forgot! This came for you by messenger just before you got home."

I slid it onto the table, startled by his grunt of surprise and a barely perceptible recoil, as if the padded envelope were alive—and dangerous. For a moment he stared, his hands still gripping the edges of *Le Monde,* his cheeks drained of even the faint color the chill April sun had given him during his morning walk.

"What is it? Alain?" I prodded when he didn't reply.

With leaden arms, he lowered the paper and ran his fingers lightly across the address label. He turned it over, testing the contents much as I had done when it had been placed into my hands. Then with a sigh he said, *"Un couteau, s'il vous plaît."*

I handed him the same small knife I had used for the string on the pastry box, and he slit open the envelope. It *was* paper, several sheets of computer printout, with a handwritten note clipped to the upper left-hand corner. I could make out nothing of the heavy script except for the signature: *LeBrun.*

I didn't need a translator. The guilty excitement in Alain's eyes told me all I needed to know. LeBrun ran Interpol. Darnay had indeed recovered enough to travel.

And they wanted him back.

CHAPTER
TWO

The airport limousine negotiated the last of the ruts in the dusty dirt road and eased into the circular drive in front of Presqu'isle. I'd had the window rolled down during the entire one-hour trip from Savannah, and I leaned out to reacquaint myself with the sight of my childhood home. The tall, square-columned house sat high on its arched foundation of tabby, its split staircase gleaming with a fresh coat of white paint in the late afternoon sun.

The driver shut off the engine then moved around to the back of the vehicle to fling open the trunk. Behind me I heard his grunts as he hefted the luggage onto the ground. I sat, my chin resting on my arms, savoring the familiar smell of pluff mud and decay drifting up from the narrow strip of marsh that bordered St. Helena Sound at the rear of the property. In the warm silence of April in the Lowcountry I heard the muted cries of the curlews and ibis, the drumlike cadence of a woodpecker attacking the bole of a loblolly pine, and the high scream of a solitary gull as he skimmed along the shoreline in search of food and his fellows.

The driver paused, one highly polished black shoe resting on the first of the sixteen steps leading up to the verandah. "Ma'am," he called, indicating with a nod the two oversized suitcases he struggled with, "you want them all up here?"

"What?" I mumbled, startled by the sharp interruption of

my dreamy reverie, then, "Oh, the bags. Sure. Up on the porch is fine. I'll be right there."

I retrieved my tote from the floor next to my feet and pulled a twenty from my wallet, glancing to the empty seat beside me. With a brief shake of my head to clear the tears I felt rising in my throat, I pushed open the car door. I slung the jacket of my rumpled suit over one arm and followed the driver up the steps.

I leaned against the railing and gazed out across the front lawn. A carpet of pink and white petals lay strewn beneath the line of shrubs bordering the road, evidence that I had missed the azaleas in bloom. If the weather gods smiled, spring almost always came early to this southernmost tip of the Carolinas, bathed in soft breezes out of Florida and nudged gently by the warmth of the Gulf Stream as it meandered by off shore.

"I can take these inside if you like."

I turned at his voice, the nasal twang and harsh vowels betraying him as a Yankee transplant, one of thousands who swelled our already exploding population every month.

"No thanks, that's fine." I reached to hand him the twenty as he set the last two smaller cases next to the larger ones, arranging them so that all the edges were perfectly aligned.

An obsessive-compulsive Yankee, no less, I thought and smiled at his nod of thanks. He'd go far in this land of "Fiddle-dee-dee, I'll just worry about that tomorrow." No doubt he'd own the limousine company one day.

The longing for a cigarette jolted me, and I actually felt my hand reaching into my bag before my conscious mind ordered it to halt. I had quit, with only a little help from the various nicotine-replacement aids, as soon as it became apparent that Darnay's damaged lung could not tolerate the intrusion of smoke—his own or anyone else's. With that kind of incentive it had been much less stressful than I'd ever imagined. Strangely emancipating as well, and not just because I was no longer burdened with the paraphernalia of smoking. For the most part I had conquered the need. Incredible, too, that I had found the commitment so easy to keep in a country where everyone lit up everywhere, and no-smoking signs were as rare as restaurants that didn't serve wine.

Darnay's image shimmered before my eyes in the waning afternoon sun, and I pushed it away with an angry twist of my head. I had known what his decision would be—would *have* to be—the moment I recognized the signature on the background material LeBrun had sent to entice him back into their deadly game. Twenty-four hours of pleading and shouting had not altered his grim determination. Nor had it changed my own.

I had watched him hover near death once before. I couldn't do it again.

"Bay?"

I hadn't heard the heavy front door swing open on its well-oiled hinges. I turned to find Lavinia Smalls, her worn hands the color of polished oak folded primly against the starched blue apron. Her deep brown eyes regarded me solemnly. We stood staring at each other for a long moment, a lifetime of shared memory hovering between us on the still air of the wide verandah.

Then she smiled and opened her once-strong arms, and I rushed into her welcoming embrace, knowing as I laid my cheek against her face that I was truly home.

IF MY father felt any joy at the return of the prodigal daughter, he managed to conceal it well behind a cloud of smoke from his contraband Cuban cigar. I found him ensconced in his favorite spot on the verandah at the rear of the restored antebellum mansion. He had settled his wheelchair in the shade to the left of the ramp leading out from his old study which we had converted into a bedroom after his last stroke.

"Hello, Daddy." I pulled up my assigned rocker and kicked off my low-heeled pumps.

"About time you quit gallivantin' all over the damn world and came back where you belong." He cast a sidelong glance at me from the corner of his clear gray eyes and lifted his glass of bourbon and lemonade from the wicker table between us.

I made no attempt to embrace my father. Ours had never been a *touching* family, and we abhorred naked displays of emotion, which was why his lack of enthusiasm didn't particularly bother me. I hitched a footstool over in front of me, propped up my stockinged feet, and let the warmth and the birdsong and the soft breeze off the Sound settle around me. Again I breathed deeply of the dank odor of the marsh.

We sat that way for some time, the near silence and the familiar serenity of the Lowcountry afternoon lulling me into a peaceful half-doze until the Judge's words jerked me awake.

"You really quit smoking?"

I rubbed a hand across my face, willing myself back into consciousness. "Yes, sir. I've been clean for three months now."

His snort spoke volumes. "Well, don't think you're gonna start in on me about it. It's bad enough havin' Vinnie dole out my cigars and measure the level in the whiskey decanter every damn day. I won't tolerate any such nonsense from you."

"No, Your Honor."

I caught the twitch at the corner of his mouth just before he turned to face me.

"You look tired," he said, his voice softening now that he'd reestablished the chain of command to his satisfaction. "Bad flight?"

"No, just long. But I'm going to have to force myself to stay awake until something resembling a normal bedtime, or I'll never get reoriented."

I waited for him to ask the obvious question. Instead he resumed his contemplation of the wide lawn rolling down to the short dock and the soft lavender of evening creeping across the water. I realized I would have to be the one to raise the painful subject and get it out of the way.

"Darnay's going back to work."

"I figured as much." He rattled the melting ice cubes

around in his glass before swallowing the last of his diluted drink. "Can't expect a man to retire at his age."

The breeze had freshened, bringing with it the lingering remnants of winter's chill, and I shivered. "He wouldn't have been idle," I said, rubbing my hands along the silken sleeves of my thin blouse. "He has the house, the farm in Provençe . . ."

On the fading smoke from the Judge's cigar I drifted back to the cold Paris nights, Darnay and I wrapped in the duvet, curled on the Empire sofa before a blazing fire. Heads close together, we had pored over his sketchpad filled with drawings, designs, and landscapes. He would transform *Le Manoir d'Or* from a drafty, seventeenth-century cottage into a comfortable, modern home surrounded by a few acres of vines. In my mind we walked there, arm in arm, as the last light of a summer evening burnished the golden stone of the manor house, and sea-eyed children with dimples in their tiny chins protested the call to bed.

"Bay?" Lavinia's soft tread on the old boards of the verandah had failed to penetrate my reverie, and I jumped. "Sorry. Telephone," she said.

"Is it . . . ?"

"No, it's Erik. Callin' to welcome you home, I expect. Shall I take a message?"

"No, thanks. I'll get it." I swiped my thumbs across the corners of my eyes and forced my swollen feet back into my pumps.

"Are you staying the night?" Lavinia asked as I followed her down the ramp and into the Judge's study.

"If it's okay," I answered, unable to contemplate the cold, yawning emptiness of the beach house on Hilton Head. Without Dolores and the cat, there was nothing and no one to care if I ever returned.

"Dinner in about an hour," she said over her shoulder as she made her way toward the kitchen. "Get changed and you can give me a hand."

As if she needed my help, I thought. My culinary skills, though vastly improved during my sojourn in the land that invented haute cuisine, were still rudimentary at best. I forced a smile into my voice and picked up the receiver.

"Hey, Erik! What's up?"

"So the long-lost Bay Tanner returns! Welcome home, partner."

Erik Whiteside was the third member, along with the Judge and me, of the loose confederation we had dubbed Simpson & Tanner, Inquiry Agents. The manager of an electronics store in Charlotte, Erik brought a sharp intellect and an encyclopedic knowledge of computers and the Internet to our fledgling enterprise which so far had failed to attract a single paying client. At least so far as I knew. I had been out of circulation for nearly five months.

"Thanks. It's good to be back," I said.

The silence grew as Erik fumbled for some way to inquire about what had sent me scurrying back to the old homestead. My e-mail to him had merely announced my intentions and approximate arrival time without offering any explanation as to the reasons for my abrupt departure from the City of Light.

I decided to let him off the hook. I was going to have to get used to answering the unasked question. "Darnay had some business to take care of, family stuff, so I decided to spend a little time at home." I lied with an ease that made me just a little uncomfortable.

"Great! So how about getting together? We could run down there this weekend, if it's okay with you."

"We?"

"Well, you know, Mercer and I. We've sort of been seeing each other now and then."

I could visualize the color creeping slowly up toward his pale blond hair, and it brought me the first genuine pleasure I'd felt in a number of days. That my flaky half fifth cousin, Mercer Mary Prescott, and my rock-solid partner had hit it off still amazed and delighted me. At least someone's love life was on track.

"Sure, that would be great. When do you think you'll head out?"

"I'll check on hotels and see what we can work out for Friday night. If I leave here around noon, I can pick Merce up at the farm on the way down."

My cousin and her mother rented a small place about halfway between Orangeburg and Walterboro. I was surprised to hear that, despite their newfound wealth, they still lived in the ramshackle old farmhouse where I had sought refuge just before Christmas last year. I turned at the hiss of the tires on the Judge's motorized wheelchair as he rolled down the ramp.

"Forget about hotels, Erik," I said, recalling the mass of humanity pressing around the carousels on the lower level of the Savannah Airport as I'd claimed my bags. "It's Heritage week. You'd better plan on staying with me at the beach house."

The annual PGA tournament, contested on the famous Harbour Town golf course in Sea Pines on the south end of Hilton Head, swelled our population to overflowing every April.

"You sure? We wouldn't want to impose."

"Not at all," I replied with false confidence. *Friday!* Which left me only a couple of days to get the house opened up and in some kind of condition to receive visitors. And then there were groceries to buy and flowers and . . . But it beat the hell out of sitting around alone and brooding. "I'm looking forward to it," I said with a conviction I almost believed.

"It won't just be all pleasure, either," Erik said with the hint of a smile in his voice. "I think we might have a client."

"Oh, really?"

"Yeah, this guy I know in Charleston called and asked if I could help him find some stuff on the Web, maybe teach him how to get into some places he couldn't access." Erik's prowess in penetrating secure servers and databases had been well established during our initial collaboration in tracking down a vicious serial killer. "It sounded pretty weird, so I pressed him for details. I know it's not exactly what we set out to do, but he doesn't want to go to the cops, and his dad's got plenty of money, so that won't be a problem. I told him all about you and the Judge, and he wants to hire us, but I told him I'd have to run it by you guys first."

Despite myself, I was intrigued. "So what is it he wants to know?"

The pause lasted just long enough to achieve the effect Erik intended. "He dug up a body, and he wants us to find out who it was."

CHAPTER
THREE

I shut off the ignition and sat for a moment in my driveway, savoring the silence. The house looked much the same, the boards replaced after the explosion already weathering into the same muted, silvery tan of the original wood siding. The shrubs were neatly trimmed, and the ever-present pine straw had been blown from the concrete pad into neat piles along its edges. Apparently the maintenance company I'd hired before dashing off to Paris had been earning its fees in my absence.

I slammed the door on the rented car then paused to allow the low murmur of the ocean to wash over me. The rhythmic *whoosh* and roll of the breakers soothed some of the chaotic jumble rattling around in my head: *Rob, Dolores, fire, explosion, Mr. Bones, pain, death . . . Darnay.*

I shook off the ghosts and began wrestling my bags from the shallow trunk. If I kept myself busy, perhaps I could hold the memories at bay. Slamming the lid, I decided the first order of business was transportation. I hated the thought of having to shop for a vehicle again, but it was something I had to face up to soon. Considering the fact I had demolished two perfectly good automobiles in a matter of six months, I hoped I would still be able to get insurance.

The stale, heavy air hit me like a slap when I stepped through into the foyer. Without hesitating I strode across the great room and flung open the French doors onto the deck, moving purposefully then from room to room until every window in the house stood wide to the cool breeze drifting over the dunes from the beach.

Two hours later I had slid the last of my French silk lingerie into the dresser drawers, stowed the suitcases in the attic, and stood leaning against the railing on the deck outside my bedroom. The evening sky over the ocean had deepened to a rich purple, and against this darkening backdrop, the lights of a freighter passing by on its way to the Port of Savannah sparkled on the horizon. Below, the rustling of the night creatures accompanied the cries of hungry gulls and the soft rattling of the wind in the palmettos.

I was home, and I wanted a cigarette so badly I could have screamed.

BY THE time I set the last pots of bright red geraniums and scarlet-throated hibiscus along the edges of the back deck on Friday night, the smoking urge had subsided to manageable proportions, and I had amazed myself at what I had accomplished in two short days. The refrigerator and larder overflowed with the results of my extended excursion to Publix; the cleaning ladies had helped me banish the accumulated dust of four months of neglect from furniture, walls, and carpets; and a call to Carolyn's Nursery on the north end of the island had brought an efficient crew to transform my winter-brown flowerbeds into spring magnificence.

I turned at the sound of a powerful engine easing up the driveway and went to greet my guests, the first I had allowed to storm the walls of my hideout without Dolores for backup. The idea of facing this weekend without my former housekeeper suddenly overwhelmed me, and I had to wipe my damp palms on the seat of my khaki pants before reaching for the handle to pull open the front door.

They looked almost like parent and child standing there hand-in-hand on my porch. Erik Whiteside, blond and tanned and well over six feet tall, towered above my diminutive half fifth cousin, Mercer Mary Prescott, whose dress and personal hygiene had taken a decided turn for the better since our last meeting. I flashed back to the first time we'd encountered each other, through the bulletproof partition of the visitor's room in the Beaufort County Jail, and marveled at the changes a few short months and an unexpected infusion of cash could make in a girl's appearance. Her mousy brown hair now sported pale gold highlights and curved softly around her narrow face. The grungy, black-rimmed glasses had obviously been replaced by contacts, and I thought I detected a hint of deftly applied makeup, especially around her eyes. The short denim jumper and white T-shirt were pressed and spotless, and I was pretty certain the navy blue Birkenstock sandals were new.

Not a hole or a rip anywhere. *How very un-Mercer-like,* I thought.

"Is there a secret password, partner, or can we come in now?"

I reached quickly to unlatch the screen. "Of course! Sorry. It's just . . . well, damn it, Mercer, I wouldn't have recognized you! Come in, both of you. I'm so glad you're here."

The moment I said the words I knew they were true. During the long Paris winter with Darnay, I had finally been able to shed the mantle of grief and guilt which seemed to have been hanging over me for years. Coming home—*alone*—had threatened to plunge me back into that pit of despair. These two would bring youth and life and happiness into this place of ghosts and bad memories, dispel the aura of sadness that seemed to permeate the walls of the beach house.

I flung open the door and embraced them both.

"SO TELL me about this client of ours," I said as I poured coffee into one of the mismatched mugs and passed it over to Erik.

Mercer had decided to join me in after-dinner tea, and the kettle had yet to whistle its readiness. I stacked the dirty dishes on the counter and returned to the table where the three of us lounged in companionable informality.

"That was quite a meal, by the way," Erik said, raising his

cup in acknowledgment. "Sure didn't take you long to pick up on this cooking thing. Did you learn all that in Paris?"

"Thanks," I replied, unexpectedly shy under his frank compliments. For years my inability to do more than punch the buttons on the microwave had been the subject of good-natured ribbing from practically everyone I knew. "I did take a couple of classes while I was there. It's hard not to get caught up in the whole culinary thing. Food and wine are some of the most frequent topics of conversation. I sort of had to get in the game or find myself with nothing to contribute."

The teakettle shrieked, and Mercer Mary Prescott leaped from her chair. "I'll get it," she offered as she crossed to the range top on the center island.

I pointed out the cupboard which held the tea bags then turned back to Erik. "Okay, enough stalling. Let's hear it."

He grinned at me and sipped his coffee, heavily laden with milk and sweetener. ' Well, it's not that I'm stalling, exactly. It's just the whole thing's sort of weird, as I told you on the phone, and I'm beginning to think we might want to take a pass."

"Why? I thought this guy was a friend of yours."

"Not exactly a friend. We went to college together, at N.C. State. We had some of the same classes, and we sort of hit it off, used to meet for a few beers on the weekends, hang out at the same parties. You know."

Mercer set a mug of tea in front of me then carried her own back to her place next to Erik. The smile they exchanged sent a stab of loneliness straight through my chest. *Damn you, Darnay!* I thought for about the millionth time since I'd boarded the huge jet at Orly Airport an ocean away. *Damn you!*

I jerked my mind back to the matter at hand. I was having difficulty understanding Erik's sudden reluctance to give me the details of this supposed new case. He had sounded so up-beat on the telephone. "Why don't you just tell me what this guy wants us to do, and let's talk about it. You said he found some bones. Where? When? Why does he think they might be human? And why didn't he just go to the police?"

Erik's deep brown eyes held mine for a moment then flicked briefly toward Mercer, and it dawned on me he didn't want to discuss details in front of her.

Too gruesome? I asked myself and almost laughed aloud at how ridiculous the idea sounded. Mercer Mary Prescott had been in her share of scrapes with the law, had even spent time in jail. She'd done some pretty disgusting things in support of her obsession with our shared ancestors, so I really didn't think hearing the details about the discovery of a few old bones would send her into a fit of the vapors or whatever else Erik feared might happen. Still, it was his story, his call . . .

I was racking my brain for some excuse to send her out of the room when she apparently caught the vibes and rose from the table. "I think I'll check in on Cat, see how she's doing on her own," my cousin said. "Is there a phone I can use?"

Mercer Mary's mother, Catherine, had a long history of mental instability, supposedly now kept under control by a new miracle drug, but I was glad to know my cousin was keeping close tabs on her.

"There's one in your room."

I turned back to Erik, remembering with a smile my dread as I'd pulled long-unused linens from the cupboard and carried sheets and towels into the guest room. I hadn't a clue of how to approach the awkwardness of determining if I needed to make up the sleeper sofa or if these two planned on sharing a bed. They had solved the dilemma before I even had an opportunity to ask by tossing both bags into the guest room and emptying two sets of toiletries onto the counters of the adjoining bath.

"So you really quit smoking," Erik said, a statement rather than a question, but I answered him anyway, my eyes following my cousin's progress toward the hallway.

"Yes, I did. Why is everyone so amazed? I thought at least some of my friends might have had a little more confidence in me."

Erik pointed at the small pile of blue paper littering the

table in front of me. Without thinking, I had taken the empty packet of artificial sweetener and systematically torn it into tiny squares. "Oh, I don't know . . . Maybe something to do with your obsessive-compulsive nature?" His bright laugh took any sting from the words. "You should think about taking up knitting."

"Go to hell," I said, returning his smile then sobering. "Tell me about the bones."

Erik straightened around in his chair and planted his elbows firmly on the glass-topped table. "Gray—that's my buddy, Gray Palmer—was doing some digging on this island, and he came across a skull. Human. At first he thought it might be Indian, maybe the site of an old burial ground or something, but then he realized it couldn't be."

He paused and glanced toward the hallway. I followed his gaze. Over the low hum of the air conditioning I could hear Mercer Mary Prescott's voice through the open door of the bedroom.

"Where was this?" I asked. I rose to refresh Erik's coffee, then my own tea, and settled back into my chair.

"Well, that's just it, he doesn't want to say. I guess he could be in trouble for even being there, so he's keeping that to himself for the time being."

"Why was he digging? Did he tell you that?"

"No. He's working with this group, but . . ."

"But he can't say who they are," I finished for him, and Erik nodded.

I flashed back to my previous involvement with one gang of pseudo-environmentalists and another of anti-nuke wackos and shook my head. "No way. I don't want any part of some bunch of nuts with an agenda. I vote for running as fast as we can in the opposite direction of whatever this guy's up to."

"How do you know they're nuts?" There was an edge to his voice I hadn't heard before, a hint of anger.

"Erik, think back to what we just went through a little more than five months ago, what happened to Mercer. We almost got ourselves killed, if you recall."

He shrugged and studied the picture of the Harbour Town Lighthouse emblazoned on the side of his coffee mug. I watched his wide shoulders relax before his face lifted to mine. The old smile was back. "But we didn't, did we? Get killed, I mean."

"That's not the point. Look, tell me everything you know about this guy and the mess he's gotten himself into. Then we can make a semi-intelligent decision."

"Okay. He found the skull, kept digging, found the rest of the skeleton. When he realized what he'd stumbled on, he covered it back up, marked it so he could find the spot again, and got the hell out of there. He won't say where he found it, and he won't say why he was there. What he wants from us is to find a way to determine who the dead guy is without alerting the authorities."

"Well that's just ridiculous! How would either one of us know a thing like that? The only way to determine the identity of a body, so far as I'm aware, is for a coroner or a forensic pathologist to examine the remains. To do that, they need to have access to the corpse. And something to compare it with, like dental records."

I turned at the sound of the toilet flushing in the guest bath and realized Mercer must be finished with her call. "I don't see how we can help him, do you? Besides I really don't like all this secrecy stuff."

Erik had heard the water running as well and rushed to finish. "He took one of the bones. He wants us to find someone willing to examine it and try to find out at least how old the skeleton is. He'll take it from there."

I sighed and shook my head. This sounded *exactly* like a case I wanted nothing to do with. "How does he know it isn't what he first suggested, an old Indian burial ground? Why does he think the corpse can even be identified?"

Erik smiled as Mercer crossed the great room and started up the three steps into the kitchen. In a voice so low I had to strain to hear him, he said, "Because he found a wristwatch still strapped to the guy's arm."

CHAPTER
FOUR

The next morning we enjoyed a leisurely breakfast then joined the long line of vehicles snaking their way around the infamous traffic circle on the south end of Hilton Head Island. As we crawled toward the main entrance to Sea Pines, I reached across from my place in the backseat of Erik Whiteside's massive Ford Expedition and handed him our tickets.

"You'll need to show these at the security gate," I said.

When Erik had expressed an interest the night before in experiencing the Heritage golf tournament in person, I had scrambled around to come up with passes to the always sold-out event. Big Cal Elliott, my best friend Bitsy's husband and a man I thoroughly detested, grudgingly parted with some spares he had not yet handed out to political cronies or potential customers of his vast used-car empire. Bits and I shared a brief hug and a promise to get together soon when I breezed by to pick up the tickets. Although she was too much of a friend to ask right then, I saw the questions about Darnay reflected in her soft blue eyes, and I knew I'd be in for an intensive interrogation over our next lunch.

Better get used to it, I warned myself. *She won't be the only one.*

We pulled up to the gate, and a guard in full Scottish regalia, from tam-o'-shanter to kilt and patterned knee socks, glanced briefly at the tickets Erik held out the window and waved us through. We crept along the two-lane road leading into the heart of the late Charles Fraser's visionary development, the first on this once-deserted island which now ranked as one of the poshest resort destinations on the eastern seaboard. Having lived in the area all my life except for my last few years of college, spent at Northwestern on the frigid shores of Lake Michigan, I sometimes forgot that this explosion of population and tourism had happened over a relatively short period of time.

"Is the traffic always like this?" Mercer Mary Prescott asked, turning in the passenger seat to face me.

"This isn't bad at all," I said as we approached the first of the designated parking areas roped off beyond a line of trees to our left. "Tomorrow, for the final round, we'd be lucky to get in the gate unless we started out a lot earlier."

"I didn't realize there were this many people so crazy about golf." Erik cranked the air conditioning up a notch as the uniformed parking attendant waved the line of cars past the overflowing lot and on toward the next.

"It's the biggest event on the island, since the Family Circle tennis tournament moved up to Charleston," I replied. "Some locals plan their vacations for this time every year and get out of town, while others consider it the social highpoint and spend the whole week partying."

Rob and I had been frequent guests over the years at the rolling parties throughout the Sea Pines community, often spending the night with friends on Calibogue Cay just to avoid having to deal with the traffic.

"Maybe this wasn't such a good idea," Mercer mumbled from the front seat, and Erik reached over to pat her tanned thigh.

Again I smiled to myself at this unlikely alliance.

Within twenty minutes, we had wound our way up to the big open area next to Lawton Stables, followed the direction of one of the many volunteers into a tight parking space, and joined the short line awaiting one of the many motor coaches pressed into service from as far away as Charleston.

Using buses was an efficient method of handling the thousands who flocked to the tournament each year, and in a short time we were whisked off in air-conditioned comfort and deposited in the heart of Harbour Town.

We followed the throng around the curve of the harbor lined with everything from small motor boats to massive, multimillion-dollar yachts. Mercer Mary Prescott's gold-tinted hair flipped from side to side as her head swiveled in an effort to take in the elegantly dressed people, the quaint shops and restaurants, and the magnificent condominiums flanking this tiny jewel of a marina.

Without conscious thought, my eyes strayed to the windows of the penthouse apartment at the far end of the promenade. For an instant, the noise and jostle of the crowd faded, and in my mind I lay again in the arms of Geoffrey Anderson, gazing out at the lights of the harbor below us. In spite of the warm midday sun, I shuddered, reliving in a kaleidoscopic flash those days of longing, fear, betrayal . . .

"Bay, is something wrong?"

I felt Erik's hand on my shoulder a second before his words registered, and I shook myself as if waking from a nasty dream.

"No, sorry. I'm fine."

His look said he thought otherwise, but I pasted a reassuring smile on my face and moved out into the lead.

"Come on, let's move up by the clubhouse. That way we can see the players on both the first tee and the ninth green without having to walk too far."

I strode off, leaving Mercer and Erik to trail along behind, weaving my way at a brisk pace through the slow-moving crowd.

Will I ever be free of the ghosts? I wondered as we stopped to have our passes inspected at the entrance to the golf course area. *So much misery and death in the past couple of years, and yet . . .*

A roar went up from the tightly packed group pressed along the edge of the number one tee to our left. Mercer's, "Oh my God, there's Greg Norman!" was followed by Erik's laughing, "I thought you didn't know anything about golf," and I was thankfully back in the sunlight of the present once again.

I CARRIED my hot dog, loaded with ketchup and onions, and an icy can of Diet Coke to a vacant table and settled gratefully into the matching white plastic chair. Despite the canopy of shade provided by the interlacing branches of the little grove of trees, sweat streaked my face and trickled down between my breasts. I popped the top on the soda and guzzled half of it down.

After giving them a quick orientation on the layout of the various holes, I had sent Erik and Mercer off to explore on their own and wandered down the concrete path to this spot where Rob and I had often rested our feet during previous tournaments. Situated between the fifteenth green and the sixteenth tee, the welcome oasis provided the perfect place to relax and watch the golfers parade by in their groups of two or three, caddies trailing behind lugging the heavy bags of clubs. Sooner or later, every one of them had to pass this spot. Besides which, S.H.A.R.E., the local senior center, manned the concession booth right behind me, and they cooked up the best hot dogs on the grounds.

I'd arranged to meet the youngsters there in a couple of hours.

Youngsters. I smiled to myself and wiped a dribble of ketchup from the corner of my mouth. Erik was only ten or twelve years my junior, while Mercer was at least in her early twenties. June would find me turning thirty-nine, with the ominous watershed of forty lurking right behind. If I ever expected to have children . . .

I glanced up as a cheer erupted from the stands surrounding the green to my left. I propped my feet up on the chair next to me, wadded my napkin and the empty hot dog wrapper into a ball, and tossed them in a long arc toward the nearby trash can. I snapped my fingers when my makeshift missile landed cleanly in the center of the opening.

"She shoots—she scores!"

I turned at the laugh which followed this announcement to find a man towering over me, his face lost in a sliver of sunlight filtering through a gap in the leaves. I tilted my head to avoid the glare just as he removed his sunglasses and moved closer.

"I thought it was you, but I wasn't certain. How are you, Bay? When did you get back? I thought I heard you'd decided to stay in Europe."

It took me a moment to place the eager, open smile and boyish countenance of the young Beaufort attorney who had handled the affairs of the Herrington family. I suffered a brief flash of guilt for not having been in touch lately with Jordan von Brandt. One of the three Herrington offspring who had inherited their late parents' hardware stores, Jordan had set in motion the chain of events that led me to Darnay.

"Chris. Chris Brandon," he said, extending his hand. "Maybe you don't . . ."

"Of course I remember. It's good to see you." I shook his hand, lowered my feet, and gestured toward the empty chair. "Have a seat. Tell me what's been happening in the old hometown."

His answering smile was out of all proportion to my casual invitation. "Thanks! Gosh, you look great," he said, running his hand through his wavy brown hair in a nervous gesture which would have identified him to me even if I couldn't have seen his face.

"Thank you." I acknowledged the compliment, recalling with discomfort that the awkward young lawyer had displayed something resembling a crush on me during our brief encounters over the Bi-Rite Hardware fiasco. "You look different though, somehow. I can't quite put my finger on it, but definitely different."

The blush started at his chin and worked its way in seconds to the roots of his unruly hair. "Laser surgery on my eyes. I finally got rid of the glasses."

"Good for you," I said, refraining from telling him the loss of his wire-rimmed spectacles made him look even younger and more vulnerable, not necessarily desirable traits in a practicing attorney. "It suits you," I lied.

"Thanks. So what brings you back? I hope the Judge isn't . . ."

I waved away his concern, although not before a little ripple of fear ran along my nerve endings. He'd been okay a couple of days before, ornery and overbearing as ever. And surely Lavinia would have said . . . I flinched, suddenly remembering the repeated questions in her letters about when I was coming home.

"Bay? Is something wrong?"

"Oh, no, Chris. Sorry. The Judge is fine. I guess I just got homesick. Paris is wonderful, but it's so hard to get a decent glass of sweet tea."

He smiled. "I can see how that would be a major problem."

Conversation halted all around as Phil Mickelson and David Duval hurried by us, their cleats clacking against the concrete of the cart path. When their respective fans and entourages had clustered around the edges of the next tee box, Chris resumed.

"Listen, this is really funny, my running into you this way. I was thinking about you just the other day, wishing you were still around." My face must have betrayed the apprehension this statement engendered in me because he stammered a bit before going on. "I mean, you know, it's really great you're back and all, and I know the Judge must be thrilled and . . . well, it's just . . . I have this client." The rambling sentence stumbled to a conclusion, and he regarded me expectantly across the table.

I waited for him to continue, unsure what sort of response I was supposed to make.

"The case is right up your alley, a possible embezzlement or at least some hanky-panky with the books, and I was thinking it would be great if you could take a look at it for me." When I failed to answer, he mumbled, "You know, like you did for the Herringtons."

The offer took me completely by surprise. I had given no thought to what I would do to occupy my time once I was back in my old neighborhood. All I had been able to think of was getting out of Paris, away from the anger and disappointment I read in Darnay's eyes every time we passed each other in the hallway or tripped over each other on the way to the bathroom. I really hadn't planned any farther ahead than the next few days. Chris's proposal had reminded me with a jolt that I would have to find something to do or I'd die of boredom. One thing was certain: I was *not* getting involved with Erik's friend and his dismembered skeleton.

"I might have time to take a look at it for you," I heard myself saying. "Yes, I think I'd like that. When can we get together?"

"Great! How about Monday at my office? Is ten good for you?"

"Sure . . ." I began when I felt a presence at my back, and a shadow fell across the white table between us.

Chris Brandon jumped immediately to his feet. "Oh, good, you're here. I want you to meet a friend of mine," he said.

The shadow moved around and resolved itself into a pretty young woman in a white sundress, her long, light brown hair topped by a wide-brimmed straw hat. She snaked one tanned arm around Chris's waist and smiled tentatively up into his face.

"Amy, I'd like you to meet Bay Tanner. I know I've spoken to you about her. She helped me with the Herrington estate last year. Bay, this is Amy Fleming. My fiancée."

I suppose the shock must have registered on my face, and I found myself uncharacteristically at a loss for words. Amy struggled to keep the self-satisfied smirk of the newly affianced from lifting one corner of her generous mouth. I waited for her to waggle an impossibly huge diamond under my nose, and she didn't disappoint.

Okay, so maybe I *had* gotten just a little too used to Chris Brandon dancing attendance on me, too smug about regarding him as a fawning puppy trotting obediently at my heels.

When I recovered my voice, I immediately wished I hadn't. "How lovely to meet you," I heard myself gushing.

"Congratulations! It's strange we've never met before. Are your people from the County?"

God, I thought, *I do not believe I said that!* Mama would have been proud.

"Amy's father's in the service." Chris broke in before his soon-to-be-bride had a chance to respond. "Career Marine. Colonel Harlan Fleming?"

He left the sentence hanging, as if I should be nodding sagely in recognition. The truth was I had no idea who Colonel Fleming was and frankly didn't care to. Except for the fact that Red, my sheriff's deputy brother-in-law, had once been a Marine, I had no connection whatsoever to the military and planned to keep it that way. Over the years I'd had more than enough experience with Citadel graduates, including my own father. The arrogance seemed to linger long after the uniform had been folded away.

"So you must have moved around a lot," I ventured, twisting in my chair to avoid the slanting beam of sunlight.

I was beginning to think the child couldn't speak as Chris replied, "All over the world. Amy was actually born in Turkey, can you imagine?"

He patted her hand, now tucked possessively into the crook of his arm, and she smiled up into his naked eyes.

"Not much different really from being born in the States," she said, the sweetness of her face now evident since she'd dropped the simper of triumph. "Except I have two birth certificates, and one of them is written in Turkish."

I was trying to think of some tactful way to extricate myself from the inevitable next act of this already-scripted exchange in which I would be expected to inquire into the details of the wedding—date, location, number of attendants, an exhaustive description of the gown, etc., etc., etc.

As if in answer to prayer, I heard a familiar voice call, "There she is!"

We all turned as Erik strode up to the table, Mercer trotting along behind. I could tell by his expression that something was very wrong, and my cousin's normally pale skin had gone ashen.

"What is it?" I asked, jumping to my feet. "What's happened?"

Erik stood awkwardly, his head swiveling from Chris and Amy to me and back again. I managed to stutter out perfunctory introductions, and everyone smiled and nodded, but the tension level had to be evident even to someone as generally oblivious as Chris Brandon.

"Well, nice to have met you both," Chris finally said, steering his fiancée toward the sixteenth hole. "Bay, I'll see you on Monday?" he called over his shoulder.

For a moment I had no idea what he could be talking about, then our pre-Amy discussion came back to me, and I nodded. "Sure. Monday. At ten."

Erik immediately sank into the chair across from me.

"What?" I demanded for the second time in as many minutes.

"I just got a call on my cell, from someone named Mindy . . . something, I don't remember now. The name's not important."

"Slow down . . ." I began, but he cut me off.

"She's a friend of . . . works with . . . Gray Palmer. Remember the guy I told you about?"

"The one who found the bones?" A shiver of fear skittered across my scalp and down my back.

"Yeah, him." Erik paused to run a hand over his sweating face. "They just pulled him out of the water south of Charleston. He's dead."

CHAPTER FIVE

Back at the beach house, I abandoned my newly acquired passion for culinary experimentation, and we called Giuseppi's for pizza. Once again Mercer was on the phone checking up on Cat, and Erik and I sat huddled together over the kitchen table.

"Tell me again what this Mindy person said," I urged him. "Word for word if you can remember."

"Why? I mean, what does it matter?"

I had never seen my partner so downcast. Even in the darkest times—his grandmother's murder, the incredible scene high in the three-story house where it seemed as if we might watch each other die—Erik Whiteside had been confident, upbeat, optimistic. This was my first experience with his sullen, defeated side, and I didn't know how to react to it. So far I'd tried cajolery, sympathy, and businesslike brusqueness. Nothing had worked. Time to try another tack.

"What does it matter?" I parroted his question. "It matters because I want to know! Now quit acting like a baby and answer me!"

His head snapped up at the anger in my voice, and his response was just as intense. "You didn't want to help him in the first place! What the hell difference does it make what his moronic girlfriend said? Dead is dead. End of story. Case closed."

Erik dropped his face into his hands in a gesture at once

exasperated and pathetic. In spite of his recent brushes with death, the drowning of his old college drinking buddy seemed to have unnerved him completely. I reached to lay a hand on his muscled forearm and forced him to look at me.

"What has you so upset?" I asked softly. "It's a shock, of course, especially since you just talked with him a few days ago. But you weren't that close, were you?"

I didn't notice Mercer had slipped into the chair next to his until her thin, childlike hand joined mine on Erik's arm. The possessive look my cousin shot me stirred the simmering resentment I usually managed to control whenever she was around. In my mind I knew her dropping into our lives on that stormy night the previous November had not directly caused the misery that followed it, but my gut blamed her anyway.

Erik slid his arm out from under our hands and crossed the kitchen to throw open the refrigerator door. "I need a beer." He twisted off the cap, tilted a slug down his throat, and flopped back down in his chair.

"Look," I said as he studied the wet rings the sweating bottle left on the shimmering glass tabletop, "I understand it's not pleasant when someone you know dies." I gulped a little at that masterpiece of understatement. "But it's not as if you could have done anything . . ."

"How do we know that?" he asked, some of the anger easing out of his face. "I mean, God! We . . . we made fun of him, almost. Like he was some sort of kook or . . ."

"Hey!" I interrupted him. "That wasn't *we*. That was *me*. So if you want to beat someone up about it, get the guilty party." I paused to let some more of the tension drain out of the air. "If you like, we can step outside and go a couple of rounds."

He almost smiled. "Nah. I guess I'm being a jerk. I just wish . . ."

"You wish you could change things. You can't." I knew I didn't have to explain to Erik Whiteside why this had become the bedrock of my personal philosophy. He understood. He proved it by nodding gently; and his eyes, when he raised them to meet my own, were clear and steady.

I opened my mouth to ask again for the story of the phone call when the peal of the doorbell interrupted. I grabbed my wallet, and traded money for pizza in the time-honored tradition of my pre-Paris days. I sent Mercer scurrying for plates, napkins, and cutlery as I set the large box in the center of the table. Whatever Erik had to tell me, it would sit better on a full stomach. At least that's what I told myself as I licked dripping mozzarella off my fingers and tried to turn the conversation to something suitable for the dinner table.

"Did you guys enjoy the golf today?" I pulled an errant slice of pepperoni from the bottom of the box and popped it into my mouth. When neither of them responded, I pressed on, determined to keep us away from unpalatable topics. "I've always thought it was a boring game to watch. Especially on television. I put it right up there with billiards and bowling as far as spectator sports are concerned."

Again I got no response. Mercer crossed to the refrigerator and returned with two cans of Diet Coke. She set one in front of me and popped the other open. The silence settled around us. I forced myself to finish another slice before I slid the last of the pizza onto Erik's plate and carried the empty box to the counter. I busied myself with tidying up around the sink while Mercer brought the used plates and silverware to the counter. Over the racks of the dishwasher I saw her nod.

In for a penny, in for a pound, I told myself, not for the first time in the past several months, and sat back down at the table across from my partner. I felt the nervous flutter just beneath my breastbone which signaled my body's craving for nicotine, and I pushed it viciously away. "Okay, tell me about the phone call."

"It's pretty gruesome," Erik said, his eyes darting to Mercer.

"I figured that. You up for it?" I asked her.

"I can handle it," my cousin said firmly, tossing the dish towel onto the counter as she crossed back to the table. "Y'all need to quit treating me like a baby."

"Fair enough. Go ahead, Erik."

"You sure?" He reached for her slender hand.

"God sakes, I used to work in a nut house! You really think you can shock me?"

I winced, but her candor had apparently made its point.

Erik shrugged. "Okay. Mindy Albright. She and Gray work . . . *worked* on some kind of project that involved the Sea Islands, up and down the coast, from Charleston to Jacksonville. She didn't say what they did or what they were looking for. She just wanted me to know that Gray . . . that Gray had gone out yesterday on his boat, to check something out, she said. When he didn't come home last night—I got the idea they lived together—she didn't panic at first because he's apparently done this before, gotten on the trail of something and lost track of time."

Erik paused and swiped his napkin across his upper lip. He did look flushed even though the air conditioning was blowing full blast. Mercer seemed on the verge of asking something, but I quelled her with a pointed look.

"Go on," I said.

"The police showed up at her door around noon to tell her . . . tell her someone had spotted his boat running in circles and called the Coast Guard. It had run out of gas by the time they got a patrol out there."

He didn't flinch, but I could tell it pained him to relate the rest of the story told to him by a perfect stranger over the phone. The Coast Guard had boarded the drifting boat and found it empty, although a local fisherman had reported seeing the seventeen-foot Sea Pro spinning in circles just an hour or so before. While Erik confessed to knowing absolutely nothing about boats—an ignorance I shared—apparently the professionals took to wondering why someone would have abandoned a craft with the throttle set at full, especially since a rope dangling over the side seemed to indicate the anchor might have been deployed. When they hauled up the line, they found their answer.

Gray Palmer had somehow become entangled in the rope and gone overboard. Dangling helplessly underwater, he had come in contact with the propeller. Repeatedly.

Erik stopped, and the air seemed to vibrate with the ugly picture his words had conjured up. Mercer and I exchanged looks of horror.

"Do you mean . . . ?" I began.

"Yes," he said between clenched teeth. "The props nearly chewed his face off. The only way they could identify him was by his clothes and his wallet."

The silence lasted several minutes. Mercer quietly left the table, passing her hand gently across Erik's shoulder before trotting down the steps and disappearing into the hallway. I hoped she wasn't in the bathroom, losing her pizza, which was exactly what *I* felt like doing. I swallowed hard and asked the question that had been nagging at me almost from the first.

"Why did this Mindy person call you?"

"What?"

"Mindy Albright. Gray's girlfriend or whatever. Where'd she get your number? Why did she call *you*?"

Erik shrugged. "I don't really know for sure. She was pretty upset. I didn't want to press her."

"But surely the question occurred to you, too?"

"Sure it did. All she said was Gray had told her about the . . . bones and all, and that he'd been in touch with me about identifying them. She found my numbers in his Day-Timer, tried the store, then my cell. She said she thought I'd want to know."

"Strange behavior for a woman whose boyfriend just died. I mean, you'd think she'd be out of her mind with grief or whatever, wouldn't you?"

An image so vivid it nearly took my breath away flashed briefly in front of my eyes: *Rob's plane exploded in a thunderous roar . . . flaming debris and body parts littered the small country airstrip . . . my own flesh smoldered under the assault of white-hot metal falling from the sky . . .* Without conscious thought my hand moved to touch the scars on my left shoulder, the ridges of the mangled tissue discernible to my fingers through the thin fabric of my cotton shirt.

Erik shrugged again. "I suppose. Her voice was pretty

rough, as if she might have been crying a lot. But she wasn't babbling or anything. Gave me all the details in logical order."

The details. I shivered, praying Gray Palmer had drowned or at least been unconscious long before his face ever made contact with the deadly propellers.

"So did she say *why* she thought you'd want to know? Aside from the fact that you and Gray knew each other?"

Erik fidgeted, tapping his fingers in rhythmic succession against the glass table. The sound sent little shivers of annoyance up my spine, and I reached across to still his hand.

"Erik?"

The look he gave me was half apology, half defiance. "She thinks it might not have been an accident, and she's afraid. She asked me to help her." He paused and leveled his clear brown eyes at my face. "And I told her I would."

NONE OF us had the heart for any more detailed discussion of the horror of Gray Palmer's death, but we kicked it around in generalities awhile before deciding to call it a night. Sometimes Scarlett O'Hara's method of dealing with trouble—*I'll just worry about that tomorrow*—seemed the best course of action. I sent the young people off to their room, tidied up the kitchen, and carried a steaming cup of Earl Grey with me out onto the deck.

I shivered a little in the salty breeze floating in off the Atlantic and curled myself onto the brightly flowered cushion of the chaise. I half expected Mr. Bones, the scruffy tomcat I'd adopted after Rob's murder, to come bounding up into my lap as he had on so many other soft nights when I'd taken my problems to the solitude of the stars and the ocean. But, like so much else in my life, he was gone, disappearing into the palmettos as unexpectedly as he'd once emerged. He was a good hunter, as the tiny skeletons that once littered my yard could attest, so I knew he would survive. I missed the warmth of his sturdy body, the reassurance that here at least was one creature who demanded nothing of me except my presence and an occasional scratch behind his battle-scarred ears. I could almost feel his full-throated purr against my chest . . .

I must have dozed in the late-night stillness, because the shrill of the phone inside the house took a long time to register. When at last I came fully awake, I could hear my voice on the answering machine inviting the caller to leave a message. I kicked over the half-empty mug of tea in my haste and sprinted through the French doors just as I heard the unmistakable *click* of a receiver being replaced.

Darnay? I wondered, staring at the silent telephone as if it might somehow reveal its secrets.

How many nights had I waited for his call, for some acknowledgment that he had survived his wounds? I'd never fully understood his bosses' insistence on restricting their most valued undercover agent's contact with me during the period of his convalescence. Had they seen his involvement with me as a threat to their plans? Had they even then anticipated luring him back into their dangerous game, knowing a lover—a *wife*—would be an entanglement from which they might not be able to woo him?

I wandered the house, securing doors, shutting off lights, and setting the alarm system before padding wearily down the hallway to my empty bed. I peeled off my clothes and burrowed under the sheets. With my mind full of death and loss, I expected to fight for sleep, but exhaustion won out.

Sometime in the night I dreamed of Darnay, floating peacefully on a teal-green sea, his arms outflung in a mockery of joy, his slashed, ruined face staring sightlessly into a boundless sky . . .

CHAPTER
SIX

I sneaked out early on Sunday morning for quick stops at the French bakery and the pharmacy, returning laden with warm croissants and the local papers. I made coffee, another lesson learned at the feet of Madame Srabian in Paris, and arranged sliced strawberries and melon on a serving platter. I was just setting the basket of fragrant pastry on the round table in the screened-in area of the deck when Erik and Mercer emerged, hand-in-hand, from the guest room. The softness of my cousin's face and the tender manner in which Erik gazed down at her made me pretty sure they'd just had sex.

The little ripple of annoyance that rose in my chest was tinged, I had to admit, with just a hint of envy. "Good morning," I said, forcing myself into a cheerfulness I didn't feel. "Your timing is perfect. There's coffee or tea, take your pick."

Erik's fingers trailed across my cousin's arm as he seated her, then flopped himself into a chair. "Coffee, please," he said, flashing me his devastating smile. "And quickly."

Mercer reached to pick up the carafe and serve him, then pour tea for herself. "Bay?" She extended the flowered teapot toward me, and I lifted my cup.

"Thanks."

It may just have been my imagination, but her simpering look from beneath partly lowered lashes seemed mocking and more than a little smug. For a moment she reminded me of Amy Fleming, Chris Brandon's fiancée. Did every female on the planet—except me—have an actual functioning love life? And were they all determined to rub my nose in it?

I checked that descent into rampant paranoia and offered my cousin a croissant. "Sleep well?" I asked sweetly.

"Fine," they answered in unison, grinning at each other.

"Speaking for myself, I should have stopped about two beers before I did," Erik said, blowing gently across the top of his cup. "I must be getting old. In college, Gray and I used to . . ."

The introduction of his former drinking buddy, the late Gray Palmer, brought conversation to a screeching halt. We ate and sipped in silence, avoiding each other's eyes, and pretending to be absorbed by the doings of the town council and the school board as enumerated in the Sunday *Island Packet*. When we'd been reduced to picking pastry crumbs from the napkin in the bottom of the basket and passing around the advertising inserts and classifieds, I reasserted myself as hostess.

"What's on your agenda for today? Do you have to head back early or can you stay for lunch?"

My two houseguests exchanged a look which told me they'd already had this discussion.

"We thought we'd get going pretty soon," Erik said, glancing at Mercer, but failing to meet my eyes. "It's a long drive, and I want to spend some time with Cat when I drop Merce off."

Erik Whiteside is a wonderful, caring young man, kind and considerate, and a really lousy liar. It was the main reason his contributions to our investigative enterprise were designed to keep him in front of the computer screen and away from contact with actual clients. Every thought that passed through his mind found expression on his face.

I, on the other hand, was getting depressingly good at lying.

"You're stopping in Charleston," I said, freshening my cup from the teapot. I tried hard to keep anything resembling disapproval out of my voice. "Have you been in touch with this Mindy person to arrange a place to meet? You probably should, you know. It's a confusing town if you're not familiar with all the twists and turns of the old streets. I can help if you need directions. We . . . I used to live there."

His smile of chagrin told me I'd hit the mark. "In the lobby of the Fort Charles Hotel downtown. Shouldn't be too hard to find, should it?"

"We didn't mean . . ." Mercer began, but I cut her off with a wave of my hand.

"Not to worry. I know you both mean well, but have you really thought this through? I won't bore you with lectures about the police and the Coast Guard being far better equipped than we are to investigate Gray's death. You know that already. What I will say . . ." Again I forestalled my cousin's attempt to interrupt, this time with a finger pointed squarely in her face. "What I will say is your assumption that Mindy Albright's fears may be valid is precisely the reason you should *not* get involved."

"I don't get it," Mercer said.

"I do." Erik spoke before I could launch into my well-reasoned argument. "Bay is saying that, if Mindy is correct about Gray's death not being an accident, we'll be hanging out with someone who may be another target."

"You'll be adding yourselves to the list," I said. "Assuming, of course, this girl isn't just paranoid, or some kind of nut case. Either way, it's a bad idea. You're walking into what could be a dangerous situation, with a person about whom you know absolutely nothing, in a setting with which you're completely unfamiliar. Sounds to me like a recipe for disaster."

I rose and began gathering the loose newspaper pages. Mercer stacked plates and cups, Erik picked up the two pots, and we carried the silence along with us into the kitchen. I knew he was giving serious consideration to everything I'd just said, while my cousin was barely containing her desire to tell me to mind my own business. As I filled the dishwasher, Erik cleared his throat.

"Okay, what you say makes good sense." He offered me

his killer smile. "But I promised I'd at least talk to her. She's pretty shaken, and it sounds as if she doesn't have anybody else to rely on. What can I do?"

I turned to face him and leaned back against the sink. "You can go back to Charlotte, run your business, take Mercer out to dinner on Friday nights, and put this out of your mind."

"And what about Mindy Albright?" he asked.

"Oh, don't worry about Mindy," I said brightly, wiping my hands on the dish towel. "I'll just tell her you couldn't make it."

"*You'll* tell her?"

"Sure," I said, patting his arm gently. "When I see her this afternoon. Now what time is my appointment at the Fort Charles?"

I DECIDED to take the back way, jumping off I-95 at Point South and skirting Beaufort on Route 17. Traffic sped along at well over seventy until we reached the spot where the road narrows to two lanes near Gardens Corner. From there, the way meandered on toward Charleston, the blacktop seeming to dance in the alternate dappling of shadow and sunlight filtered through swaying pines and sweet gums overhanging the road.

Erik Whiteside and Mercer Mary Prescott had finally left the beach house some time around noon, refusing my offer of lunch, saying they'd grab a sandwich on the way back to Charlotte. I knew my partner didn't like handing over the job of interviewing Mindy Albright to me, but I'd given him little choice.

Something about the whole episode rang false, although I couldn't have said exactly what at the time. Perhaps it was our ready acceptance of everything this unknown young woman had told us. We had no reason to trust her, and yet here I was dashing off to meet someone whose motives might not be entirely pure. *She* believed Gray Palmer's death might not have been an accident. *She* expressed fear that she herself might somehow be in danger. No proof, just feelings. Since I had never spoken to her myself, I wondered how much Mindy Albright had preyed on Erik's sympathy, his innate sense of honor. I wondered how she'd react to encountering, not a chivalrous young man ready to ride to her defense, but a pragmatic woman who'd been led down way too many garden paths in her lifetime. A few snuffling tears and a little-girl-lost look were not going to get her far with me.

I decided I'd find those answers soon enough. As I moseyed my way north in the dowdy four-door sedan, I forced myself to put out of my mind any expectation of what my meeting with Mindy Albright would bring. As it turned out, that was probably a good thing.

CROSSING THE bridge into the outskirts of Charleston brought such an unanticipated flood of memory washing over me I almost had to stop the car in the middle of the highway. As I navigated through the surprisingly light weekend traffic, everywhere I looked brought flashes of Rob and our life here in this treasure of the antebellum South. Even something so mundane as the Exxon gas station, devoid of customers in the lull of midafternoon, brought a vision of my dead husband, filling the tank and checking under the hood before sliding back into the seat of the white convertible.

In my mind I reach again to wipe the smudge of oil from his tanned cheek, and he captures my fingers in his hand, bringing them to his lips with a mischievous grin . . .

Bad idea, bad idea. The words reverberated in my brain. Nearly two years since I'd tossed everything we owned into the back of a rental truck and raced out of the city we had both loved so well. Two years, one brief, disastrous love affair, and the joy of finding Darnay—and still the pain of Rob's memory held the power to reduce me to this state of ragged breathing, racing heart, and . . .

Screeeeech! Without conscious thought I stood on the brakes, sliding to a stop with the front of the car just nosing out into the intersection. Horns blared as angry drivers

mouthed obscenities at the idiot woman who had almost run
the red light.

For the nine millionth time since returning from France, I
reached toward my bag with the intention of grabbing a cigarette, only to recall, just in time, that I no longer smoked. I
wondered how long it would be before I ceased thinking
about nicotine as the panacea for all my nervous reactions.

Instead I drew a long, shuddering breath and eased sedately across Coburg Road when the light changed. I ordered myself not to think about Rob, to concentrate on
negotiating the narrow, one-way streets that drive visitors to
Charleston frantic with frustration, and pulled up ten minutes later into the courtyard of the Fort Charles Hotel. Leaving the car with a smiling attendant, I made my way past the
statue of rearing stallions and into the stately magnificence
of the downtown landmark.

Scanning the clusters of chairs and tables drawn up into
intimate groupings scattered around the lobby, it occurred to
me neither Erik nor I had thought to request a description of
our potential client. My gaze lighted on a young woman, her
long blond hair splayed out across the back of a maroon-
and-green-flowered wing chair, her eyes closed in either
boredom or sleep. But as I watched, a dashing young son of
old Charleston, dressed in the approved uniform of blue oxford cloth shirt, sharply pressed khakis, and Topsiders, approached the girl and swept her into an exuberant embrace.
Arm in arm they wandered toward the exit onto King Street.

I took a leisurely stroll, examining the displays in the
windows of the shops lining the long hallway while at the
same time surreptitiously checking out my fellow browsers,
eliminating them one by one by reason of age or gender.
And my quarry would be looking for a handsome young
man about the age of her dead boyfriend, so there was no
use expecting her to leap up and announce herself to me.

I wandered back into the resplendent lobby, admiring the
split spiral staircase rising elegantly to the second floor.
Above me, two huge crystal chandeliers cast a glow over the
green marble counters of the reception desk, as well as a pair

of perfectly formed topiaries flanking the main entrance, and a stunning flower arrangement in a mammoth Chinese vase.

When the tap came on my shoulder, I jumped about a foot off the Italian marble tiles.

"May I be of some assistance?"

He wore the livery of the hotel—white dress shirt, black pants, and a deep green blazer with a discreet logo. His name tag proclaimed him to be Robert . . . *something*, whose native language contained way too many consonants and apostrophes and a decided dearth of vowels.

"Uh, yes," I stammered, "perhaps you can. My friend was supposed to meet someone here . . . in your lobby, but he couldn't make it, so I came instead." The brilliant white smile never wavered, and his brown eyes regarded me expectantly. But I could tell he was thinking about calling security to have this nut case removed from his hotel. "So, you see, the young lady would not be expecting me, and I don't . . ."

"Ah, it is a young lady you seek, no doubt the one from the foundation."

Foundation? I had no idea what he was talking about, but I had no opportunity to voice a question, for he had turned and was moving across the expanse of tile. "This way, madam, if you please. She will be waiting in the lounge, which you see there before you. Please to go up."

The formal, almost British cadence of his voice and manner of speech made questioning his statement seem unconscionably rude, so I nodded my thanks and stepped around him toward an elevated area marked off by a polished brass railing. Dimly lit, the lounge was dominated by a baby grand piano. High-backed leather chairs were drawn up around both dining- and coffee-type tables creating a variety of groupings where one might take Sunday afternoon tea with the family or enjoy an intimate tête-à-tête without fear of interruption.

As I stepped up, I noticed only one occupant, and she turned to stare. It took me a moment to adjust to the dimness, but the woman had already returned her attention to her book. I moved around the table for two at which she sat, just in front of a lacquered Chinese screen, and laid my hand on the back of the chair across from her.

"Mindy? Mindy Albright?"

The young woman raised her head from the paperback novel and regarded me solemnly. "Yes?"

"I'm Erik Whiteside's partner. He couldn't make it this afternoon, so I've come in his stead. May I sit down?"

A nod of the regal head was followed by the extension of a slender arm bound from wrist to elbow in a winding coil of gold.

"Araminda Albright," she said, shaking my hand and flicking aside a fall of straight, blue-black hair.

"Bay Tanner," I replied, and stared into the clear gray eyes of one of the most stunningly beautiful women I had ever encountered.

CHAPTER
SEVEN

Araminda Albright definitely came from a varied lineage, as evidenced by the straight, aristocratic nose and a slight up-tilt at the corners of her unusual eyes, heavily outlined in black like those of an Egyptian goddess. I hooked my bag over the arm of my chair and ordered a soda from the waitress who had materialized at my shoulder.

I crossed my legs, adjusting the crease in my tan linen trousers, decidedly uncomfortable with the poise of this striking young woman now regarding me coolly from across the table. I cleared my throat, unsure how to begin the interview. I had envisioned some puffy-eyed beach girl with a mane of sun-bleached hair and a head as empty as her wallet. Instead I found myself the subject of a frank appraisal by a woman whose mixed heritage had given her not only an astonishing beauty but a studied confidence as well.

"I'm sorry about your friend," I began as soon as the waitress had deposited my soda and departed.

"Thank you." Araminda Albright adjusted the bracelet twisting its way up her arm, and I realized it was in the form of a serpent. If it were in fact real gold, and if its sparkling eyes—one red, one blue—were real stones, the piece had to be worth more than the price of my last car.

Curiouser and curiouser.

"Erik sends his condolences as well, although he and Gray hadn't seen each other in some time." When my companion failed to respond, I continued, "Miss Albright, I'm a bit confused . . ."

"Mindy," she interrupted, her husky voice inviting intimacy. "Please call me Mindy."

"Mindy," I echoed, although I couldn't help thinking how inappropriate a nickname it was for such an exotic creature. *Araminda* suited her much better. "At any rate, as I said, I'm confused as to what it is you think Erik—or I—can do for you."

Again I felt myself being inspected—*assessed*—by those knowing eyes. Her next words told me I had passed whatever unspoken test she had set for me.

"I want to hire you to find out who murdered Gray. And to keep them from killing me."

I FOLLOWED the bright yellow PT Cruiser through the winding streets of old Charleston. Araminda Albright had given me just enough information to pique my curiosity without divulging any specifics. Despite my warnings to Erik, I found myself trailing along behind this stranger to an undisclosed location, without so much as a nail file for protection or a phone call to let someone know where to start looking for my body. I tried to find that last thought outrageous and managed only limited success.

We skirted the Slave Market and the Four Corners of Law, including the grandeur of St. Michael's Church. This symbol of the old Confederacy had just recently been restored to splendor from its devastation during Hurricane Hugo. When we finally gained the highway, I realized she had taken me on a roundabout tour of the downtown area in order to head back south, exactly the way I had come in. I made a mental note to ask her if the maneuver had been intended to confuse me or to throw off a possible tail. If she was seriously worried about the latter, she needed to find herself a less conspicuous vehicle. Like mine.

We took the turn toward the beach and a short time later pulled up in the sandy yard of an ancient but well-maintained cottage whose boards had been weathered to a silver patina by the relentless assault of sun and ocean spray. I maneuvered the rental car in beside her and stepped out into a brisk, on-shore breeze and the smell of dead fish.

Shaded by one stately live oak and surrounded by a tangle of sea grape, oleander, and crape myrtle run wild, the old single-story house stood wrapped in porches and the silence of the late Sunday afternoon. I trekked through the loose sand behind Araminda Albright, pausing to shade my eyes from the glare off the ocean. A few yards away, a narrow strip of beach lay littered with seaweed-draped driftwood and the usual debris abandoned by a retreating tide.

I turned toward the sound of jangling keys then followed my hostess across the wide, open verandah and into the cool dimness of the house. The tap of her high-heeled sandals and the *clunk* of my tasseled loafers on the worn pine floor broke the stillness. In the sparse light filtering through narrow slats of bamboo, I could just make out the shapes of bulky sofas and overstuffed chairs scattered around the single, large room. When Mindy moved to raise the blinds on the front windows, I smiled in pleasure at the eclectic chaos of her home.

"Would you like a tea?" she asked, dropping her keys into a sweetgrass basket perched atop a mahogany console table against the near wall.

"That would be great," I said, and she disappeared through a curtain of glass beads that rattled softly as she passed into what must have been the kitchen at the back of the house.

I wandered the room, amazed at the extent and variety of the objects displayed across the surfaces of a hodgepodge of furniture periods and styles. Rattan sat coolly alongside Queen Anne; the stark beauty of a Shaker chair nestled against the gilt magnificence of a French armoire which reminded me of the Paris apartment. Intricately carved jade figurines shared space with bleached sand dollars; a ruby-and-sapphire cloisonné egg on a filigreed stand lay nested within a collection of feathers. Book-filled shelves lined one entire wall, and an antique, hand-crank Victrola cabinet served as the stand for an ultramodern metal sculpture, twisted ingeniously into the shape of a dolphin.

Nothing matched, and yet everything fit, as if each piece had been chosen for the particular spot it now occupied and would have looked jarringly out of place in any other.

Encouraged in my snooping by the *clink* of ice still emanating from the kitchen, I inspected the spines of some of the books. Most appeared to be used, outdated textbooks, at least on the shelf I was studying, and I pulled out a few to riffle the mildewed pages. Several dealing with archaeology and anthropology had large blocks of text underlined in heavy black ink. Biology, philosophy, medicine. Jane Goodall's book on primates, one of the few that looked as if it might have been bought new and not at some flea market. No light bedtime reading here. There wasn't a John Grisham or Stephen King in the lot.

"Here we are."

Araminda glided soundlessly into the room on bare feet, her voice causing me to jump like a burglar interrupted in the act of sliding the jewel case out of the safe.

"Sorry," I said, accepting the tall frosted glass as I slid a volume back into its slot. "I have this thing for old books."

Mindy set the tray on the sideboard. Carrying her drink she settled herself into a rocker draped with a colorful Southwestern throw. "No need to apologize," she said.

I sank onto soft chintz and waited for her to begin. When she didn't, turning her elegant head to stare out the windows toward the ocean, I said, "You have a wonderful variety of things here. Are you a collector?"

"My parents," she replied, her gaze still locked on the soft rollers washing up against her private beach. "They traveled all over the world. My father was a professor of archaeology at the University of Edinburgh, and my mother taught English literature. She was Lebanese."

The short genealogy explained both her strange name and exotic face.

Her gold-wrapped arm gestured to encompass the array of treasures scattered around the room. "They planned to retire here. This was their refuge, the place they retreated to when things got . . ."

She let the sentence trail off, and once again her wondrous eyes sought the sea. I itched to press her for details, but the tone of her words held me back. Her continued use of the past tense made it pretty obvious her parents were dead, and I didn't want to add to her sorrow. Somewhere, between the hotel bar and this isolated beach cottage, the haughty, confident Araminda Albright had disappeared, replaced by a young, vulnerable, and intensely sad girl called Mindy.

"Look," I began, hoping to break the mesmerizing effect of the heat and the silence and the strange woman rocking rhythmically across from me, "I can appreciate how upsetting Gray's death has been for you." When she looked up, as if to challenge me, I hurried on. "Believe me, I do. My husband was . . . killed a couple of years ago, and I spent a good bit of time trying to find someone to punish. I even proved, at least to my own satisfaction, who was responsible. But that's as far as it's gone. I've had to resign myself to living without retribution."

I paused, brought up short by that statement which had slipped from my mouth without conscious thought. *Could it be true? Had I finally come to terms with never seeing Rob's murderers brought to justice?*

"You think that's what I'm after? Vengeance?"

Her gray eyes flashed, and the force of her emotion brought a blush of color to her sculpted cheeks. It was the first hint of any strong emotion I'd seen her display since we entered her sanctuary, and it gave me hope. I'd begun to wonder if she were on some sort of downers.

"I don't know. Maybe not. But you haven't been very forthcoming, at least not so far. As I told you at the hotel, I came up here to meet you in person and tell you that our firm . . ." I almost choked, on the idea as much as on the word itself. Considering our only investigation so far had ended in dismal failure, it sounded pretty damn presumptuous to refer to Erik, the Judge, and me as a *firm*. "That our firm is not equipped to investigate a murder, if that's in fact what this is."

"You think I'm lying?" With a flip of her ebony hair, she rose from the rocker, her fist clenched so tightly around the iced tea glass I flinched in anticipation of its splintering in her hand.

I tried for a calm, nonthreatening tone of voice as I said, "Well, look at it from my point of view. The Coast Guard tells you your boyfriend died in a tragic boating accident, and the first thing you do is ask complete strangers to investigate the death as a homicide."

"I didn't call *you*." *Araminda* had resurfaced, her voice icy with contempt. "I asked for help from Gray's friend, someone he trusted. Whether Erik doesn't have the balls for the job, or you decided to butt into it on your own, I don't really care. But if you aren't interested in hearing my side of things, if you're convinced I'm a liar—or a lunatic—then feel free to haul your arrogant ass back where you came from. I'll handle it on my own."

Araminda Albright glared at me across the wide expanse of pine floor, her proud head jutting out defiantly on her slender neck, and promptly burst into tears.

HALF A box of tissues later, I pulled on my navy blazer and joined Mindy on the beach. I left my shoes on the backseat of the rental car, rolled up my pants legs, and swung into step beside her. We turned south, keeping the wind at our backs. Though the young woman was a few inches shorter than my five-foot ten, I had to lengthen my stride to keep up with her determined pace.

We rounded a small headland, having encountered no one but the ever-present sandpipers skittering across the hard-packed beach. As we approached a narrow copse of palmettos a few yards up from the tide line, my companion veered away from the edge of the water and led the way toward a weathered wooden bench nestled in among the trees. I flopped down beside her, breathing a little more heavily than I would have liked to admit. The months in Paris—the languid decadence of rich food and good sex—had taken their toll on my physical fitness. A new regimen was definitely in order.

"Okay," I said, as we watched the sky deepening to a rosy purple out over the water, "tell me everything you know. No snap judgments until I've heard you out."

Araminda peered out at me from around her curtain of hair and nodded.

"But no promises, either," I added, digging my bare toes into the loose sand and wishing I had a cigarette.

"Gray and I work . . . *worked* for his father," Mindy began, stumbling a little over the past tense. "He's Gray Palmer, too. Senior. He owns boats—container ships, actually. His offices and warehouses are down at the Port of Charleston."

"Palmer Shipping," I said, surprised at not having made the connection before.

"Right. But we didn't work for the company."

I remembered then that the man at the hotel had referred to Mindy as the young lady from *the foundation*. "What's the purpose of his foundation?"

If my knowledge of Gray Palmer's other interest surprised her, she didn't let on. "Lots of things. Archaeology, history, ecology. He's especially interested in native cultures, the Indians and then the Gullah, the descendants of the West African slaves. How they lived, how they're being affected by all the development and the loss of their family lands."

"Why?"

The question seemed to unnerve her, and she leaned back to study my face in the gathering dusk. "What do you mean?" she asked.

"Why is he interested enough in this subject to fund an organization and hire people to gather data for him? It must cost a great deal of money."

"I guess. Although he doesn't pay us much. Gray had to move in with me because he couldn't afford his own place anymore."

"He lived with you here? At the beach?" When Araminda nodded, I hurried on. "Are his things still intact? I mean, the police or the Coast Guard or somebody hasn't already been through them?"

Her puzzled frown lasted only a moment. "No, of course not. They're all convinced he just got drunk and fell off his boat. No one official is going to do anything about whoever killed him."

I still didn't understand her willingness—hell, it was almost *eagerness*—to believe her boyfriend had been murdered. "So tell me why you're so certain it wasn't an accident."

"It's the grave. The skeleton," she said. "Gray knew it wasn't an old Indian burial, because of the watch. And he said there was some material in there that didn't jibe with a death which would have occurred over two hundred and fifty years ago."

"What kind of material?"

"He didn't tell me. He thought the information might be dangerous, that someone wouldn't want him out there digging around where he wasn't supposed to be in the first place." She swallowed hard and rubbed her hands across her glistening, almond-shaped eyes.

"Out where?"

"I don't know! Don't you get it? He . . . he went out on his own that day, said he had something he wanted to check out. I didn't think much about it—he's done that before. But when he came back, he was . . . I don't know, *excited* isn't the right word. He was nervous, scared almost, but exhilarated, too. He told me about the grave, about the skeleton, then went right in and called Erik. He said this was too big for him to handle on his own, and his old college pal was 'in the business.' That's what he'd heard, anyway."

I could read in her eyes that some or all of what she'd just said had been a lie. How much or which part I couldn't tell.

"Why didn't Gray just go to the police if he thought there was something fishy about the corpse?"

"I don't know!"

"Did he tell his father what he'd found?" It seemed to me it would have been the next logical step if the young man felt threatened and believed he couldn't trust the authorities. Why call someone you hadn't been in touch with in years, someone you'd known primarily as a college drinking buddy?

Araminda shook her head as if I were a backward child. "Gray hated his father. You remember you asked me why GS . . ."

"GS?" I interrupted her.

"Gray Senior. That's what my Gray called him. You wanted to know why GS was spending all this money investigating abandoned islands and the remains of old cultures? Well, Gray wanted to know that, too. He took his father's money and did the work, because it's what he was trained to do. But he didn't understand it, either." She sighed and pulled the sweater more tightly around her slim body. "GS never did anything that didn't make him a buck. That's what Gray always said."

I filed the son's bitterness toward his father away for future reference, but I didn't think it probably meant much. Name me a young person who hasn't at one time or another despised one or both of his parents. The thought hit a little too close to home, and I changed the subject.

"So you know absolutely nothing more about where this skeleton is located or what else Gray might have found in the grave. Does that about sum it up?"

"He went back out there on Friday to get more proof, but he wouldn't tell me anything more about it until he had solid evidence. He said he didn't want me to be vulnerable, too."

"But you still think you are."

She snuffled, pulled a wad of tissues out of the sleeve of her baggy sweater, and wiped her leaking eyes and nose. "Listen. Gray Palmer grew up on the water. He knew more about boats than anyone else I've ever met. There is no way he got tangled in the lines and fell overboard. There is no way he would have tried to set the anchor with the throttle running full-open. Someone else did that, someone who didn't want him to get to the gravesite. Or didn't want him to get back." She stuffed the sodden Kleenex into her pocket and stood up. "Come on. I'll let you see his room, although I don't think it will do much good. I've already been through it all myself. But I'm sure he didn't put anything on paper. There was no entry in his site journal. I'm sure he kept it all in his head."

The image of the damage done to that head by the boat's propellers sent a shiver through me which had absolutely nothing to do with the falling temperature, nor with the freshening wind off the ocean. In silent agreement we turned back toward the cottage.

The one thing I had going for me was the fact that Araminda apparently knew nothing about the bone. Gray Palmer had told Erik he'd removed a bone from the gravesite. If it were in his room, surely she would have found it. So her boyfriend had stashed his grisly find somewhere for safekeeping and taken the secret of that location to his death. Or someone had taken it from him.

Araminda, walking slightly ahead of me, sighed deeply and straightened her shoulders, not only physically, but—it seemed to me—emotionally as well. I remember thinking I wouldn't be surprised if those were the last tears, the last display of weakness I would see from Araminda Albright.

I wish to hell I hadn't been so wrong.

CHAPTER
EIGHT

The drive back from Charleston seemed to disappear in a whirl of speculation, my conscious mind worrying away at the thin threads of Gray and Araminda's story, while some instinctive portion of my brain kept the car on the road and my speed somewhere under eighty.

I hadn't found the bone. I hadn't found much of anything other than the usual assortment of clutter one would expect to encounter in the room of a young man who had neither mother nor wife to pick up after him. Clothes were strewn across the unmade bed, and papers and notebooks littered every flat surface. I glanced through a couple of them, but Gray's shorthand defeated me. Araminda claimed he hadn't made any notes about his most recent discovery, and I couldn't find anything to contradict her statement. I checked his camera—an expensive Nikon with a telephoto lens attached—but there was no film in it. I also recognized one of the handheld GPS gizmos Erik had introduced me to the past winter. All in all, the search had pretty much been a waste of time.

Both Erik and I had made the assumption that Gray and Araminda had been more than friends—*why*, I couldn't exactly put my finger on right then—but the evidence in his room and the girl's own demeanor seemed to indicate she had taken on a boarder rather than a lover.

Darkness had fallen completely by the time I turned onto

Route 17, and the headlights of the small car cut only a narrow swath through the gloom of the nearly deserted roadway. For long stretches I appeared to be the only one alive as I hurtled down the smooth macadam hemmed in on both sides by endless stands of towering pines. I was grateful for the sudden appearance of the occasional hamlets with their clusters of roadside amenities and scattered houses which disappeared into the distance behind me in a matter of seconds.

Reception was terrible in the no-man's land between Charleston and Savannah, so I switched off the radio and tried making a mental list of exactly what I knew. The enumeration was pitifully inadequate. From Mindy I had learned the foundation set up by Gray Palmer, Senior, was a nonprofit organization funded entirely by Palmer's shipping company. Basically, he was studying the history, ecology, and fauna of the small islands dotting the coastline between Charleston and Jacksonville, Florida. Not the developed ones like Hilton Head or St. Simon's or Amelia, where most remnants of the previous tenants had disappeared under the foundations of sprawling resort complexes and the feet of millions of tourists.

The goal was to determine how these inaccessible little tufts of land had first become inhabited, how the animal population was introduced, and how life there progressed. I'd never given much thought as to how places we now routinely visited had supported life, human and otherwise, before the advent of causeways and humpbacked bridges. I guess I'd just assumed that Indians in canoes and the Gullah in their flat-bottomed boats had traveled easily from the mainland, and that deer, rabbits, bobcats, and the other denizens had simply swum over.

Obviously my assumptions were way too simplistic, otherwise what was the point of investigating? In a way I admired Gray Palmer, Senior's willingness to expend some of his accumulated wealth on a purely academic pursuit, in spite of the son's conviction that the father's motives had to be monetary rather than altruistic.

I hadn't managed to ferret out exactly what Araminda's

educational background was, but Gray Palmer had earned his degree from N.C. State in archaeology, with a minor in biology. He and Mindy—along with several other young people the foundation employed—traveled by boat to these isolated islands, gathering spoor, observing and recording the various animal populations, and taking soil and plant samples. They also searched for evidence of past human habitation, sometimes encountering the foundations of abandoned houses or the rotted remains of old cabins. Occasionally they recovered artifacts—arrowheads and rusted implements along with more modern leavings such as tin cans and beer bottles.

At any rate, they recorded their findings, labeled their samples, and turned them over to the foundation for analysis and classification. Sounded pretty mundane, perhaps even boring, at least to me. Why anyone would find these two young people a threat still eluded me. And yet, Gray Palmer was dead, and Araminda Albright was scared she might be next. I knew I had already made up my mind to pursue it, even though I had no real idea of where to begin. Or even of what a satisfactory resolution might look like.

It was an intriguing enough puzzle to keep me from spending every waking moment obsessing about Alain Darnay and his return to active duty in Interpol.

At least I hoped it was.

I HAD nearly forgotten my commitment to meet with Chris Brandon.

It dawned on me as I puttered in the kitchen next morning, trying to decide where to begin my investigation into the death of Gray Palmer. I'd reported in to Erik the night before, downplaying my stupidity in allowing myself to be lured to Mindy Albright's beach cottage, telling myself it didn't matter because nothing bad had happened. Still, I made a mental note to get my head in the game if I were serious about pursuing this case.

I should probably think about retrieving the 9mm Glock from its nesting place in the floor safe in my bedroom closet,

I thought, as I split an English muffin and dropped the halves into either side of the toaster. I assumed my permit was still valid, although I hadn't had occasion to carry the weapon in the last several months, most of which I had spent in Paris.

Erik committed to gleaning as much information about Palmer Shipping and its CEO's strange foundation as he could coax from the Internet, as well as any background material about Palmer, his son, and the girl. He sounded resentful that I had pretty much shanghaied the legwork and left him only the butt-in-the-chair part of the job, but he finally agreed we each had our own individual area of expertise.

What mine was, exactly, I had yet to figure out.

We hung up, our relationship frayed a little around the edges, but basically intact, with a promise to get together online and compare notes in a day or so. Though Mindy had more than once expressed fear her own life might also be in danger, I had a difficult time accepting that in my gut. I'd been in enough tight situations lately that I'd learned to trust my instincts, at least to a certain extent, and I just couldn't work up any real urgency in regard to this investigation. We didn't have anywhere near enough information to make a rational decision at this point, so I decided to defer judgment until we did.

It was after eight-thirty when some random electrical impulse in the back of my brain kicked the Chris Brandon appointment up into my consciousness, so I had to scramble. I tossed on a slim black skirt and white silk blouse and forced my protesting feet into pumps. I hadn't wanted to bother with stockings, but my painfully white, pasty legs sent me digging into the lingerie drawer. I definitely needed sun, the sooner the better. I resurrected my old briefcase from the back of the closet, tossed in a faded legal pad and a couple of pens, then slathered peanut butter on the cold English muffin and hit the road.

The golf tournament crowds had scattered back to their homes and offices, and traffic was just the usual mayhem of a Monday morning in the Lowcountry. The worst stretch, as always, was from the foot of the Cross Island Parkway to just past the intersection at Moss Creek. As I idled in my drab rental car at the traffic signal at Spanish Wells Road, the image of Dolores Santiago flashed into my head.

How many times had I turned left at this light, following the meandering two-lane road back to the Santiagos' neatly kept home on the marsh?

Not nearly enough, I chided myself, drumming my fingers on the steering wheel while visions of my friend and housekeeper unrolled behind my suddenly misty eyes . . . *Dolores huddled in a pool of blood in the hallway of the beach house . . . tiny Dolores swallowed up by the paraphernalia of the hospital room, her shattered leg suspended from a tangle of wires and pulleys . . .*

I tried to shake off the guilt which overwhelmed me whenever thoughts of her crept past my defenses. Five months ago I had forced her out of my mind, fleeing to Paris and my waiting lover. In his infrequent letters, the Judge had hinted at progress in Dolores's recovery but had not provided details. And I hadn't asked. I had been home now for close to a week, and still I had not called. The truth was I couldn't face it if the outcome had been bad. Better not to know. I clung to my ignorance like a security blanket.

An ominous *whoosh* as the driver of the big concrete truck behind me released his air brakes gave me a blessed excuse to shove the guilt back into its mental storage compartment. I stomped on the accelerator, and the car lurched ahead, leaving Dolores and memory behind.

IN FITS and starts dictated by the flood of vehicles choking Route 278, I finally gained the turn onto 170, only to be stopped a few miles later by the construction at the new bridge rising inexorably over the Broad River. Only one lane of traffic was open in each direction, and I cranked up the radio and sang along to keep my mind from drifting again into painful territory. When I finally pulled into a parking space along Bay Street in front of Chris Brandon's building, the white numerals of the digital clock on the dashboard had just rolled over to *10:00* on the button.

The office décor, spare and modern, hadn't been changed since my last visit, nor had the officious little snot at the receptionist's desk. Cheryl something, if memory served, and her one-word acknowledgment and pointed glance at the round clock face hanging over her desk told me her attitude hadn't undergone any serious adjustment, either. Back in the days when Chris had been making half-hearted attempts to interest me in easing our relationship into something more romantic, Cheryl had developed an intense antipathy to my person and presence, no doubt seeing me as a threat to her own plans for the eminently eligible young attorney.

I wondered how she was dealing with the reality of a fiancée in the person of little Amy Fleming.

This thought buoyed me as Cheryl pointed me silently toward a chair in the waiting area and lifted the phone to announce my arrival. I barely had time to settle myself in the black leather chair and cross my legs before Chris Brandon popped out of the door leading to his office and waved me forward.

"Bay! Good to see you again. Gosh, you look wonderful. Please, come in."

"Why, thank you, Chris," I replied and edged past him through the doorway, unable to resist casting a smirk of satisfaction over my shoulder at the glowering Cheryl.

It was childish and unkind, and I ordered myself to grow up as I stepped into Chris's office and seated myself in one of the client chairs drawn up in front of his glass-topped desk. As on previous visits, I marveled at the dearth of paper and clutter. My mother would have said an orderly environment indicated an orderly mind, or some such twaddle. She had a cliché for every occasion, and I shuddered, thinking she would probably have applauded my attitude toward the unfortunate secretary instead of condemning it. Sometimes genes have a way of sneaking past your better judgment. At least mine seem to.

"So, what's up?" I asked, pulling my bag onto my lap and rummaging for my reading glasses. "You said something about a possible embezzlement?" I finally located the rimless, John Lennon–style frames and settled them onto my nose. "Have the police been notified?"

"Oh, no, nothing's gone that far yet. These are clients who're convinced they're being ripped off, but don't have enough accounting knowledge to prove it."

"Have they contacted their outside accountant? Their CPA?" It was generally the first course of action in cases like this. Because of his familiarity with the books, the person doing the taxes is more inclined to pick up on anything hinky, especially if he's been alerted to the possibility. Chris paused, a look of uncertainty passing across his expressive face, and I frowned. "Wait, this isn't another of those fiascos like the Bi-Rite Hardware thing, is it? Please tell me these people at least *employed* an outside auditor."

The fact that the managers of the Herrington family's hardware empire had been doing all the taxes as well as keeping the day-to-day books had led to an embezzlement scheme so sloppily obvious, a first-year accounting student could have tumbled to it inside of half a day's investigation. The biggest problem had been sorting through the tons of useless paper we had been bombarded with. Strange as it might have sounded, I hoped these next folks had been a little creative, could at least provide a challenge while I nailed them to the wall. My former partners in the CPA firm in Charleston had always looked somewhat askance whenever I'd voiced my preference for at least mildly intelligent crooks and tax evaders instead of the stumbling stupidity of most of the ones we encountered.

"Chris? Is there an accountant of record?"

"Well, yes and no."

"That clears everything right up."

"Sorry. It's a little complicated." He pulled one of the gold-plated pens from his onyx desk set and leaned back in his chair, his fingers twirling the slim metal cylinder like a miniature baton. "I don't suppose you've been keeping up with the local scandals while you've been in France, have you?"

I settled myself more comfortably into the client's chair,

prepared now for an extended story in the hallowed Southern tradition. "Only the gossip the Judge occasionally passed on in his letters," I said. "What member—or former member— of the profession has run afoul of the law this time?"

His rueful smile told me I'd nailed it in one. "Remember Worthy Foxworth?"

"No!" I shot upright in the chair, my astonishment genuine. Whether in accounting, real estate, or the law, the name Foxworth had always been synonymous with honor and fair dealing in our little corner of the world. Even my mother had been unable to find fault with anyone in the family, all the way back to their original immigrant ancestors fleeing religious persecution in England. "No," I repeated, "not Foxy! I don't believe it."

"Neither did anyone else until the State Accountancy Board revoked his license to practice. Seems he had a little problem differentiating between the money his clients had designated for their tax bills and his own investment account. The market slide last fall hit him hard."

"Worthy Foxworth." I shook my head, still staggered by the fall from grace of one of my early mentors and puzzled by my father's failure to pass along such a juicy item. Maybe he'd thought it would distress me too much. He would have been right.

"Yeah, it kind of took everyone that way. He pled guilty to embezzlement, liquidated everything he had in order to make restitution, and still fell way short. He's doing three-to-five upstate."

"And this is the 'little matter' you wanted me to look into? There's no way . . ."

"No, no," he hastened to assure me. "That's all in the hands of the state boys. Worthy's client list reads like a who's who of Hilton Head money and power. I have a feeling it's going to take years before that mess gets squared away. No, my client is a much smaller fish, so to speak. Mitchell Seafood." He smiled at his own clever turn of phrase.

"You mean the Shack? Those Mitchells?"

Damon "Bubba" Mitchell, an all-pro defensive tackle before blowing out a knee, and his equally massive brother
Dwight ran Hilton Head's oldest fishing and shrimping business from a series of docks on Skull Creek. Their dilapi-
dated, four-table bar and restaurant, appropriately named the
Shack, squatted next door to their fleet of boats and was one
of the most popular seafood places in the area. We locals
guarded its secret from the tourists with almost religious
fanaticism.

It was all beginning to make sense now. "They were Worthy's clients?"

"Right. Just for taxes. Dwight and Bubba's mother kept
the books until she got sick last fall. Cancer. Sad."

I vaguely remembered Delia Mitchell, a taciturn woman
with weather-worn brown skin and a slender frame so compact it was hard to believe she could have brought forth the
giants her two sons had grown into. "Did she . . . ?" I began,
but Chris was already shaking his head.

"No, she pulled through. Had to have a mastectomy, and
the chemo pretty well ate her up, but she made it. Problem is
the boys had to hire someone to take over the office work,
and that's where the trouble started."

It was a story familiar to every accountant who dealt with
small business: proprietors or partners whose expertise
didn't extend to the mysteries of double-entry bookkeeping
entrusting their financial well-being to a stranger who
seemed to know what she was doing, only to find out too late
their faith had been misplaced. If Worthy Foxworth had had
any inkling the Mitchells' employee was helping herself to
the profits, he had apparently been too embroiled in his own
troubles to do anything about it.

"So what is it you want me to do?" I asked with a decided
lack of enthusiasm. Visions of mangled boxes overflowing
with random receipts and ledgers, à la the Bi-Rite Hardware
mess, sent a shiver of revulsion along my arms, and my
mind began searching for some plausible excuse to renege
on my commitment.

"Take over for Worthy. The girl has to be thinking she's

all set, what with him in jail and no one lookin' over her shoulder. The boys just want you to go in, like you would if you were doing the taxes, and see if you can spot how she's getting the money out. It's almost time to file their return anyway, so it shouldn't arouse any suspicion."

"Are they incorporated? If so, they're already past the March fifteenth deadline."

"No, it's still a proprietorship, just the same as when their granddaddy started it up right after the war. That makes them good until the end of this week. April fifteenth, right?"

"Doesn't give me much time to operate. First thing I'll have to do is file an extension. Where are the records?"

"Most of them are at the docks. Delia kept an office in the back of the retail store. But I did put together a few things for you to look over."

Chris handed me a brown accordion file fastened with a matching elastic band. The label on the front had MITCHELL SEAFOOD typed neatly beneath the imprint of the Foxworth & Company accounting firm.

"Where'd you get this?" I asked, accepting the package and tucking it into my briefcase. "I would have thought all Foxy's files would be in the hands of the auditors."

Chris Brandon's smile spoke volumes about favors, connections, and the good-ol'-boy network, a concept that not only flourished, but probably originated, in the South.

I stood and brushed at the creases in the front of my skirt. "I won't ask. Do Dwight and Bubba know I'm coming?"

Chris rose and moved around to the front of the desk. He cupped a hand under my elbow and guided me toward the door. "Yes. I tentatively set you up for tomorrow at ten, but we can change that if it's not convenient."

"Nope, ten tomorrow is fine."

"Great! I'll call them and confirm. They're really happy it's you, someone they already know. It's going to be awkward for them, especially if you find out she really is skimming funds out of the business."

"Awkward?" I asked, one hand on the doorknob. "Why

would they be uncomfortable about exposing someone who's stealing from them?"

"Didn't I tell you? The woman they hired to take their mother's place is Tamika Jessup. Used to be a Mitchell. She's Dwight and Bubba's cousin."

I TOYED with the idea of running out to Presqu'isle and checking up on the Judge then changed my mind. Too many things to do, and Lavinia would insist on feeding me. Instead I headed back through the construction nightmare toward Hilton Head.

I stopped at an office supply store in one of the many shopping clusters springing up almost daily along the 278 corridor in Bluffton and replenished my depleted stock in preparation for my assault on the Mitchell Seafood books. I spent considerable time in the electronics section, astonished by the advances achieved since I'd last shopped for a computer. The sleek laptops were already lighter, smaller, and faster, and a smooth-talking youngster who couldn't have been long out of high school nearly sent me from the store with one tucked under my arm.

I resisted both his grinning charm and the lure of cutting-edge technology, at least temporarily, and settled for the boring, but functional aisles offering calculators, mechanical pens and pencils with fine points, and pale green pads lined in comforting, orderly rows and columns. These last required a dedicated search, no doubt a result of the proliferation of spreadsheet programs. But, despite my familiarity with these wonders of efficiency and convenience, I still preferred the scratch of lead on paper when it came to puzzling out the kind of accounting conundrums I expected to find at Mitchell Seafood. There was something about the activity of writing it all down that stimulated my brain in a way pounding on keys never could.

As I pulled back out into the streaming noontime traffic, I felt a familiar stirring of anticipation, not unlike the feeling you get in the pit of your stomach just before you toe the starting line or step out onto the court for a singles match against a highly ranked opponent. I certainly didn't miss advising recently retired fat cats about how to invest their millions for maximum tax advantage, or dueling with arrogant, belligerent IRS agents over the legitimacy of a charitable deduction. Those were facets of my days as a Certified Public Accountant I had cheerfully consigned to the file marked *Never Again*. But I did miss the challenge of the puzzle, the beauty and precision of the numbers. All these years and still I craved the inevitability, the predictability . . .

The certainty of the outcome, I said to myself with a mocking smile.

I gave a thought to stopping in at the Shack for lunch then decided against it as I zipped past the light at Squire Pope Road. Instead I joined the line of cars snaking its way through the Wendy's drive-up lane, and ordered a Number 7 chicken combo to go. Ironically, one of the things I'd missed most during my sojourn in France had been French fries, and I pulled a few from the bag to nibble on as I drove.

Ten minutes later, I pulled into my driveway and stopped dead, all thoughts of food evaporating in a heartbeat. I swallowed hard against the fist squeezing the air from my lungs, the knot of dread rising in my throat.

Tucked in among the trees sat a dented blue Hyundai. Dolores Santiago's spot. Dolores Santiago's car.

I shook my head to clear the paralyzing wave of *déjà vu* washing over me, eased the rental car the rest of the way up to the garage, and switched off the engine.

My day of reckoning had come, and I was not prepared.

With leaden fingers I grabbed the door latch, the chicken sandwich and my office supplies forgotten on the seat beside me. I had only one foot on the ground when I heard the kitchen window slide open above me, and a voice I thought I might never hear again called loudly, *"Señora! Gracias a Dios!* Come quick or your lunch, it will be cold."

CHAPTER
NINE

I don't remember what we ate or what we said, exactly. My strongest memory of that afternoon is one of joy—at Dolores's almost complete recovery, at her strong, sure gait with only a barely perceptible limp, at finding my worst fears unrealized. After my initial outburst, we never spoke of the past again, not about the attack nor its terrible aftermath. God had smiled, and now we were both back where we belonged. That was good enough for Dolores Santiago, and she insisted it be good enough for me.

The only topic relating to our previous lives over which we did linger was the unexpected bounty of the cupboards and pantry. I downplayed my newly acquired cooking skills as best I could, laying it off on the necessity of providing for my recently departed guests. Whether or not Dolores entirely bought my stumbling excuses, we both knew we needed her to accept them in order for us to resume our old relationship: Bay Tanner, inept bumbler in all things culinary, saved from starvation of both body and spirit by her dear friend and housekeeper, Dolores Santiago.

I allowed myself to be chased from the kitchen, retrieved my soggy lunch bag and office purchases from the front seat of the car, and carried the latter into the third bedroom. What had once been Rob's and my shared office still housed the desktop computer, printer, and a couple of filing cabinets and had now become the Hilton Head branch of Simpson &

Tanner, Inquiry Agents. I selected a manila file folder from the package I'd purchased that morning, resurrected my favorite Waterford pen from the center desk drawer, and printed PALMER/ALBRIGHT neatly on the tab.

If we were going to run this as a legitimate business, I needed to start treating it like one.

For the next couple of hours I lost myself in the familiar routine of organizing a project while Dolores's soft humming, interrupted occasionally by the drone of the vacuum cleaner, provided sweet background music. I used the word processing program to type up a detailed report on my encounter with Araminda Albright, including all my speculations, and printed it out for the file.

Next I prepared a series of forms using the green columnar pads in anticipation of my meeting with the Mitchell brothers the following morning. Though it had been several years since I had fully utilized my accounting and auditing skills, the routine felt familiar, almost comforting.

Like riding a bike, I thought, leaning back in the chair. My hand shot out, automatically seeking a nonexistent pack of cigarettes and a lighter. The need seemed as much a part of the process as the paper or the computer.

The soft knock on the partially opened door behind me checked the impulse, and I turned to face Dolores, who had a blouse and two pairs of slacks draped over her arm.

"I have finished the cleaning, *Señora*. The carpet, she is *muy sucio*," she added, shaking her head. "I call the men who do the cleaning, *si?*"

"Fine. I don't know how soon you can get someone, but I'll be out most of tomorrow morning."

"Mañana, Señora?"

Her brief laugh, the sparkle in her black eyes, made me smile in gratitude for the unexpected gift of her return.

"You're right," I said. "Tomorrow is definitely a fantasy. Whenever you can arrange it is fine with me. I'll work around them." Dolores nodded, turning toward the hallway when I called, "Wait! Where are you going with the clothes, *amiga?*"

One of our agreements before her injury had been that I took care of my own laundry. While that generally meant hauling anything which needed ironing down to the local cleaners, I handled the mundane things like jeans and underwear on my own. However, that hadn't kept Dolores from trying to sneak it by me in the past. She had often expressed her horror at the cost of professional cleaning.

"Los botóns, Señora." At my bewildered look she fingered the buttons on her own gaily striped blouse. "I fix for you."

"Buttons! Oh, okay, that'll be great. Thanks."

"De nada. Miércoles?"

Over lunch we had discussed a schedule which would accommodate Dolores's physical therapy sessions and keep her from overdoing on her still fragile leg. I had to fight to keep her from insisting on returning to her regular daily schedule. We'd start with two days a week and go from there, I'd insisted, and finally received grudging agreement.

"Wednesday it is," I replied. "Just give me a call when you can get a commitment from the carpet cleaners."

"Si, bueno. Adios, Señora."

"Goodbye, my friend. And welcome back."

Dolores ducked her head in embarrassment at the emotion I couldn't keep from my voice. A few moments later I heard the spluttering cough of the Hyundai as she cranked it over, and I allowed a few tears of relief and thanksgiving to spill over onto the desk.

I SPENT the rest of the afternoon assembling my financial "detective" kit and arranging everything in the calfskin briefcase which had been Rob's last Christmas gift to me. The memory brought a more manageable twinge of pain than usual, and I considered the possibility that I was finally coming to terms with his death. It was way past time to stop allowing grief to govern my life, to release the hard core of guilt and anger that had been my constant companion in the years since my husband's murder . . .

The welcome interruption to these gloomy reminiscences

came in the form of the pealing doorbell, and I slid my bare feet back into my loafers before heading down the hallway. I glanced quickly out the front window, surprised and pleased to find a white Beaufort County sheriff's cruiser pulled up in the driveway. I flung open the door to the slightly shorter, slightly younger version of my dead husband standing stiffly on the wide porch.

"Red," I cried, "how great to see you! Come in."

Sergeant Redmond Tanner, handsome and tanned as always in his crisply pressed khaki uniform, remained in place, legs apart, hands clasped behind his back, in the formal stance of "parade rest."

I faltered, checking my natural impulse to grasp him in a sisterly embrace. "Red? What's the matter? Is something wrong?"

My mind flew immediately to my father, to Lavinia's persistent questions at the tail end of his letters about when I was coming home from Paris. I'd put them out of my mind once I'd been able to see for myself that the Judge seemed his usual irascible, hearty self. Had I been wrong? Had I missed some sign of frailty or impending collapse? I could feel my heart kick into overdrive as I stood staring into the implacable face of my brother-in-law, imagining the worst possible scenarios of heart attack, stroke . . .

"Back nearly a week and I have to hear it through the grapevine. When were you going to be in touch, when you got yourself ass-deep in trouble again and needed a cop to bail you out?"

I swallowed the flare of anger, tinged with relief, as I watched his face break into a mischievous grin.

"Bastard!" I laughed and punched him hard, just above the gold star and nameplate pinned to his chest. "You scared me to death with that damned funeral face of yours."

"Hey, that hurt! When did you stop hitting like a girl?"

I grabbed his arm and pulled him inside the house where we finally managed the awkward, fraternal hug. Rob's murder, which had come right on the heels of Red and Sarah's painful divorce, had left him reeling, and I soon became aware his feelings for me could become more than brotherly if I gave him any indication I was interested. It had created a gulf between us I sincerely hoped my escape to Paris and the intervening months had healed.

"You on or off duty?" I asked, leading Red up the three steps and into the kitchen. "Want a beer?"

"Nope, thanks. I'm on at seven."

"How about a tea?"

"Sure."

I retrieved the ever-present pitcher from the refrigerator, dumped ice into a pair of tall glasses, and set it all on the table. "You hungry?" I asked, pulling out the chair across from my brother-in-law and dropping into it.

"If I was, I wouldn't be looking for relief here." His grin took any sting from his accustomed jibes at my lack of cooking skills.

"I could whip up a spinach quiche that'd make you think you'd died and gone to Paris," I said, my sarcasm matching his own. "I wasn't exactly idle all those months in France, *mon ami.*"

"So what are you doing back here? What happened?"

The directness of his questions wiped the smile from my face and quelled the stock lies hovering on my tongue. Like my father, Red deserved the truth.

"Darnay's back in the game. His old boss whistled, and he went running." With my index finger I traced the pattern of blue lilies on the linen place mat in front of me and avoided Red's gaze. "Or maybe I should say he went limping back. He isn't completely healed yet. He has no business getting involved with all that . . . that *crap* again!"

I could feel the heat of my anger, rising again to engulf me. Red's next words didn't help any.

"So you just ran off and left him?"

I flung back my chair, crossed the room in three strides, and dumped the remains of my tea into the sink. I fought hard to control the anger Red's question had sent surging into my throat. "I wasn't going to sit around by myself in a strange country and wait for a knock on the door, for some

officious little man to bring me the news that Darnay has
been shot again. Or worse. I won't do it. I won't!"

I hate tears, almost more than anything. In the fine tradition of my Tattnall-Baynard ancestors, I pride myself on being able to control my emotions. But anger seems to be the
one which most often creeps past my defenses. I swiped a
hand across my eyes, aware that Red had moved quietly
across the floor to stand directly behind me. I sensed a hand
hovering just above my shoulder, felt his need to comfort
and console as if it were a tangible presence in the room. I
swallowed tightly and edged away, out of his reach.

"You love him?"

The question, loaded with all sorts of implications for
both of us, hung in the air for a long time before I shrugged.
"I don't know for sure. I think. Maybe."

The smile that always made my heart ache for Rob
worked its way across his brother's face. "Then get your butt
back to Paris," he said. "Now."

AFTER HE left, I remembered I'd meant to ask Red about
Gray Palmer's death, about who had jurisdiction and which
agency would be in possession of the reports. *Later,* I told
myself. *Mañana, demain. Yes, Miss Scarlett, tomorrow is
another day.*

I found the chicken breast nestled in its bed of wild rice in
a casserole dish in the refrigerator, followed Dolores's directions for reheating it in the microwave, and made myself a
salad. The silence seemed almost overwhelming in the rambling beach house as I picked at my dinner. So different
from meals taken around the ancient kitchen table, with
Darnay insisting I speak French, then correcting my syntax
and pronunciation at every turn; the two of us giggling like
children when my barbarian's tongue mutilated the beauty
of his language, turning the name of the French Minister of
Finance into a slimy toad with the mere misplacement of an
accent grave.

I retrieved the remote control from the counter and
flipped on the small television set suspended under the cor-

ner cabinet. Dolores hated to miss her afternoon soaps, broadcast in Spanish on one of the cable channels, so the placement of the TV had been an integral part of our plans when we remodeled the kitchen. I surfed to one of the local stations and let the chattering newscasters provide diversion to my gloomy thoughts until a familiar name snapped me back to attention.

". . . held a news conference this afternoon at the headquarters of his shipping empire here in Charleston. The sixty-one-year-old Palmer, whose rags-to-riches story was the subject of a recent series of articles in *The Post and Courier,* pleaded for information regarding the tragic drowning death of his only son early last Saturday morning."

The scene switched from the studio to what looked to be the lobby of a large hotel or office building. The camera focused on a tall, good-looking man in an impeccable navy blue suit and maroon tie, who leaned into the bank of microphones sprouting from a polished mahogany lectern. His dark brown hair, streaked with gray, had been combed straight back from a broad forehead. The picture zoomed in on a face dominated by an aristocratic nose. Hazel eyes squinted against the glare of the lights, and a mouth which was probably generous when he smiled was clenched in a tight grimace that might have been pain. Or anger. When he spoke, his voice carried a hint of his Southern origins, subdued but not entirely eradicated by either a Northern education or dedicated effort.

Much like my own.

The videotape editor had picked up his speech somewhere in the middle.

"While I have every confidence in the ability of the local authorities, as well as the Coast Guard and the Department of Natural Resources, I am convinced my son's death was not an accident. Therefore, I am offering a reward of twenty-five thousand dollars for information leading to the arrest and conviction of those responsible for this heinous crime. Anyone with knowledge of my son's whereabouts or activities on the night of his death should contact the special toll-free number you see on your screen. For those of you in the print media, a copy of my remarks will be available immediately following this press conference. Thank you."

I lifted the remote, my finger poised on the channel selector to check out the other local stations' coverage, when the camera pulled back from the determined face of the grieving father. A slender hand lay clasped in his. The ruby and sapphire eyes of the serpent winked in the strobe of still camera flashes, and its gold body wound up the olive-skinned arm.

"Despite Mr. Palmer's eloquent plea and generous offer, a Charleston police spokesman reiterated the department's belief young Gray Palmer was a victim of an accidental drowning. The autopsy, due by the end of the week, will determine if alcohol or drugs played any part in the tragedy.

"In other news, the stock market edged up today . . ."

I mentally tuned out the voices, my mind racing with the implications of the fade-out shot of Gray Palmer, Senior, comforting a weeping Araminda Albright.

CHAPTER
TEN

The next morning began well enough. I arrived, laden with briefcase and calculator, at the docks on Skull Creek at precisely ten o'clock to be engulfed in a bear hug that might have shattered bones on a daintier woman. Damon "Bubba" Mitchell and I had known each other a long time, his hole-in-the-wall eatery a regular stop whenever Rob and I had traveled down from our home in Charleston to the beach house for the weekend. It wasn't the type of greeting I usually got from my clients, but the Mitchell brothers and I had broken bread together, and that created a special bond.

"Damn, Bay, it's been too long. Where the hell you been keepin'?"

Bubba's huge black hand engulfed my upper arm as he steered me up the rickety steps and into the cramped little room which served as the office for his business. Tucked in behind the converted single-wide containing the retail shrimp and fish store, the narrow space was clean and orderly and held a surprising amount of modern equipment: computer, printer, fax machine, copier. Neatly labeled file folders stood aligned in a rack on the scarred oak desktop, and a pristine calendar lay open to the day's date.

I set my briefcase on the floor and turned to Damon Mitchell. "I've actually been out of the country for a few months," I said, shrugging out of my linen blazer and draping it across the back of the swivel chair tucked in to the desk. "Just got back last week."

"What you want to do a damn-fool thing like that for? Ain't nowhere better than the good ol' U. S. of A."

"Business," I replied, cutting short any additional questions about my temporary defection to the hinterlands of Europe. "How about you? How's Delia getting along?"

Bubba's naturally genial countenance darkened, and he shook his head. "I tell ya, Bay, that cancer's the Devil's work. Mama was a skinny little thing to start off with, but now . . . Well, she looks plain deathly, and that's the truth of it."

"But she's feeling better? Chris Brandon said . . ."

"Oh, yeah, they say they got it all. But all them chemicals sucked the life right out of her. Just lays around most days, watching the TV and readin' some. Now you know that don't sound like my mama."

"It sure doesn't." Delia Mitchell had been the driving force in holding together her father-in-law's business over the years. As I recalled, her late husband hadn't been good for much except fishing, and that more for pleasure than for producing income. "But she's earned her rest, don't you think?"

"Oh, surely. I'd just like to see some spark in them eyes again, hear her threaten to switch me and Dwight for cussin' like she used to."

I smiled at the picture of the reed-thin matriarch of the Mitchells taking on her mammoth offspring with a hazel branch. I had been emptying the contents of the briefcase onto the desk as we chatted and decided we needed to get down to business. I settled myself into the chair and pulled my reading glasses from my bag.

"So, what's been going on here, Bubba? Chris says you think your cousin has been stealing from you?"

Damon Mitchell perched his massive bulk precariously on a wooden chair which disappeared beneath him and shook his head. "I don't wanna believe it, but it seems like she must be."

"What does your mother say?"

"Mama don't know nothin' about it! I won't have her worryin', hear?"

"Sure, Bubba, no problem. Just between us. I promise." It would have been helpful to have Delia's take on the situation from her unique perspective of having kept the books all those years, but her son had a point. Recovering from cancer and a mastectomy was burden enough, especially for a woman no longer young. "So what roused your suspicion in the first place?"

The former pro-football tackle told his story with a minimum of words. In a nutshell, the catches had been of near record proportions lately, the boats requiring remarkably few major repairs, the longtime employees' working hard and efficiently. They'd even had to take on some high school kids to help out on the weekends. Like this morning the parking lot in front of the retail store was almost always full, and it was not a rare occurrence for folks who arrived late in the afternoon to go away empty handed because the day's catch had been sold out.

"And yet every week seems we're scramblin' to make payroll, pay the bills," Damon Mitchell concluded. "Tamika says we're doin' fine, not to worry. But I call the bank every once in a while, to check the balance, and it just keeps goin' down. Seems like we can't get ahead of the game no matter what. It just don't seem right to me." He shook his large, shaved head at the perplexity of the situation and raised his troubled eyes to my own. "Just don't seem right."

"Calling Chris Brandon was the smart thing to do, although I'm sure Mr. Foxworth would have brought it to your attention if he had noticed anything untoward."

"Ol' Foxy's got his own troubles," Bubba said with another head shake and a rueful grin. "Though maybe he woulda been a good one for it. Set a thief to catch a thief, ain't that what they say?"

I smiled back and nodded. "Could be. Well, let me get started here and see what I can find. Is there anything locked up here in the office? Any cabinets or cupboards I'll need keys for, or maybe a safe?"

"I opened it all up this mornin', first thing. Safe is over there underneath that lamp and the cloth Mama crocheted for it. It's closed, but not locked. Same with the files and such. Anything you need you can't find, you just give a holler. I need to be gettin' the lunch started. Folks start showin' up at the Shack sometimes right after eleven."

"What about your cousin?" I asked as I unbuttoned the cuffs on my long-sleeved shirt and rolled them up in anticipation of getting down to work. "Where's she today?"

I didn't relish the idea of an irate Mitchell woman storming in on me in the middle of my investigation, particularly if she carried any portion of her cousins' girth and height.

"Tamika don't come in on Tuesdays," Bubba replied, hoisting his three hundred-plus pounds out of the chair. "Monday, Wednesday, and Friday, that's it."

"Does she know I'm going to be looking at the books?"

"Sure. I told her you were takin' over for Foxy, I mean Mr. Foxworth. For the taxes and all. You don't have to worry about puttin' things back exactly like they was."

I nodded again at Bubba's insight. Folks who assumed he was just another washed up ex-athlete seriously underestimated his native intelligence and savvy.

"Well, I'll let you get to it. You holler if you need anythin'. I'll be just across the way there, gettin' the pots boiling."

"Thanks," I called as he lumbered down the steps.

I pulled open the bottom drawer on the right side of the desk—the one with the lock and the place I'd keep the checkbook if I were arranging things in the office—and smiled as I lifted out the black binder with blank, three-to-a-page checks and the green stubs of those already written. I plugged in the calculator, arranged my spreadsheets, wished for about the millionth time I hadn't quit smoking, and got busy.

TAMIKA JESSUP wasn't nearly as clever as she undoubtedly thought she was, nor as inept as I'd imagined her to be. I found the legitimate work she'd done to be neat, orderly, and precise. Her printing was legible; her math, accurate. Problem was, she was skimming money at such an alarming rate I wondered if she had a gambling debt or a drug habit she was financing. Damon and Dwight paid her a good salary, especially for a part-time employee, and they picked up her medical insurance as well.

Ungrateful little wretch, I thought, leaning back and tossing my pencil onto the pile of paper strewn across the desk.

I had taken a quick break around one o'clock and wandered across the driveway where the lunch activity at the Shack's four tables and cramped bar was still in full swing. I'd carried a plate of steaming shrimp and a diet Coke, none of which Bubba would let me pay for, out to an old-fashioned park bench set beneath the sheltering branches of an ancient live oak. I ate looking out over the docks and the creek to the green serenity of uninhabited Pinckney Island just across the way. The mid-April sun, filtered down through leaves quivering in a light breeze off the water, felt warm against my upturned face. The peace and beauty of my Lowcountry settled over me as gulls and pelicans swooped and called, and I had to force myself back to the task at hand.

By the end of the day, I was pretty confident I had Tamika's scam nailed. I gathered up my work papers and notes, made several copies of cancelled checks and some other pertinent documents, and returned it all to my briefcase. I would write up a complete analysis of my findings at home then deliver the report to Chris Brandon. It would be up to the Mitchell family to decide if they wanted to involve the sheriff.

I would have liked to avoid Bubba, but I couldn't. My affection for him and his brother, as well as Delia, made confirming their fears more difficult than if they had been simply clients, strangers. No one likes to hear they've been cheated and robbed, especially when the perpetrator is one of their own. But despite my reluctance to be the messenger who brings the bad news, I had to discuss the tax situation with someone. I would have preferred Delia, but Bubba had let me know in no uncertain terms she was off-limits.

He came after I called to him across the driveway, his shaved head glistening in the combined heat of the spring afternoon and several hours spent over boiling kettles of seafood. He took the news surprisingly well, asking only a few questions. I was more convinced than ever he must have known the answer before he asked the question, simply needing someone from outside to confirm his fears.

"I'll put it all in writing, and you can discuss your next move with Chris Brandon," I said as the huge man mopped sweat from his face with a crumpled white handkerchief. "What I do need is for someone to write a check to the IRS and get it in the mail ASAP. I've prepared a 4868 for you— that's an extension of time to file the tax return—but you can't get an extension for payment of the tax. I've estimated the amount due based on the prior years' Schedule C's from your mother's returns I got from Chris, so this may not be all of it. It's hard to tell when the books are in this state. You're going to need a full-blown audit and a reconstruction of the records before you can file an accurate return."

"Can't you do it?" Bubba's voice seemed diminished, lacking its usual force and timbre.

"I don't have the time to devote to it," I said honestly, my thoughts running to the press conference I'd witnessed on television the night before. Erik Whiteside had committed us to an investigation, and Gray Palmer's performance had kicked my curiosity level up a few notches. I had a feeling I might be spending a lot of time in Charleston over the next few weeks.

"Chris can recommend a competent firm to do the reconstruction for you." I had to suppress the urge to pat the former tackle on the head, so forlorn did he look at the news. "You also need to find someone to replace Tamika. There are a couple of good temp agencies here locally. I can give you a few names . . ."

"You want me to fire Tamika?"

It took me a moment to comprehend the question. "Of course. Why wouldn't you?"

"She's family," Bubba said simply.

"But she's been stealing from you! She created false employees and phony vendors, recorded that information on the stubs then made the checks out to herself. Or to cash. She's been averaging at least a thousand dollars a week, sometimes more. Why on earth would you *not* fire her?"

His look held genuine puzzlement. "She's Uncle T's daughter. Daddy's brother's girl."

"And?"

Again Bubba wagged his bald black head at me. "You don't understand, Bay. Family don't fire family. Tamika musta needed the money for somethin' important. I'll just ask her what it is, and we'll give her whatever she needs." His final statement seemed to settle it, at least in his mind. "That's what families do."

"Of course, it's up to you," I said, unrolling my sleeves and slipping on my blazer. "I'll give my report to your attorney, and you can take it from there. I'll send my bill to him as well. Be sure and get the extension and the check in the mail by Friday."

I could tell by the look on Bubba's face that my brusqueness had hurt him in some way, but I couldn't help it, and I wasn't sure why. Anger at a criminal's getting away with it? The feeling that my efforts had been for nothing?

Honesty compelled me to consider the emotion rolling around in the pit of my stomach just might be envy. How many people in this world had the luxury of knowing their families would forgive them anything, even stealing from their own kin? Not many I knew of, that was certain. Maybe not even my own.

Bubba Mitchell and I finally parted on an upbeat note, my genuine smile and firm handshake apparently erasing any bad feelings. He insisted Red and I stop in soon for some oysters and shrimp or maybe a bowl of his renowned Frogmore stew, and he promised to give his mother my best regards.

As I pulled out of the bumpy dirt driveway onto Squire Pope Road, I wondered if Tamika Mitchell Jessup had any idea how lucky she was.

• • •

I SET the carryout bag on the counter next to the telephone and punched the message playback key. I brought a plate from the cupboard and emptied the foam container of grilled chicken Caesar salad onto it as I listened to a honey-voiced woman try to sell me on the joys of timeshare investment in Myrtle Beach, and a fast-talking guy who promised to improve my golf game in just three short lessons. I had arranged the slices of garlic pita bread along the edge of the dish and poured myself a glass of tea before we finally got to the good stuff.

I recognized Gray Palmer's voice from his television appearance the night before. For some reason, I wasn't surprised to hear from him.

"Ms. Tanner," the message began, and I noticed his non–press conference voice held more of the South in it. "This is Gray Palmer, Senior, of Charleston. My late son's roommate has informed me that Gray had engaged your, uh, firm to do some investigative work for him. She is unaware of the nature of that work, but I did want to make it clear any relationship you may think you have with my family has, of course, been rendered null and void by my son's unfortunate death. If you will present your bill to my office here in Charleston, I'll be happy to see that you're properly reimbursed. I trust this will effectively terminate any contract, either implied or written, which my son may have entered into. I look forward to receiving your invoice. Have a pleasant day."

Whew! I thought, mopping up the last remnants of the Caesar dressing with the remaining sliver of pita bread. *That was interesting.*

I carried the plate to the dishwasher, added my fork, and tossed the foam container into the trash. In the bedroom I pulled out my favorite sweats, which had lain neglected in the dresser since my defection to France. The pants felt a little tight around the waist and hips, a condition I intended to remedy immediately. I laced up my battered, disreputable

Nikes, did ten minutes of intense stretching, and ran down the steps from the deck and onto the beach.

A light breeze lifted my hair as I turned left, away from the Westin Hotel and its early spring tourists, and set out in a light jog. Despite my warm-up, I could feel the long unused muscles in my legs and back protesting as I picked up the pace. When I had finally gained my rhythm, settling into a comfortable lope, I turned my mind loose on the puzzle of Gray Palmer's message.

First off, poor little Araminda Albright, grieving friend of the deceased, had lied through her teeth, either to me or to her employer. Palmer had said his son's roommate had no idea why Gray had hired us, yet she had been perfectly lucid on the subject as we'd sat together on the beach near her house. She had stated unequivocally Gray's discovery of the skeleton on one of the islands he'd been investigating for his father had been the cause of his murder. And might endanger her, as well.

What had happened to change her mind? And where had this sudden allegiance, evidenced by her appearance at the press conference with Gray Senior, come from? She had told me in no uncertain terms that Gray hated his father, even though he worked for him and took his money. She hadn't seemed to be his biggest fan, either. Then why the public display of support? Had she run to her employer after our meeting, or had he somehow found out about it on his own? What was the game here, and who exactly were the players?

I tuned back in to my breathing and the light burn beginning in the backs of my calves and decided to head toward home. My watch told me I'd been out for a little over twenty minutes, and the soft graying of the light across the ocean signaled that nightfall was fast encroaching. I cut the return trip by five minutes, sprinting the last hundred yards just to prove I wasn't completely out of shape, knowing I would pay a price for it the next day.

Still, it felt good to have worked up a sweat, although it

was rapidly cooling in the darkening twilight as I plodded up the steps onto the deck. The interior lights, connected to a sensor, popped on just as I inserted my key, and I felt again the stab of loneliness I'd experienced when I'd stepped back into my home after the long months away. The house looked warm, inviting, and yet I would walk inside to yawning emptiness, with only the comfort of the TV to banish the silence.

Quit whining, I ordered myself. Dolores was almost fully recovered and back in my life, and for that I would be eternally grateful to whatever Power had made it so. I had friends, family, financial security, and an interesting new career, if I could ever manage to get the damned thing off the ground.

This newest case had proved to be a bust, Gray Palmer, Senior, blowing us off with a brusque determination couched in Southern gentility, and Araminda Albright proving herself to be a beautiful, charming liar. The picture of her exotic, multiethnic face, strained with what I had believed to be genuine grief and fear, floated ahead of me down the hallway to my bathroom where I stripped off my running clothes and tossed them into the hamper.

I had been wrong about a lot of things lately . . . about a lot of *people,* actually.

Which is why you should stick to numbers, my girl, I told myself, setting the hot water to run in the whirlpool tub and pulling on my old chenille robe. In the kitchen I nuked a cup of hot water, dropped in a tea bag, and carried it back with me. The aroma of eucalyptus steaming in the bath was already easing the strain in my unused muscles when the telephone interrupted.

I gave thought to letting the machine pick up, until another face—last seen glowering in anger as I handed my bags to the Parisian taxi driver—materialized inside my head. I dropped onto the closed lid of the toilet and picked up the extension from the marble vanity.

"Bay," an excited Erik Whiteside shouted into my ear, "you'll never guess what I just got in the mail!"

I swallowed my disappointment, forcing my mind away from a thousand images the thoughts of Darnay had conjured up, and said, "Hey, partner! Before you tell me, I have to give you some news, too."

"Wait, mine's better."

I laughed. "You sound like some kid who just got a new bike. This is business. I had a message on my machine tonight from Gray Palmer, the father. Apparently the lovely Araminda spilled her guts to him about his son hiring us and all, and he called to bounce us off the case. Pretty adamant about it, too. Told me to send him a bill and basically take a hike. I'm sorry, but . . ."

"Well, you can tell him to take a walk, too."

"What do you mean?"

"I'm trying to tell you. This package. It was waiting outside my door when I got home tonight. It's from Gray." He sobered suddenly, and my breath quickened. "And guess what I found inside?"

It took only a moment to figure out what was the one thing which could have engendered this much excitement in my young associate.

"A bone," I said, the implications of it sending all thoughts of a long, soothing soak whirling away with the steam.

CHAPTER
ELEVEN

As the water in the tub cooled and my muscles tightened, we wrestled with what to do about the strange contents of the package dropped by the door of Erik Whiteside's apartment.

"Does it . . . smell?" I asked at one point.

"No, not at all. Well, just kind of musty. Sort of like a damp basement, or the ground under a rock when you roll it over. You know."

Actually, I didn't. No one in his right mind would build a house with a basement in the marshy, flood-prone area in which I'd lived most of my life, and I hadn't had many occasions to be turning over rocks, at least not literally. My late husband's passion for *Law and Order* reruns had given me my only insight into dead bodies and how they deteriorated. I was pretty certain the local bugs and worms would have quickly stripped the body of any tissue or ligament, but we had no idea how long the remains had been in the ground.

I ventured another grisly question. "There isn't anything attached to it, is there?"

"You mean like flesh or anything? No. It's pretty clean, except for some dirt and a few leaves. It came wrapped in a material sort of like oilcloth and then canvas, maybe from a sail or something else nautical."

"Nothing else? No note or letter of explanation?"

"Nope." Erik cleared his throat, stumbling a little over his next words. "I guess he figured he'd explain everything when he saw me."

I gave him a moment to get himself back together. I had to keep reminding myself this was his friend we were discussing.

"About the bone. How big is it? Can you tell what part of the body it's from?"

I couldn't believe I was sitting there on the lid of my toilet discussing human remains over the telephone. Perhaps I needed to rethink this new profession of mine.

"Well, I don't know squat about biology, but I got onto a Web site that had a detailed diagram of the human skeleton. The bone is long and narrow, so it looks like it could be from either the arm or the leg. Humerus or femur, maybe. Sucker's heavy at any rate."

I swallowed against the sudden image of young Gray Palmer gently extricating the bone from the disturbed gravesite, carefully wrapping and packing it, then trotting down to the nearest FedEx location to ship it off to Erik. The smile hovering on my lips disappeared, however, when I remembered this boy lay dead in the Charleston County morgue, his face slashed beyond recognition. That grim thought triggered an idea which had been hovering in the back of my mind, just out of reach, since we'd heard the details of his death.

"How do you suppose they identified him?" I asked, as much to myself as to Erik, whose quick response surprised me.

"You mean Gray? Yeah, I wondered that, too. Maybe by clothes or jewelry? I guess they could have assumed it was him because it was his boat. Or they could have done dental records."

Again my television training leaped to the fore. "But they'd already said it was him immediately after they pulled the body out of the water. They wouldn't have had time to do any dental comparisons, even if they could have contacted his dentist on a Saturday afternoon. When was the package mailed? You don't suppose . . . ?"

"I thought of that, too. No, the date on the shipping label is Friday, just after nine A.M. A Mailboxes office in downtown Charleston. He probably dropped it off on his way to the boat."

We both digested the implications of the timing. According to Araminda Albright, Gray Palmer set off on Friday to revisit the nameless island where he had discovered the skeleton. And never returned. Of course, she hadn't proved herself to be the most reliable of informants, and I said so to Erik.

"You think there's something fishy about her relationship with the old man?"

"I really don't give a damn if she's sleeping with him or anyone else. My point is she lied about it, which makes me wonder how much of her story we can rely on at all."

"Well, it's kind of pointless to worry about it now, don't you think? I mean, if she's gone over to the enemy and GS doesn't want to fork over any fees to find out what his son was involved in, we're sort of up the creek without a client, aren't we?"

"Technically speaking. But you're forgetting about the bone. What do we do about that?"

"We could always turn it over to the authorities."

I sensed a hesitation in his voice which mirrored my own thoughts. "Do you really want to do that?"

"No, but I don't see how we have any choice."

"No one knows we have it, so I don't suppose we need to make a decision on it right this minute. Do you have a safe place for it?"

His laugh brought a welcome break in the gruesome conversation. "You bet. Ever since I was a teenager and Mom started making me do my own laundry, I've always stashed stuff in the bottom of my dirty clothes hamper. So far it's been better than a safe. I figure if anyone's brave enough to dig through my sweaty socks and used under . . ."

"Okay, I get the picture."

"So then what? I mean, what's the plan?"

I stood and stretched, easing the stiffness in my back and

thighs. "I don't have a game plan. Yet. Sit tight and let me think this through. I'll get back to you tomorrow."

"Okay, you're the boss. I'd feel kind of bad just letting it drop, though. Because of Gray and all."

"I understand. By the way, they said something on the newscast yesterday, the one that had Palmer's press conference, about an article the Charleston paper did on him not long ago. Would something like that be on-line?"

"Should be. Want me to check it out?"

"No, thanks. I think it's time I learned a little more about how to navigate my way around the Internet. What should I do?"

I heard the disappointment in his voice, but I felt strongly about not relying entirely on my young partner whenever something needed to be checked out on the Web. He had a full-time job and responsibilities and an actual functioning love life, none of which troubled my existence at the moment.

"Just do a Google search for the name. Or better yet, find the Web site of the paper and search the archives. Most larger papers have their primary articles out there."

"Google?" I hadn't even started and already I was behind the curve.

"Google dot com. It's a search engine, probably the best one."

"Okay, I'm on it. Come to think of it, I may not get back to you for a day or two. I have to do something about getting myself a car. I can't keep running around in this little cracker box forever."

"Got any particular model in mind?"

"Not really. Maybe something a little bigger than the Zeemer. But definitely a convertible."

"You should check out the new Jags."

"Thanks, pal. Maybe if I hit the lottery." I thought of Worthy Foxworth, cooling his heels in a state prison for appropriating client funds to cover his own investment losses. The stock market had not been entirely kind to me, either, during the past few months. I leaned over to let some of the tepid water out of the tub then turned the hot tap back on full blast. "You're sure you're okay with holding onto the . . . thing?"

"Don't worry. It'll probably improve the smell in the hamper. Talk to you soon."

I hung up laughing, peeled off the robe, and slipped into the steaming whirlpool, marveling at the progress I had made in becoming a real private eye. I could joke about bones. Maybe I just might succeed at this after all.

INSTEAD OF relaxing me, the half hour in the tub seemed to rejuvenate both mind and body. I pulled on my old flannel pajamas, made a pot of tea, and hunkered down in front of the computer. My initial intention was to dive into the quest for more background information on Gray Palmer and his shipping empire, but first I forced myself to type up my report on the Mitchell Seafood embezzlement. I printed it out and slipped the pages, along with an invoice, into an oversized brown envelope. I slid my feet into sandals and pulled my robe back on, then trotted out to the mailbox at the end of my driveway. A choir of tree frogs serenaded me in their piercing voices as I hurried back into the house.

Back at the computer, I tried *The Post and Courier* first and struck pay dirt almost immediately. Apparently the paper had run a series of articles on local movers and shakers during the February tourist doldrums, and Gray Palmer's had required two successive Sunday feature pages to do him justice.

I scanned the columns, interested to learn he hailed from Yemassee, a tiny crossroads town northwest of Beaufort famous for its old gas-station-turned-steakhouse restaurant. After a brief stint in the Marine Corps, Palmer blasted through the business curriculum of the University of South Carolina, graduating with honors in less than three years. After two failed attempts to start his own enterprises—a nautical supplies store and an ill-fated excursion boat venture whose principal asset sank before the first tourist ever stepped on board—Gray Palmer found the perfect solution to his entrepreneurial ambitions.

He married money.

Anne Compton Whitley's family rose from relative financial and social obscurity to incredible wealth and power on the polished decks of their sleek sailing ships. Not nearly as dashing as Scarlett's Rhett, to judge by the grainy photos accompanying the *Post* article, the Whitley blockade runners bribed and fought their way to glory by regularly penetrating the nets thrown up around vital Confederate ports such as Charleston. Ironically, their wealth grew in direct proportion to the misery and deprivation of the local populations whose desperation for foodstuffs and other goods drove prices to dizzying heights. Despite this, they earned themselves the everlasting admiration of their countrymen and untold riches with which to begin a new life when the South had finally been reduced to ashes.

Apparently the heroes had not been as adept at procreating as they had been at slipping past gunboats in the dead of night. Anne had been the last Whitley, her only brother having died in infancy. Enter Gray Palmer—charming, handsome, ambitious. Whitley Maritime became Palmer Shipping, and everyone's problems were solved.

I printed out the pages, scanning them as they slipped from the printer. The only other item of immediate interest I found was the mention of another child, a married daughter living in California, and the sudden death of Anne Compton Whitley Palmer when Gray the younger was in his teens. No mention of cause of death, which I found curious, and I made a note in the margin to see if I could track down her obituary. Not that it probably had any bearing on anything, but the omission intrigued me. I added the sheets to the thin PALMER/ALBRIGHT file and went to make more tea.

I settled on the white sofa in front of the television in the great room and tried to give my brain a respite. I surfed idly through the dozens of channels, finally coming to rest on a PBS rerun of an old *Mystery* episode. While Jeremy Brett had always seemed to me the quintessential Holmes, I couldn't seem to concentrate on his crisp delivery of the familiar lines, his scathing repartee with the bumbling Watson. My mind kept wandering, my outer gaze drifting to the deep gloom just outside the partially closed drapes, and my inner eye to the darker void around my heart.

Damn it, Darnay, where are you?

CHAPTER
TWELVE

I have no idea what possessed me to solicit my father's advice on the subject of a new car, but I knew it had been a serious tactical error the moment the words were out of my mouth.

We sat glowering at each other across the scarred oak table in the kitchen, our hands and arms washed in patterned warmth from the late morning sunlight streaming through the mullioned windows. Lavinia, neutral as usual in the silly confrontations which erupted regularly between the Judge and me, ignored us, humming softly to herself as she worked biscuit dough with her strong brown hands. Something redolent with garlic and sea creatures bubbled gently on the stove.

"Just borrowin' someone else's miseries," my father said for what I seriously believed might have been the tenth time in as many minutes. "I have never bought a used vehicle. Buy new and buy American, that's been my credo, and it's stood me in good stead, daughter. All these damned Germans and Japanese dumpin' their inferior products on our markets, that's what's wrong with the whole country!"

I'd tried to point out earlier that his thinking was about thirty years out of date, that some of the finest automobiles now rolled off American assembly lines with foreign nameplates decorating their trunk lids. My beloved little BMW Z-3 had been put together right up the interstate from us in Greer, South Carolina. Besides which, since his last stroke had rendered his left side virtually useless he hadn't even been a passenger in a car, let alone a driver. Rob and I had ordered and equipped the handicapped accessible van which sat out in the driveway, the one Lavinia used for shopping and errands. The number of times my father had even set foot or wheel inside of it could be counted on the fingers of two hands. But the Judge never let facts stand in the way of his firmly entrenched opinions, so I sipped tea and let him rant until he finally had to stop for breath.

"I'm going to buy an American car, Your Honor, so save the closing arguments. And I've decided it's going to be one of the new T-Birds. But the company seems to be restricting production, no doubt to keep the demand up, and the only one the dealer has is a program vehicle." As the young female salesperson at Island Ford had explained it to me, these were cars driven briefly by company bigwigs then sold to dealers at closed auctions. "It's only got six thousand miles on it."

And it's yellow, I wanted to add, a beautiful, creamy, butter-yellow with a tan leather interior whose bucket seats and retro styling fit me perfectly. Admitting to my father that the color of the car was influencing my decision would have been like pouring gasoline on an already roaring blaze. Instead I had been enumerating the many safety and engineering features of the resurrected classic of the late fifties, rattling off crash-test and performance statistics I'd memorized from the brochure.

"Besides," I added, saving my most devastating salvo for last, "it's almost eight thousand dollars less than the sticker price on a new one."

I had rendered him speechless. I sat back in my chair and crossed my arms over my chest in satisfied triumph. I so seldom won an argument with the Judge.

He *harrumphed* a couple of times, cleared his throat noisily, and reached for another of the blueberry bran muffins from the plate we'd been working on.

"No more of those. Lunch will be ready in less than an hour."

Lavinia's voice, though soft, crackled with the authority she had exercised in this house since before I was born. Emmaline Baynard Simpson had found the perfect housekeeper in Lavinia Smalls not long after she inherited Presqu'isle, and the calm, stately black woman had ruled as a benign dictator ever since. Not that my mother didn't run the show. Her autocratic demands for perfection echoed throughout the massive old mansion, her pride of heritage and its trappings evidenced in every room. But it was always Lavinia, subservient but never servile, who carried out the commands from on high, administering justice and keeping the wheels greased amid the day-to-day messiness of raising a child. If anything about my early years resembled a normal home life, it was due to Lavinia.

"You stayin'?" she said to me, sliding out an oven rack and setting on it the pan of biscuits she'd rolled out.

"What's in the pot?"

"A gumbo. I had some shrimp and a few other things I needed to use up. Thad and Isaiah brought us over a mess of oysters, but I'm saving those for supper."

Lavinia's only child, Thaddeus, worked for the post office and lived in Bluffton. Although my mother had always addressed her as *Mrs*. Smalls, I had never once heard either of them refer to Thad's father, and the mysterious progenitor of the boy who had shared my childhood remained a subject about which we did not speak. Her grandson, along with my best friend Bitsy's son CJ, was a star athlete for Hilton Head High. Both boys would be graduating this year, if memory served me right. A light shiver traveled down my arms as I recalled how close they had both come to spending this past year in jail instead of piling up touchdown statistics.

"Is there okra in it?" I asked, getting back to the topic of lunch.

"Of course there's okra in it. Wouldn't be a gumbo without okra." Lavinia shook her head at my aversion to all things green.

"Just pick it out, like you do the peas." My father had apparently recovered from his humiliating defeat in the auto wars.

"Okay," I said. "Thanks."

"You can set the table then," Lavinia replied, wiping her floury hands on her ever-present apron.

"Yes, ma'am."

"I'll go wash up." The Judge toggled his wheelchair controls and beat a hasty retreat out into the hallway. Over the soft whirring of the motor, I heard him mutter, " 'Any coward can fight a battle when he's sure of winning.' "

I stepped into the doorway and called, "George Eliot. Pen name of Mary Ann Evans. No doubt the coward she was referring to was a man."

He stopped and maneuvered his chair around to face me. " 'Winning isn't everything . . .' " he began.

" '. . . it's the only thing!' " I crowed. "Vince Lombardi. Two for two, ladies and gentlemen, the little lady is two for two!" I pumped my fist in victory, and my father shrugged good-naturedly as he swiveled back around toward his study.

"I don't know why the two of you can't be in the same room for more than thirty seconds without getting into some kind of hoop-de-do." Lavinia sprinkled herbs over the surface of the pot and stirred them in while inhaling the fragrant steam which rose in a cloud around her face.

"*Hoop-de-do?* What the hell kind of word is that?" I laughed as I popped back into the kitchen and began distributing place mats and the everyday china and silver around the table.

"You know what I mean. And there's no need for profanity."

I suffered the oft-repeated rebuke in silence, finished laying out the table, and dropped back into my chair. "Anything else I can do?"

Lavinia turned from the stove. The look she cast over my head and out to the doorway brought me snapping to attention. She was obviously checking on the whereabouts of the Judge, and there was something furtive, almost conspiratorial in her eyes. The memory of her postscripts to my father's letters surfaced again in my consciousness, and I was suddenly afraid.

"What?" I demanded in a forced whisper.

"I've been wanting to talk to you, but I don't quite know how to . . ."

"Is he sick?"

"No, nothing like that." She said it offhandedly, a throwaway line that made anger rise into my throat.

"Well, it's not exactly an unwarranted fear. He is pushing eighty, if you recall, and you certainly planted enough hints in his letters."

My sharp tone surprised her, and I watched comprehension, then remorse chase each other across her face. She dropped into a chair and reached for my hands.

"Oh, Bay, I'm so sorry! What a fool I am! I had no idea you'd interpret my words that way. And I should have." She shook her elegant head in dismay. "I surely should have."

It was my turn to feel bad, for challenging her, for doubting for a moment that, if the Judge had serious medical problems, she would have called me in Paris and demanded my immediate return to the States.

"It's okay," I said, patting her hand where it lay next to mine on the table. "I shouldn't have jumped to conclusions. So what is the problem?"

Again she stared past me, her head cocked to one side, listening for the soft *whoosh* of tires on the heart pine floor which would announce my father's return.

"Do you know anyone named Felicity Baronne?"

I studied Lavinia's face, wrinkled in worry, and shook my head. "No, not that I'm aware of." *Felicity* did scratch a little at the back of my memory, but it may have been because it was an unusual name, anachronistic in a pleasant sort of way. "Why?" I asked.

"She's been coming here. To the house."

The statement itself wouldn't have caused an eyebrow to twitch in most homes in Beaufort County, but it made mine rise almost to my hairline.

"Here? To Presqu'isle?"

When I told people my father had become housebound after his strokes, it was something of an under-exaggeration. He had, in fact, become a virtual hermit, refusing to allow any but his most intimate friends of very long standing see him brought to the sorry physical state to which he had been reduced. Lavinia and I had become accustomed to his left hand lying curled and useless in his lap, his once powerful legs shriveled to sticks. Although he retained his full head of thick white hair and the sparkle in his piercing gray eyes, he was most distressed by the flaccid, drooping left side of his face. I had said on more than one occasion he should be thankful his mammoth intellect had been unaffected, as evidenced just a few minutes before with his rattling off obscure quotations without a moment's hesitation.

It was a concession to good fortune I could never get him to acknowledge.

"He never mentioned her in his letters," I went on in the face of Lavinia's silence. "Who is she?"

"She called one day, right after the first of the year, and asked to speak to your father. Referred to him as 'Tally.'"

Lavinia paused to let that sink in. Again, no one but people he had known for dogs' years called him by that nickname. To most residents of Beaufort, he had been simply "the Judge" for as long as I could remember.

I caught some of her apprehension, glancing quickly over my shoulder at the empty hallway. "What did you do?"

"Told her he wasn't available, just like I always do, unless I recognize who it is. She said if there was a more convenient time she'd be glad to call back. I asked her what her business was with him, because you know these days we get so many of those annoying people wanting to sell stocks or vacations or whatnot."

"What did she say?"

Lavinia pulled her narrow lips into the line of disapproval I remembered so well from my childhood and said, "Personal."

"That's it? Just 'personal'?"

"All I could get out of her. Said to give your father her

name, even spelled it out for me as if I was some illiterate high school dropout, and then said she'd call back later in the day."

"And did you? Tell him, I mean?"

"Of course I did. And the look on his face! As if he'd seen the ghost of one of his dead ancestors or something. 'I'll talk to her.' That's all he said. So when she rang again, about four that afternoon, I took him in the phone and left him to it. Next thing I know, he's telling me she's coming to visit, the following day, and would I be so kind as to make certain we had some refreshment to offer her." The snort of derision was pure Lavinia. "Would I be so kind! I wanted to shake him until his teeth rattled!"

I had no idea where this story was going, but I was beginning to get an inkling. Lavinia had ruled Presqu'isle—and my father's life—for the more than fifteen years since my mother's death. That their relationship might have been more than employer and housekeeper had been brought home to me in a very poignant way last summer, and the shock of it had strained my relationship with Lavinia for some time afterwards. We had promised each other a long talk, but the truth of it was I hadn't really wanted to know. I preferred that both Lavinia and my father stick to their assigned roles as I perceived them, and counted myself happy in my ignorance. Over time, our avoidance of any direct reference to our confrontation on the back verandah those many months ago had allowed us to drift easily back into our old relationship without looking too closely at what the new one should be.

Of course, the truly adult part of me recognized this situation couldn't go on forever without some clearing of the air between Lavinia and me. But, despite Plato's warning, both of us seemed content, at least for the moment, to find our unexamined lives quite worth living.

"What happened when she showed up? What was she like?"

I figured it was the appearance of an attractive female which had so rattled Lavinia, especially one who had obviously once known my father well enough to call him Tally.

"White. Pretty, in a hard sort of way, lots of makeup and clothes way too young for her. But still in decent shape, considering her age."

I nearly laughed at Lavinia's grudging description until I noticed the anger in her eyes. Both our heads snapped up at the creaking of the floorboards at the far end of the hall. The Judge's tuneless humming could be heard just over the whirring of the wheelchair mechanism as he neared the door to the kitchen.

"Quick! Tell me what happened! Did he say where he knew her from?"

"No," Lavinia whispered, leaning in so close our noses almost touched. "But I did eventually find out what she came for."

"What?" I urged.

"Money," she announced triumphantly. "Your father is giving this floozy money!"

APPARENTLY THE strain of getting through lunch after that bombshell didn't register at all on my father. He chattered away about local gossip, culled from the many phone conversations he had with his old cronies over the course of a day. Several times I opened my mouth to bring up the subject of the *floozy,* only to be quelled by a dagger stare from Lavinia. I'd hoped for the opportunity to pump him once we'd left the table for his customary post-meal cigar and bourbon on the verandah, but he expressed himself tired after a restless night and whirred off to his afternoon nap.

I cleaned up the dishes while Lavinia got him settled. I managed to scrape into the garbage the untouched okra, which I'd cleverly camouflaged under a partially eaten biscuit, before she returned. I dried while she washed; and, though I questioned her at length, she had seemingly given me all the information she possessed.

"How do you know about the money?" I asked, vigorously attacking one of the silver knives with the dish towel to insure against water spots as I'd been taught at Lavinia's knee.

She transferred soapy dishwater from the sink to the big cooking pot and set it on the counter to soak. When she didn't meet my eyes, I was pretty sure she had been doing a little old-fashioned snooping of her own.

"It's okay," I said. "Whatever you did, I know it was done out of loyalty and . . ." I was about to add *love* and thought better of it.

"It's just that he kept giving me envelopes to mail, the small kind, like you use for checks. They were addressed to her at a post-office box in Hilton Head."

"How many?" I asked.

"Six, so far, that I know of."

"How much money?"

Lavinia ducked her head and scrubbed unnecessarily hard on the pan she'd used for the biscuits. "How would I . . ." she began, but I wasn't having any of that nonsense.

"You would know by going through the bank statements when they came and adding up the cancelled checks made out to her," I said matter-of-factly. "Now don't try to BS me, Mrs. Smalls. I know you have access to the statements, and it's what any concerned person would do. So how much?"

She straightened her shoulders and looked me squarely in the eye. "Three thousand dollars. Six checks for five hundred each. Since the middle of January, and the last one bein' about two weeks ago."

"And you asked him about it? Asked him what was going on?"

"Of course I did no such thing! Is it any of my business what he spends his money on?"

"Come on, Lavinia, this is crazy! You've been worrying yourself into a decline about this mystery woman, and you haven't just come out and asked him?"

"No, and you won't either. I mean it, Bay Tanner, I won't have you pickin' at him about this."

"Then why the hell did you tell me about it in the first place?" My voice rose, and she shushed me with a wave of her hand. "I swear I don't understand either one of you most of the time."

Lavinia sighed and finally turned from the sink to face me squarely. "If he wanted me to know, he would have told me right away. He knows it's gnawing at me. I can tell when I glance up sometimes, sudden-like, and find him looking at me in that way he has. You know, as if he's trying to read my mind."

"Yes, I know what you mean. But answer my question. What was the point of all the hints in the letters and the whispered conversation before lunch if you don't want me to confront him about it?"

She nodded her head, as if coming to some conclusion. "I want to hire you. To investigate." I opened my mouth to point out the utter stupidity of her statement, but she overrode me. "Yes, and I want you to charge me, just like you would anyone else."

"Don't be ridiculous! First of all, I wouldn't take your money if you held me down and stuffed it in my pockets, and secondly this is my father we're talking about. If he's gotten himself into some kind of mess, I'll get him out of it. Free. Gratis. No charge. Are we clear?"

It might have been the first time I'd ever really asserted myself with Lavinia Smalls, and I watched grudging admiration dawn in her eyes. "As you like, Bay. Thank you."

"Get me the address and the cancelled checks and I'll see if I can track this woman down."

"Why do you need the checks?"

"To see where she cashed them or deposited them. When's the last time you saw Ms. Felicity Baronne?"

"A few days before you came home. I served them tea and carrot cake in his study." Amazingly there were tears forming in Lavinia's deep brown eyes. "He asked me to close the door behind me."

I resisted the urge to put my arms around this wonderful woman who had been my refuge and my salvation, but I knew she'd soon regret her moment of weakness and resent my witnessing of it. Instead I slid the last of the silver into its lined drawers and hung the dish towel on the hook next to the sink.

"Okay, then," I said, "go find me that information, and I'll get busy."

Lavinia Smalls gave me a watery smile and bustled out of the kitchen.

"Lord help me," I muttered and collapsed into a chair.

CHAPTER
THIRTEEN

I had to hustle to get back to the car dealership before they closed for the evening, but I made it with about half an hour to spare. After dropping off the rental car in Beaufort, I'd paid them an additional fee to be ferried back to Bluffton just ahead of the nightly rush hour. The young man who delivered me safely to the front door of Island Ford said his company had a policy against accepting tips, but I folded a ten and slipped it into the pocket of his crisp blue oxford shirt anyway.

I had made all the arrangements with the young saleswoman by phone from the Judge's house, and she had the T-Bird shined up and waiting just outside the showroom. I wrote out the check, wincing a little at the dent it put in my brokerage cash account and signed more papers than I thought could possibly be necessary for a relatively simple transaction. But, shortly before six, the convertible top stored neatly under the boot, I roared onto Route 278 in my fabulous new wheels.

The bean counter in me acknowledged I should have done more research, considered more options. Done a few test drives, whipped up some lists, and made detailed comparisons. But there's something visceral about vehicles, at least to me. Maybe it harks back to the days when our personal mode of transportation was a living, breathing creature, with a face, a personality, a name. The car simply replaced the horse, and I still needed a connection in my gut with whatever pile of steel and fiberglass and plastic was going to haul me from place to place. Not exactly logical, but there you are.

We caught a lot of stares, this sleek yellow beauty and I. My dark brown hair had regained some of its reddish-gold highlights after a few days' exposure to the Lowcountry sun and had grown back in enough to stream out behind me when we finally got up to speed. The sheer joy of it lifted my spirits to a level I hadn't experienced since I'd fled Paris.

As we idled at the stoplight at Moss Creek, my words to Lavinia came back to me, and I realized I needed to take my own advice.

And you asked him about it? I'd demanded, and been astounded to find the answer was no. I had been waiting for more than a week for Alain Darnay to call, for him to come to his senses, realize the folly of his decision, and beg me to return. Obviously that wasn't going to happen. So, unless I intended to spend the rest of my life waiting and wondering, I was going to have to make the first move.

If I remembered correctly, the time difference between Hilton Head and Paris would be five hours now that Daylight Savings Time had gone into effect, so it would be well past midnight there by the time I got home. Still, if I stayed up late enough, I could catch him before he left the apartment next morning for . . . well, for wherever he was spending his time now. The decision made, I cruised on over the bridges, delighting in the glistening mud of the marshes at low tide and the reflection of pristine sailboats in the clear waters of the Intracoastal Waterway.

My bridge, my ocean, my island. The old, familiar litany ran through my head, and I wondered again what it was about Hilton Head that had made it home, despite my many years in Charleston and my growing up on St. Helena.

When I stepped into the house, I realized Dolores had worked her magic with the carpet cleaners. The whole place smelled fresh and slightly damp, and I found several of her wonderful bilingual notes tacked up at the entrance to almost every room: *Is no dry. Not walking hasta noche.*

I slipped off my shoes and tested the condition of the great room rug, finding it satisfactory. In the bedroom it was still a little squishy, but I changed quickly and headed back to the kitchen. I had consumed enough biscuits and gumbo at Lavinia's table to live off for at least a couple of days, so I threw together a salad and ate it standing at the counter. One bowl and one fork into the dishwasher and I was done.

I slid onto the chair at the built-in desk and lifted the local phone directory from the center drawer. I felt a little foolish as I thumbed my way to the beginning pages, but stranger things had happened. I ran my finger down the tightly packed names. There were several one-*n* Barones listed, but none with two. If it had been that easy, Lavinia would have found the woman herself, but it had been worth a try.

I carried tea into the office and settled myself in front of the computer. I signed on and typed in *www.google.com,* the search engine Erik had suggested I try when I had been looking for information on Gray Palmer. *Felicity Baronne* kicked up a couple hundred responses, but most of them had to do with street names in New Orleans and other obscure references. I gave up after scanning through the first thirty.

So apparently Felicity Baronne hadn't done anything to warrant mention on any of the gazillions of Web sites out there in the great void. Just for fun I typed in my own name and was astounded by the number of references. Upon investigation I discovered that many came from articles in the local papers, mostly to do with the Judge rather than with my own infamous exploits. I resisted the temptation to explore further and logged off.

The next order of business would be the cancelled checks. Lavinia had slipped me the packet after rifling my father's desk while he napped. She'd also enclosed the post-office box address to which she'd sent the envelopes, and I noticed the ZIP was 29938, indicating the box was at the branch on the south end of the island. The handwriting on the endorsement looked ordinary enough, neither flowery and flowing nor cramped or illegible. They had all been cashed at Bank of America.

I pulled the desk lamp closer and examined the jumble of numbers encoded on the back of the first check. There was no indication of which branch of the huge financial conglomerate she had used, and there were at least three or four on the island. One thing was certain, though: she had an account there. I'd stood in line at my own bank many times waiting while non-account holders produced their identification and inked their thumbs to place an impression on the document they were presenting. There was nothing resembling a smudgy thumbprint on the face of these checks.

And there was no way Bank of America or any other financial institution was going to give me information about an account holder. Good thing, too, since I'd be the first one screaming bloody murder if accessing my own personal records were as easy for some stranger as simply inquiring. The only real clue of any value to me was the date stamped on the reverse. By comparing that with the day the check was drawn in my father's spidery handwriting on the face of the document, I realized Ms. Baronne must hotfoot it to the bank the same day she picked up the envelope. Every check had been cashed within two days of its having been mailed.

I leaned back in the chair and stretched to loosen the kinks settling into my shoulders from hunching over the desk. A sore back and a cramped neck had been occupational hazards back in my full-time accounting days, but I'd been relatively free of those pains since I'd given up my practice and begun exercising regularly. I touched the ridges of scar tissue on my left shoulder through the fabric of my shirt. I worked hard to keep the shiny, ugly skin loose with special creams and lotions, but it still seemed to be stretched too tightly across the flesh beneath. Nearly two years, and the healing was not yet complete.

I shook my head to chase those gloomy thoughts away and contemplated the six checks spread out across my desk. I had exhausted just about every avenue for identifying my father's mystery woman short of asking Erik Whiteside to hack into the bank's computers. I smiled at the idea. Erik would no doubt jump at the challenge, but I had no intention of putting him into a position to get nailed by what had to be an extremely sophisticated firewall system. I could envision his being hauled out of his apartment by two burly Treasury agents and carted off to federal prison.

No, I told myself, *we'd have to do it the hard way.* I'd advise Lavinia to alert me the next time she mailed a check to the elusive Felicity Baronne, and I'd stake out the post office. Though how I'd manage to make myself inconspicuous in that relatively small area for extended periods of time escaped me at the moment. And I had just purchased a vehicle which would attract attention wherever it was parked.

I carried my empty glass back toward the kitchen, detouring on the way to peer through the gap in the great room drapes out into the fading light. The outdoor thermometer attached to the railing directly across from the French doors hovered just a little below seventy degrees. I opened the door a crack, sniffing the air like a bloodhound seeking his quarry. It smelled like spring: warm, damp, loamy. Too pleasant an evening to be shut up inside.

I put my glass in the top rack of the dishwasher, grabbed a sweatshirt and my bag, and trotted down the steps into the garage.

THERE REALLY wasn't anyplace other than a few stretches on the interstate to let my new baby have her head, so I settled for roaming up and down the island, top down, heater cranked up to drive off the chill breeze blowing in off the ocean. I cruised 278 from end to end, the traffic sparse on a weekday night. I cut down side roads I hadn't been on in years: Union Cemetery, Dillon, Fish Haul, Baygall. I explored some of the new condominium and apartment complexes which had sprung up in the months I'd spent in Paris. They seemed to explode from the stands of palmettos and chinaberry trees, all natural wood and muted trim, low-impact lighting and carefully camouflaged parking lots. They were well conceived and every attempt had been made to make them blend in with their environment, but nothing could disguise the fact that progress was slowly eating away at the natural beauty of my island.

I tried not to let it depress me, turning back onto 278 and eventually onto the Cross Island Parkway, another blight on the landscape which nonetheless helped keep the hordes of tourist invaders moving along during the summer. I paid my dollar at the toll booth. Cresting the bridge over Broad Creek, I slowed to take in the breathtaking beauty of the vista spreading away on either side of me: the vast expanse of star-studded sky arching overhead; the smooth flow of the waterway as it widened into Calibogue Sound; the lights of Shelter Cove Harbor twinkling in the distance off to my left and those of the smaller, snugger Palmetto Bay Marina casting a soft glow on my right.

Tourists be damned, I thought, *it's still a wonderful place to live.*

Approaching the traffic signal at the foot of the bridge, I suddenly remembered Miss Addie. Adelaide Boyce Hammond. Thanks to her having been duped into a shady investment the past summer, I had found the courage to slink from my hiding place at the beach and face the world again after Rob's murder. I had been unable to refuse the plea of one of my late mother's oldest and dearest friends, and it had been the saving of me. I checked the clock on the dashboard and realized it was much too late to go calling on octogenarian ladies. Besides, the upscale retirement community where she resided, just down the road, had a twenty-four-hour security gate. Tomorrow would have to do.

I pulled through the light and headed for home, making a mental note to call Miss Addie first thing in the morning. If anyone knew what Felicity Baronne had once been to my father, it would likely be Adelaide Boyce Hammond.

THE BASEBALL season had just gotten underway, and many of the games were being postponed due to cold, rainy weather in the northern cities, so I had to content myself with a re-viewing of *Raiders of the Lost Ark* for about the hundredth time on one of the movie channels. I dozed off somewhere after Indiana Jones's famous gun-versus-scimitar scene in the marketplace and woke just as the Nazis were being consumed and melted by the guardian spirits. Thankfully I'd missed the part with the snakes.

I rubbed my eyes, squinted blearily at my watch, and swore. Almost two o'clock, approaching seven in Paris, and Darnay might already have been up and about his business. Still, I didn't want to make such an important call with only half my brain engaged, so I stumbled into my bathroom and threw a few handfuls of cold water over my face.

I needn't have bothered.

I sat on the sofa listening to the hollow ringing, imagining the shrill sound echoing off the silk-covered walls and the wonderful old fireplace framed by original Delft tiles, the sound sliding across the Empress Eugénie chaise longue and the faded green Aubusson carpet beneath the old casement windows.

I don't know how long I huddled there before the realization hit me, and I finally brought my thumb up to depress the off button on the portable handset.

No answering machine had picked up; no bright, *"Allô, je ne suis pas chez moi maintenant"* in Darnay's soft, rolling French had invited me to leave a message.

"Gone," I murmured into the dead telephone and dropped it into my lap.

Somewhere I had written the number for the manor house in Provençe. No doubt his sister, Madeleine, had been given a way to reach him in an emergency. But I had neither the will nor the desire to run the gauntlet of her haughty demeanor and obvious disapproval. It would probably give her a great deal of pleasure for me to come begging for a way to contact her brother, and I'd be damned if I'd give her the satisfaction of refusing.

No, the painful truth was Darnay had disappeared once again into the great void of his undercover world, and he'd gone without a word to me.

Bien. Fine. So be it.

CHAPTER
FOURTEEN

I tried to sleep, failed miserably, and spent the remainder of the night tossing on the wide cushions of the sofa in the great room, staring through the open drapes toward the sea. As soon as the first soft glints of dawn touched the horizon, I pulled on my running clothes and punished my body for the better part of an hour.

One of the things you have to develop in the accounting business is the ability to compartmentalize. You have to learn to put away all the numbers associated with the current project running around in your head and clear the mental decks for the next one. By the time I came pounding back over the dune and up the steps onto the deck, my mind had constructed a steel-walled chamber, shoved the memories of Darnay's loving smiles, sweet caresses, and lying words inside, and slammed the stout door firmly shut.

If I occasionally heard him scratching faintly to get out, I promised myself to ignore it.

Ravenous after a steaming shower, I dressed hurriedly and wolfed down a huge mushroom-and-cheese omelet accompanied by English muffins slathered in blackberry jelly. I left the dirty dishes on the table and dialed Adelaide Boyce Hammond.

Her soft, tentative, "Hello?" brought a smile.

"Miss Addie? It's Bay. Bay Tanner."

"Oh, Lydia . . . I mean, Bay, how delightful to hear from you, my dear."

"It's good to talk to you, too."

"Surely you're not calling me from France, are you? Does this mean you have some word about Win?"

Oh, God, I thought, and mentally smacked my forehead. How could I have been so stupid!

What now seemed a lifetime ago, Miss Addie had asked me to help her locate her brother, Edwin Hollister Hammond, who had disappeared more than twenty years before. During her recent troubles the past summer, she had received a cryptic postcard from Win, indicating he had been aware of all the news from the old hometown, but neglecting—intentionally or otherwise—to disclose his whereabouts. Miss Addie had professed a desire to find him before, as she put it, he had to come home for her funeral.

I'd set Erik Whiteside on his trail, figuring he, with all his computer skills, would have a better chance than I of tracking down a man who apparently didn't want to be found. In the chaos which had been my life in the months preceding my pilgrimage to Paris, neither one of us had given the task the slightest priority. Now it was time to pay the piper for that neglect.

"No, Miss Addie, I'm sorry. I don't have any news about Win." I heard her soft sigh of disappointment, and I added, "But we're still working on it." The lie only made me feel worse.

"Well, I always knew it was a long shot, as Daddy used to say. And how is Paris, my dear? I was there once, in my girlhood. Did I ever tell you?"

"No, I don't believe you ever did," I replied, settling onto the chaise at the edge of the deck. This could be a long story, and I owed Miss Addie the chance to tell it to me. I had no trains to catch. In fact, I had nothing now but time.

Her rambling tale of a pre–World War II Paris delighted me, and I let her reminisce to her heart's content. I did manage to squeeze in a couple of comments in an attempt to make clear that I was back in the States, but I'm not sure she heard me. Her voice had taken on a girlish quality, and just for those few moments, she seemed to have slipped back into a time when the idea of love, husband, and a family of her own had still been very real possibilities in her life.

Eventually she wound down, and I said into a brief silence, "Thank you so much for sharing that with me. When . . . if I return, I'll be able to look at things in a vastly different way now."

"You're quite welcome, my dear. It's so rare these days for young people to have the slightest interest in the memories of an old woman. Thank you for taking the time."

"No problem. Listen, Miss Addie, I wonder if you could answer a question for me."

"I'll certainly try."

"Do you know someone named Felicity Baronne? A friend of the Judge's from the old days, I'm guessing. Or maybe an acquaintance of my mother's. Does the name do anything for you?"

She was quiet for so long I thought we might have been cut off.

"Miss Addie? Are you still there?"

"Yes, of course, Lydia. I'm sorry. *Felicity.* Lord help me, I haven't heard that name in years! At least thirty, maybe more. It quite took me back."

"Who was she? *Is* she, I mean."

Again Miss Addie hesitated.

"Oh, come on now," I wheedled. "If Felicity was a former flame of my father's, an old girlfriend or something, it can't really matter now."

"Why are you asking?"

All the teasing and sweetness was gone from her voice, and the simple question hung in the air for the few moments it took me to decide how much of the present situation to reveal to my mother's oldest friend.

Tough call. I settled on, "She's been in touch with the Judge recently, and Lavinia is concerned."

"I don't wonder," I thought she said, but the murmur had been so low I wasn't positive I'd heard her correctly.

"Excuse me?"

"Oh, it's nothing, my dear. I'm not quite clear on why you're asking me about this. Your father knows perfectly well who—and what—Felicity is, although I believe her name was Starks in those days. Strange, I can't believe she married." The pause was infinitesimal, but laden with meaning. "Is there some reason you're hesitant to ask him yourself?"

Again I faltered, unsure how much of this Lavinia would be comfortable with my sharing. Then, though no one could see me, I shrugged in a what-the-hell manner and plunged in. "He's being very secretive about it, offering no explanations whatsoever. And he's giving her money."

I was expecting a shocked gasp of dismay, but Miss Addie disappointed me. Instead—inexplicably—she laughed, a dry chuckle I couldn't quite interpret.

"You find it amusing?" I asked with perhaps a little more acerbity than I should have.

"I'm sorry, my dear. Of course I don't find it amusing if it upsets you and Mrs. Smalls. But really, it is ironic. 'The more things change . . .'" she began and let the rest of the quotation dribble off into silence.

"It could be blackmail."

It was what Lavinia had been hinting at and the idea which had first sprung into my own mind when she'd first broached the subject. It wouldn't have been the first time someone tried to hold past or even recent indiscretions over my father's head.

"No, Lydia, I don't think it's blackmail, at least not in the sense you're implying. Why don't you just ask the Judge? I'm quite sure he'll tell you anything you want to know."

"And if he doesn't?"

"Well then he must have an excellent reason, and it would be most improper of me to gossip with you about personal matters he prefers to keep private. I'm sure you understand."

Of course I didn't understand, but I could tell it wasn't going to make a damned bit of difference to Miss Addie. I mustered up my early childhood training, thanked her graciously for her time, and promised to stay in touch regarding the search for her brother. Mad as I was at her old woman's coyness, I still owed her that.

The phone rang almost the second after I hung it up.

"Mrs. Tanner?" a bright female voice I didn't recognize chirped into my ear. "Mrs. *Bay* Tanner?"

"Yes?"

"Please hold for Mr. Palmer."

Before I had a chance to stutter out any response, the line switched to canned hold music, something Broadway and innocuous, with lots of strings. I swallowed my surprise along with the last of the tea in my glass, moved back through the house and up the steps into the kitchen. I dropped into the chair which matched the built-in desk and pulled a small pad and a pen in front of me. I had no idea what this was all about, but I had a feeling note-taking might be in order. I'd straightened and aligned every item on the granite surface and was starting in on the drawers when the remembered voice from my answering machine cut into a haunting rendition of "If I Loved You."

"Mrs. Tanner? Sorry to keep you waiting. Had to take an emergency call from one of our overseas offices. This is Gray Palmer. Senior."

The last was added in a tone which made me swallow hard, recalling that the other person entitled to the use of those names no longer existed.

"Yes, Mr. Palmer. How may I help you?"

I kept it strictly business, the memory of his message basically telling me to butt out of his son's affairs still fresh in my mind. If he was calling to rant some more, I'd cut him off in a second. But kindly, of course. Allowances had to be made for grief.

"I hope my previous communication didn't offend you. I certainly meant no disrespect."

"None taken, Mr. Palmer. While my partner was initially contacted by your son, the relationship necessarily terminated upon his unfortunate death." I had no intention of revealing anything about the strange contents of the package Erik had received. If Araminda Albright had spilled everything to GS, as she referred to him, I'd let him broach the subject first. "So you had no real need for concern, and there will of course be no bill."

"The money is of no concern to me, Mrs. Tanner," he snapped.

"Then I'm afraid I don't quite understand the purpose of your call," I replied in a voice frosty enough to match his own.

The pause lasted several seconds. When next he spoke, his tone had softened considerably. "Again, let me apologize. I'm sure you of all people must understand how something like this . . ."

He let it hang there, inviting me to comment on his unfinished thought. Two things flashed immediately across my mind: he was trying hard to elicit my sympathy, and he had checked me out. His oblique reference had to be about Rob's murder.

"Of course."

Two could play the waiting game, and I felt certain I was at least as good at it as Gray Palmer, Senior.

"I seem to have made a complete muddle of this," he finally said. "Could we start over?"

"Of course," I repeated.

"Look, Mrs. Tanner, I understand from Miss Albright that she spoke with you at some length last weekend about my son and the circumstances surrounding his death. She told me you expressed an interest in helping her to some resolution of her concerns."

I thought that a strange way to put it, but I got his drift. And this would have been the perfect time for him to mention the bone. I waited a few seconds to give him a chance to jump in, but he didn't. "What Miss Albright and I discussed is confidential, Mr. Palmer. If she chose to reveal the particulars to you, that is certainly her right. I'm afraid I cannot."

Again I had given him the perfect lead-in, but he ignored it. Perhaps, for some inexplicable reason, Mindy had held out on him about his son's grisly find. What the hell was her game?

"Understood. What I'm calling for is to take back the

condescending message I left for you, and to engage your services on my son's behalf."

That took me by surprise. "To what end?" I asked.

"You may be aware from the local news coverage that I am firmly convinced my son's death was not an accident."

"Yes. I did happen to see your news conference the other night."

"Good. Then you know I've offered a substantial reward for anyone with information concerning his death to come forward."

"Yes."

"I'm afraid I've been inundated with calls and messages, at both my office and my home, although I installed a special toll-free line to deal with any responses. How these . . . these *maniacs* managed to track me down I don't know, but I'm being harassed day and night by people claiming all sorts of bizarre things."

"Bizarre?"

"Absolutely! Everything from his having been zapped by an alien death ray to being executed by some paramilitary group, to someone claiming he was killed by drug dealers because he owed them fifty thousand dollars."

"And they wanted you to settle the debt?"

"Exactly. I had no idea my offer would engender these kinds of cruel hoaxes. I suppose I should have, but I didn't."

He had my sympathy now. "What can we do to help?"

"I'd like to hire your firm to track down all these people and weed out the obvious crackpots. I know you probably think I'm incredibly naïve, but I can't help believing there just might be a legitimate lead somewhere in all this madness." He paused for effect, and it worked. He had my complete attention. "I'm determined to find out what happened to my son, and I don't care how long it takes or how much it costs. Will you do it? Will you help me?"

Without the first idea of how Erik, the Judge, and I could possibly live up to the commitment, I said, "Of course."

CHAPTER
FIFTEEN

I sat for a long time staring at the wall behind my desk after Gray Palmer hung up.

He had a record of all the call-back numbers left by the reward-seekers, whether on the toll-free line or his private and business numbers. He promised to have his secretary fax me the information as soon as he could have it collated into a useable list. I had no idea how to go about putting names and addresses with them, but I was pretty sure Erik Whiteside would.

My sleepless night had begun to creep up on me, and I stifled a yawn as I carried my scribbled notes into the office. I opened the Word program and transcribed them, printing out a copy and adding it to the file. Then I picked up the phone and dialed Chris Brandon's office.

Of course Gray Palmer had forced me to discuss money, and I didn't want it to appear as if this were our first legitimate case, even though it was. So I'd quoted him a daily rate gleaned from countless PI novels and television episodes, and he hadn't flinched. What I needed now was a contract. I wondered if there was a standard document for engaging the services of an accountant-turned-gumshoe. The thought made me smile, even through the ill-tempered Cheryl's veiled attempts to make me go away. In a matter of moments, Chris came on the line.

"Bay, good to hear from you. How goes the investigation?"

That stopped me in midsentence. How the hell did he know about the new case? Then I realized he must be talking about the Mitchells.

"Oh, fine. All done. Didn't you get my report?"

"No, I didn't. Maybe it's languishing in the mail somewhere. I swear, sometimes I think it would be faster just to walk the paperwork from town to town."

"Well, I'll give you the thumbnail version. Tamika is definitely embezzling, creating phony employees and vendors then cashing the checks herself. Not very original, but she's draining a lot of money out of the business."

"That's too bad. How did Bubba react?"

"He doesn't want to prosecute, says families don't treat each other that way. I don't agree, but it's not my call. Maybe you can convince him. At any rate, they're going to need a complete audit. First priority would be the payroll taxes. With nonexistent employees, they're going to be totally inaccurate and will need to be re-filed."

"Can you do it?" I started to enumerate the reasons for my inability to oblige him when I heard him say, "Oh, hi, sweetheart! Come on in. I'll be done in a minute." Then, "Sorry about that, Bay. Amy's here. We're headed for lunch with her mother and the Colonel. Wedding plans, you know?"

"Sure, no problem. We can finish this up . . ."

"No, go ahead. We've got plenty of time."

"Okay. I was just saying I don't have time to take on that extensive an operation. How about the firm that did the Bi-Rite audit?"

"I'm sure they'll be glad to help. I'll give them a call after I get your report."

"Great. Listen, Chris, I need to retain your services to draw up a contract for me. It's kind of complicated, so maybe we should make it another time if you're in a rush to get to lunch."

"What kind of contract?"

I don't know why I hesitated to reveal the nature of my new venture to Chris Brandon. Now that the formerly amorphous idea had actually become reality, I suppose I felt a little silly about my decision to become a full-fledged investigator. In the cold light of day, it seemed somehow childish, a game I'd decided to play to keep myself busy. Not unlike an old widow-woman's learning bridge. Or taking a lover.

"Personal services," I replied, hoping the generic term would keep him from probing any more deeply into specifics. "Is there some standard form I could use, maybe a fill-in-the-blanks kind of thing?"

"Well, I don't see why you couldn't use whatever you had for the old accounting practice. You'd have to change the names and all, but it should work. Are you going back into business?"

"In a manner of speaking. So you think that would fly?"

"I don't see why not. If you like, I could look it over for you, make sure there aren't any ugly loopholes for potential deadbeats to wriggle through. The main goal is to protect you from unnecessary liability. If the contract was vetted by your attorneys before, I think you'd be pretty safe in using it again."

I hadn't thought of that, and it seemed a good suggestion. Change some wording, print it out from the computer, and I'd be in business. Literally.

"Thanks, Chris. It's a great idea. I'll give you a holler if I run into anything I can't figure out."

"Not much chance of that," he said, and once again I basked in the glow of his boyish admiration. "Did you include an invoice for the Mitchell thing in with your report?"

"Yup. Hope it's okay with you, but I took it easy on them. I'm not looking to make money on these kinds of things, and Bubba is my friend. If I thought he'd let me get away with doing it for nothing, I would."

"Understood. Thanks again for taking it on."

"No problem. Thank you for the referral and the advice. Be sure to bill me."

"Don't hold your breath. Best to your father."

"And tell Amy I said hello."

"Will do. She wants the two of you to get together some-time soon. I'll have her call you for lunch."

What the hell for? I asked myself, but upbringing won out again. "Lovely! I'll wait to hear from her," is what came out of my mouth.

In a pig's ear! I thought, hanging up the phone. Why on earth would Chris Brandon's fiancée want a cozy little tête-à-tête with me? I vowed to use every excuse in my consider-able arsenal to avoid having to sit across the table from a simpering Amy Fleming and her massive engagement ring.

I SIGNED on again to my Word program, located a copy of my old contract, and spent the next two hours cutting and pasting until I had a document I thought would be sufficient to mollify Gray Palmer. I also played with a couple of graphics programs I found lurking on the hard drive, and ended up designing a logo for Simpson & Tanner, Inquiry Agents I thought was pretty damned clever. I had no idea how my father and Erik would feel about it, but since I seemed to be doing all the grunt work they'd just have to live with it.

I printed off two copies of the contract onto the new let-terhead, filled in the appropriate blanks, and signed them. Then I whipped out a cover letter asking Palmer to return one signed copy to me, along with a retainer, and slid it all into a manila envelope. If we really decided to go full steam ahead with this business, we were going to need clerical help. And someplace for her to operate.

I pushed those unpleasant thoughts aside and went to the kitchen for a sandwich. By two o'clock I was back in the of-fice watching several pages of phone numbers and repro-duced messages roll off my fax machine. Gray Palmer's secretary was not only accurate, she was fast. Maybe I should think about luring her away to man the imaginary of-fice which was taking shape and form in the back of my mind. I tapped the pages to straighten the edges and dropped into the chair in front of the computer.

There were sixteen entries in all, far fewer than I had

been led to believe. The three Palmer had mentioned were there, along with a couple who might be legitimate. A weekend father, out fishing with his sons, thought he had seen young Gray's boat anchored just about dawn on Saturday morning. The vessel looked abandoned, no one visible on deck as he and his boys passed by about thirty yards off his stern. He couldn't be positive until he'd verified the name of Gray's craft. One of the kids remarked on the unusual name, although the father hadn't seen it himself: *Arky Olly Jist.* The man had been forced to think about it himself, until he finally caught on and explained it to his son.

"Clever," I muttered, although it seemed like something you'd put on a vanity license plate rather than a name for a boat. Still, Gray Palmer, Senior, should certainly have recognized it.

I circled that entry. The Good Samaritan and reward-seeker had left his name—Delbert Pidgen—as well as home, work, and cell phone numbers and an e-mail address. I could tackle him myself, though how I would go about verifying his story escaped me for the moment.

The other intriguing message came from another weekend boater, this one a woman traveling from Hilton Head up the Intracoastal Waterway to Charleston. She had left Skull Creek Marina well before first light in order to rendezvous with some friends and had observed a craft matching the description of the *Arky Olly Jist* pulled up alongside another boat. Young Gray, if in fact that's who it was, seemed to be carrying on a conversation with two men. Although they had to shout to be heard above their respective idling engines, she couldn't make out what was being said. Her impression, however, had been that the exchange of words being hurled across the narrow gap between the two boats had been angry. She had not observed the name on either vessel, opting to give them a wide berth. Ms. Cynthia Sellers professed herself completely disinterested in the reward, her only goal to be of some assistance to the grieving father.

Right. There are a lot of wealthy people on Hilton Head, but I couldn't seriously envision anyone turning down twenty-five grand. That kind of money would buy an awful lot of gas or finance a few barnacle-scrapings—or whatever it was one did with boats. Or maybe Ms. Sellers had discovered Gray Palmer was a widower—a wealthy widower. Maybe her game was passing up the little fish in order to land the big tuna.

The remainder of the list consisted of numbers left without name or detailed message attached, except that most of the callers had hinted at valuable information to be imparted, but only if Palmer coughed up some good-faith cash in advance. I thought we'd probably check these out, but not until we'd eliminated the quasi-legitimate ones.

The alien death-ray guy intrigued me, but he'd no doubt turn out to be one of those fruitcakes who think the CIA is stealing their thoughts through microwave towers or radio antennae. The drug deal gone bad theory didn't sound so far-fetched now that I'd read Ms. Sellers's account. This had possibilities on two fronts. The paramilitary hit I dismissed out of hand. We would probably check it out, just to be thorough, but I felt it probably ranked right up there with the Venusian laser-zapper guy.

I typed it all into a file, organizing and prioritizing as I went. It occurred to me that if I had one of those scanner thingys I wouldn't have to keep re-entering this kind of information. I'd have to ask Erik. It was also probably time I caved in to his repeated insistence I avail myself of a cell phone. I supposed if we were actually going to get this enterprise off the ground, it would become a necessity rather than a nuisance.

By four-fifteen, I'd had it with playing secretary/typist. I saved all my files after printing hardcopy and placed a call to Erik Whiteside in Charlotte. It was time to let someone else's fingers do the walking.

THE CALL came as I stood before the open refrigerator door trying to muster up some enthusiasm for defrosting something for dinner. But it wasn't Erik, back from whatever errand had lured him out of the store. It was a very agitated Lavinia.

"Bay! She's here!" Her words, urgent and excited, came through in a tight whisper. "I just left them in the study—with the door closed!" I knew immediately who "she" was: the mysterious Felicity Baronne. "Can you come?" The plaintive voice cut straight into my heart.

I glanced at the clock over the sink. Just after five. Rush hour. Even if I made every traffic light, and there were no major pileups, it would still take me the better part of an hour to make it to Presqu'isle.

"How long does she usually stay?" I asked.

"It varies. Sometimes fifteen or twenty minutes. Never more than an hour."

"There's no way I can make it there in time, Lavinia." I paused, hesitant to make the suggestion. "Have you tried eavesdropping?"

Her own hesitation confirmed my suspicion that this idea might already have occurred, even to the painfully honest Lavinia Smalls. "The door is over a hundred years old and solid oak. Don't be ridiculous, child."

"Well, I don't see any way I can get there before she leaves."

"I know. I can't think what's gotten into me."

"You're worried about the Judge, that's what's gotten into you. And I have to admit you're making me pretty damned nervous, too. Do you seriously think this woman can harm my father in some way?"

"I'm telling you, I just don't know! It's the sneaking around, closing doors, and pretending like everything's just like normal that worries me. I don't for one second think your father has to tell me every last detail of his personal life. But we . . . that is, we've shared most everything in these last years, and I have to believe it's something he thinks will hurt me in some way. And the only thing that could do that is if it's something that could hurt him!"

I promised myself I'd examine this extraordinary outburst when I had the opportunity to think about it more clearly. What I did recognize was that this was about as much revelation on the subject of her relationship with my father as I'd heard her divulge—ever.

"Let me think a minute," I said to cover my own confusion.

A sharp click followed by a deep humming made me realize I'd been carrying on this conversation with the freezer door hanging open. I pushed it closed and settled myself onto one of the chairs ranged around the glass-topped table in the bay of the kitchen window. I glanced out toward my shiny new T-Bird pulled up in the drive, and inspiration struck.

"How did she arrive?" I asked.

"What do you mean?"

"By cab, or did she drive herself?"

"She drove. I saw the car when I opened the door for her."

"What kind is it?"

"Lord, girl, I don't know anything about cars!" I could feel Lavinia's frustration level rising. Then, "Wait!" I heard her whisper. "She's comin' out!"

"Don't hang up!" I ordered. I found myself lowering my own voice, though I had no idea why. "Follow her outside and get the color and make of her car. License plate number, too, if you can manage it."

She hesitated for only a moment. "I understand. I'll call you back just as soon as she's gone."

I hung up the phone, abandoning all thoughts of an early dinner. As I passed down the hall to my bedroom, I found myself smiling.

You're in this investigating thing up to your neck now, my girl, I told myself while I stripped out of my clothes and surveyed the contents of my walk-in closet. I had about half an hour to select an appropriate outfit for my first genuine stakeout and figure out the best place to lie in wait for the unsuspecting Felicity Baronne.

CHAPTER
SIXTEEN

I pulled the sweating can of diet Coke and a handful of pretzels out of the brown paper bag beside me and shifted around again in the seat. A glance at the dashboard clock told me it was a little after six, and I was beginning to worry.

I'd settled the T-Bird under the canopy of a spreading sweet gum just inside the driveway of the Gullah Flea Market on the north end of the island. Carolyn's Nursery next door would have offered more cover, but they had closed and locked their gates sometime before I arrived. A few stragglers had still been wandering the colorful stalls of the long rambling market which housed everything from native island crafts to used lawn furniture and exercise bikes, but by five-thirty most of the customers had headed off. The wide wooden doors had been lowered across the open-air building, and mine had become the only car in the lot.

I'd left the motor running, the local oldies station playing softly during the first half hour of my inaugural stakeout, in order to be able to jump into traffic the moment I spotted Felicity Baronne's car. The problem was I had spotted *dozens* of white Ford Escorts, most flying through the intersection at such a clip I had no time to check out license plate numbers. I'd considered the Gullah Market a good choice because it sat right at a traffic signal where vehicles would be slowing in anticipation of having to stop. Apparently I'd been in Paris too long. I'd forgotten no one on Hilton Head obeys the forty-five mile per hour speed limit, and the lights on 278, especially during rush hour, turn red only about once every half hour.

I grabbed another handful of pretzels without taking my eyes from the road. A Beaufort County sheriff's cruiser leading a parade of suddenly law-abiding motorists rolled sedately through the light just as it changed. I saw the officer glance briefly over at me then continue on his way.

Admiring the T-Bird, I thought, then gasped as I realized the car I had been seeking had landed practically in my lap. The little white four-door sedan sat almost directly in front of me on the inside lane. The profile of the driver was partially concealed by a mass of red-gold hair teased into the kind of bouffant you only see in old Gidget and Elvis Presley movies. Exactly as Lavinia had described her to me. As I watched, she leaned over toward the center of the dash then straightened to touch the car's round lighter to an impossibly long cigarette.

Another clue confirmed. "Smells like you used to." Lavinia's terse description of my quarry's reeking clothes had made me blush in embarrassment.

I shook off my astonishment and put my plan into action. I jerked the gearshift into drive, turned right onto the main drag, and eased over into the middle lane. I let my speed settle in at about thirty-five, slow enough for everyone behind me to pull around and ahead, and not so turtle-like that I risked getting myself rear-ended. At least I hoped not. I had to stay flexible because Ms. Baronne could make one of several moves at the next intersection, the one at Spanish Wells Road, and I had to be ready for any eventuality.

Behind me the light changed, and vehicles shot past like drag racers coming off the line. Felicity Baronne moved more sedately by me on the left. I let a couple of cars get between us, after noting with satisfaction that her license plate number jibed with my information, then darted into the left lane in front of a minivan from Ohio. The poor guy at the wheel was so confused by all the road signs dangling overhead he didn't even take the time to blow his horn at me.

I followed the Escort through the light and onto the Cross Island Parkway. Another guess confirmed. If she used the south end post office, Felicity probably lived in that vicinity as well. I stayed behind her through the toll gates, handing over my dollar through a rolling stop which earned me a glare from the lady in the glass-enclosed booth. At the foot of the bridge she again moved to the left. By this time only one car separated us, and I tried to hang back. But when she flipped on her signal at the light, I had no choice but to move right up behind her in the turn lane. When she made another hard left, I breathed a sigh of relief. This road dead-ended at Palmetto Bay Marina, and there were a limited number of places she could be heading. I slowed enough to let her get a little ahead then watched as she eased into the parking lot of the high-rise condominium building in the heart of the marina.

I pulled into the area reserved for guests of the Chart House restaurant and got out of the car. I slung my bag over my shoulder and stuck my hands in the pockets of my jeans. Felicity Baronne was a small woman, dwarfed even more by her riotous hair which made her easy to keep an eye on as she tottered on three-inch heels toward the glass entrance doors. Her bright purple knit top strained across an ample bosom which may or may not have been real, and her white stretch Capri pants revealed way too many bumps and bulges.

A floozy indeed, I thought, at least to judge by outward appearances.

I lurked outside while she waited for the elevator to arrive then stepped in to watch the indicator until it stopped on the third floor. I searched the foyer for the bank of mailboxes, but Felicity's name appeared on none of the little slots. Of course, she had a post office box, so I supposed she had no need of a receptacle on site, although that, too, seemed a little odd.

I debated whether or not to hang around to see if she went out again, but my rumbling stomach decided me against it. Besides, I knew where she lived, and I had her box number.

What good it was doing me I hadn't quite worked out yet, although I supposed a confrontation would be inevitable. If Lavinia refused to let me ask my father why he was paying off this woman, I would have to get it from the horse's mouth. Now that I knew where to find her, it didn't seem quite so imperative.

I turned back toward the restaurant, realizing with sadness the name had been changed to Eugene's. Another landmark altered. I wandered inside anyway to find to my delight that the spectacular view of the sunset over the marsh and the wonderful food had both survived the change intact.

I AWOKE Friday morning to lowering skies and a pounding headache. I'd stayed up late waiting for Erik to return my call but had heard nothing from him. No messages, no e-mails, nothing. My first thought was he'd gone down to visit Mercer Mary Prescott, but he was usually so paranoid about checking his answering machine from his cell phone I couldn't quite shake a feeling of unease. Especially when I remembered he had a human bone, recently stolen from a disturbed gravesite, stashed in his clothes hamper.

I popped three aspirin, showered, and tried Erik's home number again. The machine engaged after only one ring, so there had to be a lot of messages waiting for him. It was too early for him to be at the store, and I realized I'd never gotten his cell number from him. Lots of things needed to be much better organized if we ever hoped to pull off running an investigation agency.

I made tea and studied the weather from the comfort of the great room. A line of gray clouds hung along the horizon, and the ocean looked dark and angry. I paced, craving a cigarette, frustrated by my inability to formulate a coherent agenda for dealing with Gray Palmer's death or my father's duplicity. I flopped down onto the sofa and promptly fell asleep.

"SEÑORA? SEÑORA!"

I waved a hand in front of my face, trying to ward off the

annoying intrusion into my fractured dreams of Darnay standing in the doorway of the house in Provençe, sunlight bathing the golden stone and his wonderful blue eyes . . .

"*Señora, qué pasa?* You are ill?"

I rolled onto my back and forced my gummy eyes open to find Dolores leaning over me, concern deep in her voice. I stretched and forced a reassuring smile.

"A headache, is all. I must have needed a little catnap." I sat up and rolled my head on my stiff shoulders. "What time is it?"

"*A las cuatro.*"

"Four o'clock? In the afternoon?" I swung my legs to the floor as Dolores stepped back. "How is that possible? I've been asleep the entire day!"

"*Necesario,*" she replied, nodding, which I took to mean something like, "You must have needed it."

The storm appeared to have passed, because sharp needles of light were bombarding my eyes through the shimmering glass of the French doors. I groaned and dropped my head into my hands.

"Is good I come," Dolores said, patting my back reassuringly before turning toward the kitchen. "I bring *la cena* for you, *Señora*. Roberto and Alejandro, they catch many shrimps."

I didn't want to think about dinner or eating or anything which required dragging my butt off the sofa at that moment, but I knew I needed to break the lethargy that lay over me like a sopping blanket. I pinched my cheeks a couple of times and forced myself to my feet.

"What is it?" I asked, trying to fake some enthusiasm as I staggered up the steps.

"Ah, you will like. The garlic, the *vino blanco*. Many things *muy bueno*."

"Thank you," I said, mustering a smile. "Just put it in the fridge."

"I fix for you?" Dolores stood in the middle of the kitchen, the casserole dish held out to me like an offering to an angry god.

"Later," I said as I punched the play button on the answering machine. "I need to take a shower."

The messages were all junk, and I deleted them immediately, amazed the phone had rung that many times and I had failed to hear it.

Dolores slid the dish into the refrigerator and lifted her worn black handbag from the counter.

"Thank you," I repeated, with genuine feeling this time.

"De nada."

"I'll see you on Monday then?"

"Si, Señora. A lunes."

I followed her out to the door, then reset the alarm and hurried into the office. I signed on and scrolled through more spam, but found no message from Erik.

"Damn you!" I said aloud.

I peeled off my sweaty, wrinkled slacks and sweater and headed for the shower, hoping I'd be able to wash away the growing knot of anxiety which seemed to have taken up permanent residence in the bottom of my stomach.

CHAPTER

SEVENTEEN

Dolores had been right about the shrimp casserole—*muy bueno*. In the spirit of my grumpy mood, I ate it straight out of the dish while standing on the deck staring out toward the ocean. Wisps of mauve-and-orange-tinted cloud drifted out from the mainland along with the deepening twilight. The line of demarcation between sky and water slowly blurred, then disappeared altogether into the night.

The lights in the house clicked on behind me, the timers connected to the security system performing their assigned task as I lowered myself onto the chaise. I tucked my hands behind my head and tried to force myself to relax.

In the years since Rob's murder, I had learned how to be alone. Not the kind of solitude I used to crave when the demands of my own business and my husband's relentless drive to nail every drug dealer in the state had seemed to occupy us twenty hours a day. Back then I would simply toss my handbag into the front seat of the car, let down the top, and take myself off to the beach. I had favorite spots, secluded inlets and tiny strips of sand unknown and often inaccessible to the casual visitor. For a stolen hour or so I'd simply toss aside my shoes and my harried life and contemplate the water, the sand, the sky.

But since the day I had watched my husband's plane explode on takeoff, had felt the hot metal pieces striking my own cowering body, I had resigned myself to being alone. True, there had been that one, unguarded moment of passion, dying quickly when it became apparent I was only being used. With Darnay I had been more cautious, testing, yearning forward, only to draw back at the point of intimacy, of real connection. Paris had been a test, not only of his feelings for me, but of my ability to accept them, as well. And again I had failed. At the first sign of stress, both of us had bolted—he to the work that defined him, and I . . .

To this, I told myself, *this place, this life. This loneliness.*

I never cry. Well, almost never. It seems to me a pointless exercise, messy and not the least productive. I sniffed loudly in the darkness and was saved the ignominy of making a liar out of myself by the sharp ringing of the telephone.

I sprinted across the great room and snatched up the handset.

"Hey, partner, it's me."

I bit down hard on the stream of invective waiting to leap from my lips, the natural outlet for all the day's miserable frustration. Instead I forced myself to say calmly, "Hey yourself. Where have you been? I've been trying to reach you."

"Have you? Sorry. Something's wrong with the damn cell, and I've been out of touch for the last few hours. What's up?"

"Where have you been?" I repeated.

"On the road."

"To where?"

"Well, right now I'm parked outside your security gate. The guy inside let me use his phone. Can you tell him it's okay to let me in?"

"Here? You're here?"

Erik Whiteside hesitated a moment before replying. "It's okay, isn't it? I mean, you don't have company or anything, right? I would have called first, but the cell . . ."

"Don't worry about it," I interrupted, the idea of sharing the lonely night with another living, breathing, human being overriding all the annoyance I had been building up against my partner and friend. "Let me talk to the security officer."

I authorized Erik's entrance into the sanctity of Port Royal Plantation, then scurried around plumping up the cushions on the sofa, crushed and dented from my day-long sleep, and tossing the morning paper into the trash. In the bathroom I slapped on a little lipstick and mascara and ran a brush through the usual tangle of my hair. By the time the sweep of the headlights on the monstrous SUV finally cut across the kitchen, I had glasses of beer and iced tea poured and waiting on the table.

"so it just made sense to come straight down here and talk it all out with you. If you agree, we can run over there tomorrow." Erik leaned back in his chair and wiped his mouth with the blue linen napkin. "Thanks," he added, "that was great."

I'd thrown together an omelet when he'd finally confessed to being hungry, and I had sat listening to his story between bites.

"So this guy, this retired professor, lives on Hilton Head?"

"Not exactly. It's another island, he said, close by. Some place called Daufuskie?"

"Right. It's just off the 'toe' of Hilton Head, between us and Savannah." I carried his plate and silverware to the dishwasher and poured myself more tea. "Ready for that beer now?" It had seemed not entirely the correct accompaniment to the eggs.

"Sure. So how do we get over there? Is there a bridge?"

"Nope. You have to go by ferry. The landing's down at the south end, by Palmetto Bay Marina."

"So that's what he meant when he said he'd make arrangements for us. We have an appointment tomorrow morning at ten."

"Why the rush?" I asked. I still didn't understand the urgency which had sent Erik tearing down from Charlotte, turning the operation of his computer store over to the assistant he usually claimed didn't have the brains God gave a goat. And this would make twice in one week he'd done so.

"Doctor Douglass and his wife are leaving for Asheville

on Monday. Something to do with one of their grandkids. Anyway, he agreed to run some preliminary tests for us before he goes. I just thought we should take advantage of the opportunity."

Erik had apparently not been idle in the days since receiving the grisly package from young Gray Palmer. Through some alumni contacts and a good deal of Internet sleuthing, he had discovered Dr. Denton Douglass, late of the anthropology department of Erik's alma mater and currently an occasional consultant to various police agencies on matters of forensic pathology. I didn't quite understand how my partner had convinced this obviously upright citizen to involve himself with a gruesome artifact from a robbed grave. Then again, perhaps he hadn't.

"Does he know the circumstances?" I asked.

"Not exactly," he said, dipping his head in that way he had when he'd been caught out in some fib or obfuscation.

"So what parts did you leave out?"

Erik fidgeted with his glass, tilting it at various angles and sloshing the beer around inside. I had to force myself not to reach over and take it away from him. Finally he glanced up to find my gaze fixed on him, and he grinned.

"Just about all of them," he said.

"I can't wait to hear the story myself."

"A variation on the truth, a lesson I learned at an early age. I told him I used to be one of his students."

"And were you?"

"Yeah, technically. At least for a week or so. See, Gray talked me into taking the course. It was required for him because he was an archaeology major, and he convinced me it would be cool to learn about bones and all that."

"No doubt in the midst of one of your drinking dates." I smiled to take the sting out of my words.

"Probably. Anyway, I was already up to my eyeballs, and I just couldn't cut it. Tons of reading and fieldwork. I dropped the class and picked up a management course instead. I figured, since he's taught there for so many years, he wouldn't remember me one way or the other."

"So what yarn did you spin him?"

"I said I'd dug it up while gardening in my backyard. Just the one bone, not a whole skeleton. I said it was probably a dog or some other animal, and I didn't want to look like a fool by calling in the cops. At first he said I should just send him a picture and he could tell from that, but I told him I was going to be on Hilton Head visiting a friend for the weekend and couldn't I just run over and show it to him. I offered him a hundred dollars for his time. He said okay."

Erik looked tired as he worked his head and neck around on his shoulders as if to ease some tension that had settled there.

"And what do you expect to happen when he confirms that it's human?" I asked. "Assuming that Gray's story is true."

"Why would you think it wasn't?" There was a clear challenge in his voice, an edge I seldom heard. "Do you think he was lying about finding the grave? Why would he? Besides, didn't his girlfriend confirm it?"

I sighed and shook my head. "She was only repeating what she heard from Gray. You can't use her as any kind of confirmation of his story."

"You think he was involved in some sort of crime?"

I held up my hands in a gesture of peace. "No, Erik, I don't believe Gray had anything to do with this person's death. But you have to stop making assumptions based on nothing more than wishful thinking. You haven't heard from this kid in a lot of years. You're drawing conclusions which may have no basis in fact now. Today. People change."

"Not that much. Listen, if you're dead set against this, I'll just get a hotel tonight and go see the doc myself in the morning. I don't want you involved in something you're not comfortable with. I can pay his fee, no problem. I just can't drop this thing, do you understand that? I just can't."

All of a sudden I realized we'd been so busy discussing Erik's bombshell I hadn't had an opportunity to relate my own news.

"Don't be silly," I said. "We're in this together. And you

won't have to foot the bill for the good doctor's expertise. We have a client again."

"Mindy Albright?"

"Nope," I said with just a hint of smugness, "better than that. Gray Palmer, Senior, himself. Contracts are in the mail."

ONCE WE got Erik's things settled in the guest room, we adjourned to the office where we pored over the file I had compiled and especially over the list of reward-seekers. Though we chewed on the possibilities, neither of us could come up with any plausible explanation for why young Gray had kept his gruesome discovery from his father or why Araminda Albright continued to do so as well.

"Why wouldn't she just have told the old man about the bone and the grave?" Erik rose from the futon on one end of the converted bedroom and stretched.

"I have no idea. I've tried several scenarios on for size, but none of them fits. The only possible explanation is there's something in it for her, something she hopes to gain from keeping the knowledge to herself. But that doesn't wash, either, because she knows that *we* know. She has no guarantee we won't tell GS the whole story. In fact, she hasn't even asked us to keep it quiet."

"Right." Erik prowled around the room, picking up objects, tossing them from hand to hand, then replacing them on the desk in a nervous ritual that was beginning to irritate me. "What's up with this?" he asked abruptly, thrusting the heavy crystal cigarette lighter under my nose. His accusatory tone made my response more waspish than I'd intended.

"Put that down, would you? And go park it. You're making me dizzy."

"Sore subject?" he asked with that grin that could always totally disarm me.

"No," I said, returning his smile. "And no, I haven't been backsliding, though God knows I've been tempted often enough in the last week. The lighter is a way of reminding myself of how well I'm doing at holding the devil at bay."

"Sort of like a recovering alcoholic keeping an inch or so of gin in a bottle in the cupboard?"

"I suppose. Anyway, back to the matter at hand. How long were you planning on staying? Any chance you could hang on past the weekend?"

"I guess," he said, somewhat reluctantly. "I've got about a year of vacation days saved up. I suppose I could use a couple of them. What do you have in mind?"

"I thought we could tackle this list of people trying to claim the reward. If we split them up, we could eliminate a lot of them right off the bat and be able to concentrate on the real possibles."

"Sounds like a plan. Let me call Jackie and see if she can cover for me."

I tried unsuccessfully to stifle a gaping yawn. "Great," I mumbled.

"Guess we'd better turn in. Big day tomorrow." Erik extended a hand and hauled me from the chair.

As I reached to flip off the lights, I shot a glance over my shoulder at the innocuous-looking file cabinet nestled up against the computer desk. I hesitated, then crossed back over and pushed in the lock. No one probably had the least interest in my meager files, but past experience had shown me you just never knew what could happen.

Still, a casual burglar would have to share my warped sense of humor if he intended to make off with the looted bone.

I'd filed it under "G" for Ghastly.

SATURDAY MORNING should have been bottled and saved, to be opened on one of those occasional dreary days in mid-December or January when it seems as if the sun will never appear again. Very little humidity, a light breeze, and a pristine sky greeted us as we walked from the parking area to the embarkation point for the ferry. I'd heard somewhere that vehicles—except for golf carts—were prohibited on Daufuskie, and this seemed to be attested to by the number of cars shrouded in tarps and hunkered down in the tree-shaded lot.

The main building resembled a typical Lowcountry–style house with wide porches, the one facing the water complete with several rocking chairs. Inside, the reception area echoed the attempt to recreate a feel of days gone by with painted wainscoting, scattered imitation Oriental rugs, and dark green wing-backed chairs. The cherry desk was unoccupied. A discreet sign requested us to pick up our boarding passes at the small building where golfers left their bags to be transported in the closed metal containers we'd seen lined up just outside. I assumed these were also used for carrying mail and supplies to the isolated residents of Daufuskie Island.

The boat, sparkling white against the glistening water of Broad Creek, sat waiting as we made our way down the long gangway. A sign informed us the ferry left every hour on the half hour. A uniformed attendant offered us a hand as we stepped aboard and entered a snug salon carpeted in dark green with matching upholstery on wide benches. Some flanked tables, while others sat back-to-back down the center of the cabin. Several copies of the morning's *Island Packet* were scattered around, and an overhead TV set, sound off, was tuned to CNN.

We nodded greetings to several people already seated, many of whom carried shopping bags, apparently from early morning excursions to the Food Lion and Publix stores on Palmetto Bay Road. We plopped onto seats facing the open water.

"This is pretty cool," Erik whispered to me. "I mean, these people *really* live on an island."

"I'm not sure I'd like it," I said, shedding the light jacket I'd thrown on over my cotton sweater.

"Why not? Just think, you'd never have uninvited guests if you lived like this."

"True, but what happens in an evacuation? If a hurricane hit, you'd have no other way to escape except on this little boat. I don't know how many people live over there, but it seems to me it would take a lot of trips to get everyone off."

My watch read 9:29 when a man who appeared to be the captain passed through the cabin and headed forward. Lines were cast off, and the ferry edged away from the concrete dock. Erik hitched himself around to watch the land slipping away as we moved out into Broad Creek. Once we'd passed beneath the Cross Island bridge and rounded the little point on which the Palmetto Bay Marina sat, Erik turned back toward the elegant homes of Spanish Wells sliding by the wide, square windows.

"Beautiful places," he said, shifting around in an effort to accommodate his long legs in the narrow aisle.

"Bram's Point. It's not a spot for the faint of pocketbook," I replied. "The founders and heads of some of the biggest companies in America have homes over there."

" 'Them that has, gets', or so my grandmother used to say."

"Granny Pen?" I shivered, recalling with sadness the woman whose brutal murder had first brought Erik and me together.

"No, my mom's mother, Grandmother Kingman. No *Gran* or *Granny* for her. It was strictly *Grandmother* or heads were sure to roll."

I smiled, lapsing into silence while we cruised past Buck Island and out into Calibogue Sound. Off to our left the red-and-white-striped column of the Harbour Town Lighthouse rose into the clear warm air. Beside me, Erik maneuvered the black nylon case he'd had slung over his shoulder until it settled on his knees. He wrapped both arms around the carryall and pulled it close to his chest.

I tried hard to pretend I didn't know what lay tucked in the bottom of the innocuous-looking bag. We'd rolled the bone in some old towels and packed others around it in an effort not only to conceal the grisly thing, but hopefully to insure no telltale smell would escape. I wasn't sure exactly how the owners of this well-maintained little craft would react to our bringing human remains aboard, but I was pretty sure it wouldn't be pleasant.

Shaking off the chilling feeling we were also breaking about a dozen state and local laws, I lowered my voice and edged myself closer to Erik's side. "What do you expect to gain from this excursion?" I asked. "I mean, what can this Dr. Douglass tell us we don't already know?" I ducked my head as the man across from us lowered his newspaper and glanced across the aisle.

"Besides confirm it's human? He can take measurements and do some tests to determine . . ."

Again our nosy companion peered over the top of the sports section, this time fixing me with an oily smile. I nodded and turned back to Erik who said softly, "This isn't the place."

"You're right. Sorry."

I reached behind me and snagged an abandoned copy of the *Packet,* snapping it open to the editorial page. Erik levered himself around again and watched the approaching outline of Daufuskie Island growing larger as we neared the ferry terminal. I forced myself to become engrossed in a spate of letters both for and against a proposed dredging project in South Beach when the voice cut through the hum of the engines and the low murmur of conversation around me.

"Excuse me, but aren't you Bay Tanner?"

I rattled the paper, hoping the thin sheets of newsprint would protect me from this unwanted intrusion. No such luck.

"I'm sorry, but I'm pretty sure I remember you from Beaufort. Well, St. Helena, actually."

I drew a deep breath and lowered the paper. Beside me I felt Erik stiffen and turn back around on the bench.

"Harry. Harry Simon," the man said, one hand extended across the aisle which separated us. "Beachside Realty. I'm workin' outta Hilton Head now."

"I'm sorry, but I don't remember you."

"Oh, sure ya do! We used to run into each other a lot at

your daddy's political rallies. Back in the old days, when he was runnin' for solicitor and then judge. I swear your mama could flat-out throw a party! Why, I remember one time . . ."

I tuned out the good-ol'-boy rhetoric, noting the rustling of those around us as the ferry sidled up to the landing on Daufuskie Island. I gathered my jacket and bag, nodding all the while at this fool man's scattered reminiscences. I still had no idea who the hell he was.

". . . and then Law Merriweather chucked the whole damn thing right off the dock and into the Sound!" He slapped his thigh, but the hearty laugh which accompanied it never reached his eyes. "Remember?" he prompted me.

"No, sorry, can't say that I do."

My curt response didn't slow him up at all. "You by any chance lookin' for property over here? I have some great listings . . ."

"No. Thanks."

"Visiting friends?"

"Something like that. Nice to see you again."

I grabbed Erik's arm and jerked him to his feet, sliding around in front to place his not inconsiderable bulk between me and Harry Simon. We moved in single file through the narrow doorway and onto the dock. I set a brisk pace up the slight incline of the gangway, and soon we had left the garrulous, overweight real estate agent puffing some distance behind us.

"How do we get to this Doctor Douglass's place?" I asked as we passed the enclosed waiting room at the top of the walkway.

"He said he'd meet us."

Several people hoisted their grocery bags and other purchases into waiting golf carts and sped away, while others boarded what looked to be a converted school bus. I glanced back over my shoulder, pleased to find Harry Simon had stopped to chat with one of the uniformed crew members off the ferry.

"What's up with that guy?" Erik asked as he hefted the bag containing the bone up onto his shoulder.

"Beats the hell out of me. So far as I know, I've never met him before. But some of those fund-raisers for the Judge's campaigns used to be real madhouses. Sometimes two hundred people or more would show up for one of his barbecues or oyster roasts. Simon couldn't have been much of a player, though, or I'd remember him. I used to keep all the financial records of my father's contributors."

We moved up toward what appeared to be an inn or some sort of restaurant as the last of the passengers on the 9:30 ferry climbed onto the bus which then lumbered slowly out onto the road. There didn't seem to be anyone waiting for the return trip.

"Hello there! Are you the folks from Hilton Head?"

The man approaching wore green plaid golf pants and a brilliant yellow shirt. Beneath a white billed cap with the Nike swoosh emblazoned across the front, a few wisps of curly gray hair fluttered in the light breeze. "I'm Denton Douglass."

"Erik Whiteside. This is my friend, Bay Tanner."

We shook hands all around.

"Pleased to meet you. Sorry I'm a little late. Tried to get in a quick nine holes this morning and had a bunch of hackers in front of me the whole way. We're over here."

The retired anthropologist bustled off toward one of the ubiquitous golf carts with a gleaming set of clubs strapped onto the back ledge. He moved with the energy of a much younger man, a testament no doubt to the benefits of regular exercise on the Haig Point course. A little below average height, with the deep tan and spreading crow's feet of someone who spent a lot of time in the Lowcountry sun, Denton Douglass seemed an unlikely candidate for a career spent carving up dead bodies in the bowels of some dingy science building.

"You'll have to take the rumble seat, young man," he said, offering me his hand as I slid into the passenger side of the compact vehicle. "It won't take us but a couple of minutes to the house. Martha will have the coffee on, and maybe some of her special cinnamon buns. She does love to bake, that woman. Amazing I don't weigh three hundred pounds."

The doctor kept up this running commentary as we circled around and headed out in the same direction the bus had taken. Almost immediately we were into heavy stands of live oak, the resurrection fern clinging to their twisted limbs glistening bright green after the recent rains. Pines and sweet gums and cedars concealed massive homes, the sweep of their front entrances merely a flash of color as the cart chugged down the path. More houses, no doubt much less expensive, many with the distinctive porches and dormers of Lowcountry architecture, nestled closer to the road. It was into the short driveway of one of these, pale yellow with gleaming white trim, that our host pulled to a stop.

"Here we are," he announced, sliding from the golf cart. "Mmmm. Smell that? Fresh rolls. Lord, I love that woman!"

We followed Dr. Denton Douglass up the steps and into a high-ceilinged great room furnished comfortably with loveseats and overstuffed chairs which had probably made the trip with them from their college housing back in North Carolina. Wide windows across the back wall overlooked a small lagoon. In a brilliant patch of sunshine filtering down through the limbs of the shade trees surrounding the house, a baby alligator took his ease along the near bank.

The doctor followed the direction of my gaze. "Ah, Freddie! He shows up just about every morning, at least when the sun's out. He's cute now, but Martha won't be so inclined to coo over him when he gets to be eight feet long! Martha!" he yelled, making both of us jump. "Where are you, woman? Company's here!"

Mrs. Douglass bustled in, wiping her hands on the dish towel tucked into the waistband of her polyester pants. As wide as her husband was narrow, she beamed and held out her hands.

"Young people! How wonderful! Everything's set up on the back porch. Just come right on out."

We followed Mrs. Douglass onto a screened-in room furnished with obviously new rattan furniture with brightly flowered cushions. The yeasty smell of something not long out of the oven mingled with the pungent aromas of pine and newly mown grass.

"Sit," Mrs. Douglass ordered then turned to her husband. "Denton, you pour. I have more buns ready to come out." She showered us all with her smile and turned back into the kitchen.

I declined coffee, and the professor filled bright blue mugs for himself and Erik before settling back in his chair. "Can't say that I remember you, young fella. Sorry. But then I was at N.C. State for the better part of twenty years, so I guess it's not surprising. Archaeology major or pre-med?"

The question took Erik by surprise, and he stumbled a little over his answer. "I changed majors a lot, sir. Couldn't seem to make up my mind."

"Always a lot of that goin' on back then, though not so much these days. Lots of kids come in hell-bent on getting into business or computers or some other such nonsense. Know exactly what they want to do. Only interest is in making a bundle of money. Hardly anyone cares about science anymore."

He paused, although neither of us had a clue what he expected us to say. Erik slurped coffee, and I stuffed a section of the delectable cinnamon roll into my mouth to avoid answering.

But apparently the former professor was used to carrying on conversations with himself. "So let's see it," he said abruptly, with an air of anticipation which sounded, at least to me, a little too gleeful.

I selected another of the warm buns from a cloth-draped basket and rose to stand looking out the screened window. The nylon bag rustled as Erik handed it to the professor. I forced myself to tune out the low conversation of the doctor's murmured questions and my partner's well-rehearsed story.

"Well, let's see what we can do."

I turned as Denton Douglass disappeared through the door, the black bag swinging jauntily from his hand.

"Shouldn't take too long," he called over his shoulder. "Make yourself at home."

Erik and I exchanged looks as he crossed his long legs and settled back into his chair.

THOUGH WE could hear the professor's wife humming tunelessly in the kitchen, she never reappeared during the half hour or so we cooled our heels on the porch. I ate enough cinnamon rolls to wipe out at least a week's worth of beach runs while Erik became engrossed in several back issues of the N.C. State alumni magazine spread out on a side table. Neither of us seemed inclined to break the silence of the warm South Carolina morning. The atmosphere felt like that of a surgical waiting room, hushed anticipation mixed with large doses of dread.

When the doctor finally spoke from the doorway, his voice sounded like a crack of thunder.

"Where in hell did this really come from?" he barked, all trace of the mild-mannered, bumbling professor wiped from his tone. "And I'd better like the answer, or I'm going to be on the phone to the authorities before you can spit."

CHAPTER
EIGHTEEN

By the time we stepped off the ferry onto the dock at Hilton Head, the sun had retreated behind a bank of clouds building up off toward the mainland, and the temperature had dropped considerably. A chilly breeze lifted the strands of hair that had curled and frizzed against my neck in the dank humidity of Daufuskie.

We had remained silent throughout most of the ride back, the import of the doctor's revelations and the crowded salon of the small boat combining to thwart conversation. As we trudged up the gangway toward the parking lot, Erik voiced my thoughts as if he could read them inside my head.

"We've gotten ourselves into a real mess this time, haven't we?" He stood alongside the T-Bird as I unlocked the doors. "Or rather, *I've* gotten us into a real mess. What the hell was I thinking? We should have turned the damned thing over to the cops the minute it landed on my doorstep. If Dr. Douglass decides . . ."

"Quit beating yourself up," I said, unconsciously parroting Red Tanner's oft-repeated order to me whenever I'd stuck my nose into something which had the potential to turn into a disaster. I slid behind the wheel and cranked the powerful engine to life. "What's done is done. We've got a window of opportunity here, although a pretty narrow one, and we need to take advantage of it."

I negotiated the roundabout at the entrance to the Haig

Point facility, made a couple of turns past the new Crossings Park, and pulled out onto Palmetto Bay Road before adding, "We're fortunate the good professor took a shine to you. I think it's what tipped the scales in our favor."

"I think it has more to do with the fact he's enamored of Indiana Jones movies. I think he fancies himself in the Sean Connery role as Indy's father."

I turned to smile at Erik, whose optimism could never be squelched for long, and a lot of the tension evaporated.

The retired anthropologist's findings shouldn't have been as shocking as they seemed when you applied a little logic to the situation, but we had both reacted with dismay when he announced his conclusions. I was particularly astounded to hear all he had been able to determine during his brief examination in the small lab he had set up in his garage.

In a nutshell, Gray Palmer, Junior, had shipped us a human femur, the long bone between the knee and the hip and the largest, heaviest one in the skeleton. It was also the one from which the most information could be gleaned. As an archaeologist, he would have known that. Gray's selection had not been a random one.

The corpse was a male, probably African-American, approximately twenty to thirty years of age at the time of his death, and somewhere in the neighborhood of six feet tall. Of course Dr. Douglass had no access to any really sophisticated equipment, so his estimate as to how long the body had been interred was a guess at best. He did seem fairly certain burial would have taken place somewhere within the past fifty years.

How the body came to be where Gray had discovered it and how the unfortunate young man had died were topics of complete conjecture at this point.

Early afternoon traffic was heavy as we negotiated the Sea Pines Circle, and I spared a moment to lament once again the annual onslaught of tourists this congestion heralded. In a matter of weeks we permanent residents would be back to scheduling our trips and errands around the least likely times for our tens of thousands of visitors to be on the road. My months abroad, where Darnay and I had used the Mètro to avoid the clogged streets of Paris, seemed even more like a distant memory. I gunned the T-Bird into the narrow gap between two vanloads of bewildered Northerners before replying.

"When he challenged you about there being just the one bone, I almost fainted. He could actually tell it hadn't been . . . What was the word he used?"

"Disarticulated," Erik replied.

"Right. Disarticulated more than a few days ago."

"Apparently it wasn't as clean as we thought. He managed to detect enough cartilage or ligament or whatever to tell it had been disconnected from the other bones only a short time ago." He paused, thinking something through. "I'm surprised there was any of that left, if he's right about it being in the ground for fifty years."

My stomach did a few flips, and I swallowed hard against it. "No more than fifty, he said. Could be less. We're just damned lucky he's heading out of town tomorrow, or I'm convinced he would have insisted on turning the blasted thing over to the coroner's office. He's basically given us until next weekend to come up with a valid reason for him not to, and I haven't a clue what our next move should be. Any brilliant ideas?"

"Any place along here to get something to eat? I'm starving."

The non sequitur stopped me for a moment. "Sure." I flipped on my left turn signal and waited for a long line of cars to clear before turning into the entrance to the Hilton Head Diner. "This okay?"

"Great." I caught his glance and smiled back. Apparently all our talk of cartilage and disarticulated bones hadn't affected his appetite. "I know, I know," he said. "I ate practically my weight in those fabulous cinnamon buns, but what can I say? I'm a growing boy."

When we were settled in a booth and Erik had ordered his second complete breakfast of the day, I leaned toward him across the wide expanse of Formica. "Okay, I'm still soliciting brilliant ideas about how to proceed."

"I think we need to make one of your famous lists. Let's get down everything we know about the . . . *item*," he said, checking the area for potential eavesdroppers. "Got any paper?"

I rummaged in the oversized canvas tote which doubled as my handbag and pulled out the small notebook I used for my grocery lists. Locating a pen in the jumble of used tissues, loose change, and stale peppermints took a while longer.

"Okay, shoot."

We were interrupted by the arrival of two heaping platters bearing Erik's eggs, pancakes, sausage, grits, and various other accompaniments along with my English muffin and hot tea. While he attacked the mountain of food, I took notes.

The result was a pathetic enumeration of just how little we had to go on. It could be condensed into a couple of simple sentences: On an island, probably isolated and uninhabited, located somewhere between Beaufort and Charleston, Gray Palmer the younger had uncovered the grave of a black man, approximately six feet tall and between twenty and thirty years old at the time of his death. He had been buried hurriedly and without benefit of casket or formal service. Artifacts found in the grave would no doubt confirm Dr. Denton's assumption he had been dead no more than fifty years.

That his death had been the result of foul play of some sort seemed to be without question, although Erik hesitated a bit over this last conclusion.

"Why?" I asked, watching him use his last sliver of toast to mop up the bright yellow and amber swirl of egg yolk mixed with maple syrup.

"You're always telling me not to assume," he replied. He wiped the corners of his mouth then held out his cup for the approaching waitress to refill with steaming coffee.

I waited until she'd cleared the table and set the bill down in front of Erik. "I don't think it's any kind of leap in logic. Araminda Albright said their research involved the undeveloped islands along the coast, so Gray didn't stumble onto some kind of illegal family burial plot. The fact that the corpse was apparently fully clothed, including a watch, when it went into the ground seems to indicate a certain amount of desperation on the part of whoever did the burying, don't you think?"

"Yes and no."

"That's helpful."

"What I mean is, the grave had to be pretty deep or animals would have disturbed it long before now. So that says to me the gravedigger spent a lot of time making sure no one would stumble across it accidentally. That doesn't square with someone in a panic to conceal a murder."

"Maybe he wasn't in a panic. Maybe he chose that spot to kill our guy because he knew he'd have lots of time to work and no fear of being interrupted. He could do the job right."

"Then how did Gray find it?"

"Good question."

Erik reached for the bill, but I snatched it out from under his fingers then fished a credit card from my wallet. "Business lunch," I said as we slid out of the booth. "Deductible, at least partially."

Outside, the clouds had moved off over the ocean, and a surprisingly warm sun beat down once again. I put the top down and eased us back onto Route 278. Erik studied our meager list and picked up the conversation.

"Then we appear to have a contradiction in our assumptions."

"Elaborate."

"I see one of two scenarios. Either the death was accidental and whoever was responsible panicked and tried to conceal it by burying the corpse on the spot, or it was a cold-blooded murder, and the killer meticulously planned to make certain no one would ever find the body. You can't have it both ways."

"Why not?" I waved to Jim, the guard on duty at the entrance to Port Royal Plantation, and eased through the checkpoint. "We're theorizing based on way too little concrete evidence, projecting logic onto a situation which by its very nature defies rational explanation." I eased into my driveway and turned toward Erik as I hit the button on the garage door opener. "I suppose even Jeffrey Dahmer or those two dolts who shot up the Washington, D.C., area had some sort of rationale, at least in their own twisted minds, but it isn't something a normal person could probably deduce."

"Did you see that?" Erik shot up in the bucket seat, his finger pointing at the open garage beneath the house.

"What?" The sudden edge to his voice sent memories of fire and devastation on this very spot tumbling through my head. "What?" I repeated, more urgently this time.

"There was something written on the door. Didn't you see it before you hit the button?"

"No. What kind of writing?"

"Looked like spray paint. Put it back down."

How we had missed it that morning I couldn't imagine, except I had probably backed the T-Bird around and headed out before lowering the garage door. Some of the red letters had run, long swirling blobs of paint giving the whole thing a cartoonish, written-in-blood look. However, the message, though lacking the finer points of spelling and syntax, certainly managed to convey the sentiments of its author in a concise and very convincing manner.

The words WHITE BITCH covered the top half, while I thought the bottom line intended to label me a racist whore. I wasn't positive, because the wielder of the spray can had left the W off the final word, and the E was truncated where he—or she—apparently ran out of room, failing to heed that age-old admonition to plan ahead.

"Jesus!" Erik expelled a breath and jumped out of the car. He approached the door and gingerly pressed a finger into the paint. "Dry, except for the globs. Must have been done last night. Jesus!" he repeated.

I turned off the engine and slid out of my seat, moving around the front of the car to stand next to Erik. "A pretty sad commentary on the state of our educational system, don't you think?" I remarked, mimicking his gesture by touching my own index finger onto the paint. "Stupid bastard can't even spell 'whore.' "

"You think this is funny?"

"Not particularly."

"You're awfully damned calm about it. Doesn't the thought of some lowlife skulking around here last night while we were sleeping a few feet away give you just a little chill?"

I couldn't explain my lack of surprise or indignation to myself, let alone to the earnest young man standing beside me. I suppose it had something to do with the complete lack of any validity to the charge, the fact that the whole idea of my being either racist or a whore was so completely ludicrous I had a hard time taking the whole thing seriously.

"You going to notify the cops?"

"And tell them what? That some kids defaced my garage door? That I heard nothing, saw nothing, have absolutely no idea who or why?"

"You can't just let it slide." Indignation vibrated in Erik Whiteside's voice. "You should file a police report."

"What for? Repairing this won't even make a blip on my homeowner's deductible. I'll call maintenance and see if they can come by and slap a couple of coats of something over it until I can get a painting contractor in here next week." I retreated to the T-Bird and depressed the button on the opener. "Relax. The morons obviously got the wrong house."

I lifted my bag from the seat as the bizarre epithets slid out of sight on silent rollers.

"I hope to hell you're right," I heard Erik mutter as he followed me into the house.

IN HONOR of the gift of a warm, sunny afternoon, we moved our office out onto the deck. I hunkered down onto the chaise with my favorite Waterford pen and a supply of yellow legal pads, while Erik balanced a state-of-the-art laptop on his knees. An extra-long modem cable snaked its way through the open French doors and into the phone jack in the great room so we could access the Internet when necessary. The file labeled PALMER/ALBRIGHT lay spread out on a low rattan table between us.

We systematically worked our way down the list of Gray Palmer, Senior's reward seekers, chewing over the possible legitimate ones for later contact while attempting to eliminate the kooks and the weirdoes. Erik managed to coax his recalcitrant cell phone back into service while I used the portable from the kitchen. In the space of two hours we had reduced the list to a manageable few by virtue of the criteria we had decided upon, primarily insisting on a description of Gray's boat and the unusual name painted on its stern. Erik proved surprisingly good at this game of trap-the-liars, and we had a couple of laughs at the expense of some of the more inventive claimants to the twenty-five-thousand-dollar jackpot.

Two of our possibles weren't at the numbers they'd provided, so my partner used his expertise to tease addresses from the Internet. The woman who had provided the information about a verbal altercation between Gray and two men in a boat pulled up alongside his lived only a few streets away in Port Royal Plantation. The second had been added to our follow-up list over my protests, but Erik had a gut feeling it had possibilities, so I deferred to his instincts. I felt certain the paramilitary angle would prove to be a dead end, but my partner stood his ground.

"There's an awful lot of bases around here, aren't there?" he asked as I returned from the kitchen with our second pitcher of iced tea. "Parris Island, the Marine Air Station. A couple in Savannah. And isn't there a Navy base in Charleston?"

I refilled our glasses and added melting ice from the bowl I'd carried out earlier. "I think the big one in Charleston got shut down in the last round of Defense Department closings, but I'm not certain. I haven't been around there much lately, except for that last trip to meet Mindy Albright."

"Well, I'm not ready to dismiss it out of hand just yet.

There's something about the story which speaks to me. I'd like for us to talk to the guy before we write him off."

"Fair enough. So where are we with this thing? Any closer to finding out what really happened to Gray?"

"Not that I can see." The admission brought a frown to Erik's normally cheerful countenance. "You know," he added, "there's something else bothering me about this whole scenario. A couple of things, actually."

"What's that?"

"Well, why are we going through all this when the authorities obviously think Gray's death was an accident? Why are his father and the Albright girl so convinced he was murdered? It seems a strange thing for a father to fixate on, don't you think? I mean, I sort of understand how he feels, because of, you know, Granny Pen. No one believed me either when I insisted she'd been . . . a victim. Everyone thought I was just delusional, overcome by grief, not able to accept her death. You know?"

I did indeed, and Erik's speech startled me into admitting I had been thinking exactly the same things about Gray Palmer, Senior. I had leaped at the opportunity to take on this case, to get our infant enterprise up on its feet and underway, but the small voice inside my head had been whispering that it was a fool's errand. Young Gray had fallen overboard, whether by sheer bad luck or from the stupidity of trying to handle a boat while drunk or stoned. We wouldn't really know which until the autopsy report was finalized. But there was absolutely no indication, at least from anything we knew for certain, that foul play had been involved. Just a father's insistence and a friend/lover's conviction. And Erik Whiteside's gut instinct. That's the one that would keep me in the game until we discovered the truth.

I glanced up to find him studying me, and I realized I had left his rhetorical question dangling. "Yes, Erik, I understand. So we'll keep going. It occurs to me we should see if Red can get hold of the official police report."

"I wonder who actually conducted the investigation."

"Good point. I suppose it could have been the local police, the sheriff's office, or even the Coast Guard. How can we find out who would have jurisdiction?"

"I suppose it would depend on exactly where the . . . accident or whatever occurred. I really don't know that much about territorial limits or any of that stuff. Would your brother-in-law?"

"Let's call and find out. If he doesn't, I'm sure the Judge knows someone connected with the Coast Guard who could help us. It's probably time we let him in on this anyway. He's going to be madder than hell if we cut him out of our first real investigation."

"Want me to give him a call? I think he's less likely to ream me out than he is if you're the one who announces we've been sleuthing behind his back."

"Good idea."

The mention of my father brought the problem of his mysterious visitor whirling back into my head. I was on the verge of soliciting Erik's advice on the best way to ferret out some information on the elusive Felicity Baronne when the sounds of a heavy truck sent me down the steps and around to the driveway.

The uniformed maintenance men, both of whom were black, made no comment on the accusation dripping from my garage door in the fading afternoon sun, but set to work silently with rollers and brushes. I felt as if I should offer some explanation, some defense against the stark red words, but I turned instead and retreated back onto the deck.

What, after all, could I have said?

Seeing the shock register in their dark, somber eyes forced me to rethink my earlier, cavalier dismissal of this attack on my property. What if it wasn't a mistake? What if the denunciation had, in fact, been intended for me?

I shook off the bizarre notion and rejoined Erik, who was just terminating a cell call when I plopped back onto the chaise. "The Judge is not a happy camper, but I think I got him calmed down. Anyway, we're invited, or rather commanded, to appear for dinner tonight at precisely six thirty.

No excuses, or so I was instructed. And we're to bring all the paperwork with us."

We exchanged smiles. Erik was beginning to understand how to deal with my father, a lesson it had taken me many years to learn: acquiescence was the only acceptable response to his pronouncements, and giving in immediately rather than putting up a fight made everyone's life a whole lot easier.

As we began to gather our things together, I remembered the thread of the conversation the arrival of the painters had interrupted. "You said there were a couple of things about the case that bothered you. What's the other?"

Erik stopped midway in the process of disconnecting the modem cable and fixed me with an intent stare.

"Just this," he said, and his tone made me sit up straighter. "Suppose the father is right. I keep coming back to Mindy Albright's idea there's a connection between these two deaths, Gray's and the poor guy he dug up."

The shiver that raised gooseflesh along my arms had nothing to do with the cool breeze off the ocean. "What do you mean, exactly?"

"What I mean is, did Gray Palmer die because he found that body? Or did someone kill him to shut him up about something else entirely?"

CHAPTER
NINETEEN

We let the topic of both Gray Palmers simmer as the cool wind whipped around us. We'd bundled up a little in deference to the inevitable drop in temperature which would accompany encroaching twilight, but we'd agreed the top should definitely stay down. I'd spared a glance in the rearview mirror as we pulled out of the driveway, relieved to be able to discern only the barest shadow of the red letters of hatred some unknown moron had spray-painted on my garage door.

That was also a subject I had forcefully put off-limits.

So we listened to the Saturday oldies show on the local radio station while I picked Erik Whiteside's brain about how to track down the scoop on Felicity Baronne, and the beauty of the Lowcountry afternoon whizzed by our open windows.

"So you did a Google search?" Erik asked, reaching down to lower the volume on the radio. "And nothing at all popped up?"

"Sure, I got lots of hits, but nothing related to this woman."

"Did you try enclosing her name in quotation marks?"

"What good would that do?" I slowed as we approached the construction area on the road-widening project which seemed to have been defacing the lovely Chechessee River area for decades. I still couldn't get used to the openness of the roadside where huge swaths of trees had been leveled to make way for the addition of two more lanes.

"It keeps you from getting hits with only one of the names in them, or from having the search engine find the first name in one part of an article and the last name in another."

"I didn't know that."

"I'll give it a try when we get back to your place. In the meantime, there are other things we can check out."

"Like what?"

"Genealogy sites, land records, Social Security. I've been doing a lot of study on this ever since your friend Miss Hammond asked us to find her brother."

The reminder stacked another layer of guilt on my already overburdened pile of regrets. "We really have to get on that, Erik," I said, then quickly added, "not that you haven't already done a ton of work. It's just I feel so damned bad about letting her down. And the truth is I pretty much blew the whole thing off while I was . . ."

I realized the trap the moment the words were out of my mouth, but it was too late to call them back. Erik pounced on the opening with both feet.

"Just what exactly happened over there, Bay?" I started to interrupt, but he cut me off. "Yeah, I know what you told me in the e-mail, about Alain having family business to attend to, or some such crap. I didn't buy it then, and I'm sure as hell not buying it now. You haven't once mentioned the guy's name since you've been back. Unless you're holding out on me, you haven't even talked to him. What gives?"

I toyed with the idea of telling him it was none of his damned business, which was technically correct, but he was my friend. I could hear the genuine concern in his voice. What I didn't hear was the naked curiosity I expected from other of my acquaintances, especially the female ones, so I made a snap decision to tell him the truth.

"He's back in the game," I said in what I hoped was a calm, rational statement of fact. "The big boys at Interpol sent him the background on a case they've been trying to crack for months, something related to smuggling. Supposedly they wanted his 'take' on their operation, but what they were really after was enticing him into another undercover assignment."

"And he agreed? I thought he was . . . you know, still banged up from being shot. I thought he couldn't . . ."

"Me, too." I forced the anger back into its little compartment and continued, "But you don't know Darnay. Once he had the details, once he'd gotten his head into the case, it was all over. He couldn't resist the challenge, missed the excitement, I guess. At any rate, I decided I didn't want to sit around Paris waiting for the phone to ring or worse yet, have him disappear into that world and never know what really happened to him. We weren't married. They would have no obligation to inform me of his death."

The last word hung between us as we eased down Carteret Street in Beaufort, swooped over the bridge onto Lady's Island, and sped on toward St. Helena. Around us, the afternoon had softened into the pale, hazy glow that presages evening in the Lowcountry spring. Wherever the wide expanse of water met the limitless sky, opalescent streaks of pink and lavender tinged the wispy clouds hovering on the horizon.

Erik mistook my sigh of contentment at the incredible beauty for one of despair.

"Want me to go over there and beat the crap out of him? Bring the man to his senses?"

It was exactly the right tone, exactly what I needed, and I laughed out loud.

"No, but thanks for the thought." Sobering, I added, "He'll come on his own, or not at all. That's what I've decided. It's his life, and he has to live it."

We lapsed into silence then, and I forced my thoughts to the upcoming confrontation with my father. I had no doubt it would be a battle. I could almost predict his reaction to our running around the countryside with a leg bone stolen from an illicit grave. He might have been inclined to bend the rules a little, especially when it involved his friends and cronies, but concealing evidence of a possible homicide would be stretching his understanding way past the breaking point.

As we pulled into the circular drive in front of Presqu'isle's stately grandeur, I drew a deep breath and strapped on my proverbial sword.

"'THERE IS no sin except stupidity.'"

It was the last straw for me, although Erik had maintained his equilibrium remarkably well during the long tirade we'd been subjected to from the moment we'd leaned back from the dinner table. Lavinia, ever the woman of wisdom and sound judgment, had retreated to the kitchen, refusing all offers of help and leaving us, in effect, defenseless against the Judge's rant.

By the time that particularly scurrilous salvo had been fired off, the party had moved out onto the back verandah where my father was performing his nightly cigar ritual. In a fit of pique, I at first refused to help him. But after watching him struggle to manipulate the cutter with only one good hand, I finally gave in and came to his rescue. I received only a grudging nod for my efforts.

When smoke was billowing around his head and swirling away into the deep night, I said, "'There is no sin except stupidity.' Oscar Wilde, *The Picture of Dorian Gray.* I'll take two points. And that remark was totally uncalled for. While it may be part of my job description as your daughter to put up with your ill humors and bad temper, Erik is not similarly burdened. That was an insult which he certainly doesn't deserve."

The Judge fidgeted around in his wheelchair, apparently fascinated by the glowing end of his panatela, and harrumphed a little before replying. "Perhaps it was a bit harsh. I apologize, young man. No offense intended."

"None taken, Your Honor," Erik said, and I could hear the smile in his voice.

I gave a thought to playacting a heart attack, brought on from the shock of actually witnessing my father's apologizing to someone, but the darkness would have rendered my performance something less than effective. Instead I re-marked, "I notice you're not including me in this magnani-mous reprieve."

"He's young and hasn't had the benefit of my tutelage over the course of his lifetime. You, on the other hand . . ."

"Do you guys always talk like this?" Erik interrupted him in midsentence. " 'Magnanimous reprieve'? 'Tutelage'? You make me feel like I should carry a dictionary around with me just so I can follow the thread of the conversation."

"Sorry," I said, settling into my favorite rocking chair and setting it in motion. I couldn't begin to explain to an outsider the depth of the competition that existed between my father and me on all kinds of levels, not just the vastness of our re-spective vocabularies or our ability to reference obscure quotations.

"The point is," the Judge continued as if the last exchange had not taken place, "you have both acted foolishly in not turning this bone over to the police or at least to the coroner. Not only is it possible evidence in the crime in which its un-fortunate owner met his death, it could also have bearing on the investigation into the demise of Erik's friend. Evidence tampering is not something the authorities take lightly. I my-self have imposed jail terms as well as onerous fines in a number of such cases which came before me when I was on the bench."

It was my father at his pompous best, and I could tell he was cranking up for another lengthy diatribe, so I cut him off at the pass. "Spilled milk, water over the dam, et cetera, et cetera," I said into the hushed night air. Down by the end of the dock, a fish jumped, slapping the water with a loud smack. "What do you suggest we do about it now?" Behind me, in the depths of the entry hall, I heard the muted peal of the doorbell.

"Ah, perhaps some of the answers are about to be made known. Follow my lead."

The Judge negotiated the tangle of legs and chairs and glided down the ramp into his room. I strained to recognize the voice responding to Lavinia's inquiries. It did sound familiar, as if I had heard the deep drawl before, but I couldn't put a name to it. Erik and I exchanged looks as the soft whirr of the Judge's chair grew louder, and the conversation came into focus.

". . . out here on the verandah," my father was saying, slightly muted, as if he spoke over his shoulder. "Lavinia will bring us some refreshment in just a moment."

He rolled onto the porch, followed by a bulky presence whose features were lost in the backlight from the doorway. But as the visitor moved onto the shadowy deck, my father said, "I believe you know my daughter, Bay Tanner? And this is our friend, Erik Whiteside."

Before my father could complete the introductions, I found myself staring into the hard eyes and oily smile of the Daufuskie real estate salesman, Harry Simon.

MY FATHER had given us no hint about what he was up to prior to the arrival of his guest. He'd probably intended to, but he'd wasted too much time showing off for Erik. Still, we managed to pick away at Simon without anyone's divulging the real reasons for our questions. No one mentioned the bone or the grave or the mysterious island. Instead, we concentrated on learning as much as we could about the workings of the Coast Guard in general and their response to the call about Gray Palmer in particular. Because, inexplicably, this overweight, unctuous man turned out to be a member of the reserve and had served in that capacity for a number of years. He also claimed to have been in the Marine Corps in his youth. Looking at the paunch that overflowed the waistband of his wrinkled black trousers, I found this assertion difficult to believe.

Over outrageously expensive cigars and a steady flow of bourbon diluted with the merest trickle of soda, we squeezed him dry of every drop of information which could prove useful to us in our investigation of young Gray Palmer's death. We learned the Coast Guard has primary jurisdiction over any crime which occurs over three miles from the shore. If such an incident involved murder, they would no doubt turn the case over to the FBI to continue the investigation.

Inside that three-mile limit, however, things got a little murky. Harry Simon pointed out that it's the natural inclination of most boaters to call the Coast Guard, regardless of where they encountered trouble. It made sense the average guy wouldn't think about exactly where he was in relation to some arbitrarily proscribed limit. Crime on the water equals the Coast Guard, at least in most people's minds.

"That's what happened with your friend," Simon offered as I splashed more Kentucky bourbon over the melting ice cubes in his tumbler. "Mostly the Intracoastal Waterway—that's where your boy was spotted—is state-controlled water, but that don't . . . doesn't register with most folks." Harry's careful syntax had deteriorated in direct proportion to the level of whiskey in his glass.

"So who does the Coast Guard hand off to?" I asked.

"State boys," he responded promptly. "Department of Natural Resources."

"I thought they just ticketed speeding boaters and checked for fishing licenses, things like that," Erik offered.

"Nope. Lots of folks make that mistake. Them boys got it all, same as the police. They can investigate stuff, got arrest powers, all that. Some of 'em even carry guns."

I detected a note of wistfulness in Harry Simon's voice, and I shuddered at the thought of this blustering salesman climbing aboard a boat, brandishing a weapon like some modern-day pirate.

"I seem to recall, though, that this particular incident ended up in the hands of the local authorities. The Charleston police, I believe." My father spoke with the careful enunciation one uses for very small children and fools. Or drunks.

"True, true. Far as I can recollect, the boat was drifting somewhere between the two juri . . . juris . . . you know, and they took it over 'cause the kid was from there. Somethin' like that. Anyway, it don't really make any difference, 'cause everyone says it was just a stupid accident. Boy shoulda known better 'n to be drinkin' while runnin' full-out in a boat like that. Stupid accident," he repeated.

"Did you or any of your buddies get in on the investigation?" I asked. "Did you interview any witnesses, collect any physical evidence?"

"None to be found, far as we could tell. Poor kid was pretty chewed up by the prop, though. Glad I wasn't one of the guys who had to pull him out. I ain't real good with blood."

"So no signs of foul play? No open bottles or drug paraphernalia found on the boat?"

The Judge's question got no immediate response, so he leaned in toward Harry Simon, lowering his tone to a conspiratorial level. "I realize this may be privileged information, but you can trust us to respect the confidence. We're just trying to find out what happened so young Erik here can gain some closure on his friend's death. I'm sure you understand."

The Judge's voice exuded respect and gratitude. Harry Simon seemed to lap it up.

"Sure, Judge, sure. Jack Kelly, who heads our reserve unit, he told me they had a devil of a time even identifyin' the kid. The props, you know. But the boat had this kinda weird name, and the kid's old man confirmed it. The girlfriend said the clothes on the corpse were the ones the kid was wearin' when he took off the day before. So . . ." Harry tried for a wink, but the coordination of his facial muscles had been compromised by the booze. "Course, that's just between us chickens, if you get my drift."

"Of course, of course. That goes without saying. But no signs of foul play, so far as the Coast Guard is aware."

"Nope, Judge, not a thing. The kid was prob'ly drunk. Maybe stood up to take a leak off the side of the boat and fell in. Or got tangled up in the line and lost his balance. Lots o' stupid accidents happen out there on the water. People got no respect for how dangerous it can be."

"Well, thanks, Harry. You've been very helpful. I surely do appreciate it."

As if on cue, Lavinia appeared with coffee and tea along with thin slivers of her famous carrot cake, and we set about sobering up our guest. Harry Simon's fawning abated as the bourbon worked itself out of his system until, by the time the Judge maneuvered his chair out of the rough circle we had formed around the low table, the man had become only marginally obnoxious. It took him a couple of minutes to realize this was the signal the meeting was over, but finally he rose and offered his hand all around. His palm was sweaty, and I resisted the urge to wipe my own on the leg of my slacks once Harry had reluctantly returned it to me.

"Glad I could be of help. Any time, you just call on ol' Harry. A pleasure, yessir, a real pleasure." He turned and the Judge followed him down the ramp and into the house.

The door had barely eased shut behind them before Erik whirled to face me. "That's the same guy who was on the boat out to Daufuskie, isn't it? The one you didn't want to talk to?"

"Yup. Good ol' Harry. God, he gives me the creeps."

"And you don't think it's strange he turns out to be involved in investigating Gray's death?"

I stood and stretched then leaned my elbows atop the railing of the verandah and studied the blackness out over the Sound. "You keep forgetting this isn't Charlotte. Beaufort, Hilton Head, Bluffton—they're all basically small towns when you factor out the tourists."

"I suppose." Erik joined me at the railing. "So that's it then. They're going to write this off as an accident."

"There's still the autopsy report," I reminded him. "If the tox screen and blood tests come back clean, how are they going to justify labeling it an accident without investigating it further?"

"Because somebody wants them to," he murmured, "and I'm damned if I can figure out exactly who. Or why."

CHAPTER
TWENTY

But all during the drive back to Hilton Head I kept worrying at the idea of Harry Simon's appearance on the Daufuskie ferry that morning as a coincidence.

"They do happen," Erik reminded me in a complete reversal of his earlier position.

"I know that!"

"And the Judge just happened to decide to pick Simon's brain when he couldn't get hold of this Jack Kelly guy. I don't see anything sinister about it."

"Just serendipity, is that what you're saying?"

Erik studied the empty road cut by the twin beams of the T-Bird's headlights before answering. I knew the sharpness of his words was engendered, in part anyway, by my own sarcastic tone. "Yeah, that's what I'm saying. And I think they call it paranoia when you see conspiracies behind every tree."

I let the silence deepen while I fought my own fear and resentment for control of my emotions. "You're right," I said, finally expelling some of the tightness in my chest with a long, slow breath. "Sorry."

I caught the edges of Erik's answering smile out of the corner of my eye. "Me, too." He shifted his long legs into a more comfortable configuration before adding, "You know what I think?"

"What?"

"I think this thing with the graffiti has you more bugged than you're willing to admit. Why don't you let me call your brother-in-law and see what he has to say? Give me the number, and I'll try to raise him on my cell."

He pulled the slim phone from his pocket and flipped it open.

I didn't like the idea Erik Whiteside could read me quite so well. And I wasn't paranoid. Circumstances over the past few years of my life had taught me that assumptions could not only be foolish, they could be deadly. Taking things for granted had gotten me and those I loved into some dangerous situations. I was trying to learn from my mistakes.

I relayed Red's number to Erik who punched it in as I negotiated the on-ramp leading to Route 278. We tried him on his personal cell first. I could never keep track of Sergeant Red Tanner's changing shift schedule, so I had an entire repertoire of phone numbers to access whenever I needed to contact him. We lucked out. He picked up after only three rings, and Erik extended the little gadget in my direction.

"No way," I said, shooing his hand away. "I'm always cursing at drivers who talk on those damned things while they're behind the wheel. You tell him."

The recitation took only a couple of minutes, and I could tell from Erik's side of the conversation Red was taking him seriously. "He'll meet us at the house. Should be there about the same time we are." He tucked the phone back in his pocket. "I'm actually looking forward to meeting the guy."

"You and Red have never met? Are you sure?"

I racked my brain trying to remember. It was inconceivable to me these two men who had both played such enormous roles in my life were virtual strangers.

"Nope," Erik confirmed. "I've heard you talk about him enough times, and I did meet his ex-wife Sarah, of course. But I don't know the sergeant except by reputation."

I mulled this strange situation over in my head as we sped along through sparse traffic past several new golf course housing developments which had sprouted seemingly overnight while I'd been in Paris. Soon there wouldn't be an open expanse of trees between Hilton Head and Beaufort. I was ruminating about the old days, back when 278 had been a two-lane road and there had been nothing to interrupt the green except an occasional cottage or trailer tucked back into the woods.

"Look out!"

The wheel jerked in my hand at Erik's shout. Then the deer came sailing into my vision from the right, soaring in a leap that cleared the hood of the T-Bird before I had a chance to react. By the time I'd stomped on the brakes and sent the car swerving toward the shoulder, the graceful creature had bounded across the remaining three lanes of the divided highway and disappeared into the blackness. Behind me I heard the blare of horns and the screech of protesting tires, but thankfully no tearing or crash of metal. I eased to a stop on the grass verge and shoved the gearshift into park before dropping my head onto hands still locked to the steering wheel in a death grip.

"Jesus!" Erik exclaimed, then I felt his touch on my shoulder. "Are you okay?"

"Sure," I managed to say around the fear constricting my throat and the roar of blood rushing in my ears. I exhaled deeply and turned toward him. "You?"

"Fine. Although I should probably check my pants."

He smiled and ran a hand through his short blond hair. I was afraid the laughter bubbling up inside me might have been hysteria, but I gave in to it anyway, and soon both of us were roaring. Anyone stopping to offer assistance would have found two seemingly normal adults whooping and gasping, tears streaming down their faces.

When I had finally hiccupped my way back to some semblance of normalcy, I accepted Erik's proffered handkerchief and rubbed at my mascara-stained cheeks. As I handed it back, he said, "You look like a giant raccoon," threatening to send me back into another laughing jag, but I forced myself to gain control.

"Live with it until we get home," I replied, checking the side mirror for traffic and easing back onto the highway.

"Nice bit of driving," Erik remarked as he searched for a clean spot on his hanky to blow his nose.

"I had nothing to do with it. All the credit for avoiding an accident belongs to the deer. Did you see if it was a buck or a doe?"

"Female, I think. At least I didn't see any big rack of antlers, although I wasn't really at my most observant in those couple of seconds."

"If we didn't keep building all these damned projects and bulldozing their habitat into oblivion, the poor things wouldn't have to keep risking their lives and ours crossing major highways."

It was probably a good thing Erik didn't reply. It was a subject about which I could speak for hours with a fine degree of passion.

The near-disaster finally sobered us into a silence that lasted until I pulled into the driveway of my brightly lit beach house. Two things immediately caught my attention. The first was the white Beaufort County sheriff's cruiser pulled up on the pine straw beneath the towering trees.

The second was the bright red letters sprayed across my garage door.

I MADE coffee, thick and strong the way Madame Srabian had taught me in Paris, and carried the pot to the breakfast alcove where Red Tanner and Erik Whiteside sat eyeing each other across the glass-topped table. I returned for cream and sugar and my own mug of steaming tea before seating myself between the two men.

After my hurried introductions beneath the light of the outdoor vapor lamp which bathed the driveway in a soft blue glow, the two men had shaken hands warily, then joined me in contemplating the new message from my nocturnal accuser. This time the sentiment was less complex, though repetitious, and actually spelled correctly: the word *BITCH* scrawled three times in foot-high letters.

"Simple, but effective," Red had remarked, unwittingly mimicking Erik's actions of a few hours before by touching a finger to the center of one of the Bs. He rubbed the stickiness against his thumb. "Fresh. Can't say for sure how long ago, especially because it's damp tonight. But I'd guess not more than an hour or two. How long you been gone?"

I had checked my watch, surprised to find it only a little past ten thirty. The day had somehow taken on the feel of an endless loop of trouble and anxiety, from the early morning boat ride and the professor's revelations, to my father's tirades and the reappearance of Harry Simon, to the deer and the return of the midnight scribbler.

Déjà vu all over again, as Yogi used to say.

"Since five or so." I had answered Red's question, then suggested we adjourn inside. I'd felt somehow strangely vulnerable standing out there in the driveway, like a target in a brightly lit shooting gallery at a carnival sideshow.

"So what have you stuck your nose into this time?" Red asked when we'd all finished our individual drink rituals. Erik and I exchanged a look which no doubt spoke volumes to my brother-in-law. "Spill it, Tanner. Stop trying to figure out how you can fudge or manipulate or manage to tell me just enough to get me off your back for a while." He held up a hand at my grunt of protest. "Save it! For once just give me the truth, the whole truth, and nothing but the truth the first time out and spare us all a lot of grief in the long run. It's been a hell of a day, and I'm not in the mood to play your games."

It was perhaps as long and as harsh a dressing-down as I'd ever gotten from Red, and I had a sneaking suspicion it had something to do with his having an audience in the person of Erik Whiteside. Although Red was well aware of my business relationship with the handsome young computer expert, I also hadn't imagined the look of distaste that flitted across his face when Erik trotted down the hallway to "his room" to leave his jacket and use the john.

"Thanks for stopping by, Officer," I said, rising from the table with such force I nearly toppled my own chair. "If I could have a copy of the report for my insurance company, I'd be grateful."

"Knock it off, Bay." Red's voice now held more resignation than anger.

"Go to hell," I snapped, not the least bit mollified by his change of tone. "It wasn't my idea to drag you into this, and I sure as hell don't need you waltzing in here and reprimanding me as if I were some naughty child. God, you sound just like my father!"

I dumped the remains of my tea into the sink, banging the mug against the stainless steel side.

"Maybe it would be a good idea to have Red's input on our other . . . problem," Erik ventured in the kind of voice usually reserved for skittish horses or snarling dogs.

"Bad idea, in my obviously flawed judgment. But you spill your guts if you want to. I'm going to bed."

I stomped down the steps into the great room, took the length of the hallway in three angry strides, and slammed my bedroom door behind me.

THOUGH I didn't expect to, I fell asleep fairly soon after stepping from a long, hot shower and arose Sunday morning feeling a little ashamed at my outburst of the night before. I brushed my teeth and threw on a pair of shorts and a T-shirt before padding barefoot into the hall. Erik's door was still closed, and a glissando of snores worked its way up and down the scale as I passed.

I had no idea what time the party had broken up, but the boys had at least cleaned up the kitchen. I made tea, slid my feet into the beaten-up pair of Birkenstock sandals I kept by the door, and carried the mug with me down the steps and outside. The wind off the ocean smelled clean and sweet as I moved around to the driveway and stood contemplating last night's message.

What in the hell is this all about? I asked myself. I had no clue as to what actions or words of mine might have prompted someone to take such extreme measures to chastise me, nor did any names suggest themselves while I stood lost in thought in the cool, bright morning.

Obviously there was no way I could dismiss this second

attack as a mistake, unless the perpetrator was incredibly stupid. I suppose he could have gotten the wrong house twice in a row, but something now told me the accusation was in fact meant for me. I wandered over to the yard and slid down next to the base of one of the massive live oaks which guarded my property from the curious eyes of random beach walkers and my widely scattered neighbors. I settled onto the soft bed of pine straw, my back supported by the trunk of a tree which had probably sprouted when only Indians and wild pigs roamed the island. As much as I loved my home on the ocean, I tried never to forget what price had been paid in the loss of trees, plants, and habitat for the deer and other creatures in order to grant me the peace and pleasure I always found here.

The thoughts took me back to my conversation with Araminda Albright. It astounded me when I realized it had been only one week ago that I had sat in her home on another stretch of beach and listened to her halting tale of the death of Gray Palmer and her fears for her own life. I tried to pinpoint exactly what part of her story had triggered this connection in my memory. I let my eyes drift closed as I sipped my cooling tea and tried to let my mind float back to that afternoon. Overhead a jay squawked, and a mockingbird took up the cry . . .

We had been discussing the foundation Gray's father ran in addition to his shipping empire. Araminda was telling me that she and Gray spent their time exploring uninhabited islands up and down the Atlantic coast, from the Carolinas to Florida, studying the old cultures and the habitats of animals and their migration from the mainland, how . . .

"I hope you didn't spend the night out here." Erik's voice sent tea sloshing out of the cup and across my hand. "Sorry! You okay?"

I shook the tepid drops from my fingers and squinted up at him. "Yes, I'm fine. It's pretty much cooled off. But try to avoid scaring the . . . scaring me like that, okay? I'm getting way too old to have to keep restarting my heart on any regular basis."

"Sorry," he repeated and extended his hand. I allowed him to help me up. "Get any more ideas about who might have done it?"

For a moment I didn't follow his thread then I realized he was talking about the graffiti on the garage door. "No, not really. Actually I was thinking about something else entirely. You up for a walk?"

His bare feet and long, muscular legs were topped by a pair of gray athletic shorts and a ratty Carolina Panthers T-shirt. He carried a mug of what smelled like really strong coffee.

"I haven't showered yet," he said, his free hand trying to tame a stubborn cowlick that stood up on the back of his head.

"I can stand it if you can," I said, and he shrugged in what I took to be acquiescence.

I turned and headed around the side of the house, pausing to set my cup on the steps up to the deck as we passed. I took the boardwalk over the dune and in minutes stepped out onto the wide, deserted beach. Sandpipers scurried frantically across the packed sand, alternately chasing and fleeing the rhythmic ebb and flow of the tide. I turned away from the Westin Hotel, its pristine whiteness visible in the soft morning glow off to my right, a cluster of early rising tourists milling around in the surf in front of the beachside pool. We walked in silence at first, Erik matching my long stride with ease.

"So how did it go with Red last night?" I finally asked without looking at him.

"Fine. He got a call not long after you . . . left us and had to take off." When I didn't comment, he continued, "He said to tell you there wasn't much he could do about your midnight prowler. He said you should spend some time thinking about who you might have pissed off recently. Should be a fairly short list this time, since you've only been back in town for a couple of weeks." Erik raised his hands in a protestation of innocence. "His words, not mine." I could tell he was struggling to control a bubble of laughter.

"I'm thrilled to find you two had so much in common. Like your biting wit, for example."

"Seriously," Erik went on, lowering his voice as we passed a slower moving tourist couple in hideously matching Hawaiian shirts, "Red said you shouldn't get the door repainted for a couple of days. See what happens."

"He thinks if the artist is deprived of his canvas he'll just go away? That's pretty stupid. All he'll do is get busy on the rest of the house."

I paused to watch a flock of geese holding formation in a perfect V that pointed dead north. *Heading home for the summer,* I thought.

I let several minutes go by before changing the subject. I found it difficult to break the serenity of the morning with talk of death.

"I've been thinking," I began.

"Always a good start."

"Thank you. Did you decide to run any of our current problems past my charming brother-in-law?"

"Nope. As I said, he got called out to an accident just a few minutes after you went to bed. And besides, I'd already figured you were probably right and we should wait until we had more to go on."

"Good call. As I was saying, I've been thinking about this whole thing, trying to lay it out in my mind in some sort of order, and it seems to me we may be going about this investigation all wrong."

"Enlighten me."

"Well, you said it first, yesterday I think, when we got back from Daufuskie."

"Hold that thought." Erik paused to flip the dregs of his coffee into the Atlantic then jogged back up to settle the empty mug into the sea oats waving along the top of the dune. "I'll pick it up on the way back," he said, falling again into step beside me. "Go ahead."

"Actually, it was two things. First, you wondered if Araminda was right that the two deaths were connected somehow. You know, Gray's and whoever was buried in the grave.

And then last night, you mumbled something about why was everyone except her and Gray's father so hell-bent on believing it was just a boating accident."

"Look!"

I turned toward the water, in the direction of Erik's outstretched arm. A few yards off shore, shining gray fins broke the surface of the placid ocean.

"Dolphins," I replied.

As we watched, three of the graceful water mammals cruised along beside us, like a family out for a leisurely stroll after breakfast. Rising to take air into the breathing holes in the tops of their heads, they dived again, only to reappear moments later in a rhythmic dance which held Erik transfixed.

"They're spectacular," he whispered, and I smiled.

"I guess we have a tendency to take them for granted here."

The trio rose once more, as if in farewell then headed back out to sea.

"That was worth the price of admission." Erik grinned and turned as we resumed our walk. "Sorry for the interruption. You were just about to give me credit for some brilliant, but unintentional deduction, I believe."

I knew his flip attitude was a cover for his sadness and frustration. Erik Whiteside didn't like displaying his emotions any more than I did.

"Let's say you and Mindy are right. Assume there's a connection. Now let's look at how the timeline of events plays out." I hadn't really given this much thought, contrary to what I'd told Erik. Somehow the connection between my bemoaning the loss of the habitat on Hilton Head Island and Araminda Albright's story last Sunday had fired off synapses in my brain.

"Sometime before last Friday, a week ago I mean, Gray Palmer was digging on some unnamed island between Charleston and Beaufort when he unearthed a grave. The contents led him to believe it was not an ancient site. For some unknown reason, he decided to remove a bone from the corpse and carry it away with him after doing his best to conceal the evidence of his tampering. So far so good?"

"I'm with you." Erik picked up the recitation. "So then he gets back to Charleston, shares his bizarre find with his co-worker/girlfriend, but not his father, and calls me. At the time, you asked me why, I mean, why he called *me,* and I just blew it off. And how did he know how to find me? Or that I would even be able to help him?"

"Albright said he'd heard you were 'in the business' or something like that."

"Who would know that? I mean, it's not as if we've been advertising in the paper or sending out announcements or anything."

"True. I don't know."

We had reached a long spit of land, actually a large sand-bar only exposed when the tide was at its lowest, and I paused there to settle onto the beach out of reach of the water. Erik dropped down beside me.

"Anyway," I went on, "on Friday he told Mindy he was going back to the island to have another look. But before he left on the boat, he took the time to package up the bone and ship it off to you at your home address. You're sure there was no note or any other kind of explanation in the box?"

"Positive. I literally tore the thing apart. There was only the bone and the wrappings, the canvas or whatever. And some newspapers stuffed down inside to keep it from rat-tling, I guess."

"Did you check them out?"

"The newspapers? I opened them up and spread them out, just to make sure nothing was written on them."

I stretched and pulled my legs up into a modified yoga position. "How did you know the package was from Gray?" I asked, squinting into the glare of the rising sun.

"It had his name on the shipping label. Besides, once I heard the girlfriend's story from you, I assumed it had to be Gray. I don't know too many other people who would be sending me parts of dead people by FedEx."

I ignored the sarcasm. "And you never got another call

from him? He didn't try to get in touch to tell you about the package or anything else?"

"No. He didn't leave a message anywhere—the store, the apartment, my cell. I checked them all again after I got the delivery, but there was nothing."

"Strange. But we're getting sidetracked here," I said. "I'm trying to nail down the timeline. So Gray mails the package on Friday, heads out on the boat—presumably back to the island where he found the body—and the next thing anyone knows about him is when he turns up dead Saturday morning." I glanced at Erik, but he was staring out across the expanse of the ocean. "So my conclusion is we have to start where the whole thing began. We have to locate that island and find that grave. It's the key to everything."

"Why do you say that?"

"Logic." I worked my feet up a little higher, trying for a perfect Lotus position, something I'd not yet been able to achieve. "If you accept my timeline, then there are huge gaps unaccounted for, as well as a ton of unanswered questions." I began to tick them off on my fingers. "First, the grave. He told Araminda it wasn't an archaeological site, and I think we can take his word for that. After all, it was his field. But what could he have seen to make him so sure the man had been murdered?"

Erik opened his mouth to speculate, but I cut him off. "These are just rhetorical questions for now. Hear me out. Secondly, he felt compelled to go back out there just a couple of days after he talked with you. Why? Supposedly he wanted information about who the buried guy was, but he didn't wait for you to get that for him. Hell, he didn't even wait long enough for you to get the package before he went tearing off in his boat."

"Okay, I'm with you," Erik said, and I took more than a little pride in the admiration I heard in his voice. "Wait, though," he added. "Here's another thing."

"What?"

"You just said archaeology was his field. He'd probably already drawn some conclusions on his own. Why did he send it to me? Why didn't he just track down someone like Dr. Douglass in the first place?"

"Maybe you're right, and he already knew all the things Douglass told us. About it being a black male and all that. Didn't he say he wanted to find out how to hack into some databases?"

"Then why did he send me the bone? I had no need for it."

"I don't know. But if he got scared, spooked by something or someone, he might have just wanted it out of his possession. Which leads me to the next question. Who else did he tell about his discovery?"

"His girlfriend said he didn't tell anyone, except her. And me."

"That doesn't make sense. If we're operating on the assumption Gray was murdered because he stumbled onto this grave, then someone else had to find out about it between whenever he unearthed the thing and Saturday morning when he turned up dead." I paused as another thought struck me. They seemed to be coming faster than I could give them voice. "What day did he call you?"

Erik didn't reply for a moment, then said, "I think it must have been Tuesday. What day did you get home from Paris?"

"Wednesday."

"Okay, then it was Tuesday. I was going to contact the Judge about what I should do about Gray's call, but then I got your e-mail, so I decided to wait until I could talk to you."

"Good! Now we're getting somewhere. I wish to hell I had some paper to take notes on. Anyway, so sometime between Tuesday and Friday, something—or someone—made Gray so nervous he decided to ship you the bone and take off for the gravesite. We have to find out who that is. And I still think we won't have a clue how to go about finding the person until we find the grave and discover whatever it is that made Gray somebody's target. Assuming they don't find anything in the autopsy that would render the whole thing pointless. See anything wrong with the logic?"

Erik whistled. "No, I think you've absolutely nailed it. God, you're really good at this."

"Thanks," I said, again glowing under his praise. "Comes from all those years of working with numbers. You can't get much more logical than numbers."

"But I think you might have left out a couple of things that could be crucial to finding the place."

"Like what?"

"Like all those people who are claiming Gray Senior's reward. If one of them did in fact see Gray alive on his boat on Saturday morning, then that should help us concentrate the search for where he was coming from. Or at least give us a good chance at narrowing down the field."

"Good point. There are lots of little hummocks and islets out there. It could take weeks to investigate them all, and I don't think we'd have a prayer in hell of keeping our interest under wraps."

"Which would be a good idea if we don't want to end up dangling from the end of a rope underneath a boat somewhere."

I shook off the fear his suggestion engendered. If we were going to become legitimate investigators, I had to learn to deal with danger.

"So how do you suggest we proceed?"

I rose as I spoke, and Erik joined me. "I think we need to track down those couple of people from Mr. Palmer's list we haven't talked to yet, then maybe re-interview the others and get a fix on just where they claim to have seen Gray's boat. Do you have access to a marine map or whatever you call it? We could do like they do on TV and put markers in all the spots where he was supposedly seen. Maybe we can triangulate from there and pinpoint the spot."

"Great idea. And your mother probably thinks you wasted all those hours glued to the tube." He laughed and stretched his tanned arms over his head. "And then I think we have one more task that will help us get off dead center on this investigation," I added.

"What's that?"

"I think we need to have another talk with Miss Araminda Albright. I have a feeling she didn't give me the whole story the last time we met. She never really explained to me why she thinks her own life might be in danger, or why she's so willing to accept the idea of murder. Maybe she can help us fill in those missing gaps."

"If she's as gorgeous as you described her, I'd like to volunteer for that duty."

"I'd watch myself if I were you. Mercer Mary Prescott has demonstrated she's not a woman to be trifled with."

I meant it as a joke, but some of the light went out of Erik's eyes. I opened my mouth to ask about the reasons for his traveling alone this time, but he cut me off.

"Care to work some of these kinks out? Let's jog a ways to get loosened up then I'll challenge you to a race back to your place."

"You're dead meat," I called, but he had already set off in an easy lope, and I had to break into a trot to catch up with him. By the time we had moved past a number of other runners getting in their morning exercise, the moment to pursue his relationship had passed, and a short while later all my concentration was centered on leaving him in the dust on our mad sprint for home.

CHAPTER
TWENTY-ONE

Cynthia Sellers was almost a neighbor, if you calculated it as the crow flies, but it took us close to ten minutes of twisting and turning through the streets of Port Royal Plantation before I finally pulled the T-Bird up in front of her two-story home. Obviously one of the older sections of the sprawling development, most of the houses along the narrow lane had been built of natural wood which had weathered to a mellow patina in the salt and humidity of the winds off the ocean. We pulled into the semicircular curve of driveway and stopped behind a gleaming red Miata convertible.

After showering and wolfing down a quick breakfast, Erik and I had decided to spend the day trying to hook up with the few reward claimants we felt might be at least marginally legitimate. We had an appointment for later in the morning with Delbert Pidgen, the weekend father, at his condo in Shelter Cove. While we didn't expect to get much more information from him about the actual sighting, we did hope to be able to use his knowledge of the local waters to pinpoint the exact location. We didn't have an official chart yet, but I had managed to unearth a map of Beaufort which showed many of the outlying islands and waterways in some detail. It was at least a place to start.

"Looks like she's home," Erik remarked as I cut the engine.

We'd been unsuccessful once again in getting Cynthia Sellers to answer her phone that morning.

"Unless she has a husband. Or a roommate," I replied, sliding out of the bucket seat. "You want to take the lead?"

Erik shrugged. "Sure. You think my boyish charm will work on the ladies better than your more direct approach?"

"Something like that," I said, smiling. "Remember, we're here as representatives of Gray Palmer. Don't mention anything about our being investigators."

"I wouldn't have the nerve."

We climbed the front steps to a wide porch devoid of plants or chairs or any other concession to decoration, and I rang the bell next to the open screen door. Peeking inside, I looked past a short entryway directly into the living room. A little to the right, a staircase rose to a small landing, disappearing quickly in a sharp left angle toward the second story. The carpet appeared to be a soft blue, faded a little, and I could just discern the delicately curved legs of a table when my vision was cut off by the sudden appearance of a presence blocking the doorway. I hadn't heard anyone approach.

"I don't mean to be rude," a woman's voice said as I stepped back away from the door, "but I've asked you people not to bother me, especially on a Sunday morning."

"I beg your pardon, but . . ." I began, but got cut off immediately.

"I'm perfectly willing to allow you the right to your religious views. Please grant me the same privilege."

Erik caught on to it a split-second before I did. "I'm Erik Whiteside and this is Bay Tanner. We're not Jehovah's Witnesses, ma'am," he said softly, reliability and trustworthiness almost oozing from his pores. "And we did try to call first. I'm sorry if we startled you."

Cynthia Sellers paused in the act of pushing the inside door closed. I took another step backward, and her face and form came more into focus. Relatively small, perhaps five-feet four or five, her blond hair was pulled up into a ponytail tied jauntily with a bright red ribbon. Compact and well-muscled, she looked to be the kind of woman who works hard at keeping in shape. Or has the kind of job that does it for her. In a white tank top and light blue denim shorts, she could have been anywhere from thirty to fifty. I needed to see her eyes more clearly to make that judgment.

"We represent Gray Palmer of Palmer Shipping," I said before she could change her mind again and swing the door shut. "You contacted him about a reward?"

"Why didn't you say so? Come in."

She stepped out of the way, and we filed into the small entry. Without a word, our hostess turned to her right and led us through an elegantly furnished dining room and pristine kitchen, then out a set of French doors onto a spacious screened porch.

"Sit." It sounded more like a command to a pair of ill-behaved dogs than an invitation to guests.

"Thank you." Erik dropped into one of a pair of cushioned, wicker chairs, and I settled myself on the matching loveseat. Cynthia Sellers took what looked to be her usual seat in a rocker drawn up beside a round table littered with magazines, books, and a tall, sweating glass of an amber-colored liquid I took to be iced tea.

"So you've come about the reward. I said in my message I wasn't interested in that. Just trying to help. So what do you want?"

Erik and I exchanged a look, and I nodded slightly. "We have a few questions, a few points we'd like to clarify," he began, correctly interpreting my intention. I could already see how our hostess relaxed when Erik held her attention.

"So you work for him? For Mr. Palmer?" She leaned over her tanned legs, crossed at the knees, to expose a nicely rounded cleavage above the edge of her tank top. The move looked far too practiced to have been accidental.

"Yes. He's asked us to follow up on the leads he received after his news conference. We did try to call, as I said before, but we never got an answer."

"Caller ID. If I don't recognize the number, I don't pick up the phone. Usually the answering machine gets it. Damned thing must be on the fritz again."

"Of course I understand. A young woman living alone can't be too careful."

Cynthia leaned over a little farther, displaying a few more of her charms, and I knew Erik had her.

"Ask me anything you like. I really don't know much more than I told them on the phone, but I'm more than willing . . ." Like the lean, I didn't think the pause had been unintentional. ". . . to help you. And Mr. Palmer, too, of course."

I had been looking out over the backyard, enclosed in a fence which matched the siding on the house and ringed with bright pink, red, and orange blooms when inspiration struck. "May I see your roses?" I interrupted Erik's reply without a qualm. "I believe you have some unusual varieties." I answered her quizzical look with an enthusiasm entirely false but apparently convincing. "I'm something of a rose gardener myself."

"By all means," Cynthia answered, her face puzzled. "Help yourself."

"Thank you. I won't be a moment."

I let myself out the narrow screen door, down two steps, and out into the yard. I actually didn't give two damns about flowers, except to admire their beauty from afar. It had been my late mother who owned the passion for exotic rosebushes and who could rattle off the names of hundreds of hybrids just by sight and smell. I knew, however, that whatever information we would be able to wrench from the reluctant Ms. Sellers would best be extracted by my charming partner—on his own, without any other female around to cramp the lady's style.

I made two complete rounds of the small area, bending and sniffing and examining each bud or bloom with what I hoped looked like genuine fascination. I needn't have bothered with the charade. Every time I glanced back up toward the screened-in porch area, Cynthia Sellers had my partner locked in her gaze. I could have dug up the damned bushes and carted them off, and she'd never have noticed.

I was just beginning to get seriously annoyed when I heard Erik call my name. As I approached them, Cynthia laid her hand on Erik's forearm and tilted her head to one side in a way I was certain she thought provocative.

"You'll call me?" I heard her ask in a little-girl-lost voice so phony I was surprised my partner could keep a straight face. "With any news? I'm so concerned about poor Mr. Palmer. All this must be just dreadful for him."

"We'll certainly be in touch if we need any additional information." Erik gently disengaged himself as I pulled open the screen door.

"Are you sure I can't offer you a drink? Or lunch?"

He shot me a look of helplessness, and I had to choke back a laugh. If Erik was going to be an active participant in Simpson & Tanner, Inquiry Agents, I was going to have to sign him up for Extricating from Predatory Females 101.

"We really do have to run, or we'll be late for our next appointment. But thanks so much." I didn't pause, but kept right on walking into the kitchen and through to the entryway. They had no choice but to follow. "Thanks again, Ms. Sellers," I said as I marched through the front door and down the steps while Erik turned to shake hands.

"Yes, thanks, Ms. . . ."

"Cynthia, remember?" She interrupted him with a dazzling smile and that restraining hand again on his arm.

"Cynthia," he mumbled, pulling away and all but sprinting to the passenger door of the T-Bird. "Thanks again."

"Bye-bye," she chirped.

The red-painted nails on the ends of her blunt fingers were still wiggling in the breeze as we eased out of her driveway.

I WAITED until we were well away from the Sellers house before allowing the shout of laughter to burst from my lips.

"What?" Erik demanded, his expression so perplexed it sent me off into another fit of giggles.

"I half expected to come back up on the porch to find she had you down on the floor, trussed and tied up like a calf in a roping contest. You do have a way with the ladies, partner, I'll certainly give you that."

"Okay, wise guy, let's see how you make out with ol' Delbert," he retorted, his natural good humor once again rising to the fore. "And don't expect me to bail you out if the guy decides he wants to grab you by the hair and drag you off to his harem."

"You mean you wouldn't defend my honor? Hell, I was ready to go toe-to-toe with Ms. Sellers back there. I would have taken her on to protect your virtue."

"Who said I wanted to be protected?" he retorted.

"The look of absolute and total panic on your face was a clue."

We rode a ways in silence, both of us enjoying the soft breeze and gentle sun. The traffic on Route 278 was sparse, not surprising for a late Sunday morning, and we pulled into the parking lot in front of the Anchorage at Shelter Cove barely ten minutes after leaving Port Royal Plantation.

"So what did you find out?" I asked, turning in my seat to face Erik. "You did take notes I trust?"

"Of course." He slipped the narrow pad from the breast pocket of his pullover and flipped back a couple of pages. "Well, nothing really more than what she said in the message she left. She's quite an accomplished sailor, you know. One of the few, men or women, who can actually parallel park her boat at the dock without any help."

"I'm impressed all to hell," I replied. As a confirmed landlubber, I hadn't the foggiest notion what that meant, except it probably sounded good when she was on the prowl for men. Some might be intimidated by the feisty Cynthia Sellers, but a lot would no doubt find her nautical proficiency attractive. No accounting for taste.

"She said she recognized the kind of boat those guys were in." He consulted his notebook. "A Grady White. About twenty-four feet. And she did give me a more precise idea of the location of her sighting." He had apparently decided to ignore my sarcasm. "I wrote down everything she told me, although I have to admit it doesn't mean anything to me. Maybe when we get that map up and working it will start to come together."

"So you stuck your head in the lion's mouth for nothing." I checked my watch, then pulled my bag from the floor of the car and slid out. "Let's go find Mr. Delbert Pidgen and see if he's any more help."

"Wait. There is something else."

I stopped and leaned over the door. "What?"

"Cynthia said she thought the men she saw arguing with Gray might have been in uniform."

"Uniform? As in what?" The suggestion by one of the callers that Gray had been killed by a paramilitary group popped into my head.

"She didn't know. She thought it was more like camouflage, you know, the kind of T-shirts and pants kids like to wear to be cool."

"Doesn't sound like the sort of thing you'd put on to go fishing, though, does it? Isn't that used more for hunting?"

Erik tucked the notepad back in his pocket. "Maybe. But then what I don't know about either one would fill an encyclopedia. It could mean nothing."

I shrugged and slung my bag over my shoulder. "Come on. Let's go see if we can pump anything useful out of our next reward-seeker."

FOLLOWING THE directions we found tacked to the door of his apartment, we located him, along with his sons, cleaning fish on the pier that ran alongside the swanky Harbourmaster restaurant. Mid-thirties, the beginnings of a serious paunch just inching over the waistband of his stained khaki shorts, Delbert Pidgen proved to be the soul of cooperation. He answered our questions in a straightforward manner.

We retreated to one of the benches bolted to the concrete pier zigzagging its way along the harbor. The adjoining docks were lined with small pleasure craft as well as several large yachts and a couple of dolphin-sighting excursion boats. Behind us the condominiums of Shelter Cove rose in long stretches of glass made opaque by the relentless reflection of the sun off the water. The ones on the third story no doubt provided a spectacular view across the Disney timeshare complex and straight out to Broad Creek.

Thankfully Delbert Pidgen didn't offer to shake hands,

and he apologized several times for the smell clinging to his clothes and person. "We just got back from fishing," he explained, "and the boys wanted to cook these up for lunch so we had to get them gutted and filleted. I need to have them back to their mother by six." At my quizzical look he added, "The boys, not the fish."

This time I pumped, and Erik made himself scarce, with about the same results. No actual coordinates, but we did get a clearer picture of exactly where the *Arky Olly Jist* had been when Delbert and his sons passed by. At one point he called to the older boy who verified his father's recollection that it had been just around seven thirty A.M.

"If you had a chart, I could show you," Delbert Pidgen offered.

I rooted around in my bag and came up with the Beaufort County map I'd pulled from a drawer in my kitchen just before we'd set out. "Will this be of any help?" I unfolded it and spread it across my lap.

Delbert studied it for a moment then flipped it over. "Ah, this'll work."

The reverse side had a detailed outline of the city of Beaufort itself as well as its immediate environs, including the larger outlying islands. He paused, running his finger along what I thought was an imaginary line from the downtown docks, up between the western edge of Lady's Island and the U.S. Marine Corps Air Station on Chisolm Island, and out into the Coosaw River. On closer inspection, aided by my having perched my reading glasses on the end of my nose, I saw that in fact the route was marked by a faint, dotted red line.

"What's that?" I asked, pointing to the dots.

"Intracoastal Waterway," Delbert replied promptly. "Runs all the way up the East Coast. You can start in Florida and go pretty much up to Maine if you follow this route."

"And this is where you saw the Palmer boat?"

"No," he said, "not exactly. Farther out into St. Helena Sound. Not too far off Monkey Island."

"Monkey Island?" I watched his finger where it tapped

against the pale blue color indicating waterways on the map. "I don't see that."

"Oh, sorry. That's what the locals call Judas Island. Right here."

Something tickled at the back of my memory, an article in the paper, or a conversation with someone, but I couldn't pull it up. "Why do they call it Monkey Island?" I asked.

Erik, who had been chatting with the boys as they split the bellies of the unfortunate fish and tossed their gleaming insides into a bucket at their feet, wandered back at that point and stood gazing down at the map. "I read about that not too long ago," he said. "Isn't that the place where they raise the rhesus macaques for research?"

"Right," Delbert Pidgen said, squinting up into the sun to nod at Erik. "Get them from Indonesia or the Philippines, or somewhere like that, and breed them over here for government labs, the CDC in Atlanta, places like that. Big scandal about it a couple of years back as I recall, but I don't remember exactly what."

The whole story sounded vaguely familiar, but I couldn't have said why. Since Rob and I had divided our time between work in Charleston and weekends on Hilton Head, I had gotten woefully out of touch with a lot of the local gossip and goings-on in Beaufort during those years. You could bet my father would have all the gory details, though, I thought.

"Good fishing spot?" Erik asked.

"Probably, but you can't get anywhere near the island itself. All kinds of warning signs about givin' it a wide berth. No one's allowed to set foot on the place except the people who feed the monkeys."

"Why not? Are they afraid of disease or something?" I asked.

"Maybe, I'm not sure. Main reason, I guess, is the monkeys roam free. Don't keep 'em in cages or anything. I guess it makes it easier for them to breed. Hey, you kids about done over there?" Delbert called to his sons.

"Yeah, Dad, last one," the older boy replied.

"So do you think I have a chance of collecting any of this reward?" the father asked, turning back to me.

I liked the honesty of his question. Unlike Cynthia Sellers, he had no qualms about claiming his interest in the money. "I really can't say," I answered, just as honestly. "All we're doing is gathering information for Mr. Palmer. The final decision will be up to him."

"Understood. But what with alimony and child support and keeping two households going . . ." He let the thought trail off as the boys, both lean and tanned and impossibly good-looking, sidled up, one carrying the shiny silver filets on the lid of a plastic cooler. "All done?" their father asked, then added, "Good job. Take them on up to the condo, and I'll be right there."

They nodded and scampered off.

"Nice kids," I said, and their father smiled.

"Thanks. They're the primary reason I'm even getting involved in this thing, you know? By the time they're ready for college, it's going to cost the damn national debt to get them through."

I rose and refolded the map. "I certainly understand. Thanks for your help, Mr. Pidgen. Someone from Mr. Palmer's office will be in touch."

"I hope so," he said, favoring us again with his open smile. "The little one thinks he wants to go to med school."

We left him dealing with the bucket of fish guts his boys had left behind and made our way back to the car.

"What do you think?" Erik asked as we slid into the T-Bird.

"I hope to hell he's the one who ends up with the money," I said. I backed the car around and headed out toward 278. "And I think I'd like to know a little more about this Monkey Island."

"Why?"

"Because it sounds like just the kind of place that might have proved irresistible to your friend Gray Palmer."

CHAPTER
TWENTY-TWO

I managed to convince Erik to stick around for a couple more days by the simple act of saying I needed him. I'd been prepared for an argument, the usual one about his having to get back to the store in Charlotte because he couldn't trust anyone to keep things going in his absence. But, after a long talk with his assistant, a conversation which was punctuated by about a dozen admonitions for her to call if she ran into any trouble, he finally agreed to stay.

I defrosted a couple of T-bones and fired up the gas grill in celebration of my victory, and we ate dinner at the round table in the screened-in area of the deck. Though we were protected from the annual invasion of mosquitoes and no-see-ums, I lit a few citronella candles for ambiance. As we licked the last of the double-chocolate almond fudge ice cream from our dessert spoons, I thought how nice it was to have someone to cook for.

"So did you find anything interesting on the 'net?" I asked, stacking the ice cream bowls on the pile of dirty plates and silverware at the edge of the table. I'd made tea in the electric coffeepot and plugged it in outside. I poured for myself, though Erik held up his hand.

"None for me, thanks."

"Shall I make you some coffee? Won't take a moment."

"No, I'm fine. To answer your question, I found lots of interesting stuff, although I don't know how much use it's going to be to us. Do you know why the place was originally named Judas Island?"

"Something to do with the slave trade if memory serves."

"Right. I found this article about it. Seems some enterprising sea captains convinced runaway slaves they'd help them escape to the North. This was in about 1850 or so, right after the Fugitive Slave Act was passed."

"I remember now. Didn't they lure the poor slaves to the island, then actually take them farther south and resell them?"

Erik nodded. "Alabama and Mississippi mostly."

"Bastards. They finally got caught and hanged, right?"

"Actually it was the local planters who meted out the justice. It never got to a trial."

"Well, that's one lynching I find it hard to object to." I stirred sweetener into my tea and settled more comfortably into my chair. "So I take it you don't share my theory."

"That Gray might have found the body on Judas Island? I don't necessarily disagree, but I don't see any proof. And from the other stuff I found on-line, we're going to need a dispensation from the Pope to gain access to that place. There's no way we could do it in secret."

"If our assumptions are correct, Gray managed it."

Erik's cocked eyebrow brought me back to the crux of our problem.

"And he got killed. I hear you." I blew across the top of my teacup before saying, "But we don't know that his death came from his just being on the island. Our working hypothesis is that it was what—or who—was in the grave that got him in trouble."

"Maybe they're related," Erik offered.

"What, the grave and the island, or the grave and the monkeys?"

In the extended twilight afforded us by the recent onset of Daylight Savings Time, I saw him shrug. "I don't know. Insufficient data, as we say in the computer biz."

"Well at least tell me what you found out on-line, and I'll fill you in on what the Judge had to contribute." I knew my

father would be a fount of information on whatever local political scandal there might have been, and he proved me
right.

"I ran across several articles, most of them from the local
newspapers. There were a couple, too, from some animal
rights groups who want to see the whole thing shut down.
From what I can gather, they're the reason for all the mystery and security around the place. The people who run the
facility are paranoid about PETA and something called
the IPPO organizing protests. Considering what they do out
there, I don't blame either side."

"I'm familiar with People for the Ethical Treatment of
Animals, but what's the other acronym stand for?" I asked.

"International Primate Protection Organization. Seems
they were involved with a lawsuit a few years back because
the company that runs the facility was importing pregnant
monkeys caught in the wild in Indonesia. Apparently that's a
no-no."

I poured myself another cup of tea. Outside, the night
creatures had begun to slip from their daytime hiding places
as evidenced by the increased rustling among the sharp-
edged leaves of the palmettos and the occasional screech of
an owl.

"According to the Judge," I said, "that was the cause of
the scandal Delbert Pidgen referred to this afternoon. Seems
one of our local politicos was also an officer of the company
which operates the facility. He and some others got sued.
My father said most of them resigned. He also said this thing
with raising the monkeys has been going on for more than
twenty years, and he can't see any reason why Gray's being
in the area should have had anything to do with his death.
Lots of folks like to take their boats out there and try to spot
the monkeys. Some have even gotten in close enough to toss
them potato chips. Feeders come out every day to leave
them food, so they're pretty used to humans."

Erik stretched and recrossed his long legs. "And eventually someone has to go out there and catch them, right? I
mean, the whole point of the exercise is to sell them to re-

search labs and make a buck. Did you know they get about five thousand dollars a head?"

I whistled. "That much? How many are there at any one time?"

"One article I found said about three thousand. You know, I'm not much of a joiner, but I think I could work up some enthusiasm for hooking up with whatever organizations are trying to put a stop to this."

"I don't like the idea of using animals for research, especially ones who exhibit a high degree of intelligence, like monkeys and dolphins, any more than you do. But let's face it: most of the strides in curing some pretty hideous diseases have resulted from animal research."

"I know." Erik leaned in toward the table, his earnest conviction evident in his wide brown eyes. "But, it doesn't seem right to let animals breed, create offspring, and then take them away to be infected with Parkinson's or cancer or AIDS. Intellectually I understand the necessity of it, but it bothers me. Here." He touched his chest in the general vicinity of his heart.

"You'll get no argument from me. I hate cruelty to animals as much as the next guy. But that's a philosophical discussion we're not likely to resolve tonight. I'm more interested in what—if anything—this has to do with Gray Palmer's death. The Judge said the Department of Natural Resources just bought a portion of the island and agreed to allow the monkey facility to keep operating. There's even talk about opening up part of the land for public use. He seemed to think that pretty much ruled out any connection, although I'm not sure I'm buying it."

"I'm inclined to agree with him." He forestalled my interruption with a raised hand. "But I'm not entirely convinced you're wrong, either. There's still the little matter of the grave. If we assume Monkey Island is where Gray stumbled across the skeleton, then we still have no idea who it was or why he was buried out there. It could have something to do with the breeding operation. We just don't know."

"Insufficient data."

"Exactly," he answered.

"I think we need to hit the road," I said, rising.

"Now? Where?" Erik stood as well.

"No, not now. Tomorrow. We need to get over to that island and check it out for ourselves."

Erik slid the door open with his foot as we both balanced dirty dishes and glasses. In the kitchen, he scraped while I stacked the dishwasher.

"And just how do you propose we do that?" he asked, resuming our interrupted conversation. "It's supposedly off-limits, isn't it?"

"Not if you know the right people," I replied. I wiped my hands on the dish towel and mopped up a few water spots from the granite counter. "I've got the name of someone who can get us in close. I swear, sometimes it amazes even me how many connections my father has. I have to give the guy a call and set it up. I think it should be tomorrow, as long as you're here, if I can work it out. And the weather cooperates."

Erik pulled a beer from the refrigerator and settled himself at the kitchen table in the alcove. "I think you're jumping the gun," he said after a few moments' hesitation.

"Why?" I leaned against the cabinets, my arms crossed over my chest in what even I recognized as a defensive position.

"Don't get your back up, partner. I'm not saying you're wrong. I'm just advising caution." The smile took any sting from his words. "You know how you bean-counters can be, running off half-cocked, doing crazy, impulsive things."

"Yeah, right. Look, I don't say we storm the island and begin hunting for disturbed graves. I just think it would be a good opportunity to check the place out, see what kind of security they have, how difficult it would really be to land a boat there undetected. The map did pretty strongly suggest Judas Island could be where Gray found the skeleton."

When we returned from Shelter Cove, Erik and I had spread out the map of Beaufort and marked as best we could the three spots we knew about: the sightings by Cynthia Sellers and Delbert Pidgen, and the approximate final location of the boat off Edisto Beach where it was found by the Coast Guard. I had used a ruler to connect the three small dots then extended the line back through St. Helena Sound toward Beaufort. Judas, alias Monkey Island, was directly in the path of that line. It had also amazed me how close it was to Presqu'isle at the tip of St. Helena.

"'Could be' are the operative words here." Again Erik checked my attempted interruption with his hand. "I know you think that little exercise in map-plotting proved something, but I don't believe we know enough about what we're doing to jump to that big a conclusion. There are lots of other little islands out there. It could just as easily be one of those."

"It could also be in the middle of Waterfront Park in downtown Beaufort, but I'd bet it's not."

I turned my back and busied myself with pouring out a large glass of Diet Coke over a lot of ice and tried to analyze why Erik's sudden opposition was pushing all my buttons. Maybe I had gotten way too used to the idea he was just a minor player in this new enterprise, someone I could use to track down information when I needed him to and then fade away into the woodwork when I didn't. It wasn't a very pleasant discovery about myself, but I had a sneaking suspicion it might be true. After all, in my initial planning, in drawing up the contracts, and even in designing the company logo, the name *Whiteside* hadn't appeared anywhere.

Maybe I had gotten too damned used to running the show.

I turned back to him with a genuine smile. "You could be right. Let's sleep on that and talk about it again tomorrow. We can arrange the trip almost anytime, at least according to the Judge. And we need to get back up to Charleston, as well. I still think we need to talk to Araminda Albright again in person. Maybe you can work your Cynthia Sellers number on her and get her to tell us the whole truth."

His answering grin made me feel a lot better. "Don't you think it's time we met up with Gray's father, too? After all, we do have some concrete information to share with him about the reward, so requesting a meeting would be perfectly legitimate. I'd like to get a handle on the guy, see if I can figure out why Gray hated him so much."

"Did you manage to get a line on the other caller you were trying to track down?" I asked.

The report of a paramilitary group's being after Gray had seemed far-fetched to me until Ms. Sellers's revelation that the men she had seen arguing with him might have been wearing camouflage.

"No luck. The number is for a cell phone, and none of my directories can cross-reference an address to that. I left him another message. I guess we'll just have to wait and see if he calls us back."

"Do we know for certain it's a man?"

"Well, no, I guess we don't. My assumption. I'd still like to talk to whoever it is."

We compromised on a plan to make appointments with both Araminda and Gray's father, hopefully for Tuesday. We'd spend Monday in Beaufort, perhaps hooking up with the guy who could take us out to Monkey Island, then head on up to Charleston the next day. We could spend the night at Presqu'isle. I headed for the office to make the calls.

"I'm going to take a quick walk up the beach," Erik said, dumping his empty beer bottle in the wastebasket. "Got a flashlight I can use?"

I cast him a quizzical look. "At this time of night? There's not much of a moon. You won't be able to see your hand in front of your face."

He shrugged. "I know. That's kind of the lure of it. Living in the middle of all the city lights you don't get much of a chance to see the stars. Or the ocean. Besides, in the heat of our mad race up the beach this morning . . ."

"Which I won, if you recall."

"Only because I'm such a gentleman," he shot back.

"Right."

"Anyway, I left your coffee mug sitting out there on the dune." He managed to look sheepish and about four years old.

"For heaven's sake don't worry about it. I've got tons of

them. Besides, the tide's probably taken it halfway to Africa by now."

"I'd still like to take that walk. And if I find the mug, I'll sleep better."

"Suit yourself," I said. "Flashlight's in the left-hand drawer under the desk."

I had already given him the security code as well as a key so he could come and go as he pleased. "Just make sure you set the alarm and lock up when you come back in. Have fun."

"I won't be gone that long," he said, heading for the French doors, the ancient Eveready in his hand.

But nearly two hours later, Erik had still not returned. I had made arrangements with Gray Palmer, Senior, to meet him at his office and had settled on a tentative time for our boat tour around Judas Island. Araminda Albright did not answer despite the lateness of the hour, so I told her machine we'd be in the area on Tuesday and I'd touch base with her when we got to town. I left a light on in the great room, washed up, and climbed beneath the sheets. I fully expected Erik's return to waken me, but I heard nothing until the scream right underneath my window sent me rocketing from the bed.

NO ONE could say I hadn't learned my lesson.

Despite the fear that threatened to choke off my breath, already coming in short, heaving gasps, I took the time to fumble open the safe hidden in the floor of my closet, retrieve the Glock, and ram home the clip. I grabbed a pair of sweat pants and a rumpled T-shirt to cover my nakedness then eased out into the hallway.

I stood for a moment trying to quiet my thudding heart and heard muffled *whumps* up against the outside wall, followed by garbled shouting. I crept to the kitchen, snatching up the cordless phone on my way by and dialing 911. I told the operator there was a disturbance outside my house, and she promised to dispatch a unit immediately.

Satisfied that I had acted in as rational a manner as I could muster under the circumstances, I disengaged the alarm and eased open the French doors. Out on the deck I could tell immediately the ruckus was coming from the side of the house facing the ocean. With the gun held slightly in front of me I crept around in that direction. What sounded like a staged fistfight from an old western was going on just beneath me. I peered over the edge of the railing just as the dim outline of a body went racing past, down the path over the dune, and out toward the beach.

"Hey, you son of a bitch! Come back here!"

The voice belonged to Erik Whiteside. I had no idea who he might be grappling with.

"Stop! I'm armed!" I tried to sound sure and forceful, but I heard the fear quivering in my words. I probably sounded hysterical, but I thought that might actually work in my favor. I couldn't imagine too many people wanting to get tangled up with a crazy woman waving a loaded gun around. Although I had proved I could use it—and accurately— when I had to, there was no way I would fire with no clear target other than the thrashing bodies on the ground beside the deck and a dim shadow running away from me into the night.

"Stay where you are! The police are on their way!"

I sprinted for the steps and bounded down them two at a time, my bare feet stumbling a little at the bottom. By the time I righted myself, the noise had stopped. I hesitated, unsure what this sudden silence might mean. I crept forward on the scratchy pine straw, whipping my head from side to side, the gun still held in the ready position as Red had taught me. Once before someone had attacked me from behind, and I wasn't about to let that happen again. Back then I had been unarmed and a whole lot more ignorant about how criminals operate.

I stopped again as a low groaning drifted out to me on the cool night air. "Erik?" I ventured in a taut whisper, but got no response.

"Erik?" I tried again, inching forward into the blackness beneath the shadow of the house.

The sound seemed closer. Again I checked to the sides and rear. *Where the hell are the damned cops?* I wondered as I strained to distinguish the outlines of shrubs and bushes which might lie in my path.

He broke from cover right at my elbow, like a pheasant flushed by a well-trained bird dog, so close I could smell the sweat of fear drenching his dark shirt. The glancing blow sent the Glock spinning from my hand and knocked me sideways onto my left knee. The pain took my breath away and forced me to roll onto my side. The toe of one of his sneakers caught my right arm as he leaped over me and sprinted away into the palmettos. For a few seconds I heard him thrashing through the razor-edged plants, then he broke free, and the sounds of his escape died in the loose sand of the dune.

I remember thinking he'd be a mass of cuts. If we ever caught up to him, he wouldn't be hard to identify.

I rubbed the spot on my forearm and felt a knot beginning to rise there. I turned back onto my knees and put my hands out to lever myself to my feet. My fingers sank into a thick puddle of something wet and sticky, and I had to clamp my teeth down over the scream hovering low in my throat.

I scrambled up, took two steps in the wide pool of wetness, and stumbled over the body of Erik Whiteside.

CHAPTER
TWENTY-THREE

"Jesus, woman, take it easy!"

I nearly fainted with the relief of hearing his voice, drowned out almost immediately by the welcome commotion of slamming doors and booted feet pounding on the driveway. The slashing beam of a powerful flashlight cut through the night, and a commanding voice ordered us to stay where we were.

"I'm Bay Tanner," I called, rising slowly with both hands clearly visible out to my sides. I knew how the police operated, and I didn't want to give them any reason to see me as a danger to them. "This is my house."

Blinded by the glare, I couldn't make out who was advancing cautiously toward us, but there was no mistaking the business end of the pistol pointing directly at me.

"Stay where you are," he repeated, "hands where I can see them."

One officer approached from the side, making a wide berth around the puddle with Erik's inert form stretched out in the middle of it while the other held us in the circle of light.

"Okay," I said, "okay. But my friend is hurt. We need to get an ambulance in here."

"I don't need an ambulance." Erik rose to a sitting position and reached up to touch the side of his face.

Immediately the officer with the gun pointed at us took a

step back and yelled, "Don't move! Hands on the back of your head! Do it!"

It seemed as if I'd been in this exact position before, being threatened by the very people who were supposed to be helping me. I bit back the tide of fury which had overtaken my initial fear.

"He's not the intruder. There were two of them. They ran away over the dune and onto the beach. Quit wasting time! This man needs medical attention."

"Shut up, Bay! I don't need medical attention. Nothing's hurt but my pride."

"Sir, I want to see those hands on the back of your head, fingers locked. Now!"

"Just do it," I hissed down at Erik who glared back at me but finally complied.

The light advanced again in our direction as the officer with his gun drawn moved toward us. The other one pulled his flashlight from his belt and began playing the beam over the ground.

"Weapon here," I heard him say as the light fell on my Glock gleaming black against the pine straw.

"It's mine," I said. "One of them knocked it out of my hand when he ran into me. I have a permit."

Although that carry permit had been illegally obtained thanks to my father's connections, I didn't think that was a piece of information I really needed to share. At least not at the moment.

"Anybody got any I.D. on them?" the gun-toting deputy asked.

"I do," Erik replied promptly. "Wallet in the back pocket of my jeans."

"Okay, stand up. But slowly."

I stepped back a little to give him room to maneuver. It's tough getting to your feet from a sitting position without using your hands for leverage.

"Turn around," the officer ordered him. "Left hand down, slowly, and pull the wallet out."

Erik did as instructed, and the second deputy reached out to take it from his outstretched hand.

"Erik," I said into the silence as the two men came together to study the contents of the slim, black wallet. "If you're okay, where did all the blood come from? Did you get one of them?"

"I'd like to know the answer to that one, too, Mr. White-side." He spoke from much closer this time and had thankfully redirected the beam of the flashlight from my face to the squishy mess around us.

"It's not blood. It's paint," Erik said, sounding almost apologetic. "I came back up from the beach and caught the two of them leaving you another love letter, this time on the side of the house."

He gestured with his head toward the deck, and one of them slid a light over it. The still-dripping red *B* could be seen quite clearly against the weathered boards.

"Did you say your name was Tanner?" the first deputy asked.

I felt enormous relief his tone had retreated from powerfully commanding to something more conversational.

"Yes. Bay Tanner. My brother-in-law is Sergeant Red Tanner."

"Okay then." He lowered his gun and the tension level along with it. "You can put your hands down now," he added, almost as an afterthought, and holstered his weapon. "What happened here?"

I could feel the anger rolling off Erik, and I stepped up to nudge him gently. I had, on several occasions, given voice to my frustration with the tactics of local law enforcement and had been forced to acknowledge the futility of it. They had their methods, no doubt intended to protect them as well as innocent citizens from imminent harm. I didn't like their rules, but I understood their necessity.

So I gave them the gist of the previous two graffiti incidents, and Erik finished up with his own account of the night's adventure. In a nutshell, he had encountered two people slopping paint on the side of my house as he came up the beach path. He'd crept up on them, counting on his size and the element of surprise to corral at least one of them and wring an explanation from his prisoner before alerting me to call the police. He hated admitting to it, but they had gotten the better of him, which resulted in the fist-fight and assorted grunts and screams I'd heard from my bedroom. He felt pretty certain one of them had struck him in the side of his head with the old flashlight he'd dropped in the scuffle.

And he'd been doubly certain one of them was a girl.

AFTER THE cops left, Erik and I took turns using the outside shower I'd had installed for the purpose of washing off the salt and sand of the beach. It worked just as well for paint. When we finally located the little hoodlums who had decided to use my beautiful house for a billboard, I made a note to thank them for choosing the latex rather than the oil-based variety. I don't think I would have felt quite so magnanimous if I'd been forced to douse myself in turpentine.

Over coffee and tea, we chewed on the events of the night which was even then beginning to pass into morning.

"So you have no idea what this could be about?" Erik slouched in the chair at the kitchen table, his long legs and bare feet stretched out in front of him.

"No. Why do I have to keep answering the same damned question? Doesn't anyone believe me?"

The deputies had pounded on that theme for quite some time, but I didn't have any better answer for them than the one I'd just given Erik. I personally remained convinced it was a case of mistaken identity, but no one else seemed willing to accept that. Taking into account the bizarre things that had happened to me over the past year or so, I supposed I couldn't entirely blame them.

"I believe that's what *you* believe," he answered, "but not necessarily that it's the right explanation. Isn't there anyone you can think of with a grudge to do something like this?"

I truly couldn't and said so. The problem was, this whole thing was more an annoyance than a genuine threat. The people I had tangled with in the past had been more interested in plastering *me* all over the countryside than in just defacing my house. I seriously couldn't see any of them resorting to something so childish.

That thought struck a chord. "You said to the cops you were certain one of the two was a girl."

"Either that, or it was a guy with a really big set of boobs."

He blushed and ducked his head, and I smiled. "It's okay, Erik. I've actually heard the word 'boobs' before. But what I'm getting at is, you didn't say 'woman.' Do you think they were both kids?"

"Now that you say it, I guess I did sort of have that impression. Not that I got a look at either of them. Too damned dark. Maybe it was the voices while we were wrestling around. I don't know. It's just a feeling. Although the guy was plenty big enough. Sucker tackled me like a linebacker."

The solution hit me with the same force.

"The piece of cloth they found out there in the paint. The deputy said it looked as if it had been torn from a shirt pocket or something. What were the letters on it?"

The officers, Erik, and I had examined the small strip under the flashlight beam after one of them had picked it up out of the muck.

"It looked like a *t* and an *o* to me. That's what they thought, too. Why?"

"Could the second letter have been a *c*?"

"I suppose so. What difference does it make?"

"Nothing," I answered. "Never mind."

I found I wasn't ready to give voice to my theory, at least not right then. I felt certain I had the cause of this graffiti business figured out, but I was damned if I knew what to do about it.

BY THE time I'd fixed us some breakfast and tossed a few things into an overnight bag, Erik had pronounced himself packed up and ready to roll. I left a note for Dolores, explaining my absence and telling her to take the rest of the week off. Not that she'd probably listen to me. My house-keeper/friend had a way of smiling beneficently and nodding agreement when she had no intention of complying. I would no doubt return to find she'd cleaned all the closets or the cupboards or done up all the stored linens or taken down and rehung all the drapes. I wanted her to take it easy on her still unhealed leg, but I knew she wouldn't.

She had the Judge's number, and I added that of Erik's cell phone to the note.

The morning had broken on a high overcast, not exactly cloudy, but not the brilliant sunshine we natives of the Low-country generally take for granted except during the dreary days of late December and early January. We had decided to take Erik's hulking Expedition rather than my Thunderbird, primarily because my companion didn't particularly like being a passenger. I shared his aversion to abdicating control of anything to someone else, but I decided he deserved his turn in the driver's seat. In more ways than one.

"How's the face?" I asked as we pulled out of Port Royal Plantation and merged into the heavy Monday morning traffic on Route 278. The small cut just beneath his right eye rode atop a welling lump which had begun to take on a royal purple tinge. Despite my attempts to play nurse, fussing at him with antiseptic cream, Band-Aids, and ice packs, he was going to have one hell of a shiner.

"Fine."

Erik's terse reply let me know that subject was still off-limits. He had consistently refused to discuss his injury, even as I was trying to minister to him in the early morning hours. He couldn't get past the fact that a couple of teenagers—and one of them probably a *girl*—had gotten the better of him.

We rode in silence then for the next couple of miles, managing to hit the red on every one of the traffic lights. As we approached Squire Pope Road, which branches off to the right just opposite the Gullah Market, another of the loose threads which seemed to be tangling my life snapped into my head.

"Did you ever get a chance to check out Felicity Baronne on the Internet?" I asked, glancing to the left and the large tree under which I had conducted my stakeout a few days before. The woman who seemed to regard my father as her own personal cash cow had pretty much slipped my mind in the chaos of the Gray Palmer investigation.

"Damn it, yes I did! I'm sorry, Bay. I just completely forgot, what with everything else going on."

"What did you find?"

"Not a whole lot, but I printed the stuff out. It's in the pocket of my laptop case in the backseat."

I unhooked my shoulder harness and squirmed around to unzip the black leather carrier.

"Three sheets, I think. Should be right in the front."

I pulled the papers out, closed the case, and buckled back up.

"What is all this?" I asked while I dug my reading glasses out of my bag.

Erik sped up as we crossed the first bridge and left the town limits of Hilton Head behind. "A couple of credit reports which aren't too favorable, a notation of a lawsuit she was involved in as the result of an accident . . ." He glanced at the tightly packed printing on the single-spaced pages and pointed to an item about a third of the way down the second sheet. "And this. This one is what I thought you would find most interesting."

I began reading where he indicated and stopped short after the first sentence. "Felicity Baronne is a prostitute?" I don't know what I had expected, but it certainly wasn't that.

"Keep reading," Erik said.

"She's been arrested several times in towns all over the Southeast: Tallahassee, Jacksonville, Charlotte, Greenville. I don't believe this! The last time was six months ago in Atlanta."

"So maybe she's decided to move her business interests to Hilton Head."

"But that's not the point. Six months ago? You haven't seen her, Erik. The woman must be pushing sixty!"

"And you think guys over sixty aren't interested in sex anymore? Boy, you're going to have a rude awakening by the time you're eligible for Social Security. I bet the Judge would find that downright insulting."

His grin invited me to share the joke, but I couldn't bring myself to see anything the least bit amusing about it. Not only was the whole idea repugnant to me, I also felt a fleeting sympathy for a woman who had apparently spent her entire adult life selling herself to men for money. And the sudden implications this information evoked about the nature of her involvement with my father . . .

"Are you implying Felicity Baronne and the Judge . . . ? While Lavinia cooks his dinner in the kitchen? That he's paying her for . . . ?"

If he hadn't been driving I would have added another black eye to his collection.

Erik seemed genuinely shocked. "Of course not! I didn't mean any such thing, and you know it! I have nothing but complete respect and admiration for your father. I would never suggest . . ."

"Then knock off the wise-ass remarks about prostitutes and old men. It may be a subject you and your buddies can wink and jab each other about over a few beers, but I don't find anything funny about it at all. In fact, it's pretty damned pathetic, if you ask me, from both sides of the coin."

"I didn't . . . oh, hell, let's just drop it."

Which we did for about the next ten miles. I studied all the information Erik had gleaned about Felicity Baronne, and gradually a picture began to form of a transient life lived on the fringes of society: no home, no apparent family, no connections. Why had she suddenly decided to return to her hometown? Didn't the woman have any shame? And why was my father paying her off?

As the big SUV slowed entering the road-widening construction area, I sneaked a glance at Erik's profile, his lips set in a hard line, his chin jutting out pugnaciously. Sometimes I wish I would just think a moment before I open my mouth. I took a deep breath and let it out slowly.

"I'm sorry," I said, meaning it.

He paused just long enough to make me fear he wasn't going to accept my apology. "Yeah," he answered, and I could feel him relax. "I know."

"Can I blame it on the case and last night and almost no sleep?"

"You can try." The smile removed any sting from the words.

"So how did you find out all this stuff? What was I doing wrong that I couldn't get anything to come up on my search?"

We came to a complete stop while a lumbering dump truck, piled high with dirt, backed around from beneath a huge shovel mounted on caterpillar tracks and ground its way down the highway.

"I didn't have much luck either on a standard Google search, but I have some resources the average person doesn't have access to," he replied.

"Like what?"

"Like a locator service I pay to do background checks on prospective employees and vendors. For a fee, they can find out just about anything about anybody."

"Is that legal?"

"From my end it certainly is. They guarantee they break no laws, so I'm covered no matter what. Mostly it's just a matter of having access to huge databases, newspaper files, public records. Finding out that Ms. Baronne has been arrested numerous times for prostitution isn't violating her civil rights or anything."

"She might feel differently about it," I remarked, and we fell silent again.

And so might the Judge, I thought and added a very unpleasant confrontation with my father to what was quickly becoming a seemingly endless list of things to do. As we inched along in the clogged traffic, I leaned back in the high bucket seat and planned my attack.

CHAPTER
TWENTY-FOUR

The *Wanderer* sat high in the water, its once white hull faded to a mellow cream as it rubbed against the weathered dock in downtown Beaufort. As we climbed the gangplank and stepped aboard the large sightseeing vessel, a brisk wind off the Beaufort River lifted my hair and sent goose bumps racing along my arms. Above us, the sun struggled to break through the overcast.

"Glad you convinced me to throw my windbreaker in the car," Erik said, helping me shrug into Rob's worn bomber jacket.

"Sixty-five degrees on land can feel a whole lot colder on the water." I didn't remember from what part of my distant past I had dredged up that tidbit of information. I only knew it to be true.

Ron Singleton stepped out of the forward wheelhouse and raised a hand in greeting. "Bay!" he called. "Welcome aboard."

His warm brown hand clasped mine, and I introduced him to Erik. Ron and I had known each other since middle school, although I'd had no idea prior to my father's announcement that he ran this tourist service.

"I really appreciate your taking us out this morning," I said as we followed the short, compact sailor into the cabin and mercifully out of the wind.

"Not a problem," he said. "I always run a couple of shakedown cruises before tourist season gets into full swing. Another two weeks, and we'll be doing three trips a day with a full load."

"At least let me pay for the gas," I said, moving up beside him to stare out toward the bridge arcing over the river on its way to Lady's Island. Somehow from down here the span looked much more impressive than it did from a car.

"Nope," he replied. The big diesel engines roared to life at his touch on the control panel, and I felt the deck begin to vibrate under my feet. "I was goin' out anyways. And besides, after what the Judge did for my mama, there aren't enough ways I could repay him. This one doesn't even count."

I had no idea what service my father might have rendered to Ron's mother, or in what capacity, and it seemed ill-mannered to ask. So I simply nodded my thanks and stepped back out of his way as he leaned out to call to one of the dockhands who cast off the ropes looped around the pilings in the front and back of the boat. Or fore and aft, I supposed, if you wanted to get technical about it.

We eased out into the river, and Erik and I settled ourselves in the spacious cabin lined with cushion-covered benches and wide windows, not unlike the much smaller ferry we had taken over to Daufuskie Island a few days before. This boat was built to accommodate many more people and included a snack bar in one corner which no doubt did a brisk summer trade in soft drinks. The vibrations increased as we glided under the massive bridge and rounded the Point where the cluster of magnificent summer homes built by antebellum planters sat tall and proud in the thin morning light.

"I still don't know what you hope to accomplish by this." Erik had to raise his voice to be heard over the thrumming of the engines as we picked up speed.

"I just want to see the place," I answered, "get some feel for what it looks like and how difficult it would be to get close. We can also check out some of those other islands you mentioned, all the little ones with no names on our map. I'm not ruling out the possibility one of them might be the place."

"But you're still pretty convinced this Monkey Island is our spot."

"Gut feeling. I can't explain it. Call it woman's intuition, though, and I'll belt you one."

He grinned and shrugged then turned back to his observation of the river sliding by on the right side of the boat.

Once the pillars and porches of the homes on the Point and the austerity of the land comprising the Marine Corps Air Station had slipped behind us, I found myself completely disoriented. The river twisted and turned along marshy bottoms filled with birds swooping or wading in search of food, and here and there a glimpse of the shimmering green of a golf course or the pitched roof of a Lowcountry mansion could be seen through the thick screen of trees lining the banks.

I stepped up toward the front of the boat where Ron stood with his hands resting lightly on the wheel. "Do you have any charts or maps I might have a prayer of reading?" I asked.

He turned briefly and nodded toward a wooden locker built into the side of the wheelhouse. "In there. Help yourself."

"What am I looking for?" I lifted the lid to uncover a stack of spiral-bound books which appeared to be about a foot and a half square, along with several laminated charts rolled up and fastened with rubber bands.

"One of those books, the big ones. Get out the one that says Norfolk to Jacksonville on the top."

I located it and pulled the cumbersome thing out onto the floor.

"There's an index," Ron said, "on the back. You want the page for the Beaufort River."

"Thanks."

I carried the bulky book back into the passenger cabin and spread it out on one of the benches. Erik moved across from the other side to stand over me. I flipped to the indicated page and located Beaufort with no problem. With my finger I traced our route up the Intracoastal Waterway.

"Where are we now?" I called to Ron.

"Just turning into the Coosaw River," he yelled over his shoulder.

I located the spot and glanced up as we moved right into a much wider expanse of water. "Lady's Island," I said confidently and pointed to the land visible out the windows behind Erik. "Next comes Coosaw Island, then Judas. Shouldn't be too much longer."

I lowered the chart book onto the floor, and we settled back to enjoy the ride.

"COMIN' UP on it," Ron Singleton called about twenty minutes later, snapping me out of a half-doze.

The rhythmic humming of the engines and the beauty of the scenery had combined with the warmth from a strengthening sun to lull me into complete relaxation. I felt the boat slow as Ron eased back on the throttle. I shook myself awake and reached in my bag for the compact binoculars I'd tossed in before we'd left the house.

"Come on," I said to Erik, "let's head out on deck."

We pushed open the heavy door and stepped over the raised threshold. Outside, the wind hit us, chilly after the drowsy warmth of the cabin. We climbed the steep stairs up to the top deck. Folding chairs were stacked neatly on one end and lashed with a series of ropes to keep them secure. I could imagine a horde of pasty-faced Northerners packed into them on a mid-July afternoon, their pink skin blistering under a relentless sun. We moved to the rail on the right side, and I trained the glasses toward the green canopy spread out before us.

"See anything?" Erik asked after a couple of minutes, and I shook my head.

"Just trees." I handed over the glasses, and he scanned the endless stands of fir and hardwoods.

"Did you tell your friend down there what we were looking for?" He lowered the binoculars and leaned his forearms on the rail.

"No. And I don't know exactly what the Judge told him,

either. Maybe we should let him in on our interest in how someone would go about landing on the island. I could make it seem like just idle curiosity."

"He doesn't appear to be a stupid man. I think he might make a few connections we don't exactly want him to."

"And if he did, he'd keep them to himself. Especially if I asked him to."

"Your call." Erik raised the glasses again and made a smooth sweep from left to right.

We were edging in closer to the shore, and even with my naked eye I could make out indentations in the thick canopy where small streams and rivulets cut into the interior. We had already passed Parrot Creek which formed the western boundary of the island. I had my hand on the railing, ready to descend the steps to the wheelhouse when I heard Erik cry out.

"Bay! I see them! Come here!"

I whirled to take the binoculars from his outstretched hand and aimed them in the direction of his pointing finger.

And there they were. From a distance the motion had appeared to be natural, the ever-present wind in the tops of the oaks and pines. But abruptly the movements took on shape and definition, and I realized we were looking at hundreds of rhesus monkeys, darting from tree to tree, clambering up and down the trunks, and scrambling across the floor of the island forest.

"Amazing," I breathed, completely captivated. "Look! On that live oak limb hanging out over the water."

I thrust the glasses back at Erik who trained them on the branch. A mother nestled a tiny infant in one arm, while with the fingers of her hand she picked at the shock of hair standing straight up on the tiny monkey's head. As we drifted along in the slow-moving river, the sounds of their screeching gradually drifted across the water to us.

Erik and I exchanged a look, and I said again, "Amazing."

"It's like *Jurassic Park*," he murmured, as awestruck as I. From the pocket of his windbreaker he pulled a small video camera and trained it on the island. "I've got it set on maximum zoom, so we should get some good images."

I could tell by the sun which now shone directly into my eyes we were rounding the eastern side of the island when the noise level rose dramatically. Ahead I could see a small dock jutting out into the narrow channel. As we neared it, dozens of monkeys swarmed out of the forest and across the hard-packed earth of a small clearing next to the landing. Through the binoculars I could see several of the larger ones, probably territorial males, jumping up and down in excited agitation, their lips pulled back in menacing sneers. They kept back from the dock, though, as if they knew precisely where their boundaries lay, despite the lack of fences or any kind of barrier.

I left Erik topside, his little camera running continuously, and climbed back down to where Ron lounged comfortably in a high swivel chair, one hand carelessly on the wheel, the other clutching a long, thin cigar. The heavy smoke drifting out of the wheelhouse seemed sweet and familiar.

"Those smell just like the Judge's," I said, then, "Sorry," as he jumped in his seat.

"I can put it out if it bothers you," Ron offered, but I waved the suggestion away.

"I've recently become reformed, but I'm not above satisfying my cravings with a little secondhand smoke. Just blow a few puffs over in my direction once in a while, and I'll be fine."

He laughed and turned his attention back to the river. "This what you wanted to see?" he asked.

There was just a hint of challenge in his voice, an invitation to share what this trip was really all about, but he didn't press me when I failed to rise to the bait. I decided to risk probing a little more.

"Pretty much," I said and moved into the narrow cabin. "Who uses the dock?"

I kept my gaze on the island, hoping my question would be taken as polite curiosity, but out of the corner of my eye I saw his head swivel in my direction.

"The feeders," he said. "Come around eight every morning to leave some sort of special food for them."

"Who?" I asked. "Who comes to feed them?"

"Company that owns the place, owns the monkeys. Some bunch of *scientists*." He said the word as if it were a profanity.

"I take it you don't approve."

He drew long on the cigar before answering, his words floating out on a cloud of smoke. "It doesn't seem right to me, raisin' these creatures just so some other folks in white coats can infect 'em with AIDS or TB or some other god-awful disease, and then cut 'em open to see what made 'em die. It's not right."

His response mirrored the discussion Erik and I had gotten into the night before. It had been easy then to debate such concepts in the abstract, yet quite another to envision that tiny baby I'd seen cradled in its mother's arms dying in agony in some laboratory in Atlanta or Washington, D.C. As much as I could accept the necessity of it intellectually, my heart still cringed at the innate cruelty.

I shook off the morbid thoughts. We weren't here to get tangled up in a dialogue on animal rights. "Can just anyone dock there?" I asked, and again Ron Singleton fixed me with that curious gaze.

"See those signs?"

I followed his pointing finger. I didn't need the binoculars to read the large posters, the ones Delbert Pidgen had referred to: WARNING! PROPERTY OF U.S. GOVERNMENT. NO TRES-PASSING! It would have taken a moron not to get the message that unauthorized persons were not welcome on the island.

"Do they have security?" I asked, hoping Erik was getting the panorama drifting by us on tape.

"Naw. Nothing 'cept the usual, you know, DNR and sheriff's patrol boats. 'Course kids used to try to use it for beer parties and such, but they prosecuted a few of 'em, and the fines were stiff enough to discourage the rest. Once in a while you hear tell of some of the Marines from Parris Island havin' a few too many and tryin' to practice their landing tactics." He laughed and rolled his large brown eyes. "Military doesn't take too kindly to that, either."

"So the company that runs the place, they don't have any guards or anything like that?"

We were moving past the landing area, and the acres of tightly packed live oaks and palmettos were closing in again.

"Not that I know of. They run the thing out of Yemassee, so they're not exactly right next door."

Yemassee, I thought. Where had I heard mention of the little crossroads town just recently?

My head snapped up at Erik's shout, barely heard above the idling engines. "Bay! Get up here!"

I heard the sound as I climbed the steps, a boat motor running full out. As I stepped out onto the upper deck, Erik motioned me to join him at the rail. I noticed his hands were empty, so he must have stashed both the binoculars and his video camera in the pockets of his windbreaker. The boat roared toward us from around a headland, its two occupants standing upright in the well. As they neared the *Wanderer,* the pitch of the motor changed, and the smaller craft slowed. Below us, Ron Singleton gave a single blast on the horn in what sounded more like a greeting than a warning of our presence. The big excursion boat would be hard to miss.

Erik and I exchanged glances. "Be a tourist," I said, and he nodded.

The glint of light reflected off lenses told me we were being observed through field glasses. Erik must have caught it, too. He raised his hand in a friendly wave, and I joined him as the boat slowed still more and moved in closer. The driver lifted his arm in acknowledgment while his passenger kept us in his binoculars. I saw them exchange a few words, and the craft suddenly accelerated and veered away in a long arc, pounding off in the direction from which it had first appeared.

Below us, Ron Singleton increased power to his engines and began a wide turn of his own, heading back toward Beaufort.

"Did you get the name on their boat?" I asked. "Did it fit Cynthia Sellers's description?"

Erik leaned down toward a chair I hadn't noticed he'd

opened in front of the rail and came back up with the video camera in his hand.

"Was that running?" I asked, and he nodded. "Way to go! We've got the bastards on tape."

Neither of us had any doubt that Monkey Island held the key to what had happened to Gray Palmer. The video would be helpful if it ever came to a prosecution, but we already had enough information to satisfy us.

Both of the men in the fishing boat had been wearing camouflage fatigues.

CHAPTER
TWENTY-FIVE

We pulled into the semicircular driveway in front of Presqu'isle just before one in the afternoon. Since we'd finished our boat tour so early, I had been agitating to head on up to Charleston, get a couple of hotel rooms, and hit the ground running. Erik wanted to mull things over with my father, map out a plan of action, and make the one-hour drive first thing in the morning. I was having a really difficult time getting used to being the fly-by-the-seat-of-your-pants member of this organization.

We carried our overnight bags with us up the steps and through the massive oak door into the entryway. The beautiful proportions of this central hall, neatly bisected by the grand sweep of the freestanding staircase, never failed to inspire my admiration for the incredible talent of the craftsmen, both free and slave, who had achieved such perfection without benefit of modern tools.

I dropped my case on the first step and turned at Lavinia's voice as she emerged from the kitchen. "There you are! Lunch has been ready for more than half an hour. Good thing I decided on a cold collation. Welcome back, young man." The disapproving frown she had been directing at me softened into a warm smile as her gaze swung around to my partner.

"Thank you, Mrs. Smalls, ma'am. It's good to be back."

"Now, I thought we had decided you were to call me

Lavinia, just like everyone else around here. You're practically family, leastwise in all the ways that matter."

Erik grinned. "Sorry. Thank you, Lavinia."

"Now set those things down and get yourselves in there. Bay, your father has been fidgeting all morning waiting to hear what you have to tell him. Man has liked to drive me crazy."

We followed her retreating back down the hall and into the hazy warmth of the kitchen, its round oak table set for four. My father's wheelchair was already pulled up in his usual place, and I could tell by the glower on his face I was in for one of his infamous tongue-lashings.

"First Alexander Graham Bell and then generations of folks after him spent their entire lives perfecting a technology so you could call and let folks know where the hell you are," he began even before I'd had a chance to sit down. "Hello, Erik," he added, barely pausing for breath. "I know he carries one of those damned fool cellular things around with him. Thirty seconds, that's all . . ."

"Oh, stuff a sock in it, Daddy," I said, with more humor than rancor. "I'm thirsty and hungry. If I'm going to be forced to listen to any more of this nonsense from you, at least let me do it on a full stomach."

We gnawed on cold chicken legs and redskin potato salad along with an assortment of pickles and sliced vegetables. Into the uncomfortable silence, broken only by the clatter of our respective silverware against the everyday plates, Lavinia finally spoke.

"Have you returned your R.S.V.P. to Mrs. Quintard yet, Bay?"

I had no idea what she was talking about, and said so.

"For the bridal shower? Now, quit scowling at me like an angry dog. I know you received an invitation because Mrs. Quintard called and specifically requested your address in Hilton Head."

"Why would Bitsy's mother be giving a bridal shower?" My best friend since first grade, Elizabeth "Bitsy" Quintard, the only daughter of the house, had been married to the detestable Big Cal Elliott for nearly twenty years. And, to the best of my recollection, her own two daughters were way too young even to be contemplating the big plunge.

"For Amy Fleming, of course," my father chimed in. "She's marrying the Brandon boy, the one you got mixed up with in that Herrington mess last fall."

"I didn't get 'mixed up' with Chris Brandon." I could hear the defensiveness in my own voice, but I didn't care. "He hired me to do a job, which I did very well, thank you, and for which I was paid quite handsomely."

When he stuffed a forkful of potato salad into his mouth instead of whipping off a snappy retort, I knew he'd exhausted his vitriol on that particular subject. I glanced at Erik in time to see him trying unsuccessfully to stifle a grin.

"Why would anyone think I had the slightest interest in *any* bridal shower, let alone one being held in honor of someone I don't even know and given by a woman who has hated my guts since I was in grade school?"

"Really, Bay, such talk. Mrs. Quintard always speaks very highly of you." Lavinia had almost perfected my father's disapproving scowl. She still needed a little work on the scrunching eyebrows part, but it was pretty close.

"We had quite an interesting boat ride this morning," Erik began, and I flashed him a smile for his gallant effort at changing the subject and thereby rescuing me from being battered to a verbal pulp from all sides. I could have told him it was pointless.

"Mrs. Quintard and Regina Fleming, young Amy's mother, became fast friends during the Colonel's second tour of duty at Parris Island," the Judge chimed in, uninvited. "They were part of your mother's circle of acquaintance for a time if I recall."

I looked to Lavinia who nodded in agreement. "Well, sorry, I don't remember any of them. I met Amy with Chris at the Heritage Golf Tournament last weekend, but only for a couple of minutes. She doesn't know me from Adam. I'm sure my presence will not be missed."

"You will go."

The bald statement brought everyone up short, even Lavinia. While we had both gotten used to my father's peremptory commands over the years, not many of them were delivered with such force and assertion. He tended to favor sly manipulation when he really wanted something.

"Why should I?"

"I had a lot of dealings with Colonel Fleming back in the early days when he was at Parris Island. Basically a fine officer. Sometimes overly harsh with the men of color under his command . . ." He glanced obliquely at Lavinia as if in unspoken apology. "An unfortunate symptom of the times, I'm afraid. Occasionally the local law enforcement community had to make allowances for the military's priorities regarding certain . . . incidents. But I always found him to be a man I could work with, a man who understood how the world operates."

"In other words, you and he would put your heads together and circumvent the law when it served your mutual purpose," I said.

His chin trembled with the effort to control his irritation with me. "As you say. At any rate, I want you to represent the family."

"Why?" I repeated.

His anger-management exercise failed. "Because I owe him that courtesy," he snapped. "And because I asked you to."

"I didn't hear anything resembling a request," I said, tossing my napkin on the table. "It sounded to me like an order. And I'm not going to spend an eternity with a bunch of simpering girl-children and doddering old ladies over weak tea and cucumber sandwiches just to placate your sense of honor. If it means so damned much to you, go yourself."

I pushed back from the table and stomped from the room. I flung myself out the front door and dropped onto the top step of the verandah, my chest heaving in righteous indignation.

I would have sold my soul for a cigarette.

•   •   •

WHEN ERIK emerged about half an hour later, he found me wandering the hedge of azaleas which bordered the edge of the lawn where it ran alongside the rutted lane. I'd been pacing the perimeter of the property, front to back, calming my inner self while working up a considerable sweat in the afternoon sun.

"All clear," he called as he approached in that languid stride of his, loose-jointed, hands thrust in the pockets of his Dockers. "The other combatants have retired from the field, so it's safe to come back in."

I smiled and shook my head, more at my own foolishness than anyone else's. "I have no idea why I let him do that to me," I said, tossing aside the twig I'd been chewing on. As a substitute cigarette it was pretty useless. "I'm pushing forty years old, and he still has the power to reduce me to a snotty teenager."

"Genes," he said, and I turned to face him. "Too many of his in you, would be my guess."

"You could be right. Or maybe too many of Emmaline's. I notice lately that a lot of our arguments have that *déjà vu* quality, as if I've heard them before." I shivered in the sunlight. "God, what if I'm turning into my mother? I'll have to shoot myself."

Erik dropped into stride beside me as I set off on another circuit of the grounds. "I filled the Judge in on what we discovered this morning," he said.

"And?"

"And he pretty much agrees with you, much as it pained him to admit it. He thinks we should concentrate on Judas Island. He says Ron Singleton would take us over there, but he can't think how we'd go about pinpointing the exact site of the grave."

"We need Araminda Albright to cough up what she knows," I said. "I just don't believe Gray Palmer made this fantastic find and kept it all to himself. Did he strike you as that kind of guy? From what you remember?"

We wandered down toward the marsh and the short dock

which jutted out into St. Helena Sound. I wondered if the line of green, barely visible on the horizon off to our left, could be Judas Island. I'd never paid much attention to it before. I settled onto an old wooden bench, and Erik dropped down beside me. We contemplated the placid water, broken occasionally by a diving pelican, each absorbed in our own thoughts. He took a long time to answer.

"Gray wasn't above a little cheating, if it got him what he wanted. And he was always eager to impress the girls. I suppose, unless there was a good, sound reason not to, he wouldn't have been able to resist bragging to his current woman about his big find. Of course, he could have become a completely different person by now. But that would be my best guess."

"So why would she be keeping quiet about it? That's the part of this whole scenario I just can't get a handle on. I'm willing to bet just about anything Gray Senior knows nothing about the grave and the bone his son removed from it. Unless he betrays something when we meet him face to face. But Araminda knows. Why hasn't she told him? If that is, in fact, the reason Gray died, why hasn't she told his father?"

As if on cue, both of us slouched down against the back of the bench, our legs stretched out in front of us. I peeled a little more bark off the twig with my thumbnail and stuck it back in my mouth.

"Well, let's run that down," Erik said, clasping his hands behind his head. "What kind of motive could she have?"

"Okay, good plan. Let's see. If Monkey Island was off-limits, as I'm certain it was, she could be afraid of losing her job. Except, judging by her cozy little scene with her employer after his press conference, I don't think there's any danger of that."

"You think she and Gray's dad are . . . you know?"

Even after everything we'd been through together, Erik Whiteside still felt a need to protect my feminine sensibilities. You just had to love the kid.

"What? Shacking up? Sleeping together? You can say it out loud. I think it's a possibility."

"I thought she was Gray's, I mean my Gray's, girl."

"I could have been wrong about that. There really wasn't any evidence at her place they were anything other than roommates. I guess I got the impression they were more than that to each other by her passion about finding out what happened to him. Maybe I misread her. I did feel all that hand-wringing about being afraid she was next was just a trifle overdone."

Erik kicked off his deck shoes and ran his bare feet through the soft grass.

"So you think she's really just worrying about losing her job with this foundation? But that doesn't wash because *she* didn't break the rules, Gray did."

I shot upright on the bench. "But what if she *did*? We only have her word for it Gray was alone when he found the body! What if she was there, too? That would explain everything—her fear, her staying close to his father, all of it."

Erik turned to face me, his brow wrinkled in concentration. "And that's why she called me. She knew Gray had been in touch with me after his first trip to the island, and that he was trying to get me to help him find someone who could identify the body, to date when it might have gone into the ground."

"And after he was killed, she couldn't find it. The bone, I mean. So she jumped to the logical conclusion he had somehow gotten it to you. What she's really been after all along is finding out how much *we* know, not providing us with information herself."

"And that also explains why she hasn't told the old man. She truly doesn't know who to trust."

I saw my own elation at this epiphany mirrored on Erik's face. Both of us were grinning widely. Then another thought sobered me. "But that means I did misread her. She is afraid for her life. And with good cause, it would seem."

"It also means she thinks Gray's father could be involved. We need to get up there," Erik said, and I nodded.

He slipped his shoes back on, and we headed for the house.

• • •

THE FORT Charles was completely booked, so we settled for a chain motel just a few blocks away in downtown Charleston. The adjoining rooms, while certainly not opulent, were clean and well-appointed and about one-third the price of the landmark hotel where I'd first met Araminda Albright. We settled in quickly since neither of us had brought more than a change of clothes and a few toiletries.

It was close to five by the time we'd checked in, and a quick call verified Gray Palmer had left for the day. But we had an appointment for ten the next morning; and besides, the dead boy's father wasn't our prime objective anyway. I tried Araminda twice from the room phone, but again got no answer. Her lack of response didn't yet have me alarmed, but I had to admit, at least to myself, that her silence was making me a little apprehensive.

I voted for jumping right back in the car and trying to locate her beach cottage while it was still light. I knew I could find my way to the general vicinity, but I was pretty certain I'd need time to locate the precise house.

"Let's grab a bite to eat first," Erik suggested as we stood alongside his black Expedition in the motel parking lot. "If she's working, she won't be home for a while. Besides, it's going to stay light outside for at least another two or three hours. We've got time."

I fussed and argued a little, but finally gave in to the insistent rumblings of my partner's stomach. I tried to sell him on a quick burger, but he was having none of that.

"You must know tons of places around here," he said. "Let's go somewhere really local, somewhere we can walk to."

I figured the sooner I got him fed and watered the sooner we could get underway, so I set off at a brisk pace in the direction of the old slave market a few blocks over. The long brick buildings which today house rows of vendors of every kind of souvenir and trinket imaginable had at one point, a couple of centuries before, served exactly the function its name implied. Despite the throngs of chattering tourists who regularly packed its narrow aisles, I always found the place depressing.

Thankfully its doors were shuttered for the evening, so we took the narrow sidewalk alongside, stepping shortly up to a maitre d's stand set out in front of an old building whose entrance rose a couple of steps up from the street. A pretty blonde armed with menus asked if we were interested in being seated for dinner, and I nodded.

"Follow me," she said, glancing slyly up at Erik from interesting hazel eyes.

I probably only imagined her swaying walk, emphasized by a tight black miniskirt, was being exaggerated for his benefit.

"We'd like the roof," I called as she led us inside, up a steep flight of stairs next to the bar, then out onto a wide seating area to a small table near the balustrade.

"This okay?" she asked Erik.

"Fine," I answered for him, amazed at how invisible I became to young, attractive females whenever I was in his company.

Erik studied the tall menu while I set mine aside without glancing at it. Rob and I had eaten here many times in years past, and I always ordered the same meal. If the wait staff didn't change with every season, someone here would surely have remembered.

"What's good?" he asked over the top of the bill of fare.

"Everything. Anything seafood. I'm having she-crab soup and a Caesar salad."

Thankfully our server turned out to be a male, making the ordering process a little speedier. Erik mimicked my selections, adding a pound of peel-and-eat shrimp and an order of fried oysters.

The view from the second-floor dining area was impeded by roofs and steeples, but still provided a nice panorama of the old city whose charming, other-century ambiance was guarded with fervor by several historical and preservation societies. Very little changed in Charleston, primarily because gaining a variance from the strict codes for restoration on any of the antebellum buildings could take a lifetime.

I wolfed down the creamy chowder and attacked my salad. Across from me, Erik savored every bite of his meal. When I had speared the last bit of romaine out of the large white bowl in front of me, the little patience I had been clinging to evaporated.

"Come on, Erik, it's almost six. We're going to be caught in the rush-hour traffic now, and I'm not really sure how long it'll take to get out to the beach. We need to get moving."

"They have a rush hour? I haven't seen anybody move beyond a slow amble since we got here."

"Cute. In case you hadn't noticed, the whole damn place is full of narrow one-way streets. It doesn't make for a quick exit from the city." I signaled our waiter who wandered over to clear. "I'll take the check, please," I said, and he nodded.

When he returned, I handed over my platinum card then added a tip and scribbled my name on the ticket he brought back. All that, and Erik still picked the pale, translucent shells from his plate of rosy shrimp.

"Okay, okay," he said, cleaning his messy fingers on the wet-wipe provided with his dinner. "You sure do make it difficult to enjoy a meal."

"We're not here to eat," I snapped, more worried about Araminda Albright than I cared to admit. "Let's hit it."

I rose without giving him a chance to reply and led the way back onto the street. The hazy glow of late afternoon bathed everything in a gold mist which made even the most desolate of buildings on the side streets seem to reflect the radiance of this wonderful old city. I fidgeted beside the Expedition while Erik released the locks, then scrambled up into the high passenger seat and buckled up. I could feel his annoyance at me, but I brushed off any guilt I might have felt. With each passing minute, my anxiety grew. If pressed, I couldn't have said why I felt such urgency.

In fairness, most of the evening traffic had dissipated, and it took us only fifteen minutes to gain the turnoff which led to the beaches and the outer islands which guarded Charleston. I tried my best to gauge the distance I had followed Araminda down this narrow road on that Sunday afternoon. Twice I had Erik slow so I could peer out the open window at a home tucked back in among riotous bushes and a single live oak. We were the subject of more than one horn blast and barrage of angry words as the vehicles behind swerved out and around us.

We hit it on the third try.

Erik pulled in beside the bright yellow PT Cruiser. As he cut the engine, he leaned across to lay a hand on my arm. "Before we go bursting in on her, can we at least agree we need to go slowly? She has no real cause to trust us, and there has to be some legitimate reason she didn't level with you before."

I gritted my teeth and told myself not to get upset just because my formerly silent partner had decided to step into a more vocal role in our detecting enterprise. I told myself that, but I didn't listen.

"No, Erik, I think I'll just throw her down on the carpet and beat the truth out of her, okay?"

Wisely, he didn't dignify my outburst with an answer. I resisted the urge to slam the heavy door closed, and he followed me through the loose sand and onto the porch. There were no lights burning, despite the deepening of the twilight out over the ocean a few yards away. I rapped lightly on the silvered wood panel, and a few seconds later knocked again. Erik and I exchanged a look.

"What do you think?" he asked. "Maybe sleeping?"

"Or out walking."

"You'd think she'd leave a lamp on for herself."

"I know." I tried the ancient metal doorknob. It turned in my hand, but the door remained tightly closed. "Always works in the movies," I said and earned a smile.

"What now?" he asked, leaving my side to peer into the long, narrow window beside the door.

"See anything?"

"Nope," he replied. "It's completely dark in there. Want me to try around back?"

I had no idea if there was another entrance to the ramshackle old place, but I shrugged and nodded. "Sure. In the meantime, I'll take a look down the beach, see if I can spot her."

We each set out on our appointed tasks, both of us moving carefully down the front steps. Perhaps it was the silence, broken only by the wash of the waves against the sand and a light breeze ruffling the tops of the pines, but we both seemed to feel the need for stealth. Erik disappeared around the back of the house as I followed the well-used path over the low dune and onto the beach.

At first I thought it might have been a dolphin, although I'd never known one to beach itself, the long body draped in seaweed. As I stepped closer, I realized it wasn't seaweed, but hair.

Long, shining, black hair.

In the last slanting rays of the sun, one red eye gleamed at me from a tangled coil of gold.

CHAPTER
TWENTY-SIX

I didn't hear Erik's approach in the soft sand, and his startled yell finally forced my frozen legs into motion. I knelt beside the body, unsure of what to do. With trembling hands, I rolled Araminda Albright onto her back and pushed the wild mass of hair away from her face. I gasped at the sight of the purpling bruise that covered one entire cheek.

"Is she dead?" I could barely hear Erik's whispered words above the *shushing* of the waves that lapped at the girl's feet and splashed up over her ankles.

"No," I said, removing my fingers from her neck where the pulse beat steadily. "Help me get her out of the water."

Her clothes were sodden and stuck to her body, and it took both of us to half-carry, half-drag her dead weight back to the higher ground of the dune. "We need to get her warm," I said. The slender body trembled, and a low moan escaped her salt-caked lips. "We have to get in the house. Break a window if you have to, but find a blanket."

"I don't have to break in," Erik said softly, "someone already did that. The back door is standing wide open, and the whole place has been ransacked."

"Are you sure they're gone? Whoever did this?"

"Positive. I checked all the rooms."

"Then you'd better go get that blanket. And call an ambulance."

I gasped as icy fingers suddenly closed around my wrist. Araminda Albright coughed once, and her eyes flicked open. "No," she managed to croak.

"No what?" I asked, my head bent low over hers in an effort to make out her garbled words.

"No doctors," I thought she said.

"You're hurt. You need medical attention." Erik had squatted next to me, his tone calm, but firm. "I'll get on my cell. It's in the car."

"No! Wait!" Strength was fast returning, both to her voice and to her limbs. She struggled to sit up, but I held her down.

"Araminda—Mindy—you have to stay still. You have a head wound. We need to call an ambulance. And the police."

Her gaze kept wandering in and out of focus, and I was certain this was a sign of concussion. But she managed to shake her head with such vehemence I thought she might pass out again. "No! No police!"

I looked at Erik who shrugged and sat back on his haunches. "We can't force her," he said.

"The hell we can't," I began, then caught myself up short, flashing back to my own near brush with death. I saw myself strapped to a gurney, staring at the ruins of my car and one side of my house. Heard Red and the paramedics urging me to get checked out at the hospital and my own stubborn refusal to be driven from my home by the animals who had attacked me. I of all people should have some sympathy for Araminda Albright's position.

"Okay," I said, more calmly, "okay. It's your call." Araminda seemed to relax at my words. I turned to my partner. "Get a couple of blankets. It'll make it easier to carry her."

"I can walk." She pushed my hand away and rolled onto her knees then used my shoulder to lever herself to her feet. She swayed a little, and Erik reached to grasp her around the waist. She struggled in his arms for a moment then let him take her weight as they hobbled back toward the cottage.

• • •

IN HER bedroom, I stripped her of the remnants of her shorts and T-shirt, helped her peel off her underwear and bra, and supported her as she stood for what seemed to me like an eternity under the needle spray of the shower. I was pleased to see some pinkness returning to her skin as the hot water cascaded over her slender body and sluiced away bits of kelp and sand from her luxuriant hair. I left her alone long enough to make an ice pack then returned to help her into a fiery red kimono I found amid a pile of clothes someone had dumped from her bureau and closet onto the floor. I tried to insist she should climb into bed, but the haughty Araminda Albright surfaced again, and I was forced to follow her out onto the chintz sofa in the living area where she collapsed onto a pile of cushions with the ice bag held firmly against her badly bruised cheek. I pulled the Southwestern throw from where it lay crumpled under the rocking chair, tucked it around her, and earned a fierce scowl for my trouble.

Erik came in from the kitchen carrying a tray heavy with mugs of steaming tea and a sugar bowl. I accepted mine gratefully, although Araminda made only a token effort at sipping from her cup. I settled myself in the rocker she herself had occupied just a little more than a week before, and Erik pushed aside a few scattered books and papers and sprawled on the floor next to the raised hearth of the fireplace.

"So let's have it," I said when several moments had passed in silence.

"I don't have to tell you anything."

I gave thought to resurrecting my plan to throw her on the floor and pound the truth out of her, but it looked as if someone had beaten me to it. Literally.

"Who did this to you?" Erik spoke softly, but there was steel there as well. I had a feeling his sympathies were being exhausted about as fast as mine. When he got no response, he sat up a little straighter and fixed our patient with an un-flinching stare. "You can tell us or you can tell the police. Your decision."

Something in his posture or his tone must have penetrated

Araminda's defenses. "I can't tell you! They'll come back!"

"What makes you say that?"

Erik continued to speak in a firm, but soothing voice. He seemed to have her attention, and perhaps her confidence, so I sat back in the rocker and let him take the lead.

"They tried to kill me! I want them to think I'm dead. If they find out I'm not, they'll come back and finish the job."

"Who?"

That seemed to make one question too many. Araminda turned her head away, cushioning her cheek against the melting ice pack. Erik looked at me and nodded as if tossing the ball into my court.

"How did you escape?" I asked. "What happened, exactly?"

Strangely, this was apparently firmer ground. "They just burst through the back door. Around six o'clock tonight. Two of them. They wanted . . . something. They never said what, just kept insisting I knew what they were after. But I didn't! I told them! But they wouldn't believe me. I tried to run, but the big one grabbed me and hit me with some sort of . . . I don't know. It looked like a sock filled with something heavy. It didn't knock me out, but I pretended it did. I thought if . . . I figured if I just played dead, they'd find what they were looking for and go away."

The monotone in which this horrible tale was delivered made me question again whether Araminda might have a serious head injury.

"Then how did you end up . . . ?" I began.

"When they went into my bedroom, I jumped up and ran outside and into the water. They thought I was out cold, and I took them by surprise. I swam straight out from the shore, and I could hear them cursing and trying to start the boat. I'm a strong swimmer, and I can hold my breath for a long time. I'd stay under until I couldn't take another second, then surface to grab a breath. They looked for me for a long time."

She paused in her tale of playing cat-and-mouse with a speedboat and took a sip of tea from her mug. I wondered if,

like me, she was thinking of Gray and his poor face, mutilated by the propeller of his own boat.

"Then what?" I prodded her.

"Finally I surfaced once more and realized the boat was
moving away. By then I was really dizzy, but I kept swim-
ming underwater, coming back up until I couldn't see them
anymore. Then I struck out toward shore. But I ran out of energy. In the end I just floated on my back, hoping the tide
would take me in. I don't remember landing, but I must have
been tossed far enough up on the beach to keep me from getting pulled back in. That's all I can remember."

"Do you think these are the same people who killed
Gray?" I asked.

She took a long time to answer. "Yes," she murmured into
the back of the sofa.

"And it's because you were with him, weren't you? You
saw the skeleton as well."

The fight went out of her then, and she nodded once before turning her back to us.

I motioned for Erik to follow, and we stepped out onto the
front porch. The moon had risen, casting a shimmering glow
across the gently rolling ocean.

"She needs to see a doctor," I said, wrapping my arms
around one of the thick balusters which supported the roof
of the verandah and laying my cheek against the roughness
of its peeling paint.

"And the cops." Erik sat on the top step and let his hands
dangle between his knees. "Jesus, Bay, that's an incredible
story. It's a miracle she survived." When I didn't answer immediately, he said, "Isn't it?"

"I'm not sure I'm buying it."

"What? You think she's making it up?"

"*Sshh!* Keep your voice down," I whispered.

"She sure as hell didn't imagine that bruise on the side of
her face. And we found her down there by the water, just like
she said."

I knew it would take more than I had to offer to convince
even myself of my suspicions, but something about the story

didn't scan for me. I had no idea what it was exactly. Maybe too pat, too rehearsed. Only a couple of pauses for breath, no shudders of remembered fear. I'd been in her situation before. I had to admit I'd been pretty calm in the thick of things, some inner strength I never knew I had rising to take control of my brain and my actions. But when it was over . . .

And maybe that wasn't fair, I told myself, swinging away from the baluster to join Erik on the top step. Mindy Albright wasn't me. Wasn't I. Whatever.

"I could be full of it, Erik," I said. "Who knows? Maybe after she has a chance to sleep and heal a little we'll be able to get more out of her." I sighed and ran a hand through the tangled mess of my hair, beginning to curl around my face in the dampness of the night air. "What are we going to do with her in the meantime?"

"What do you mean?"

"We can't leave her here alone! And I don't think it's a good plan for any of us to stick around. She could be right. Her pals could come calling again."

"They'd have no reason, would they? If they think she's dead?"

"Unless they're watching the house. Even from pretty far out in a boat, they could see the lights on here." I rose and dusted off the seat of my pants. "And she says they didn't tell her what it was they were looking for. I'm not buying that. You know as well as I do the only thing they could have been after, and so does she."

"The bone," he said.

"And, if they're convinced she doesn't have it, and they spot us here, where do you think they'll look next?"

I HAD a difficult time convincing Araminda Albright her safest course was to come with us. In the end I gave up arguing with her about getting dressed. We wrapped her in the Indian throw, and Erik wrestled her out to his car while I gathered up what necessities I could find, including her purse and keys, and tossed it all in a grocery bag. In ten minutes we were back on the road to Charleston.

"What about my car?" Mindy asked as we sped off into the night.

"It's locked. Besides, you won't be going anywhere for a while without us."

I'd given thought to driving her Cruiser into town myself, but we decided it was too distinctive. Even in the crowded parking lot of the motel, anyone familiar with Mindy and her bright yellow wagon would have no trouble finding it. And her. Besides, if we left everything just as we had found it, they might just be convinced they'd succeeded in killing her. Moving the car would be a sure sign they needed to give it another try. If she was telling the truth. If, if, if . . .

We bundled her inside with a minimum of fuss and settled her in one of the two double beds in my room. While I spread her meager toiletries on the shelf in the bathroom, Erik made a run to the nearby convenience store for aspirin and ice packs. He returned laden with those as well as sodas, an assortment of chips, and a bag of apples.

Araminda had dozed during the short trip to the motel and now seemed restored, so it seemed like a good time to push her for more answers. I perched on the end of the bed in a pose I hoped would remind her of middle-school sleepovers where the girls stay up all night and reveal their darkest secrets while sipping Coca-Colas and stuffing themselves with junk food. The ugly bruise darkening on her face reminded me this game was a lot more serious.

"Tell me about how you and Gray found the grave," I began, sliding off my shoes and tucking my feet up under me.

Erik had tactfully retreated to his own room, but I noticed he'd left the connecting door open.

I confronted Araminda's stony silence and pulled a handful of corn chips out of the bag. I extended the package to her, but she shook her head. I washed the chips down with a swig of soda and pressed ahead.

"Okay, fine. I'll tell you what I think happened. Feel free to jump in and correct any errors." Again I met the stubborn set of her mouth which remained firmly shut. "In your investigation on behalf of the foundation you encountered Judas Island, or Monkey Island as the locals have dubbed it. I'm guessing you were warned off it by Gray's father because it's government property. Even without that, it could have taken you only about two minutes to realize from all the signs the place was off-limits. But from what I know of your partner, both those things probably only served to egg him on."

The thin smile softened Mindy's solemn face. "Gray hated to be told no."

I nodded. "You probably argued against it, because you seem like a nice, law-abiding kind of girl—" I broke off at her ladylike snort of derision. "Okay," I said, "you could be right. At any rate, the challenge was just too much for Gray to resist."

I paused, hoping she'd pick up the tale. Again I extended the chips, and this time she reached into the bag. Not wanting to break the tenuous truce, I held my silence. Araminda Albright licked salt from her fingers and leaned back into the pillows bunched against the headboard.

"We hung around until just before dusk, checking out some of the other little islets in the area." Her voice sounded small, almost childlike in the chill air of the impersonal motel room. "I was tired and hungry, and I wanted to go home, but Gray was determined to go snooping around Judas. He'd located this little creek on the back side and decided we could land there, poke around some, and be out before dark, before anyone knew we'd been there. Could I have a drink?"

I jumped at the unexpected change of subject. "Certainly. Glass? Ice?" I popped the top on a can of soda.

"No thanks. This is fine." She took it from me and swallowed delicately before continuing. "Gray hauled out the metal detector and all the other equipment, and we followed this narrow path toward the interior." She paused to sip again from the can. "Spooky. The animals . . . Anyway, we stopped at this clearing because he thought the ground didn't look natural. He had a real talent for that, you know. An instinct or something. And then the detector indicated metal, and he got excited, so we started digging . . ."

When she seemed hesitant to continue, I prompted, "So you found a skeleton. What on earth made Gray take the bone away? I know you said the body had remnants of clothing intact, and of course there's the wristwatch. Probably what set off the detector. But what so intrigued him he would disturb the remains?"

I felt as if she wanted to tell me, as if she needed to be relieved of the knowledge of whatever horror she'd witnessed on Monkey Island. "Come on, Mindy. One way or the other we're going to find out. We have a meeting with Gray's father tomorrow. Don't you think he has a right to know why his son died?"

At the mention of Gray Palmer, Senior, her face crumpled, and I watched tears well up and spill over onto her bruised cheek.

"Mindy? What is it?"

Her whole body began to tremble. She reached out a hand, and I grasped it tightly.

"Tell me," I said.

And she did.

CHAPTER
TWENTY-SEVEN

I waited until an hour after I heard Erik switch off ESPN and saw the thin band of light disappear from the crack in the connecting door we'd decided to leave partially open. In the bed beside me, Araminda Albright slept quietly, her injured cheek cradled in her cupped hand. I flung back the sheet and slipped on my sneakers, then eased into the adjoining room. As I'd hoped, Erik had left his keys, along with his wallet and the change from his pocket, lying in plain view on the low bureau. I scooped up the keys, leaving a brief note to explain my absence, then tiptoed back into my own room and out into the dark.

The dashboard clock glowed 3:11 as I cranked over the Expedition's powerful engine. Its roar sounded like a jet landing in the hushed stillness of the motel parking lot. Once on the street, I was surprised by the number of vehicles cruising along with me at this ungodly hour. I wondered if any of my fellow travelers were on missions as clandestine as mine.

We whizzed through traffic signals blinking yellow in the predawn blackness, and in less than half an hour I pulled up into the sand next to Mindy Albright's darkened cottage. I sat for a long time, my eyes focused on the shadows cast by the bushes hugging the porch and the sides of the house, my ears straining through the open car window for any sign I was not alone. The motor ticked loudly as it cooled in the light breeze off the ocean.

Satisfied as I could be, I pulled Mindy's house keys from the pocket of my jacket. After her revelations, I'd had no compunction about lifting them from her purse as soon as she'd finally dropped off to sleep. On the other hand, I felt bad about deceiving Erik, but I knew what his reaction would be to my plan. As I clicked on the pocket flashlight I'd also found in Mindy's cluttered handbag, I paused to consider again the irony of my having somehow become the risk-taker in this venture. Older, supposedly wiser, and conservative both by nature and profession, I had nonetheless slipped easily into the role. Maybe Bay the Wonder Woman had been lurking all along under the placid façade of Lydia Baynard Simpson Tanner, girl accountant. I chuckled to myself as I mounted the steps, crossed the porch, and inserted the worn key into the lock. Somehow I couldn't quite picture myself in tights and bullet-deflecting bracelets, though God knew the latter would have come in handy a couple of times in the past year.

The door opened silently, and I slipped inside. I flicked off the flashlight and let my eyes become accustomed to the dim interior. We had done nothing in the way of righting overturned chairs or cleaning up the mess left by the invaders. If they came back, I wanted them to see things exactly as they'd left them. As I picked my way gingerly through the debris, I hoped Araminda wouldn't be too crushed when she realized how much of her parents' wonderful collection had been damaged or destroyed.

I used brief bursts from the flashlight to guide me to the bookcases, although the pearly rose of dawn had already begun to push against the night-dark still hovering over the ocean. I made a quick check of the few books the would-be thieves had tossed onto the floor, but the one I sought wasn't among them. If they had been after the bone, as we suspected, they would have been looking for a safe or some other hidey-hole concealed by the thick volumes.

But Gray Palmer had been smarter than that. He'd gotten

the bone out of his possession and in such a way it would have taken a lot of manpower and luck to track it down. Next he'd made certain someone would be able to relocate his grisly find in case anything happened to him. And he'd done it in such a way Araminda Albright could have truthfully sworn not to know the details, although I had every confidence she would have eventually figured out the cryptic clue on her own.

I knew I'd passed over the worn spine of the book I sought during my perusal of Mindy's library that Sunday afternoon more than a week ago. Where exactly I couldn't be certain, but I knew I'd seen it. I felt along each row, stopping to flash the light on anything that felt wide enough. My frustration level grew as I worked my way around the room, only checking those shelves at or near my eye level. I didn't remember having done any reaching up or bending down during my previous snooping.

I finally located it to the right of the fireplace, a massive volume which required both hands to lift it from its shelf. I tucked the flashlight in my pocket and carried the book to the chintz-covered sofa. I ran my hand along the top edge, feeling for any irregularity that might indicate something had been slipped inside. When that failed, I riffled the pages, but again found nothing.

For a moment I wavered. I'd been so sure I had the hiding place figured out. When Mindy had finished pouring out her bizarre story, I'd latched onto the one verifiable piece of information she'd given me. Before venturing out on his ill-fated return trip to Judas Island, Gray had left her a strange message: a biblical citation he'd told her to memorize and then destroy.

I'd immediately snatched up the nearly pristine Gideon Bible from the drawer in the motel nightstand and verified my recollection of Genesis 2:23 which detailed the creation of Eve from Adam's rib. I wondered if the Judge could be badgered into giving me a couple of points since I'd remembered it exactly: "Bone of my bones, and flesh of my flesh . . ."

The solution had seemed so clear to me in that moment I'd dashed off in the middle of the night, returning to a scene of recent violence with little fear of danger. The pressure of the Glock in the right-hand pocket of my jacket gave me some comfort, but if I'd had any sense at all I would have taken the damned book with me back to the motel. I decided to give myself five more minutes before admitting defeat.

I risked clicking on the flashlight again and this time ran my finger down the index. Gray Palmer was an intelligent man. If he'd used this book as his hiding place, he wouldn't have made it easy for potential searchers like those who had attacked Mindy. My finger seemed to stop of its own accord, although my eyes must have registered the faint pencil mark, nearly invisible in the soft circle of light. I flipped to page 612, and there it was: a tiny scrap of paper with one set of coordinates—longitude and latitude in degrees, minutes, and seconds—clearly marking the location of the mysterious grave on Judas Island.

It had been tucked into the section on the human femur in an outdated copy of the bible of both medicine and archaeology, *Gray's Anatomy*.

Not only was he smart, but the boy definitely had a sense of humor. I wished I could have known him.

"I DON'T know whether to congratulate you or throttle you."

"I wouldn't try the latter, my friend. I'm armed." I tried to keep it light as I perched on the edge of the desk chair in Erik's room. I'd sneaked back in just before five and gone immediately to waken him. Perhaps it was just a bit of showing off, but I couldn't even contemplate keeping the news to myself until he had come to on his own.

I'd crept back to my own room while he pulled on a pair of pants. I slipped Mindy's keys and flashlight back into her purse, relieved to see the gentle rise and fall of her chest beneath the sheet. By the time I'd splashed some cold water on my face, he had coffee going in the miniature two-cup pot thoughtfully provided by the motel. I brought a warm can of

Diet Coke along with the remains of the bag of corn chips. And Gray Palmer's ingeniously hidden coordinates.

"So is that what the creeps who beat up Mindy were looking for?" Erik asked as I settled onto the foot of his rumpled bed and popped the top on the soda. He poured coffee into a Styrofoam cup and took the desk chair.

"I don't think so. According to Mindy, they really didn't know *what* they were looking for. It was actually our fault she got beaten up. At least that's my working theory at the moment."

"How do you figure that?"

"We got spotted yesterday morning, if you recall. The way I see it, those guys in the boat reported it to someone. I don't think it can be a coincidence they left her alone for more than a week after they killed Gray then all of a sudden decided to go after her only a few hours after we stupidly let them know we had an interest in the island."

I gave him the chance to remind me it had been *my* stupidity, my eagerness to prove myself right that had put us on the *Wanderer* off Judas Island on Monday morning. Ever the gentleman, Erik let the opportunity pass.

Instead he asked, "You think they followed us up here? That they knew about our trying to get in touch with her?" He rubbed his hand across his face in a gesture which told me he'd had way too little sleep. Maybe the coffee would help. As if reading my mind, he crossed the room to refill his cup and start another pot going.

"No, I can't see that unless there are a whole lot more of them than we know about. Mindy said they came by boat. From her description they sound like the same two who checked us out yesterday."

"So you're saying our snooping around Monkey Island set off some sort of alarm bells with whoever is behind all this."

"Exactly. Somebody put two and two together and got five. They figured Mindy must have told me something which sent us to that specific spot. How else could we have latched on to it? So they sent their goons to beat it out of her and ransack her place. They really didn't know what they were looking for. I think they were counting on making her give it up if they couldn't find it on their own."

I swigged down more warm Coke, waiting for my partner to make the next logical leap of deduction. He took a couple of detours, but in the end he didn't disappoint.

"So you went out there, knowing full well they could come back at any minute to continue their search."

"Not likely. They didn't know what they were looking for. Without Araminda, they didn't have much hope. I think they just busted up her place to scare her into talking."

Again I waited. I wanted him to reach the same conclusion without any prompting from me. He blew across the steaming cup and stared at the sliver of light seeping through a crack in the dark blue drapes. When he finally spoke, his words could have come straight from my own lips.

"Then as soon as they figure out who and where we are, we're next up on the list."

THE MOTEL provided a continental breakfast, served in a small room just off the lobby. Erik and I loaded up with croissants, bagels, fruit, and juice and carried it all back upstairs. I could hear the shower running next door when we stepped back into Erik's room and spread the goodies out on his dresser. I moved through the connecting door and stuck my head in the bathroom.

"Breakfast is served," I called into the cloud of steam drifting out of the enclosed tub area, but got no response.

I shrugged and pulled the door closed behind me and filled a paper plate with a warm bagel which I slathered with cream cheese squeezed from a small packet. I peeled a banana and lifted the lid from a container of orange juice. Settled at the desk, I talked around mouthfuls to answer Erik's questions.

"What exactly did she tell you last night?" he asked when he'd perched on the end of the bed with his own laden plate.

"I think it would be better if you heard it directly from

her," I said. "Some of it sounds really far-fetched. I think she and Gray may have jumped to a whole lot of conclusions based on pretty flimsy evidence. Their scenario certainly explains some of what's been going on, but there's one big stumbling block I just can't get past."

"What's that?"

"Wait until you hear her story. I don't want to influence your judgment."

He shrugged, and I could tell he wasn't happy about my reticence, but I really believed he should get the unfiltered version. I licked cream cheese from my fingers and wiped them on the paper napkins we'd brought up with us. Erik flipped on the television, and we watched the latest from the turmoil in the Middle East. Engrossed in the live broadcast from reporters in the field, it was some time before it dawned on me Araminda Albright had not yet appeared.

I eased open the connecting door. The sounds from the shower had not abated. I stepped into the room and did a quick sweep before dashing back to the bathroom and flinging open the sliding door on the tub.

"ALL HER things are gone," I reported to Erik after my shout of frustration brought him running next door.

"What the hell is the matter with her?"

I knew he didn't expect an answer to the rhetorical question, and I didn't offer one. "Okay, let's think this out. Her car's out at the house, so she's either walking or she called a cab."

"Or a friend," Erik offered.

"Good point." I picked up the phone and dialed the front desk. The clerk on duty sounded way too chirpy for a little after seven o'clock in the morning. "Hi," I said, "this is Mrs. Tanner in 206. Did my friend get her cab okay?"

"I'm sorry?"

"My friend. Tall, beautiful, long black hair? She called a cab a while ago, and I wondered if she got picked up okay. I was down at breakfast when she left."

If the pleasant young man on the other end of the phone

found my request strange, he had been too well trained to let it show. "Why, yes, ma'am, she did. About fifteen minutes ago."

I wanted to ask if the helpful desk clerk knew which way she'd headed, but I thought that might be pushing his cooperation just a bit too far. "Thanks," I said and hung up.

"Where could she have gone?" Erik ran a hand through his tousled hair.

"I don't think we'll be able to find that out," I said, flopping myself down on the bed again. "I know the cops can get info from cab companies about where they took their fares, but there's no way anyone's going to share that with us."

"You're probably right. Do you think she went back to her house?"

"Maybe. If she did, I'd bet she's only there long enough to throw some things in a bag and hit the road. The girl is seriously frightened."

"So you've given up on your idea her story about the break-in was a fabrication?"

"Pretty much. From what she told me last night, she probably has reason to be afraid, if everything she and Gray suspected is true."

"You ready to share the fruits of last night's little tête-à-tête with me?" he asked.

"Absolutely. Let's get packed up first. I need to make a couple of calls, then we can get out of here and find someplace to plan our strategy. I don't think we should stay in one place too long, and we need to have it together before we meet with Gray, Senior."

"Why? What's he got to do with last night?"

I paused in the doorway before I spoke. "Araminda Albright thinks he might be responsible for his son's death."

CHAPTER
TWENTY-EIGHT

We took a couple of wrong turns, primarily because it had been a number of years since I'd had any reason to visit the Port of Charleston. Rob and I had always intended to check out the new aquarium and the nearby IMAX theater, but our weekends always seemed to have been spent at the beach house on Hilton Head rather than exploring the attractions of the town in which we lived the rest of the week.

As we approached the actual harbor, Erik let out a low whistle. "Wow! Look at the size of those cranes!"

Off-loaded containers were stacked all along the wide concrete dock near the towering blue-and-white behemoths rising almost a hundred feet in the clear morning air. Palmer Shipping's vessels were container ships, the goods they carried already packed into the large metal boxes which could be hooked up to tractor-trailer rigs and sent on the way to their ultimate destinations without further handling.

"Look there," I said, pointing to one of the giant ships lumbering its way from the ocean up the sparkling Cooper River and on to a terminal farther up the waterway. Erik slowed the car, and we watched the huge yet graceful vessel glide toward the massive bridge which connected the peninsula that was Charleston to the mainland. It was a route I generally refused to take, my obsessive fear of bridges with any kind of superstructure making my driving across it completely impossible. In fact, even as a mere passenger, I had to keep my eyes closed until the wheels of the car had rolled onto solid ground once again.

"That's it," I said, indicating a tall, modern building sitting incongruously next to the brick debarkation terminal for the boats which carried tourists out to Fort Sumter. Every school child knew cannonballs crashing into the walls of the federal garrison on that tiny island had been the flashpoint for the start of our bloody Civil War.

Erik, however, found the present-day wonders more engrossing. "Think what it must be like driving one of those things," he said. His eyes were still fixed on the giant container ship moving past the decommissioned World War II aircraft carrier *Yorktown* moored just across the way at Patriots Point, a poignant reminder of yet another conflict. Despite its beauty and serenity, Charleston seemed to be steeped in monuments to war.

He pulled into the parking lot in front of the office building and cut the engine.

"The captain doesn't actually get to 'drive' the ship in here," I said as we both climbed down from the Expedition.

"What do you mean?" Erik shaded his eyes against the brilliant glare of sun on water.

"Rob had a good friend who's a harbor pilot. They take a small boat out to those big boys and guide them in."

"Sounds like a cool job."

"It takes a long time to get certified, around six years I think, at least until you can work on something that size. They have to bring in over fifteen hundred ships or some incredible number before they're considered qualified."

We fell silent then, neither of us making a move toward the building which housed Gray Palmer's office. I knew Erik was dreading this encounter as much as I was.

I had made my phone calls—one fruitful, one not—and we'd checked out of the motel around seven thirty. I directed Erik to a small coffee shop in the heart of the historic district down near the Battery and its stately antebellum mansions facing the water. Amazingly most of these pastel-colored monuments to a long-dead Southern aristocracy showed no scars from the pounding they'd taken during Hurricane Hugo.

The narrow café was nearly deserted, but we asked for the last booth in the back just to be safe. Once the waitress had deposited our respective cups of tea and coffee in front of us, I leaned in and began my story.

Or rather Araminda Albright's story, for I related it as best I could without embellishment or comment. Erik, sensing the importance of letting me get it out, refrained from interruptions. When I finally sat back, he shook his head as if to clear it.

"That's just nuts," was his initial assessment, and I had to nod.

It had been my first reaction as well. Still, the girl and Gray had been a lot more intimately involved in the situation than either of us. And we had the added disadvantage of not knowing all the players. But that was about to change. We had had less than two hours at that point before we would be confronted with the supposedly grieving father, and Araminda's revelations had tossed all our carefully planned strategies into the toilet.

"She seriously believes Gray Palmer had his own son murdered?"

I shushed him with a wave of my hand. "You have to admit there's a certain logic. If young Gray had become convinced his father was involved in smuggling and had stumbled across the debarkation point on Judas Island, his father might have panicked. Or maybe his associates took it into their own heads the kid was a danger to the operation. It's possible Gray, Senior, had nothing to do with it."

"I can't believe a father could order a hit on his own kid. I know the damned world has gone crazy lately, but I'm just not prepared to believe that until there's irrefutable proof."

"I'm inclined to agree. But Mindy has herself convinced that's what happened. Her Gray's theory was that this foundation thing was just a cover to have them scout out possible new locations for the drop sites. A lot of those little islands we sailed past yesterday morning used to be havens for pirates and slavers back in the old days. When the State of South Carolina bought Judas Island, there was all kind of talk about developing the place. They figured GS needed to find another spot before that happened."

"But why not pick someplace completely deserted? Why Monkey Island in the first place?"

"Maybe that was the point. Someone goes over there every day to feed the macaques. And they must have to mount some kind of expedition to round up the ones they've sold. It wouldn't be as noticeable for boats to be hanging around that area as it would for the totally uninhabited ones. The fact the place is off-limits to the general public would also prevent their being surprised in the act, so to speak, by some fisherman or tourist."

"I suppose that makes sense. What is he supposedly smuggling? I assume we're talking drugs."

"No. She told me Gray thought it might be people."

"People?" Again I had to quiet Erik down. The waitress ambled by and offered him a refill. When she'd moved off, he said, "You mean like illegal aliens? Foreigners? Terrorists? And the grave they found was supposed to be one of these guys who died or got killed in the process?"

"God, Erik, I don't know, and neither did she. I never said this made a whole lot of sense. I just believe they took a bunch of circumstances and came to a set of conclusions that fit the evidence they thought they'd gathered. If it weren't so tragic, this entire thing could be classified as a comedy of errors."

"Okay, wait." His forehead furrowed in concentration. "Here's what shoots that whole idea out of the water. Doctor Douglass told us the bone had been in the ground for forty or fifty years, so there's no way it could have been some victim of this supposed smuggling operation."

"Exactly my point this morning when I told you there was one big stumbling block in their whole scenario. But Gray didn't know that. He was dead before you ever got the bone in the mail."

"But wouldn't he have figured it out? The same way Dr. Douglass did? He had the background."

"I don't think so. As I said before, he might have tagged the gender and race, but he didn't have any equipment for the other tests."

It felt as if the temperature had dropped ten degrees in the cozy restaurant as we both contemplated the validity of my statement. We'd fallen silent then. I had sipped my cold tea while Erik tapped his spoon against the side of his cup. When I couldn't stand the rhythmic banging any longer, I reached across to still his hand with my own.

"I still won't believe Gray Senior had anything to do with killing his own son," he said for what must have been the third or fourth time. "What reason did Mindy have for buying into something so disgusting?"

This had been another revelation I'd had trouble swallowing, but again I had no way to dispute their conclusions. "Apparently Gray blamed his father for his mother's death. I suppose that's when he first began hating him, and it doesn't appear to have abated over the intervening years."

When Mindy had floated this explanation for Gray's hatred of his father, my mind flashed back to my Internet research on the elder Palmer and the lack of any mention of his late wife's cause of death. "According to Mindy," I went on, "Gray's mother committed suicide. He blamed his father. She seems to think it isn't much of a leap from driving someone to kill herself and being capable of ordering the murder of your own child."

"God," was Erik's only reaction.

"Did he ever mention any of this to you? About his father, I mean?"

"No. All he ever said was his old man was a rich bastard and his mother was dead."

"Anything about a sister? The article I read mentioned she lived in California."

Erik shook his head. "Not that I can remember. Is it important?"

"Probably not. It's just another bit of confusion. I swear I don't know what to believe."

I had checked my watch then and realized we had only a short time before our appointment with this man whose son's friend was convinced he was a smuggler and a murderer.

"Listen," I had said, leaning in toward Erik again, "this is what I think we have to do . . ."

I REALIZED with a start I had been standing frozen next to the front fender of the Expedition, mentally rehashing earlier conversations, for quite some time. I glanced across the expanse of gleaming black hood to find Erik studying my face.

"Cold feet?" he asked, and I shook my head.

"Just gathering my thoughts. Ready?"

In answer he pushed himself away from the car and walked resolutely toward the building.

Our plan, devised hurriedly in the short time we had, was basically to operate without a plan. We could hardly charge into Gray Palmer, Senior's office and accuse him of having ordered a hit on his own son. Conversely, we certainly couldn't spill our guts to him about everything we had actually learned in the brief course of our investigation. We decided to play it by ear, to give him the report on the reward seekers, trying our best to ignore Araminda Albright's contention that the posting of the offer and his subsequent hiring of our neophyte firm to follow up had simply been a smoke screen to divert attention from himself and his illegal activities. While I still couldn't bring myself to believe her wild story completely, parts of it had enough ring of truth to make me tread cautiously. The opening lines of our script had been planned, but from there on we were pretty much going to have to wing it.

The reception area had the expected nautical theme, with framed color photographs of what I assumed were the ships of the line taking up one entire wall of the spacious room. To the left, a small antique desk, empty at the moment of our entrance, was shaded by several tall tropical plants in large clay pots. The ubiquitous computer screen sat in a matching hutch over a beautifully carved cherry credenza, and the multiline telephone *chirruped* softly as we stood waiting on a muted red carpet which looked to be either a genuine Persian or an excellent reproduction. The phone call must have been automatically transferred over to voice mail because the measured ringing abruptly stopped.

I was studying a chart of the local waters hanging just in front of us when the door next to it slid open. A compact woman who looked to be about my age pulled it closed behind her and moved around behind the desk.

"I'm so sorry to keep you waiting," she said in a voice mellow with the honey of the South. "You must be Mrs. Tanner and Mr. Whiteside. I'm Linda Marean, Mr. Palmer's secretary."

Ah, I thought, *the efficient one who faxed me the list of names.* In her tailored navy blue suit and prim white blouse, she appeared perfectly cast for the role.

"Nice to meet you," I said.

"Won't you have a seat? Mr. Palmer is running a little late this morning, but I'm sure he'll be with you very shortly."

"Thanks."

We sank down into matching overstuffed chairs upholstered in dark blue. Linda Marean pulled a slim file from a drawer next to her and swiveled her chair around to face the computer. Erik reached for the current copy of *Time* from the neat stack of magazines on the low table beside him while I fidgeted.

I had to admit I was having serious doubts. Not just about trying to bluff our way through a meeting with a man we seriously considered capable of causing his own son's death, but about the whole idea of being an investigator. Who did we think we were? A kid who knew his way around computers and a widowed accountant. What business did we have snooping into things that might have gotten people killed? I had to admit I loved the idea of solving the puzzle, but this wasn't some mystery novel or made-for-TV movie. If any part of Araminda Albright's story came even close to the truth, our butts should be planted in chairs across from the nearest police detective, not parked primly outside the office of a man who could be responsible for smuggling illegal aliens into the country and God knew what else.

I had almost made the decision to offer Ms. Marean some generic excuse, grab Erik, and bolt when the door to the inner office suddenly banged open. It bounced off the wall and rattled the framed photographs of the Palmer Line's ships. I jumped to my feet as if I'd been yanked from the chair.

The man who nearly bowled me over was in full military uniform, his peaked cap tucked under his arm. Behind him, framed in the doorway to the office, a figure I recognized from his television appearance as Gray Palmer, Senior, carried a look I couldn't quite identify. Something between anger and fear, I decided. His skin had that blotchy red color you associate with high blood pressure. Or someone about to have a heart attack.

"Harlan, wait!" he called to the stiff, retreating back.

Erik and I might have been invisible for all the attention anyone paid to us.

"Mr. Palmer . . ." Ms. Marean began, but she, too, was ignored.

"Pardon me," the military man said as he brushed by me, but he didn't slow his determined stride. I had a brief glimpse of blazing blue eyes under closely cropped gray hair before he pushed through the outer door and disappeared.

Employer and secretary exchanged a look I couldn't quite interpret before Palmer closed the door, much more gently than his visitor had opened it. He hadn't once acknowledged our presence. I collapsed back into the chair like a deflated balloon.

"I'm so sorry." Linda Marean had moved from behind her desk and stood guard before the entrance to Gray Palmer's office. "The Colonel just popped in for a minute. They're old friends, and . . ." Her explanation was cut short by the buzzing of the intercom. "Excuse me," she murmured and scurried back to her station.

I watched her listen and nod, then pull a pad of paper toward her and begin scribbling hurriedly. Once or twice she tried to interrupt, but her employer apparently cut her off in midsentence.

"What was that all about?" Erik whispered, his head bent close to mine.

Across the room I saw Palmer's secretary hang up the phone and turn back to the computer. In a few moments, the printer whirred into life.

"Beats me," I replied, but my brain was spinning.

What possible connection could there be between Gray Palmer and Colonel Harlan Fleming? I had no doubt this was the identity of the man who'd barely missed running me down, even though I'd never laid eyes on him before. The combination of his rank and his unusual first name made the deduction less than brilliant. But what was the father of the smug Amy, Chris Brandon's fiancée, doing here? Coincidence or . . . ?

I didn't have time to finish the thought.

"Mrs. Tanner?" Linda Marean beckoned. I rose to stand in front of her desk. "I'm so sorry, but Mr. Palmer is unable to keep his appointment with you. An emergency with one of the ships. I'm sure you understand."

I glanced over my shoulder at Erik, who had also risen from his comfortable chair to join me.

"That's okay. We'll wait," I said. Some part of my subconscious had apparently decided to ignore all my good intentions of just a few minutes before.

"I'm sorry, but that won't be possible."

Linda Marean drew herself up and took my stare without flinching. She couldn't begin to match me in height, but I had a feeling we'd rank dead even on the stubborn scale. The moment of silent confrontation held until Erik cleared his throat.

"Could we reschedule, ma'am? Perhaps for later in the day? Or maybe tomorrow?"

Erik's soft voice and calm demeanor melted some of the tension. The line of her shoulders eased, and her smile made it to just short of pleasant. "I don't think so. Mr. Palmer asked me to give you this." She thrust a sealed white envelope into my hand. "I apologize as well for any inconvenience. Please have a safe trip home."

With that Linda Marean took her seat, deliberately turned her back, and resumed her rhythmic attack on the keyboard.

Erik's face mirrored my own confusion, but there seemed little we could do outside of physically storming Gray Palmer's office. I shrugged, and he turned to follow me out of the building and into a glaring sun.

"Don't even ask," I said, holding up a hand to forestall the questions ready to burst from my young partner. "I don't have a clue what's going on. Maybe this will prove enlightening."

I pried up a corner of the envelope flap and ripped it open. The single sheet of paper was folded in thirds as proper correspondence etiquette required. The message was terse and unequivocal. I summarized for Erik as I read.

"He's firing us again. He says the autopsy report indicates young Gray had alcohol in his system, so Daddy thinks he's been wrong all along. Looks like it was just a stupid accident. 'Thank you for . . .' blah, blah, blah. He hopes we haven't been *terribly* inconvenienced. Yeah, right."

I shook my head in disbelief at the effrontery of the man. "'The attached should cover your time and expenses. If not, please submit an invoice for any balance, and I will be happy to . . .' This guy sure has balls."

Erik winced at the crudity, then gasped as I turned the paper around for him to see.

The company check neatly stapled to the bottom of the letter was made out to Simpson & Tanner in the amount of ten thousand dollars.

CHAPTER
TWENTY-NINE

We held our council of war over cheeseburgers and fries in a McDonald's on the way out of Charleston. I'd deliberately chosen a table next to the brightly colored playground equipment where any conversation we didn't want overheard would be drowned out by the squeals of half a dozen kids clambering over slides and swings.

We had taken a detour after getting bounced out of Gray Palmer's office, but that too proved fruitless. Araminda Albright's house stood empty, the bright yellow splash of her PT Cruiser gone from the sandy yard. The place was locked up tight, so we'd walked the perimeter, peering into cracks in the blinds and drapes, able to see enough to convince us she'd probably thrown some necessities together and bolted. Neither of us had the foggiest idea where she might have flown to, no clue as to what friends or relatives she might have sought refuge with. Although I knew she had all my contact numbers, I had added Erik's cell phone to the list and slid the piece of paper under the crack beneath the front door.

"So, back to square one," Erik said, wiping mustard from the corner of his mouth.

"Not exactly. We know a lot of things we didn't know yesterday. The trouble is, I'm damned if I can figure out exactly what to do with them."

"But I'm sure you're working on it. Refill?" he asked,

rising from the molded plastic chair affixed to the table. At my nod, he carried our cups to the row of self-serve drink dispensers.

Despite my earlier misgivings, I wasn't yet ready to admit defeat in the matter of the two Gray Palmers. I had the distinct feeling my partner had already begun to tire of the game, but was hanging on because of some sort of warped idea that I needed protecting. I thanked him when he set the brimming container of icy soda back in front of me.

We continued eating in silence for a few minutes, my racing mind proposing and rejecting possible scenarios. I knew the one I kept coming back to wouldn't sit well with my partner. I was right. Before the entire plan was even out of my mouth, he had rendered his decision.

"You're nuts," he said, the oozing sandwich hovering halfway between the table and his mouth.

"You're dripping that on your shirt," I pointed out. "And I'm not nuts. If you just apply a little logic to the process, you'll see I'm right."

Erik dabbed at the combination mustard/mayo stain on his blue denim shirt and shook his head. "If *you* apply a little logic to the process," he mocked me, "you'll see that our mounting some sort of daring midnight raid on an island crawling with wild monkeys and patrolled by a couple of armed goons in a speedboat ranks right up there with some of your all-time stupider ideas."

I tried to make light of our disagreement. "Come on. Where's your spirit of adventure?"

"Where's your spirit of self-preservation?" he countered.

We left it there and slipped the remains of our wrapped and boxed meals into the trash container before climbing back into the Expedition. We had left most of the midday traffic behind us by the time Erik spoke again.

"I didn't mean to say 'stupider,'" he said.

"What are you apologizing for, the insult or the bad grammar?"

He laughed. "Both, I guess. But are you really serious? How would we get out there?"

I was tempted to give him a smart-ass reply, but I knew he wasn't really questioning the method of transport. "Ron Singleton will take us. There isn't anyone who knows the waters any better. And he does seem to feel beholden to the Judge."

"We can't go cruising up to Monkey Island in that huge tourist boat of his."

"I agree," I said, "but I'm sure Ron will arrange to get something smaller. We can even rent one for him if we have to. And I'm thinking we'll leave from Presqu'isle."

"Why?"

"Because I checked out the map. It's a lot closer to Judas Island than the Beaufort marina. Ron can tie the boat up at our little dock, and we can approach the island from the back side. I'd be willing to bet that's where Gray landed."

I watched him mull it over. His eyes kept jumping to the rearview mirror, and I turned in my seat to see what was occupying so much of his attention. The road stretched clear behind us except for an SUV almost identical to ours a few hundred yards back.

"Something the matter?" I asked.

"I don't know. That big Chevy has been behind us ever since we left McDonald's."

"You think he's following us?" I stared out the rear window. "You know, except for the Interstate, this is the most direct route between Charleston and Beaufort. Anyone making the trip would normally come this way."

"You're probably right," he said, but I noticed he didn't stop checking the mirror every few seconds.

"So what do you think?" I asked, attempting to steer us back on topic.

"Let me see if I have this straight." An eighteen-wheeler zoomed by us heading north, the wash of its passing rocking us just a little. "You propose we hire this guy Ron to take us from Presqu'isle in a small boat, land us on Monkey Island, and wait to take us back. You and I will use the coordinates you found in that anatomy book and my GPS unit to locate the spot where Gray found the skeleton, dig it up, and . . ."

"What?" I asked when he paused, his gaze intent on the road behind us again.

"I've slowed down to fifty and speeded back up to seventy, and we haven't lost him."

Again I looked at the huge vehicle, its massive chrome grille gleaming in the afternoon sunlight. "Forget about him," I said, turning back around in my seat. "Finish your thought."

"I was finished. I can't get past the part where we dig up the body."

"We're not going to dig it up. Well, I guess we are, technically, but I don't intend for us to load it up and cart it away with us."

"I'm relieved to hear that."

"We just need to see whatever it was Gray saw. Maybe take some pictures."

"Why do I have the feeling this is already a done deal?"

I sat demurely in the passenger seat, my hands folded in my lap. "What do you mean?"

"Oh, please! Don't play Little Miss Innocent with me. Those phone calls you made this morning. Was one of them by chance to our intrepid captain of the *Wanderer*?" When I didn't reply, he went on. "No, wait. You wouldn't have wasted time trying to arrange this yourself. You talked to your father."

"Let's just say we explored the possibilities."

"You really are crazy, you know?" He smiled to take the sting out of his words. "Okay, so when is the big expedition set for?"

"Tonight."

"And after we locate this skeleton, assuming of course those numbers you found in Gray's book weren't just the coordinates of a great fishing spot, then what?"

"Like I said, we take a few pictures and get the hell out of there. And then we turn the whole thing over to the authorities."

"I know you love this sort of thing, this skulking around and playing detective, but why don't we do that right now?

Give all this information to your brother-in-law and bow out?"

"Think about Judas Island," I said. "Part of it's privately owned, the rest just acquired by the State of South Carolina. Even if we could convince the authorities there's anything to investigate, how long do you think it would take to get permissions or warrants? Whoever is involved in killing Gray Palmer could remove the skeleton, cover their tracks. This might be our only chance."

Erik sighed and nodded. "I see your point. Okay, good."

I understood the abrupt change of subject as the vehicle which had been trailing us suddenly sped up and moved out to the left. Because of the glare off the watery marsh bordering both edges of the road, I couldn't see the driver through the windshield. All the side windows were deeply tinted, although the passenger one appeared to be sliding down as the vehicle roared past.

"Satisfied?" I asked.

Erik turned to shrug just as the big vehicle pulled back into the right-hand lane. Neither of us recognized the distant popping sound that preceded the Expedition's lurch to the left, but the bright flash of brake lights registered on my brain a split-second before it did on Erik's.

"Watch out!" I screamed.

Erik stomped hard on his own brake pedal. The huge vehicle jerked under his hands as he fought for control, but it was already too late. The car began a long, lazy slide into the opposite lane. I had a brief glimpse of our former pursuers speeding away just before the grille of the oncoming cement truck filled my vision and the world exploded in a cacophony of air horns and screeching metal.

I CREDIT the driver of the cement truck as much as Erik with saving our lives.

His reactions bordered on incredible. He registered the road behind us was empty and, by flinging his mammoth vehicle to the left, avoided slamming us broadside. His rig did catch the right rear of the Expedition's bumper, ripping it completely off and sending us into a series of spins. We came to rest pointing back toward Charleston, our front wheels buried in the soft mud at the edge of the marsh.

The sudden stop had hit me like the punch of a giant hand, slamming me back against the seat. Dazed, I don't really remember anything for the next few minutes except black eyes round with fear and the gentle pressure of even blacker hands unhooking my shoulder harness and easing me out of the car. Other vehicles and other concerned faces swam before me as passing motorists pulled over to offer assistance.

Other than what I was certain would turn out to be massive bruising over every square inch of my body, I appeared to be unhurt, as was Erik, who came quickly around to join me on the narrow grass verge. The truck driver kept insisting we had to lie down, but neither of us complied. When it became apparent no one required immediate medical attention, many of the drivers who had stopped to help moved off. In the distance, the muted wail of a siren drifted across the expanse of swampy water.

Two hours later we had been checked over by the EMS unit and pronounced fit enough to travel. After an efficient tow truck driver from AAA had cranked the vehicle out of the mud and replaced the blown tire with Erik's spare, we remounted the Expedition and moved sedately on toward Beaufort. I had the name and address of our savior in the cement truck, and I had vowed to myself his children would never want for anything. Tons of paperwork had been filled out, and heads had been shaken over the vagaries of Fate which had allowed us to come through the blowout and subsequent accident without a scratch.

Neither Erik nor I ever mentioned the popping noises just before the crash, but both of us knew exactly what they had been.

CHAPTER
THIRTY

We didn't discuss the Palmers or our brush with death. Erik found the classical music station, something soothing with a lot of strings drifting softly from the speakers, and I lay my head back and feigned sleep. Though I kept my eyes firmly closed, I could feel his head move to check on me from time to time.

I tried to wipe all the violence of the past two days out of my mind, but images still played out against the inside of my eyelids like a bad dream. I could tell by the firm set of Erik's jaw as we'd climbed back into the car that I would have no more problems convincing him of the rightness of our cause. Having people trying to kill you can be a sobering experience. It can also seriously piss you off.

I came close to suggesting we postpone our planned excursion, but then thought better of it. The sooner we got the evidence, the sooner we could remove ourselves from Gray Palmer's radar. I squirmed in the seat trying to relieve some of the soreness in my neck, and Erik took it as a sign I had awakened for good.

"Almost there," he said, and I opened my eyes to glance at him.

We had passed over the Lady's Island bridge and were moving toward the causeway out to St. Helena.

"Good," I said, pushing myself into the full upright and locked position. "You're sure you're okay?"

He smiled. "Yup, I'm fine. You?"

"I'll make it." I paused, unsure how to open the discussion. "Hell of a job back there," I said, staring straight ahead at the soft green of spring unfolding along either side of the narrow road. The serenity of the scene belied the turmoil of the past few hours.

"Not any better than you and the deer," he replied.

I cleared my throat nervously. "The deer didn't shoot out our left front tire."

"So you noticed that, did you?"

I looked over to find him grinning like a child. A laugh bubbled up from deep inside me, again part hysteria, part relief, but I bit it back down. I had a feeling this one might turn into sobs before I could catch hold of it.

"Why didn't you say anything to the sheriff's deputy?"

"Why didn't you?"

I had the answer to that one ready. "Because we would have been there till this time tomorrow trying to make them believe us. We probably would have spent the night in the psych ward."

"Agreed. So now what? You think it's time to bring Red in on this?"

I eyed him as he made the turn into the rutted lane that passed for a road up to Presqu'isle. "No. We go ahead as planned tonight, get our evidence, and then let Red and his pals have at it. Even with the grave we've still got nothing like actual proof, but I think it will go a long way toward validating our theories. There might still not be enough for a prosecutor to take to a judge. Especially with the autopsy report stating young Gray had alcohol in his blood. I'm trusting Daddy will be able to enlighten us on that point."

He looked at me then in a peculiar way, as if he were appraising me or seeing me in a different light. Maybe he'd never heard me refer to my father as *Daddy* before. I only tend to do that in moments of stress. It isn't necessarily a term of endearment. At least that's what I tell myself.

I ignored him and plunged ahead. "No, I think we have to have something to make them sit up and take notice, something they won't be able to sweep under the carpet. Don't forget Gray Palmer is a prominent citizen in Charleston. No one's going to investigate him for murder, attempted murder, smuggling, and whatever else he's been up to just on our say-so."

"You know we only have his word on the coroner's report."

Even a close brush with death couldn't dull the quickness of his mind. "Right. You know the other phone call I made this morning?"

"You mean besides the one to arrange tonight's rendezvous?"

"Yes. I called Red and asked him to get us a copy of the autopsy findings."

"Why? We hadn't even heard Gray's father's version then."

"I was hoping to use it for ammunition, but Red told me it would take a few hours to process the request. He wasn't even sure if the Charleston police would release it to him. I asked him to leave a message with the Judge."

"Good."

I winced as the right wheel bounced out of one of the innumerable holes in the sandy dirt road. Everything hurt. I hoped a hot shower would restore me enough to get me through what we had to do in just a few hours' time. "So are we on? For tonight?"

"Okay." His capitulation seemed too easy, and he correctly read the suspicion in my eyes. "Hey, I don't like getting shot at any more than the next guy. I got into this whole mess to try and help out a friend. Then, when he died, I wanted to find out what really happened to him. Now it's personal. I want to nail that lying bastard father of his as much as you do."

"Okay." I softened my mockery with a smile. "I'll get the Judge to confirm things with Ron, see if he's found a suitable boat, and we'll . . . Son of a bitch!"

"What is it?" Erik asked as he pulled into the semicircular driveway behind a small white car parked just in front of the steps.

"Felicity Baronne."

"The hooker?"

"Yeah, the hooker." I closed my eyes, drew a deep breath, and stumbled out of the mud-spattered truck.

LAVINIA PULLED the door open just as I placed my hand on the knob, nearly jerking me off my feet. I saw her eyes flash past our shoulders to the Expedition.

"Lord, son, what happened to your car?"

Her remarks came out in a rushed whisper. Before he could respond, I grabbed his hand and pulled him after me down the hall and into the kitchen, Lavinia on our heels.

"How long has she been here?" I asked before Lavinia could start in on her own inquisition. The less we said about our afternoon's adventures, the less grief I would be subjected to.

The question served to divert her attention, as I had intended it should. "About half an hour."

The anger in her voice made Erik take a step backward, then decide on a total retreat. "I'll go wash up, if I may?"

Lavinia nodded and waved her hand in his general direction as if she were swatting at a pesky insect. "Guest bath, upstairs, second door on your right."

"Thank you. I remember." Erik shot me a look mingled with compassion and confusion and bolted.

"If things run true to form, she'll sashay out of here in a few minutes, and your father will have another check for me to mail."

"Why doesn't he just give them to her while she's here?" It hadn't occurred to me before, but it seemed a legitimate question.

"Why is grass green? Why don't you ask me something I might possibly know the answer to, you silly child?"

Lavinia was so rarely given to sarcasm or nasty temper I simply stared at her in disbelief. I couldn't remember a time when I had seen her this upset, not even during the chaos of my mother's sudden death or the agony of my father's strokes.

It was the last thing in the world I wanted to do, but I couldn't let her suffer any longer. "I'm going in there and find out what's going on."

"Bay, wait!" The hand she laid on my arm was as strong and firm as it had been in the remembered days of my childhood, but I shook her off and stomped toward my father's study. Enough was enough.

I nearly collided with Felicity Baronne as she emerged from the Judge's study. Resplendent this time in an emerald green silk sheath which had seen better days, she tottered toward the front door on stiletto heels that had to be leaving deep scars on the boards of the heart pine floor. Without a word she brushed past me.

"Wait!" I called, but she kept on moving away. "Felicity, wait!"

I didn't hear the wheelchair until the footrest bumped against the back of my legs, almost sending me sprawling. By the time I righted myself, my quarry had clattered across the verandah and stumbled down the steps, leaving the front door wide open. Our eyes met for a brief instant as she wrenched open the door of her little car. Then she ground the engine to life and sped off toward the lane in a shower of pebbles and dust.

I whirled to find my father glaring up at me. I could feel him gathering himself for an attack, but this time I was not having any of it. I grabbed one of the handles on the back of his wheelchair and spun him around. Without a word I propelled him across the faded Aubusson carpet and down the hall to his study. I pushed him into the room and kicked the door shut behind me. When I turned him again to face me, his look held both astonishment and anger.

"Okay," I said, my chest heaving with the effort to control my own fury, "that's enough! You're not putting Lavinia through any more of this crap. Spill it! Now! And I'm telling you, Father, it had better be a damned good story!"

ERIK HAD the good sense to make himself scarce. Either he was hiding in the bathroom, or he had sneaked out the front door while I had gone to drag a protesting Lavinia from the kitchen. Either way, I felt relieved not to have to deal with him for the hour or so it took me to wring the truth out of my father.

We assembled in his study, the Judge's wheelchair pulled up in front of the cold fireplace, Lavinia in one of the wing chairs to the right, facing him. I found I couldn't settle, so I spent the time pacing back and forth, ignoring both their entreaties for me to park myself somewhere. An observer might have thought the scene resembled an abbreviated courtroom, with my father as the accused, Lavinia the jury, and myself as the prosecuting attorney. If so, the roles had been fairly allotted.

"Bay, this isn't necessary," Lavinia said for about the third time. Ankles crossed primly in front of her, her back ramrod straight as usual, only her worn brown hands twisting a handkerchief in her lap betrayed her agitation.

"Yes, it is," I replied. I paused then to gather my thoughts, and what came out of my mouth surprised me as much as it did my listeners. "This house has always been about secrets. At least in the years I spent in it. And it's time it stopped."

I waved off the Judge's attempt to interrupt me. Now that I had begun, I realized I had an opportunity to say some things I hadn't even acknowledged to myself.

"As a child, I always felt left out of everything, as if I were an outsider and not a real member of the family. Conversations stopped when I came into rooms. Looks were exchanged . . ."

This time my father did manage to cut me off. "That's ridiculous! You were a child. You had no right to be privy to grown-up talk."

"No right. Yes, that pretty much sums it up. But it didn't stop after I grew up, Daddy. You still act as if I'm seven and need to be sent from the room because the adults are discussing sex."

The response fell short of his usual bark of contempt. "Nonsense."

"It doesn't matter whether you believe it or not. It's what I felt. What I *feel*. For God's sakes, I'm nearly forty years old! I watched my husband and two other people die in front of me! Haven't I earned the right to be treated like an equal?"

The muted ticking of the grandfather clock provided the only background. A tiny voice in the back of my head told me to leave it alone, not to open the Pandora's box of our family's history. *Maybe secrets aren't such a bad thing,* it whispered, and I faltered.

"Your father has a right to his privacy," Lavinia said softly. "We all do."

As reprimands go, it was pretty mild, but it had the desired effect. I felt the anger seep out of me like a long, slow exhalation of held breath. "Okay," I said, turning to my father. "Okay. But you do owe us an explanation about this woman and why you're paying her money." In a courtroom tactic I knew he had perfected, I paused for effect. "If not me, then you certainly owe it to Lavinia."

He tried for his usual bluster and again fell a little short. He would tell us. It just had to be on his terms.

"Forty years ago," he began, wiping the corners of his mouth with a pristine white handkerchief, "Felicity Baronne was a stunningly beautiful teenager."

He looked at Lavinia and me, defying us to contradict him. I nodded for him to continue, though it was hard to associate that description with the ravaged woman who'd just fled Presqu'isle.

"But wild," he went on. "Her daddy had run out on the family years before, and she had several brothers and sisters. The mother took in laundry, as I recall, or maybe cleaned houses. It doesn't matter. The point is there was no money. They were on the county a good part of Felicity's life."

"So she became a hooker?" This trite, maudlin tale grated on my nerves. A lot of people grew up in poverty and went on to make something of themselves. It seemed fairly obvious what Felicity Baronne had chosen to do with her life.

I couldn't quite read my father's stare. A mixture of sadness and disappointment, perhaps. "You can be as hard as your mother sometimes, Lydia." Two insults in one sentence. I had definitely angered him.

"Were you one of her clients? Is she blackmailing you? It seems a little late for that, don't you think? I mean, why should you worry about it now? No one's going to give a damn after forty years."

"Hush, Bay," Lavinia said from across the room. "Let him tell it in his own way."

I dropped onto the loveseat and wished for a cigarette. "Fine. Let's just move it along, okay? I have things to do tonight."

He knew exactly what I meant. We locked stares for nearly a full minute before he shook his head. "No, I was not one of her 'clients.'" The pause this time came from reticence, not from calculation. "But others were."

"Who?"

"That is none of your concern. Suffice it to say there are those whose families are still intact, men who don't wish to bring disgrace and unhappiness upon their wives."

A lot of candidates flashed through my mind, cronies and lifelong friends of the Judge who might call on him to rescue them from this dilemma: Law Merriweather, the attorney who had helped us with Mercer Mary Prescott; Charlie Seldon, the former county solicitor; Boyd Allison, whose daughter and son-in-law still operated the East Bay Book Emporium he had founded. These were just the first who leaped to mind, probably because they had been my father's poker buddies up until the last few months when the ill health of several members had forced them to disband their Thursday night ritual. But my father knew hundreds of people. It could have been any number of them, names I might not even recognize.

"So this has all been done out of altruism? You're paying this woman thousands of dollars of your own money to keep her from blackmailing your friends?"

He shook his head, and again I thought I detected disappointment in his eyes. "It's not blackmail, daughter. It's . . ."

He hesitated, and it struck me how old and frail he looked. I opened my mouth to stop him, to call a halt to the inquisition. But I glanced quickly at Lavinia and remembered why I had started this in the first place.

"It's what?" I prompted.

He took a long time to answer. "There was a child."

CHAPTER
THIRTY-ONE

Twenty minutes later I left them alone and dragged myself up the steps to my old room. I stopped on the way by in what had become my private bathroom to set the plug in the old claw-footed tub and turn the hot water tap on full. I dropped my wrinkled clothes on the floor next to my four-poster and pulled on the threadbare chenille robe I kept hanging on a hook behind the door before padding back to the bathroom. I eased myself into the soothing, scented water and lay back against the cushioned headrest.

Secrets, I thought, feeling my battered muscles begin to relax, *always secrets.*

In those days before DNA testing, no one could be certain who had fathered Felicity Baronne's child, my father had said, so several of her regular customers discreetly provided a substantial stake and sent her on her way. Perhaps there was a spark of honor or conscience in the girl, for she had gone willingly and never looked back. If the child was born or aborted, no one ever knew for certain. Until now.

I lifted the bar of lavender soap from the wire holder hanging on the rim of the tub and lathered my body.

Lavinia believed him, although I wasn't sure I did. If Felicity Baronne had indeed come back to ask for help for her daughter—as alone as her mother and ravaged by ovarian cancer—why hadn't the Judge just quietly canvassed the likely candidates and come up with another joint payoff?

Why did the woman continue to haunt Presqu'isle? Once she'd made her pitch, my father or the others could just as easily have given her a lump sum and sent her packing again.

"She isn't good with money," my father had replied when I'd posed the question. "This way she's assured of its being available when she needs it."

He had a ready answer, too, for why Felicity made the hour-long drive to St. Helena rather than simply telephoning and asking for a payment.

"Because it's more . . . civilized. She enjoys talking about the old days. As do I."

His eyes had gone wistful then, some of the ravages of the years and the strokes slipping away from his drooping face, and again I'd wondered if I could trust his insistence that he had not been involved with the wild, beautiful teenager. Hadn't Lavinia said Felicity called him Tally? No one but his wife and his intimates had ever referred to him by that name. Why should my then vigorous, handsome father have been immune to the girl's charms? God knew his home life hadn't been any bed of roses.

"Then why didn't you just give her the money while she was here? Why involve Lavinia in something that was certain to upset her?" I'd asked.

"Handing her a check would have been . . . demeaning to her. Believe it or not, Felicity Baronne is a woman of considerable dignity."

My laugh of derision had gone unchallenged, although my father had shaken his head sadly.

You can be as hard as your mother sometimes, he'd said to me. I shivered in the cooling bathwater. Tough to escape genetics, but I had spent a lot of years trying. Maybe you couldn't. Maybe those twisted little strands of DNA were bound to win out in the end no matter what you did.

I rinsed out my hair and pulled the plug. As I wrapped my head in one towel and dried my aching body with the other, I could at least smile at the picture on which I had closed the study door: Lavinia's sturdy brown hand clasped in my fa-

ther's, their heads close together as she knelt on the floor by
his chair. It was the first time they'd ever let me see a display
of physical affection between them. I sincerely hoped it
wouldn't be the last.

APPARENTLY I was the only one feeling the least uncomfortable as we gathered around the kitchen table. Lavinia had recovered her old, brusque efficiency. Never given to overt
displays of any emotion, I could tell nonetheless that she
was happy again by the way she bullied my father and by her
insistence that Erik fill his plate a second time. I ate mechan-
ically, my mind on the upcoming expedition, and to this day
I couldn't say for certain what we had for dinner that night.

Over coffee and tea we talked about the case. No one suggested Lavinia leave the room, and she bustled around behind us, arranging the few leftovers in plastic containers and
washing up the dishes.

The Judge had been as astounded as Erik and I by Gray
Palmer's check. Like us, he interpreted the inappropriate
size of it as an admission he seriously wanted us to drop the
investigation and go away. Red's phone call while I had been
drowsing in the tub only added more substantiation.

"Point-oh-two," my father said. "That's what the boy's
blood alcohol level was. I'm no expert on the matter, but I
wouldn't think that would be much more than a beer or two.
You have to hit point-one-zero to be considered legally in-
toxicated in this state. And no sign of drugs."

"What does Red think?"

"I didn't pursue the matter with him, daughter. The less
he knows about your scheme, the less likely he is to come
charging to your rescue."

I had to admit this new attitude surprised me. Usually my
father stood in the forefront of those warning me off my
more harebrained ideas. If he were going to become a fully
engaged partner, we just might get this detecting enterprise
off the ground after all.

"So what time will Ron get here?" I asked as Lavinia refilled Erik's coffee cup, poured one for herself, and joined us again at the table.

"Around midnight," he said. "That should get you to the island sometime after one. I figured that would give you plenty of time to find the . . . uh, location, take your pictures, and get away well before first light." I smiled, and he raised an eyebrow. "What?" he asked.

"I have to say, Your Honor, I'm really enjoying having you as a co-conspirator instead of a nagging, overprotective father."

"I'll take that as the compliment I'm sure it was intended to be."

He had obviously forgiven me for my inquisition earlier in the study. Perhaps he was even glad I had taken the initiative in forcing him to tell Lavinia the truth about Felicity Baronne. Both his honor and his happiness had been well-served.

"Well, young man," my father said, turning to Erik, "are you prepared for this adventure?"

"I guess so, Judge Simpson," Erik replied. "I've got film in the Nikon and fresh batteries in the GPS unit. Bay says you have a couple of powerful flashlights." My father nodded. "I guess the only thing I'm missing is a warm jacket and a way to get these damned knots out of my stomach."

We laughed, but I knew exactly what he meant. Like so many other things in life, contemplating this trip intellectually had been exciting. Now that the time for action was drawing near, my mind kept dwelling on all the things that could go wrong.

"Ron Singleton will have a radio in case you run into trouble. He's sworn to me he won't leave the island without you, and at the first hint of trouble he'll call in reinforcements." A note of something I thought might be fear had crept into his voice. "You'll take your pictures and get the hell out of there as fast as you can."

"No argument here," I said. I hugged my arms as a chill ran up them.

We sipped our drinks in silence for a few moments, each

of us no doubt wondering what revelations the night's work might bring. I sent up a short prayer we would all be sitting here discussing it like this come morning.

My father broke into our thoughts. "Vinnie, would you be so kind as to fetch me that box from the top of my desk?"

I loved the look which passed between them as Lavinia rose and left the room. He turned then to Erik.

"Tell me again what this professor friend of yours had to say."

"About the bone?" Erik looked at me, but I could only shrug. I had no idea where the Judge was going.

"Yes. He said it had probably been in the ground for how many years?"

"Forty, maybe fifty. Somewhere around that. He said he couldn't be certain without running some further tests."

We waited for a response, but my father seemed deep in thought. Finally he mumbled, "Hmm. That would be about right."

"What are you getting at?" I asked, leaning toward him. "Do you have some idea about who it could be?"

Lavinia's return forestalled his immediate response. She set a small wooden box in front of him and resumed her seat.

All eyes focused on the Judge as he made a ceremony of raising the lid. The small leather holster he lifted out fit neatly in the palm of his hand, as did the miniature weapon he slid from it.

"Tally! Dear God, put that thing away!" Lavinia leaped to her feet, backing up until the sink stopped her.

"Vinnie, hush now. It isn't loaded. Come on, sit back down here."

Reluctantly she obeyed. Erik and I exchanged a look of surprise.

"It's for you, Bay," my father said, turning the little pistol over and handing it to me, grip first.

"Why? I have the Glock."

He raised an eyebrow in unspoken question.

"Yes, I carry it. Especially since . . ." I let the thought trail off. No sense in bringing up unpleasant memories. Much as

I had resisted his first insistence that I learn to shoot, the weapon had been instrumental in the fact I was still here to talk about it.

"You'll give that to Erik. Can you handle a gun, young man?"

"No, sir. And with all due respect, I won't carry one. I'd probably shoot myself rather than a bad guy."

"As you wish, although I'd feel much better if you were both armed."

"Why can't I just use the Glock?" I asked, fingering the miniature weapon.

"Smaller, easier to fire, single-action. It can fit in your pocket, and no one will even know you have it."

I had to admit the gun felt comfortable in my hand. I tried not to think too much about what that said.

"I'll load it up for you and give you a quick lesson. It's a Seecamp, completely handmade. They're very rare. And very expensive."

"Where . . . ?"

"A friend of mine gave it to me. I was able to help him out with a small problem some years back. A barber named Len over on Hilton Head. He's also a registered gun dealer."

He paused and extended his hand to me. Reluctantly I surrendered the weapon. In those few short minutes it seemed to have become mine in a way the Glock never had. He placed the pistol back in its holster.

"I hate all this talk of guns. I'm going to make sure Erik's room is in good order." Lavinia rose and marched out.

"Sometimes unpleasant things are necessary," my father mumbled to no one in particular. He paused to follow the sound of Lavinia's soft tread as she mounted the staircase, and I thought I detected a look of relief on his face. Before I had a chance to examine that too closely, he hurried on. "Listen to me now. After you told me what the professor had to say about that bone, I had Law Merriweather do a little checking for me."

"About what?" I asked.

"Missing persons cases, still open. From the late fifties, early sixties."

"Did he find anything?"

"He came up with quite a few possibilities, I'm afraid."

"How many?"

"Eleven which were suspicious over a period of five years or so."

"Really?" I asked, surprised. "I wouldn't have thought there would be that many in this little area. Anyone who fits the professor's profile?"

"Three," he answered, and cast a look over his shoulder. I could feel the tension in his voice. "That's the only reason I'm giving my sanction to this scheme of yours, Bay. Because I have a terrible feeling there might be more than one grave over there."

"You think all three could be buried on Judas Island? But why? What could they possibly have to do with Gray's death or his father's smuggling? And you don't even know if these people are actually dead. They could be anywhere."

"You're right," he said, "but the coincidence is just too much to ignore. All of them were young black men in their early twenties. They all disappeared on the same night, and I'm very afraid one of them may be . . ."

I whirled at the low moan.

Lavinia stood in the doorway, her face a mask of fear and stunned disbelief. "Dear God, you don't think . . ." she began, but her words were cut off by the crash of the crystal vase of wilted roses as it slipped from her trembling hand and shattered against the gleaming wood floor.

CHAPTER
THIRTY-TWO

Ron Singleton offered me his hand as I stepped down into the narrow aluminum boat and crawled toward the cushioned seat at the bow. I felt the rocking as Erik clambered in after me. He carried a backpack, resurrected by Lavinia from some storage box in the far reaches of the attic. It seemed familiar, as if it might have been the one I toted around with me at Northwestern half a lifetime ago. Into it we had stuffed the flashlights, camera, a couple of spare jackets, and a few other things we'd need to complete the night's work. At the last minute, I'd shoved in the Glock.

"All set?"

At our nods, Ron slipped the single rope from the piling at the end of our small fishing dock. The scream of the outboard motor as it roared to life seemed loud enough to be heard in Charleston. As we eased out into St. Helena Sound, I looked back toward Presqu'isle. Silhouetted in the spill of light from the Judge's study, Lavinia stood on the back verandah, arms folded across her chest, a solitary sentinel to our departure. I felt as if her gaze held mine, even though her face was lost in the shadows, and mine could have been no more than a blur in the meager light of a thin moon. Nonetheless, I kept my eyes fastened on her retreating figure until we rounded a small headland and the house was lost to view.

The outcome of our expedition had become as important to her as it was to us. Maybe more so.

Ron revved the engine, and we moved out into the current, headed directly for Judas Island. With the tide coming in, the trip should take no more than twenty minutes. It was one of the reasons for waiting until after midnight to set out. The other had been the belief that any patrols might be relaxed in the hours when most sane people were in their beds.

Erik had voiced the concern that the attack on Araminda Albright—and the senior Gray Palmer's sudden about-face regarding our employment—might have engendered a heightened presence in the area. My father and I were of the opinion just the opposite might be the case. Again, normal people would have taken the not-too-subtle hints and moved on. They also had no way of knowing if their attempt on Erik and me earlier that day had been successful or not. For all Palmer's murderous associates knew, we might be lying in the hospital. Or the morgue. At any rate, if things went according to plan, we'd be in and out of there too fast to alert anyone to our presence. If . . .

In spite of our heavy sweatshirts and jeans and the warmth of the evening breeze as we'd waited for Ron, the air out on the open water cut through to my bones. In only a few minutes of running flat-out in the small motorboat, with no screen to cut the bite of the wind, my eyes were streaming and my teeth chattering. I hung on as long as I could.

I had just turned to ask Erik to pull one of the fleece jackets out of his pack when the engine speed dropped. I glanced past him to Ron Singleton, seated at the tiller, and he gestured with his free hand. I followed the direction of his finger and saw a solid bank of trees rising off to our right. He cut the engine altogether. It amazed me how fast the temperature of my skin rose once the wind no longer buffeted me.

I righted myself and watched the island loom closer as we drifted silently on the incoming tide. I couldn't believe how fast we were moving without the motor. As we drew nearer, I saw a narrow ribbon of water open up to our right. Parrot

Creek, if I remembered correctly from our brief study of the charts during our first trip out with Ron.

He reached under the seat and pulled out two long oars. Mutely he fitted them into the locks on either side of the boat and signaled Erik to change places with him. Our captain positioned himself on the center seat and dug the oars into the water. We glided into the stream, the only sound an occasional grunt as Ron moved us closer. I saw Erik remove the GPS unit from his pocket and tap the button to illuminate its face. In answer, I patted the Seecamp tucked snugly against my right hip.

The next shallow creek seemed little more than a trickle as Ron maneuvered us into its channel. Again we drifted on an unseen current. A few hundred yards in, the boat nosed its way toward the barely perceptible shore then bumped against solid ground. Ron leaped out, his tall rubber boots making sucking sounds in the mud as he grabbed the painter and pulled us farther up onto land. Erik and I scrambled out, our own shoes immediately soaked through.

"You got our location marked on that thing?" Ron's whisper cut through the eerie stillness.

"Got it," Erik replied in an equally hushed voice.

We took the flashlights from his pack and tested them briefly against the marshy ground.

"Look!" I said softly, pointing to the area immediately in front of us.

Several sets of footprints, confirming our guess about this being Gray and Araminda's own landing site, led away from where we stood and disappeared into the trees, many of their trunks stripped bare of bark. I remembered seeing that on our initial reconnaissance of the island and wondered if the monkeys had wrought the destruction. At the exact moment the thought flashed through my head, one solitary, high-pitched scream split the air.

"Jesus!" I whispered, and beside me I heard Ron's low chuckle.

"Just the locals," he said, and his gleaming white teeth

flashed in the nearly invisible black of his face. "Avoid 'em if you can. Nasty-tempered little bastards, or so they say. I'll be just offshore here, in among this marsh grass. I'll give you two hours, then I'm callin' in the Marines."

"Thanks," I said, and touched Erik on the arm. "Let's go."

He flicked on the global positioning unit, set off along a barely perceptible path, and was almost immediately swallowed up by the dense woods.

With a last look over my shoulder at the small boat drifting slowly out into the creek, I trotted in after Erik.

I FELT rather than saw the presence of the monkeys. At first it was hard to tell their furtive movements from the natural rustling of the trees in the light breeze. But as we moved farther into the interior of the island, I could sense dozens of pairs of eyes on us. It was as creepy a feeling as I've ever had. Only an occasional squeak or chatter betrayed it was not humans who monitored our slow progress.

We hadn't wanted to risk using the flashlights until we had no choice in the matter, and that point arrived within seconds. Without the sure, steady beams to guide us, we would have sprawled facedown on the squishy floor of the woods any number of times. Twisted tree roots hidden beneath a carpet of brown pine needles and decomposing leaves could easily have been our undoing.

I judged we had been walking in nearly a straight line for the better part of ten minutes when Erik stopped.

"What is it?" I moved up close behind him before speaking softly.

"The unit indicates we should move off to the right." He pointed in a direction at about a forty-five degree angle to where we stood.

"So let's do it."

"It doesn't make sense," he said, and I could hear, rather than see, his concern.

"Why? Isn't that the reason we brought the damn thing? What's the point if we don't go where it tells us to?"

"Flash your light over there."

Again I followed his pointing finger. The beam seemed to bounce right back at me.

"That underbrush is almost a solid wall. And look here," he said, scanning his own light across the tangle of thorny bushes and weeds. "There's no break anywhere along here. If Gray forced his way through here, there would be broken branches. Some of this undergrowth would be trampled. And it's not."

"So what do we do?" I surprised myself by the depth of my calm. But once before I had put myself in the hands of Erik and his magical gadget, and he had proved its worth beyond any doubt. Of course that had been in broad daylight with half a dozen people around. Still . . .

"I say we keep following this track," he said. "I'll bet it twists around and comes back to the direction we want to go. I think it's what Gray would have done."

"Fine. Let's try it."

He nodded, and we moved off. Overhead the rattling of branches grew louder, as if the monkeys leaped from tree to tree, keeping tabs on us. I tried to shut the images out of my mind and keep my eyes on the muddy path in front of me. So deep was my concentration I nearly stumbled into Erik who had come to a dead stop. I put out a hand to brace myself against his back then followed the direction of his light.

The bracken on the right side of the path opened up to a small clearing. If you weren't looking for it, the slight mound in the center would have been indiscernible from the bumpy terrain around it. I added my beam to Erik's, and together we swept the area. An attempt had been made to disguise the disturbance by scattering leaves and debris randomly across the top of the grave. Gray had done a pretty good job, and again a casual passerby would probably never have given the place a second glance.

In the dim glow reflected up from the illuminated ground we exchanged a look of satisfaction. Then Erik lowered the backpack and began removing its contents. He set the Nikon carefully to one side along with the Glock then pulled out the two folding shovels. I knelt on one of the unused jackets and brushed away the thin covering of leaves and twigs. The ground was so loosely packed we could almost have used our hands, but I took the shovel Erik held out to me, and together we began the disinterment.

I sent up a silent prayer that I wouldn't disgrace myself by doing something female, like throwing up or passing out when we finally reached the body.

I STOPPED once to stretch out my back and pull the sweatshirt over my head. I pushed up the sleeves of the turtleneck which constituted my second layer. We had to go slowly since we had no idea how close to the surface the remains might lie, and we didn't want to destroy anything vital by being careless. Still, as I paused to catch my breath and check my watch, I found we had been on Judas Island just under an hour.

Beside me, Erik kept up his rhythmic motion, gently loosening the soil and setting it aside. The grim lines of his face told me he might share some of my own misgivings about what we were doing, but that, like me, he would see it through. I set back in, matching my movements to his. In the glow of the flashlights, positioned on the ground to illuminate our work area, I finally saw a flicker of color beneath the next layer of soil.

"Wait," I whispered, but Erik had seen it too.

We tossed the shovels aside and began scooping the dirt away with our hands.

IT WAS a lot less frightening than I had imagined. The bones, though caked with dirt, seemed no more alarming than the model of a skeleton Mr. Baylor had brought in for our tenth-grade biology class. We cleared away as much of the soil as we could, my eyes avoiding the gap in the right leg where Gray Palmer had removed the femur.

"There's the watch," Erik said.

Some trick of decomposition had left the watch face stuck to the left wrist bone. We played the light over it, and I thought I could detect a few strands of what had probably been a leather band. In unspoken agreement, we set the lights back on the ground and resumed our grisly task.

Erik worked at the head and I at the feet. I felt the dirt caking my nails and imbedding itself in the pores and creases of my skin. In our careful planning we had neglected to think of gloves. Even a brush would have been of some help.

Overhead, I could again feel the eyes of the monkeys on us. The level of their chattering and screeching had increased as if they discussed this invasion of their sleep by their oversized primate cousins. I wondered if somewhere, deep in their nonhuman brains, they associated our presence with the regular disappearance of their mates and offspring.

In a few more minutes we had the skeleton completely exposed, and Erik reached for the camera. As he fussed with the lenses and attached the flash, I ran my light over the entire grave. Dark blue remnants of what must once have been a pair of jeans clung to the lower torso. It—or rather *he*—must have been barefooted, for I could detect no sign of shoes. Nothing remained of anything resembling a shirt, but there did seem to be some material near the head. Thin strands of what looked like burlap had adhered themselves to the skull, and other fibers stuck out from behind the neck. I tried, but couldn't bring myself to touch them.

"Erik," I whispered.

He slung the strap of the Nikon around his neck and knelt be-side me.

"See this stuff?" I pointed to the few frayed strands. "What do you think that is?"

"I don't know. Let me get some pictures first. We really shouldn't touch anything until we get a record of how it looked when we first uncovered it. Keep the light low so it doesn't interfere with the flash."

I moved over opposite him and trained the flashlight on the head. The strobe of the camera almost blinded me, and I looked away. Erik stepped methodically around the open grave, snapping continuously.

"There, I think that's got it," he finally said, setting the Nikon aside. "Now let's see what we've got here."

Again I fixed the upper part of the skeleton in the light. The fibers were clearly visible on both sides of the neck. I leaned in, still afraid to touch the remains. "It almost looks like . . ."

"Rope," a voice said behind me.

The flashlight tumbled from my hand into the open grave, clattering against the stark white ribs of the body, and plunging us into darkness.

CHAPTER
THIRTY-THREE

I know I didn't faint. I've never fainted in my life. But there were at least a few minutes unaccounted for by the time I had recovered my senses enough to realize what was happening.

I found myself seated on the ground next to Erik, our backs pressed up against the scratchy trunk of a pine tree unscathed by the monkeys. Across the gaping hole we'd just dug, the blinding beams of their flashlights kept the men's faces indistinguishable. I knew there were two of them only by the matching sets of black boots visible just outside the arc of the light. And by the yawning holes in the barrels of the guns they pointed at us.

I glanced immediately to the contents of the pack spread just out of reach to my right, but the Glock was gone.

"I regret I needed to confiscate that, Mrs. Tanner."

The deep, masculine voice carried a hint of an accent, and I strained in an effort to recognize it. Nothing came. I'd almost swear I'd never encountered this man before. His companion remained mute. It didn't take much of a leap of logic to figure out who they must be. And that gave me hope. The two men who had broken into Araminda Albright's house could have killed her right off if they'd wanted to. Perhaps this was only meant to frighten us off. If so, it was working admirably.

"My father knows where we are," I said, surprised by my own calm. "If we're not back . . ."

"Screw your father! Too damn bad the old goat isn't here, too. I'd love . . ."

"Shut up! Now!"

The second man fell silent at this command, but not before I'd recognized his slightly slurred voice. I knew I was right, but it made absolutely no sense.

"You're a long way from the real estate office, Harry," I said in as conversational a tone as I could muster. Beside me I felt Erik's head whip around in my direction. "I'm surprised you could haul your fat, sorry ass this far into the woods without dropping dead of a heart attack."

Harry Simon growled low in his throat, and I saw a camouflaged arm reach out to restrain him.

Camouflage! And yet I couldn't begin to imagine balding, overweight Harry Simon crawling in and out of boats, beating up young women, murdering . . .

"It will do you no good to annoy my friend here any further, Mrs. Tanner. You and your father are not exactly his favorite people to begin with. Though I was actually quite amused by his account of the evening he spent in your charming company." His laugh made my stomach knot. "If you'd ever seen Harry drink, you'd know it would take more than a few watered-down bourbons to pry anything out of him we didn't want you to know." He paused to let this information sink in then flicked the flashlight at us. "Up now. Both of you. Nice and slow."

Erik helped me to stand. The stiffness screamed in every part of my body, and I wasn't certain my legs would hold me. Strangely I felt no fear, or very little at any rate. That might have had something to do with the sharp stab of the little Seecamp pistol against my right hip as I scrambled to my feet. Removed from its holster and tucked into the pocket of my jeans, its presence was invisible. Neither of them had frisked me. Even if they had, the tiny weapon would probably have gone undetected.

Once before someone had assumed I—a mere woman— would be unarmed, an assumption they lived awhile to regret.

"We're going for a little hike," the non-Harry man said, and again he used the light to motion us forward.

"Who's in there?" I asked, my eyes dropping to the gaping hole of the uncovered grave. "Is he the reason you had to kill Gray Palmer?"

"Little bastard just couldn't leave it alone," Harry began. "We tried to warn him off, but . . ."

"Shut up, Corporal! That's an order!"

Corporal? The barked command could have come straight off the parade ground. But Harry Simon hadn't been in the military for at least thirty or forty years.

"Move! You first, Mrs. Tanner."

The man jerked his light toward the path we'd taken up from the landing, and I suddenly wondered what had happened to Ron Singleton. Surely they wouldn't have . . .

But he motioned us in the opposite direction. Harry moved out in front, his waddling bulk nearly obscuring the beam of his flashlight on the rough track. Behind me I could hear Erik's measured breathing over the crackle of our feet on the underbrush. The second man brought up the rear. I glanced back over my shoulder, but again the light kept me from seeing anything of his face.

The monkeys tracked us, their excited chattering growing in volume as we moved farther away from the grave. I stumbled frequently, my hand brushing against my pocket each time I righted myself. As we trekked farther into the dark interior of the island, I became more and more convinced the concealed pistol might represent our only hope.

I couldn't read my watch face, so I had no idea how long we marched single-file along the narrow path. It could have been ten minutes or an hour before we finally stumbled into a clearing. I thought I could make out the dim outlines of a building off to one side, and just beyond I could hear the gentle lapping of water against the shore. In my first glimpse of the sky since we'd entered the woods on the other end of the island, I noticed a small bank of clouds had obscured the waning moon.

Harry Simon lighted himself to a bench and flopped down, breathing heavily. His companion snapped off his own flashlight, leaving Erik and me standing disoriented in the open space.

"Sit," the voice ordered from behind us, and we lowered ourselves to the rough, uneven ground.

Erik shifted himself until his left leg brushed against mine. I felt his arm move to encircle my shoulders, but I shrugged him off. I knew he only meant to offer comfort, but I wanted to keep my right hand free, just in case I got a chance to go for the pistol. I squirmed around, trying for the position which would allow me the quickest access to the gun.

"Quit fidgeting, Mrs. Tanner." His conversational tone and the way he kept repeating my name were beginning to grate on me in a way Harry Simon's snarling nastiness hadn't.

"What now?" I asked, making no effort to keep the contempt out of my own voice. "If you're going to kill us, it would have made more sense to do it back there. You could have used the grave we'd already opened for you."

"Bay . . ." Erik began, but our captor's low chuckle interrupted his protest.

"I must say I do admire your sang-froid, Mrs. Tanner. You would have made a formidable soldier."

The way he spoke to me . . . The mocking, formal address . . . It was almost as if he knew me. And yet I had no clue as to his identity. In the silence that followed, I let my mind range back over the events of the past two weeks. *Nothing.* Unless . . . His use of the word "corporal." The aura of command in his voice. And that last remark about my making a good solider . . . *No! But why?*

"I can feel the heat from your mental processes all the way over here," he said. Had there been enough light, I felt certain I would have seen him smiling. "Have you figured it out yet? The Judge was always bragging about how clever you are."

So he knew my father, too. Another possible confirmation of the wild idea rattling around in my head. I had nothing to lose. And it almost seemed as if he *wanted* me to . . .

"Well, Colonel, I'd hate to think my father might be accused of hubris on my behalf."

"Colonel?" Erik mumbled beside me, but our captor's laugh drowned him out.

"Bravo, my dear, bravo! What gave me away? My unfortunate slip in addressing poor Harry here by his former rank? Or was it our accidental meeting yesterday in Gray's office? It's what I always tell my junior officers: even the most careful planning has to allow for the element of circumstance. That you and I should be in that particular place at that particular time . . . Well, who could have factored in such a twist of fate?"

"What the hell is he talking about?" Erik's voice held anger, although I couldn't be certain at whom it was directed.

I knew now how the game would have to be played. "Erik Whiteside meet Harlan Fleming, Colonel, United States Marine Corps."

"I'm truly sorry for this, young man." He sounded almost sincere. "I had hoped we could avoid further bloodshed."

"So you did kill Gray Palmer! But Gray Senior is your friend! The secretary said you'd known each other . . ."

I stopped myself, names and images tumbling around in my brain faster than I could sort them out. Harry Simon on the Judge's verandah . . . The newspaper article on Palmer . . . The connection, when it clicked into place, seemed so obvious.

"You were all in the service together. You and Harry and Gray's father. All here, I'll bet, at Parris Island." When he didn't reply, I took a second to do the math. "You would all have been what—twenty or so? In the early sixties. Just about the time that body went into its grave."

"You killed him," Erik said beside me, the wonder in his voice tinged with outrage. "You hanged a black man—or strangled him—and buried him on this deserted island."

I recalled then the Judge's remark over lunch the previous day. *Sometimes overly harsh with the men of color under his command* . . . Maybe that explained why he'd never risen any higher in the Corps. A man with his years of service should have been a general by now. Thank God there was little tolerance in the modern armed forces for men like . . .

"They deserved it." Harry Simon had been silent for so long, his sudden interruption made me jump. "Always interferin' with us. Damned King and them others riling 'em up, making 'em think they were as good as us." He spat loudly onto the hard ground at his feet. "*I have a dream.*' Shit! We gave 'em somethin' to dream about, didn't we, Colonel?"

"Shut up, Harry." Fleming's tone remained conversational, but the air of command still crackled in every word. Simon fell silent. "Go down to the dock and make certain everything is in readiness. Then contact the others and tell them we're ready to proceed."

Harry Simon moved off, using the flashlight to illuminate the path. Fleming clicked his back on, the beam pointed loosely in our direction from several yards away. In the near blackness I found Erik's face and felt my own fear reflected in his eyes. *Others.* Two on two, we had a chance. With reinforcements, the odds dropped considerably. Before I could begin to think about some way to get us out of there alive, Harlan Fleming took up the tale.

"I want you to understand, Mrs. Tanner, that all of this could have been avoided if only people would have listened to reason. I told the others there was no need to harm young Palmer. I was certain his father could make him understand the necessity of forgetting about what he'd stumbled upon." He paused, and I thought I could see him shaking his head in the dim light of the sliver of moon exposed as the clouds moved off to the east. "So tragic, really. I'm afraid Gray is devastated."

"I can tell you're all broken up," I said, then hurried on before he could comment. "So are you telling me Gray Palmer had nothing to do with his son's death?"

"Of course he didn't! And neither did I! What kind of men do you think we are?"

I knew he didn't really want the answer to that question. "Then who . . . ?"

"As I said, I'm afraid the remaining members of our little

band didn't trust Gray's influence. Apparently father and son have had some difficulties in the past."

Like believing his father had driven his mother to suicide, for one. Then another thought struck me. "Why would Palmer have been using this island for his smuggling operation when he knew full well this was the scene of your . . ." I wanted to say "killing spree," then thought better of it. ". . . of your secrets?"

His laugh, coming out of the darkness, sounded like that of a madman, and yet I couldn't bring myself to believe Colonel Harlan Fleming deranged. A racist, yes. A cold-blooded murderer, probably. But not crazy. Not unless bigotry and arrogance were mental disorders.

"Gray Palmer a smuggler? Where on earth did you get such a notion? Ah, from the young lady, no doubt. I understand the boy never quite believed his father's altruistic motives for the work of the foundation, but I assure you they were quite genuine. Poor Gray has suffered more than any of us for that night's work in 'sixty-three. I believe he's tried to atone in a number of ways. Too bad he assumed all the warning signs and threats of prosecution posted here on the island would be enough to curb his son's curiosity."

"How did you know he'd been here? Young Gray, I mean. His girlfriend says he didn't tell anyone but us."

I felt rather than saw Harlan Fleming rise. Beside me, Erik stiffened as he, too, sensed the movement. The light flickered away. In the darkness that seemed to weigh down on us like a shroud, I shifted as if seeking a more comfortable position and slid my hand into the right pocket of my jeans. I couldn't quite wrap my fingers around the pistol, but the cold metal against my skin felt incredibly reassuring.

"We keep an eye on Judas Island," the Colonel said, and I remembered the men who had checked us out as we cruised by with Ron Singleton Monday morning.

"You've been watching the place for forty years?" Erik voiced the question that had leaped immediately into my own mind.

"Of course not. We were a little concerned when they located the monkey colony here, but it soon became evident the handlers had no interest in exploring the island itself."

"Then why . . ." I couldn't believe the Colonel was being so forthcoming.

"Politics and progress, my dear, the twin banes of Beaufort County. When the State of South Carolina bought Judas, we feared they might decide to develop it in some way. Unfortunately our governments are so susceptible to the temptation to make money. I've served a long time in this area. Former subordinates are always willing to do an old commander a favor, no questions asked."

So some old buddies had alerted the Colonel to Gray's incursion onto the scene of their crime. "But why . . . ?" I began when our captor interrupted. He seemed to be tiring of the interrogation.

"One visit can be construed as happenstance. Two . . . well, I'm sure you can see our dilemma."

So calm. So reasonable. Gray Palmer had made a second visit to Judas Island and sealed his doom. His confrontation with Fleming's cohorts had ended in his death. We'd probably never know what actually transpired, if Gray had scoffed or resisted or threatened. What little I knew of him made me think he probably hadn't been intimidated.

Then I realized the import of exactly what Fleming had said. *Two* visits. Just like us. If I'd had any doubts as to just what they intended for Erik and me, that throwaway line had pretty much eliminated them. I didn't think they'd shoot us there. It wouldn't do to have two more graves to worry about. Development meant bulldozers and digging . . .

"You're moving the bodies, aren't you?" The words tumbled out the moment the thought took shape in my mind. "You didn't expect us. You were as surprised as we were."

"Actually, Mrs. Tanner, I thought you might be dead. Kramer and Parelli assured me your, uh, accident was quite spectacular." In the dim light of the moon I saw Colonel Harlan Fleming shrug. "Ironic, is it not? Another few days and there would have been nothing for young Palmer to find.

Tragic, really, when you think of it. All these casualties because of a simple matter of timing."

I had a sudden, overwhelming desire to smash in the face of this smug, arrogant bastard. I coughed to cover my movement and managed to get a firm grip on the pistol. I nudged Erik gently with my elbow, but there was no way to communicate my intentions to him. I could only hope he'd sense when it was time to move.

Again I coughed and shifted my legs. If I could just get my feet under me! I felt Erik stiffen as if the call to action had somehow communicated itself from my tensing muscles to his own. With Harry Simon out of the picture for the moment, there was no time to waste.

"Sit still!" Harlan Fleming commanded, and I could feel him take a couple of steps in our direction. The light of the thin moon glinted off the barrel of his pistol.

"I'm cold," I said, raising my closed left hand to blow on my fingers.

"My apologies, Mrs. Tanner. Perhaps you'd be more comfortable on the bench?" Erik began to rise, but the Colonel waved him back down with a flick of his gun. "No! You stay where you are!"

I scrambled to my feet at his invitation. I'd never have a better chance. I shoved my free hand into the left pocket of my jeans as if to warm it and began gently easing the gun from the right, but it snagged on the seam! I slowed my steps, trying desperately to pull the pistol out without giving myself away. In the distance I could hear the crackling of twigs underfoot as Harry Simon tromped back from his mission. It had to be now!

With one final tug, my hand and the pistol jerked free.

"Erik, down!" I shouted at the same moment I spun and sighted on the splinter of light thrown off by the gun barrel across the clearing.

The two explosions came almost simultaneously.

I don't think I screamed, but any sound either of us might have made was immediately swallowed up in the reverberating echoes of the gunshots and the frenzied screeching of three thousand terrified monkeys.

I remember thanking God I hadn't hit him when I recognized Erik's face bending over me. I remember the stabbing pain in my eyes as the clearing was suddenly bathed in searchlights, and scrambling men shouted orders.

I remember thinking how odd it was that the rest of me should be so cold when my left arm felt bathed in a warm, sticky flow.

And then I don't remember anything.

CHAPTER
THIRTY-FOUR

At least this time they didn't have to cut off my hair in the emergency room. But I did have to spend three days in the hospital, mostly to make sure the bullet had caused no more nerve damage to my already mangled left shoulder.

I felt truly touched by the steady parade of visitors who trickled in by ones and twos.

My best friend Bitsy Elliott tried hard not to cry, but lost the battle. I could tell she wanted desperately to hug me, but the stiff white sling made it awkward. She settled for a gentle kiss on my forehead and my promise to visit with her and the children as soon as I felt able to get around.

"You've lost entirely too much weight," she admonished me, swiping at the tears marring her careful makeup. "What you need is some feeding up."

Dr. Nedra Halloran, my old college roommate and one of Savannah's premier child psychologists, didn't let me off so lightly. Dear Neddie had seen me through my other brushes with violence and sat quietly next to the bed studying my face.

"What?" I'd finally said when the silence threatened to become uncomfortable.

"You've changed," she said, and I didn't think she meant it as a compliment.

"Why, because I'm not hiding out, mourning for Rob anymore? I thought that's what you wanted me to do."

"You used to be afraid," she'd said.

"And now I'm not. Isn't that a good thing?"

She'd taken a long time to answer. "I'm not so sure. Come see me when you're up to it. Or I can come to you." She, too, planted a soft kiss on my temple before pausing to turn back at the door. "Fear of death and injury is normal, Bay. Not caring if you . . ." She shrugged. "We'll talk," she said and was gone.

Erik came every day. The bullet which had struck Colonel Harlan Fleming had whistled just inches over my partner's head as he hit the ground. He tried to make light of it, but I could tell the experience had shaken him to his core. From him I first learned the details of the timely arrival of both the Coast Guard and the Sheriff's Department. Summoned by Ron Singleton, they had intercepted both Harry Simon and the two men approaching Judas Island by boat.

"Who were they?" I asked as Erik handed me the cheeseburger oozing with ketchup and mayonnaise I'd begged him to smuggle into the hospital. A girl can tolerate just so much meat loaf and lime Jell-O.

"The ones in the boat? Kramer and Parelli, the other two remaining guys from the squad that murdered those black men back in 'sixty-three."

"Why?"

"You mean why did they kill them?" Erik fished a paper napkin out of the bag and wiped a dribble of grease from my chin.

"Thanks. Yes."

"They were locals, probably the ones the Judge told us about. Your pal Harry Simon spilled his guts. Gray Palmer is standing firm, but I think he'll end up admitting his involvement. Back in the late fifties, early sixties the Marines used the island to practice amphibious landings. That was a long time before the monkeys got there. Seems the recruits got in the habit of using it for parties when they had leave time— drinking, maybe women. Harry wasn't real specific."

"Did you get all this from Red?" I asked, handing him the

empty wrapper and wiping my good hand surreptitiously on the sheet. "Thanks, that was great," I added.

"You're welcome. Yeah, pretty much. He knew you'd be driving yourself crazy stuck here without any information. He said he'd be up to see you soon."

I could hardly wait. No doubt he'd rail at me for having gone off half-cocked again, for bumbling into danger, into things I had no business being involved in. There'd be the usual ranting about leaving things like this to the professionals. I'd have to promise not to leave him out in the cold on future cases.

Assuming there were any.

"So what did the black kids do, crash the party?"

"Something like that. Apparently they had been hanging out on Judas Island since they were teenagers. They'd smoke and pass around a bottle and talk about stuff. The Civil Rights movement was just getting started then, and maybe that gave them courage. Or maybe it was the booze. Anyway, they clashed with the recruits more than once. According to Simon, the recruits just got pissed one night and decided to teach them a lesson. He says Fleming was the ringleader. Who knows? They all took part."

"There were four of them? Recruits, I mean?"

"Actually there were eight. Including Gray Palmer. Harry Simon confirms that Gray was the one who tried to 'wuss out,' as Harry put it. One guy died of cancer just a few years ago. One was killed in Vietnam, and a third was shot up pretty bad over there. Never walked again. Apparently none of them still has any use for blacks."

"Jesus," I murmured, "when will it end?"

"Pretty soon for that bunch."

"Is Fleming here? In the hospital?"

I knew he'd survived the .32 slug which passed through his side. My aim had been low and too far right.

"No. They patched him up and took him away. I don't know where they're holding him."

"Poor Amy," I said. "I hope Chris Brandon stands by her."

"He will. The Judge says there's talk around town he may help with Fleming's defense. Providing of course it comes to a trial."

"What do you mean, *if?* Surely they're not going to let . . ."

I had jerked myself upright and the sudden motion sent waves of pain shooting down my left arm. I yelped, and Erik jumped to his feet.

"Don't do that! What the hell is the matter with you?"

I didn't need his yelling at me to realize it wasn't a good idea to be bouncing around just yet. I lay back, panting.

"Okay," he said, resuming his seat. "Take it easy. Nobody's going to get away with anything. It's just a question of who has jurisdiction. Fleming's still on active duty, you know. It may be a court-martial instead of a trial."

"Just so long as somebody nails the bastards." I rang for a pain pill and lay back, exhausted.

THE MORNING of my release I tried to sneak out the back way, but the nursing staff was having none of that. They forced me to take the required wheelchair ride in the elevator, across the lobby, and out to the Judge's van which Erik had been using while his Expedition underwent repairs.

Though I had been badgered by reporters throughout my stay, no one lurked nearby as Erik handed me into the passenger seat and clipped the shoulder harness around me. I held the strap away from my injured arm.

"Sure you won't change your mind?"

I shook my head. "No. I want to go home."

Both my father and Lavinia had insisted I come to them at Presqu'isle for a few days, to recuperate and be pampered, but I'd refused. I wanted to be home. A phone call from Dolores had assured me I could expect no more loving care and attention than I would receive at the beach house. She was prepared to spend as much time with me as I needed. *Déjà vu.*

"I think they're a little hurt by your refusal," Erik said. He maneuvered the van into traffic, traveling much more slowly than he usually did in deference to my injury.

"They understand."

When I had awakened on my second day in the hospital to find Lavinia standing over me, I had at first been alarmed. She looked ten years older, her normally squared shoulders slumped, her narrow face creased with new lines.

"I didn't mean to disturb you, honey," she said.

The endearment startled me as much as her appearance.

"That's okay. All I do is sleep. Is everything okay? You look . . ."

"We're fine," she had replied, automatically including my father.

"Did they find . . . anything yet?"

She'd shaken her head, the air of sadness deepening around her. "It should take about two weeks before the results come back." The pause nearly broke my heart. "But I'm sure it's him." She touched her worn brown hand to her chest. "In here."

Confirming the fate of Eugene Smalls, the purported husband whose name was never mentioned, whose very existence many questioned, lay in the hands of a DNA lab in northern Virginia. Armed with a sample from Lavinia's son, Thaddeus, they would determine if any of the graves on Judas Island held an answer which might ease the uncertainty of forty years.

Eugene Smalls had disappeared in late October of 1963, along with two of his friends, leaving behind a pregnant bride-to-be who took his name and gave it to their son. Over time, few questioned her right to do both. During the four agonizing decades which followed she had believed he had run away, lured by high-paying jobs in the north or perhaps by the rhetoric of those who preached violence in answer to a legacy of oppression. Or even worse in Lavinia's mind, by another woman. Whatever the reason, he had left her alone to raise a bastard child, and she had hated him for it, had wiped his face from her memory—and that of his son. Never once had she considered he might be dead. Never once had she looked out from the back verandah toward the small dot of Judas Island and thought she might be looking at her lover's grave.

Even with the help of Dr. Denton Douglass who had agreed to expedite the DNA tests as much as he was able, it would still be weeks before we had a definitive answer. I couldn't spend those days watching her pain. She wouldn't want me to, for her own sake as well as for mine. And so I was going home.

"I understand," Erik replied when I finished my explanation. "I'm just surprised no one made a connection with the Smalls name."

"It's fairly common in these parts. There was no real reason for Law Merriweather to link the old missing person's case with Lavinia."

"I suppose not. Forty years is a long time. But your father did."

"Even he couldn't be sure. I still believe it's the only reason he encouraged us to go. He wanted to find the answer, spare Lavinia from having to hear the news from strangers."

Erik eased the van into the wide turn at the on-ramp for Route 278, and I braced myself with my good hand. I wondered what my mother would have done if she'd known the real story. She'd dropped hints over the years, about the elusive Mr. Smalls and whether or not he actually existed. Thank God that, in spite of her own doubts, she'd still taken on the proud black woman and her bastard son. I shuddered at the thought of my childhood without Lavinia . . .

I dozed a little, the warmth of the sun beating through the windows and the rhythmic motion of the van lulling me into sleep. I awoke with a start as we slowed for the guard house at the entrance to Port Royal Plantation. I forced my mind into gear and leaned across Erik to assure Jim it was okay to let us in.

"What happened to your arm, Miz Tanner?" he asked.

"Nothing serious," I replied and waved with my right hand as Erik pulled on through.

We rolled past the golf course, and Erik caught me studying his profile. He looked embarrassed, and I realized we'd never talked about his role in the incident on Judas Island.

"How are you holding up?" I asked.

"Fine." He replied without thinking then added, "I guess."

"This is the second time I've put your life at risk. I don't mean to do it, you know. It's not that I don't care . . ."

"I know that," he cut in. He cleared his throat nervously. "But . . ."

"But it's happened just the same," I finished for him. "Look, if you want out, I'll certainly understand. I don't think this is exactly what you signed on for last fall."

I expected him to protest, to contradict me. I was surprised how much it hurt when he didn't. We were only a few hundred yards from my driveway when he finally spoke.

"I think maybe I need some time to think about it. Not that I've made a decision. It's just . . ."

"You don't owe me any explanation," I said, mustering a cheerful tone from some reserve I didn't know I had. "When you've made up your mind, just let me know. I'll understand. Either way."

He shot me his heart-stopping smile and nodded. "Okay. Thanks."

I would miss him.

As I swallowed against the pain I felt rising in my throat, we took the right turn into my driveway and pulled up in front of my gleaming white garage door. I smiled, and Erik grinned back. All traces of the graffiti were gone.

"Dolores took care of it," he said. "Got the side of the house cleaned up, too. By the way, Red told me to tell you that you were right. It was someone from the seafood place."

I had been convinced the scrap of cloth with the small *t* and *c,* found on the night Erik tangled with the two vandals, probably had something to do with the Mitchells. I couldn't think of anyone else associated with those two letters who might have had a grudge against me.

"Who was it?" I asked.

"Tamika Jessup's daughter and her boyfriend. The kid works for your friend Bubba on the boats on weekends. Red wanted to know if you're going to press charges."

I shook my head and waited for him to come around and open my door. A week ago I would have answered a resounding "Of course!" even though I understood the girl's anger at having her mother's embezzlement exposed. On that day, after everything that had happened, it didn't seem important.

"Did anyone say why she was stealing the money?" I asked, fumbling with the seat belt release.

"Gambling. Started out a few years back with those video poker machines they've outlawed and then just escalated. The family's getting her some help," Erik added, giving me his hand as I stepped down from the van. "By the way, the Mitchells took care of the cost of repairs on the door and the siding. And the kids are going to be over here evèry weekend for the next six months keeping your yard in shape."

Bubba Mitchell is a very wise man, I thought.

Erik pulled my overnight bag from behind the seat, and I leaned on him as he ushered me toward the front door. Dolores didn't wait for me to make it to the top of the steps before her sweet smile engulfed me.

"Come, *Señora*. Let Dolores help you. I know you will not stay in the bed, so I make up the sofa for you. Is good, no? *Poco a poco, Señora*."

I eased myself onto the pillows Dolores had stacked up and leaned back gratefully. She slipped off my shoes and covered my legs with a light blanket.

"I bring the tea now," she said, glancing toward the front entryway before bustling off toward the kitchen. Erik excused himself and wandered down the hallway to the guest room.

I closed my eyes for a moment, grateful to be back. Strangely enough, despite all the terrors of the past year, I felt safe here. And at peace. No longer Rob's and my house, no longer the repository of bitter memories of what might have been. Just my home. *Mine.*

"*Señora,* many messages have come. I write them down for you." Dolores set the teacup and saucer on the coffee table along with a pad covered in her delightful if sometimes indecipherable phonetic English. "And there is the lunch soon." Again I saw her eyes dart toward the door. "You rest. *Dormirse, mi señora.* Sleep. Dolores keep watch."

"Keep watch for what?" I asked but she scurried away without answering.

I settled myself more comfortably into the warmth of the soft cushions and moments later felt my eyelids beginning to droop. I wasn't certain how long I dozed before the sound of muted voices penetrated my half-sleep, and I sensed someone hovering over me.

"*Ma pauvre petite.*"

His clothes were rumpled, and his face looked drawn with fatigue and worry.

Alain Darnay dropped to one knee beside the sofa and gently pressed his lips to my cheek.

"You need a shave," I said, and he laughed.

Behind him I saw Dolores beaming as Erik hefted the two huge suitcases and carried them down the hallway toward my room.

You're not getting involved with those people again, and that's final!"

I punctuated the shout by ripping the ball cross-court, a stinging backhand that should have left him staring in admiration as it whizzed by. Instead he dived to his left, just managed to get a racket on it, and popped up a lazy floater that nicked the tape and dribbled over to land six inches beyond my side of the net.

"Game!" he shouted, pumping his tanned fist in the air. "And set!"

He dropped to his knees and raised his face and arms skyward, like Pete Sampras at Wimbledon. The group next to us interrupted their doubles game to grin at his antics, and one of the two lanky women waiting for our court applauded.

I flashed him a reluctant smile and trotted over to gather our gear from beside the net post. "I'd be ashamed to take that point if I were you," I said, slinging a towel around my neck and swiping at the strands of sweat-soaked hair escaping from my ponytail.

"Bay Tanner, I would never have expected you to be such a bad loser."

"Alain Darnay, I'd never have expected you to be such a cocky winner."

I was also pretty amazed at how well his recovery was coming along. Less than a year before, I had worked frantically to staunch the blood pouring from a gaping bullet wound in his left side. A scant two months ago he had still looked thin and frail as he glowered from the curb in front of the Paris apartment at the taxi whisking me off to Orly Airport and home. It seemed I had been wrong, returning to his dangerous work with Interpol hadn't jeopardized his health—it had apparently restored it.

"We'll discuss it, *ma petite*," he said, mopping his streaming face.

It took me a moment to realize he was referring to my outburst just before the end of the match. LeBrun, his superior at Interpol, had sent another coded fax just that morning, one in a long stream of communications which had kept the international phone lines buzzing for the past week or so. I didn't need to decipher its contents to know Darnay's employers were angling once again to get him back in their deadly game.

"Damn right we will," I said, softening the words with a smile.

We slid our rackets into their carrying cases, and Darnay hefted the double-handled tennis bag. He flung an arm across my shoulder, being careful to avoid the tender area where my own recent wound had still not completely healed.

What a pair we are, I thought. *When we get old, we can sit around and compare battle scars.*

He nodded to the two women who had moved onto the court behind us. "Enjoy your game, ladies," he said in a thick French accent that made even the most mundane comments sound like a lover's caress.

"Quit flirting," I said good-naturedly and received a Gallic shrug from the tall, craggy Frenchman who only that morning had asked me to marry him—for the fourteenth time, if my scorekeeping could be trusted. If he wasn't careful, I thought, I'd begin to take the offers seriously.

"What can I say, my darling? It is the nature of the beast. Bred into the bones, absorbed from the mother's milk, inhaled with the bouquet of the wines . . ."

I punched him playfully in the arm with my free hand.

As we approached the canopy of live oaks under which we'd left the Thunderbird, Darnay tossed the bag into the rear seat. Turning his back on the parking lot, he leaned casually against the creamy yellow fender of my new convertible. His face had lost its bantering look, and his normally soft eyes had darkened to the steely blue which usually signaled anger.

"Keep smiling," he said, ignoring his own dictum, "and glance over my right shoulder."

I faltered a little, startled by the tone of his voice.

"Smile," he repeated, and I did my best to comply.

"What am I looking at?"

He reached out to slip an errant strand of auburn hair behind my ear. "Black Mercedes sedan at the end of the row. Young man. Dark skin, longish blond hair. Navy blue polo shirt."

I leaned in to kiss him gently on the cheek and whispered, "Got him. So what's the problem?"

Another woman might have asked more questions, been more suspicious of Darnay's sudden change of mood and urgent commands. In the two years since I'd watched my husband's plane explode in a shower of flaming debris and dismembered bodies, I'd experienced enough danger to recognize its reflection in someone else's eyes.

"Do you know him?" Darnay nuzzled my ear, momentarily making me lose track of the conversation.

"Uh, no. No, I don't think so. Why?"

"Give me the keys and get in," he said.

For a moment I balked. Taking orders is absolutely alien to both my nature and inclination. But Darnay's glare didn't waver, so I strolled around to the passenger side and slid into the sun-warmed leather seat. Without turning my head, I managed to get another glimpse of the object of his interest. Definitely young. Expensive-looking wraparound shades. Maybe Latino.

"Smile," I heard again from the other side of the car, so I threw back my head and laughed, a sound so artificial it wouldn't have fooled anyone within hearing distance. Hopefully I looked the picture of carefree, fortyish Southern womanhood: rich and idle, without a problem in the world. I carried on with the charade until Darnay backed the T-Bird around and headed us out of the small tennis complex tucked up to one of the three golf courses in Port Royal Plantation.

"What the hell was that all about?" I demanded as we pulled onto Fort Walker Drive. The sweet gums and towering pines cast a welcome shade over the sleek hood of the convertible.

"He's following us." Alain Darnay, Interpol agent and former top investigator for the Sûreté in Paris, barely flicked his eyes to the rearview mirror. "No, don't look!" he barked when I began to turn in my seat.

"You're seriously ticking me off," I said in a voice he should have been all too familiar with. Our on-again, off-again romance had been more off than on recently, due primarily to the demands of his profession. "And so what if he's behind us?" I added, glancing at the firm set of his wide mouth and the slight dimple that bisected his otherwise strong chin.

"This is the third time he's turned up in the last couple of days," Alain remarked, his tone so conversational we might have been discussing last night's Braves game or the time of the next high tide. "I do not like coincidences."

"I don't either. But Hilton Head is an island, after all, and a small one. Even with all the summer tourists here, it wouldn't be that farfetched to run across the same person a couple of times. Especially if he's staying at the Westin or renting one of the condos at the Barony."

"And you believe he just happened to be at the restaurant last night? And at the bookstore this morning?"

His questions brought me up short. I'd been so intent the previous evening on deflecting Darnay's thirteenth marriage proposal over candlelight and champagne at Conroy's that I'd been pretty much oblivious to my surroundings. He, however, had been captivated by the works of our local literary icon for whom the swanky dining room of the Marriott

Hotel had been named. It had been Darnay who insisted on running out the next morning to fill in the gaps in my collection of the works of Pat Conroy. Engrossed in my quest through the aisles of Barnes & Noble, I'd failed to notice a familiar face.

"I'm sorry. I didn't realize."

His smile accepted my apology.

"So what do you think it's all about?" I asked.

It couldn't have anything to do with the fledgling inquiry agency my father and I had established. We had been floundering since the defection of one of our founding members, Erik Whiteside. The last thing remotely resembling a case had been wrapped up months before, its only lingering remnant evidenced by the stiffness that still plagued my injured left shoulder. Having been mangled by the exploding debris of my late husband's plane, then battered again by a through-and-through bullet wound, by rights the shoulder should not have been functioning at all. I applied creams to soothe the shiny skin grafts, exercised the stiff joint every chance I got, and tried not to think about it.

"He was watching us play tennis, then hurried back to his car while we were packing up," Darnay finally answered. "Nice looking, clean-cut, maybe five-eight or -nine. You sure you don't recognize him?"

"Positive," I said as we took a left just before the overpass that led to the security gate.

The road to my beach house skirted one of the golf courses, winding its way to the ocean past sprawling Lowcountry homes nestled among stands of live oaks and screening shrubbery.

"Glance back now and see if he followed us," Darnay commanded.

I turned casually, as if surveying the scenery, just in time to see the black car disappear over the bridge and glide on toward the gate. "Nope, he kept going."

My relief proved short-lived as my companion suddenly whipped the car into a narrow driveway, reversed, and roared back the way we had come. The glint in his eye as he took the sharp turn back onto the main road made me remember that Alain Darnay much preferred the role of hunter to that of quarry.

Just outside the main gate the Mercedes made a right onto the access road to the Westin. We followed more slowly, there being no rush to close the gap since the few turnoffs all led to dead ends. We hung back and watched the young man maneuver his vehicle into a parking space near the entrance to the gleaming resort hotel.

The T-Bird leapt as Darnay gunned the engine and squealed to a halt perpendicular to the black car's rear bumper, effectively blocking it in. He jumped from the driver's seat and in one swift movement had the door of the Mercedes open and a squirming teenager spread-eagled across the trunk.

"Okay, son, I need to hear why you've been following us for two days."

"Screw you!" The voice was garbled since its owner's right cheek was pressed into the hot metal of the Mercedes's deck lid, but there was no mistaking the venom.

"Now, be nice," Darnay replied in his most sarcastic tone. "There's a lady present."

"Lady, my ass!" The boy squirmed under the pressure of Darnay's grip, but he was no match for the older man.

"Don't hurt him," I called from the passenger seat. "He's only a kid."

"Shut up! I don't need you to—" the boy yelled, but the rest was cut off as Darnay twisted his arm up higher on his back.

"Alain! Please!" I was suddenly aware that someone could come along any moment and arrest him for assault and battery. Maybe things were different where he came from, but in Beaufort County, South Carolina, the sheriff didn't take kindly to people roughing up the tourists. Bad for business.

Darnay eased up a little and flipped the young man around, allowing him to stand upright. "I asked you a question, sonny," he growled.

"I don't have to tell you shit, old man." The defiance lasted until Alain pulled off his own sunglasses, and the kid got a good look at his eyes. I could almost feel the fear rising in his throat. "Look, back off, okay? I'm not trying to hurt anybody." He paused a moment, then added, "Okay?"

Darnay glanced at me, and I nodded. He took one step back, giving the boy room to breathe but still guarding against any chance of his bolting. "Let's hear it."

"I . . . I was just curious. About her." His stammering admission made him sound even younger than he obviously was. I was guessing seventeen, maybe a year or two either way. Hard to tell these days.

I stepped out of the car, surveying the surrounding area in the hope we were unobserved. Alain was here on a tourist visa, and I didn't think it would do his reputation any good to get picked up and packed off to France. In these times of heightened terrorist alerts and a rekindled suspicion of foreigners, I was pretty sure no one would be cutting him any slack, Interpol or no.

I moved around the car until I stood facing the kid, his breath coming in short, nervous gulps. Whether they were a result of the tussle with Darnay or from the waves of anger I felt rolling off him, I couldn't tell.

"Here I am," I said softly. "What do you want to know?"

The offer stunned him momentarily, but you had to give the boy credit. He glared past the hulking, six-foot-two Darnay and straight into my eyes. He drew a long, shuddering breath and said, "I want to know why you killed my father."